BOY NEXT DOOR

HOT OFF THE ICE #5

A. E. WASP

Kelpie  Press

To Doug, Kristen, & Beth. Thank you for still answering the phone when I call.

To my brother Dave. If you ever die, I'm going to resurrect you and kill you myself.

ACKNOWLEDGMENTS

This book couldn't have happened without a whole bunch of people who supported me through my nervous breakdown. Doug Clegg, May Archer, and Beth Bolden in particular spent many, many, MANY hours talking me through things and off ledges, all while making me laugh and giving me all the emotional support I could use.

Special thanks to my daughter Maya and her friends who spent months listening to me plot outlines and put up with me using them as test subjects for different ideas.

To all the people who proofread and beta read for me and gave me all the feedback - thank you a million times.

To the kind people at Hello Fresh! food delivery service for making sure I had healthy food to eat, and for forcing me to take a break to cook.

To all the internet streaming services that supported me through this, Hulu, Netflix, Amazon Music, NHLTV.com, Facebook, and of course Bejeweled, the only phone game I play. It's perfect for shutting my brain down.

AUTHOR NOTES

Astute readers who are also hockey fans may notice I played fast and loose with real life drafts/trades and the deadlines for offers for restricted free agents as well as other dates. I claim artistic license.

Defenceman with a 'c' is use throughout this book. It is the Canadian spelling and while both defenceman and defenseman are correct, the c-spelling is used most often in articles about ice hockey.

Snoop Dogg is a huge hockey fan. I highly recommend his Hockey 101 series of videos on Youtube.

Joey's exploits, including the trade, were inspired by current Dallas Stars' player Tyler Seguin, who was traded from the Bruins to the Stars. I stole some quotes attributed to Tyler. Check out his website if you want to see how much some of these guys are in the news, doing commercials, etc.

BOY NEXT DOOR & BOY TOYS
CHARACTER LIST

O'REILLY FAMILY

Kathleen (née Dunlea) (60) – Mom, Aunt Kathleen

Robert (62) – Dad, Uncle Bob

Liam (35) – Assistant Coach Seattle Thunder

Angie (33) – Nurse, married to Kellen Bryne. Children: Nathan (10), twin girls-Jasmine & Rose (8)

Jimmy (30) – plays hockey overseas, engaged to Gabriella (engaged), Child: boy infant

Natalie (26) – U.S. Women's Olympic Hockey Team and Boston Pride Goalie

Patrick (25) –Defensive player for the Lightning & the Thunder

Brigit Dunlea (85) - also known as Nana, Bridie. Widowed

LUCIANO FAMILY

Jean (59) – Mom, Aunt Jeanie

Frankie (67) – Dad, Uncle Frankie

Gina (33) – Dancer, married to Carter Smith. Children:

Matthew (11) Maria (7) Lorenzo - also known as Pookie (2)

Sophia (30) – Forward NWHL (retired), married to Leslie Hansen. Child: Stella (infant)

Nico (28) – Shortstop, Colorado Rockies, in a relationship with Michelle D'Alto

Deano (26) – Goalie, Tampa Bay Lightning

Joey (25) – Center, Seattle Thunder

Lorenzo (87) - also known as Nonno Lollo and Enzo

Leslie Hansen (29) – Massachusetts State Police Officer, married to Sophia Luciano

Michelle D'Alto, (34) – Liam O'Reilly's girlfriend for five years. Now in a relationship with Nico Luciano. Pregnant with first child.

THUNDER ROSTER (AS OF THE EVENTS OF BOY NEXT DOOR)

SEATTLE THUNDER – NHL TEAM

Development league affiliations:

BAKERSFIELD LIGHTNING – AHL affiliate for the Thunder. Patrick O'Reilly and Paul Dyson started with the Lightning.

TEXAS TORNADOS – ECHL affiliate for the Thunder. Currently in Hidden Creek, Texas but will be moving to Bellingham, WA for the next season.

Last name, first name, (age), nickname, number, position, nationality

Abeltshauser, Konrad (22), 89, Defense, GERMANY

Anderson, William, (26), Ders, 12, Forward,USA

Chebykin, Ari (22), Chebs, 24, Forward, RUSSIA

DiDiomete, Devin (19) Triple D or D, 10, Forward, USA

Donovan, Jake (32), Donny, 17, Center – Team Captain, USA

Dyson, Paul Stonewall (22), Bama, 13, Defense, USA

Huberdeau, Alex (19), Hubs, 11, Forward, CANADA

Jansson, Gabriel (28),Gabe, 61, Forward, SWEDEN

Kaarela, Hannu (27), Hands, 71, Forward, FINLAND

Kaluk, Nick (21), Kalley, 44, Forward, USA

Lipe, Daniel (31), Lips, 26, Forward, assistant captain, CANADA

Luciano, Joey (25), Lucy, Looch, 46, Center, USA

Marchment, Jake 20), Marsha, 90, Defense, CANADA

McVicker, James (21), Vicky, 30, Goalie, CANADA

Pergov, Sergei Ivanovich (34), Pergs, 34 Goalie, RUSSIA

Pettersson, Linus (23), Peets, 20, Forward, SWEDEN

Rasmussen, Jorgen (29), Razzy, 51, DefenseNORWAY

Rhodes, Robbie (21), Roadie, 22, Defense, USA

Roberson, Sven (25), Svenny, 39, Defense, SWEDEN

Smith, Bruce (23), Smitty, 15, Defense, CANADA

VanDoren, Bradley (27) Van, 64, Center, USA

Wheeler, Anderson (30), Wheels, 3, Defense, USA

Wingerli, Fredrik (29), Wings, 82, Forward, SWEDEN

CHARACTERS' FIRST APPEARANCES

#1 City Boy – main couple: Bryce Lowrey and Dakota Wellington. First appearance for Robbie Rhodes and Jake Donovan. Takes place in Colorado on Dakota's farm.

#2 Country Boy – main couple: Robbie (Rhodie) Rhodes (also referred to as 'the rookie') and Paul (Bama) Dyson. First appearance for Sergei Pergov and Alex Staunton. Takes place in Seattle during the season.

#3 Boy Toys – Christmas novella. Main couple, Joey (Lucy, the Looch) Luciano and Liam (Judy) O'Reilly. Luciano and O'Reilly families introduced and it's all very confusing. Takes place entirely in Boston over Christmas Eve.

#4 Skater Boy – Main couple. Sergei (Sergs/Pergs) Ivanovich Pergov and Alex Staunton. Many WAGs introduced. Alex's cats, Torvill and Dean. First appearance of James (Vicky) McVicker. Sergei and Alex refer to each other by diminutive forms of their

Russian Names of varying intimacy: Serhoya, Seryozha, Seryozhen'ka, Seryozhka, and Lysoha, Lyoshen'ka, Alexei,.

HOCKEY TERMS

The A- Slang for the AHL (American Hockey League).

Bag Skate - When a coach punishes a team by making them skate hard, often until they throw up in a bag. Sometimes it is simply used to better condition a team.

Bar Down- Used to describe a shot that goes off the crossbar and in the net.

Beauty- Complimentary term used to describe an ideal hockey player, from a cultural

Can-Opener- When a player puts his stick between another player's legs and twists.

Cheese- Referring to the upper part of the net. *E.g: Man, did he ever go cheese on that goal, eh?* Also may be referred to as Cheddar or Bunk.

Cherry Picker- Player who hangs out around the red line looking for breakaway passes. They always neglect their defensive zone chores. Also known as a Floater.

Chirp/Beak- The steady flow of insults thrown at opponents throughout a hockey game. Players will chirp or beak opponents throughout a game in an attempt to throw off their concentration.

Clapper- Slap shot.

The Coast- Slang for the ECHL (East Coast Hockey League).

Coast to Coast- When a player carries a puck from his own end to the opposing team's end without passing. Also referred to as Post to Post.

Cross-checking - Hitting an opponent with the stick when it is held with two hands and no part of the stick is on the ice.

D-man - Defenceman

Dangle- A term currently used to refer to a slick stick-handling maneuver. A Dangler is a player who has great stick-handling abilities. In the old days the term was used to describe some who could skate fast. *E.g: He can really dangle.*

Deke - feint or fake technique whereby a player draws an opposing player out of position or is used to skate by an opponent while maintaining possession and control of the puck. The term is a Canadianism formed by abbreviating the word decoy.

Deuce- Two minute penalty.

The Dub- Slang for the WHL (Western Hockey League).

Dump and Chase- A tactic where players dump the puck into the opposition zone and then attack on a forecheck.

Five–Hole – The space between a goalie's legs. One of the five opportunities to score a goal.

The Gate- When a player is ejected from a game he is given The Gate.

Gongshow- A term used to describe a situation that is out of control, funny or ridiculous.

Gordie Howe Hat Trick- When a player registers a goal, an assist and a fight in one game.

Grenade- An awful pass (usually a bobbling puck). Players will say, "pull the pin on that grenade" when someone makes a bad pass.

Grinder- A player who typically plays on the dump and chase line whose role on a team is to finish his checks and wear down opponents.

Hang Em' Up- Retiring from hockey. Referring to hanging up the skates

Icing- when a player shoots the puck across both the center red line and the opposing team's goal line, and the puck remains untouched. However, it is not icing if the puck is shot from behind the halfway line into the goal; if the puck crosses the goal line completely, the goal is counted. Icing is also legal when a team is short-handed.

The IR- Short form for the Injured Reserve.

Kangaroo Court- A forum where all player fines are brought forward and tried. Usually a light-hearted affair held once a week to promote camaraderie.

Kill- Slang for penalty kill. Can also be used as slang for a sexual conquest.

Lace Em' Up- Getting ready before a game.

Liney- Linesman, can also be used as another word for one of your line-mates.

Mitts- A term referring to a hockey player's stick-handling ability. E.g: *"Johnny's got some nice mitts on him, eh?"*

Muffin- A weak shot on net.

The O- Slang for the OHL (Ontario Hockey League).

One-T- Short for One-Timer which is when a player shoots a puck that is passed to him without stopping it first. Shooting a puck as it comes in motion.

Penalty Kill – when a team is at a man or two disadvantage due to team penalties. The object is to 'kill' the penalty, run down the clock, without letting the other team (who is on a Power Play) score.

Pizza- A pass up the middle. A high risk play that often gets intercepted.

Power Play – When a team has more players on the ice than the other team due to the other team's penalities. Usually a 5 on 4 play but can also be 4-3, or 5-3

Plug- This is a term players use to make fun of or degrade another player. Calling someone a Plug basically is like saying that they are a terrible player and are just on a team to fill a slot.

Puck Bunnies - Girls who chase and hang around hockey players.

The Q- Slang for the QMJHL (Quebec Major Junior Hockey League).

Sauce- Slang for a saucer pass where the puck is feathered to clear an opponent's stick.

Shnarples- A card game that hockey players play when on long road trips.

Shnook/Shmelt- A first year player or rookie.

Shoe Check- A prank performed during team meals at restaurants where the prankster will crawl on his or her hands and knees under the table and pour ranch dressing or ketchup on an unsuspecting victim's shoes. Once back in their seat, the prankster will begin tapping their glass. Everyone else follows suit in tapping their glass while checking their shoes for sauce. The victim has to stand up and get napkins and buns tossed at them.

The Show- Slang for the NHL

Shutdown-Pre-game nap

Sieve- Terrible goalie.

Slashing - a penalty called when an offending player swings their hockey stick at an opposing player, regardless of contact, or breaks an opposing player's stick with their own. Such a penalty may range from a minor penalty to a match penalty, depending on the seriousness of the injury to the opposing player.

Slewfoot- When a player kicks the legs out from behind an opponent. A very dirty play in hockey.

Snipe- A slang word used to describe a goal, particularly a nice goal. A Sniper is a player who scores frequently.

Snipped- When a player is released or cut from a team.

Stripes- Referee.

Suey- Short form for **Suicide Pass** which is a pass made by a player to another player who is in a vulnerable position to be hit or blind-sided by an opponent.

Tendie - slang for goaltender, also Netminder

Toe-Drag- A stick-handling move where you use the toe of the blade of the stick to pull the puck back, away from an opposing player. Almost as if you are dangling a carrot in front of a rabbit and then yanking it away when it tries to bite it.

The Trap- A defensive strategic tactic where all five players pull back into the neutral zone and create a log jam, making it hard for an attacking team to penetrate.

Turtle- When a player drops to the ice and covers his head with his arms when challenged to a fight.

Tweeners- Scoring a goal between the goalie's legs.

Twig- Hockey stick.

The Wall- The boards surrounding the rink.

Wheels- A word used to describe someone's skating ability. This is also used to describe a player's ability to pick up or attract girls. *E.g: "Chucky's wheeling that broad over there."*

The Wiffle- Slang for the now-defunct WPHL (Western Professional Hockey League).

The Wire- The waiver wire. Players are put on the wire when they are being shopped around for a trade or when they are released.

Zips- Stitches. Short for Zippers.

When, in disgrace with fortune and men's eyes,

I all alone beweep my outcast state,

And trouble deaf heaven with my bootless cries,

And look upon myself and curse my fate,

Wishing me like to one more rich in hope,

Featured like him, like him with friends possessed,

Desiring this man's art and that man's scope,

With what I most enjoy contented least;

Yet in these thoughts myself almost despising,

Haply I think on thee, and then my state,

(Like to the lark at break of day arising

From sullen earth) sings hymns at heaven's gate;

> *For thy sweet love remembered such wealth brings*
>
> *That then I scorn to change my state with kings.*

- Shakespeare, Sonnet 29

AN O'REILLY/LUCIANO JOINT GROUP CHAT

(Contains profanity, misspellings, sibling taunting, & name changes because all the participant are kind of annoying.)

12/31 – 3:00pm EST

CARMEN SANTIAGO posted in **ARE WE THERE YET?**

Happy New Year! 🖼️ 💯

ANGIE: Jimmy, it's like 3pm, where are you?

GINA: I THOUGHT HE WAS IN BARZIL

CARMEN SANDIEGO: Barzil? Hitting the booze already? i'm in Sweden. Somewhere. I'm in the future!

THE CUTE ONE: what are the winning lottery##$$?!?!

GIRLTENDIE: more money

GINA: Nat, we said no mre chang gin names

GIRLTENDIE: like u need

THE CUTE ONE: we also said learn to type grandma 😂😂

GINA: 👆 can you read that, Jojo?

CARMEN SANDIEGO: This is Jimmy

ANGIE: no shit Nathan leave your sister alone or I'll fuck

THE CUTE ONE changed his name to **THE LOOCH**: voice to text again ange?

GIRL TENDIE changed her name TO **THE HOT ONE**: Joey where are you?

THE LOOCH: Hanging with some of the guys at the Warren why?

THE HOT ONE: I'm bored.

GINA: come bbysit your neice and nephews they miss you

THE HOT ONE: <insert hysterical laughter> why should I suffer for your het sins?

THE LOOCH: yeah meet me at my place bring something hot we're hittin gthe town

THE HOT ONE: fuck yeah later breeders have fun falling asleep on the couch 🐦 🍸

ANGIE: bite me

GINA: bite me

GINA CHANGED THE NAME OF THE GROUP TO **YOU'RE ADOPTED**

12/31 9:24 pm EST

THE LOOCH posted in **YOU'RE ADOPTED**:

@Liam You around?

1/1 – 12:01 am EST

THE LOOCH posted in **YOU'RE ADOPTED**:

THE LOOCH: HAPPY NEW YEAR BITCHES!

 **GINA**: HAPPY NEW YEAR SWEETIE! 🍾🍾

Where's Nat?

THE LOOCH: Last I saw with some basketball chick

ANGIE: Don't you lose my baby sister asshole

NOT THE DEAN: Happy new year losers! Where's Nico

GINA: Where do you think?

HOCKEY SUCKS: nico can't come to the phone right now unlike some people I have a date

THE LOOCH: 😡 😡

ANGIE: Boys don't start

NATALIE: fucking happy new year I'm fucking fine!! Tonya says hi and she doesn't play basketball

THE LOOCH: but she's like 7 feet tall!

NATALIE: Jealous shorty?

THE LOOCH changed the name of the group to **YOU WISH**

1/1 – 12:07 AM EST

LIAM posted in **YOU WISH**: @thelooch Who is that? And why are you naked?

LIAM: Nevermind. I don't want to know.

1/1 – 3:00 a.m. EST

LIAM posted to **YOU WISH**: HAPPY NEW YEAR

PATRICK: Happy new year bro! Shoulda come out with us!

LIAM: Maybe next year

PATRICK changed his name to **BABY O'REILLY**

1

JOEY

www.espn.com June 6, 2017 - Rangers center Joey Luciano spoke with reporter Morty Ain about what it was like to take it all off for ESPN The Magazine's Body Issue.

In the offseason, I'm thinking about: what the other best players in the world are doing right now. I think about how much I want to be better than those guys. That thought is always going around in my head.

I don't think there's anything I've ever done that I regret. Like my love for tattoos. Every tattoo has some sort of relevance to me. Every tattoo has a purpose. I can have a conversation with someone for about 20 minutes going through the meaning of them all.

One tip for preparing for the nude shot. Moisturize. And you just have to breathe, relax, and trust the people taking your photo.

JOEY LUCIANO STARED AT THE LUGGAGE GOING AROUND AND around on the baggage claim carousel in Boston's Logan airport and tried to ignore the people staring at him. Even with his eyes locked on the *fascinating* revolving display of suitcases and duffle bags, he could sense the ripples of recognition spreading slowly through the crowd.

With each suitcase the conveyor belt spat out that wasn't his, a frustrated sigh pushed its way up from the depths of Joey's being. Not having to wait for baggage was only one of the reasons he normally drove the four hours or so between his home in the city and his family's home in Southie.

But the Audi was in the shop getting a tune-up, and there was *no way* he was taking the Lamborghini out in the snow and salt. *Aaand* tiny violins all around the world were playing for him now. He snorted. That had sounded douchey even in the privacy of his own mind.

He thought about sighing or making a snarky comment to the woman standing next to him about how shitty airlines were, but the buzzing of the crowd had built enough to remind him of two things. One - everyone and their grandmother had a cell phone and two – he had signed a multi-year contract promising he would conduct himself 'on and off the rink according to the highest standards of honesty, morality, fair play and sportsman-ship, and to refrain from conduct detrimental to the best interest of the Club, the League, or professional hockey generally'.

Publicly trashing an airline would probably be detrimental to all of the above. Not to mention any endorsement deals he might have coming down the pike.

With those two things in mind, he put the brakes on his undeserved pity party. *Oh, wah, poor him. His life was so hard.*

Shifting his weight must have been some kind of signal for the fans because a bearded guy in a Boston Bruins hat broke right through his personal space bubble. "Hey, aren't you Joey Luciano?"

Joey turned with his public smile. "I am."

"Awesome." The guy grinned. "I'm a huge fan." He touched the brim of his hat. "Even if you do play for the wrong team."

Joey couldn't hold back a sharp laugh. If the guy knew how true that was, how quickly would that smile drop from his face? Talk about detrimental conduct. What would happen to his fans, his job, his endorsements, if word got out that 'the Looch' was into guys? He would get a scarlet 'G' stamped on his forehead.

Not that he was really gay, he just found some guys hot and easier to understand than women. But he didn't think hockey fans would want to split those semantic hairs with him.

Two months ago, he'd had sex with Liam O'Reilly. Liam was a retired blueliner from the Minnesota Wild, the newest assistant defensive coach for the Seattle Thunder, ten years older than Joey, crazy intense, and, oh yeah, a guy.

Joey checked his watch. *Oh, look.* He'd gone a whole three minutes and seventeen seconds without thinking about Liam. That must be a new record.

"Can I get a picture?" the Bruins fan asked.

"Sure." Joey made a show of straightening his tie, fixing his hair, and searching for the perfect angle. He dragged the guy to a window. "No, over here, the light's better."

He turned them so they faced the window and threw his arm over the guy's shoulder. "Say Bruins suck!" He grinned loudly at the guy's sound of outrage.

"I think I went to school with your sister and that O'Reilly girl," the guy said as he inspected the photo.

"Yeah? Which one?" There were five Luciano kids. Anyone who had lived in the neighborhood over the last twenty years had a good chance of crossing paths with at least one of them. And since four of them had grown up to be professional athletes, people tended to remember them.

At the collective groan behind him, Joey turned to see the baggage carousel come to a complete halt.

"For fuck's sake," a woman's voice rang out.

"Are all the bags out?" Joey asked, walking back to the claim area and searching for his box. If he'd lost the promotional posters and pucks he was supposed to be signing, PR was going to kill him.

"No," a young girl next to him sighed. "I don't see my suitcase. And it has my homework in it."

She looked to be about fourteen, with long blonde hair in a ponytail and a sweatshirt from the Revere High School athletic department. Joey leaned down to whisper conspiratorially in her ear. "Yeah, but that's a great excuse. Baggage claim ate my luggage."

She giggled.

Several irritated passengers had started crowding up to the customer service desk. The middle-aged woman behind the counter viewed them with a look of resigned desperation.

Joey nudged the girl with his elbow. "Want to help me out?"

"Yeah!" she answered wide-eyed.

Joey handed her his cell phone. "I bet you take a mean selfie." She nodded. "Good. You're the official photographer."

Joey hopped onto the edge of the baggage carousel with a clang of thin metal. "Hey!" he called over the disgruntled rumblings. "If I could have your attention for just a minute." A few people in the crowd looked his way.

"Looch!" A fan called, waving wildly.

God, he loved his fans. Their energy fed him. The louder they screamed, the better he played. It was an awesome symbiotic relationship.

Like Tinker Bell, Joey could only do his magic if someone believed in him.

"Since we're all trapped here, waiting for the lovely hardworking baggage-claim people to release our painstakingly packed suitcases from the bowels of whatever lives at the bottom of this conveyor belt, I thought we could kill some time together."

There was some scattered applause. A security guard made his way towards them.

"I have a prize package of a poster of the N.Y. Rangers—" A chorus of boos interrupted him, but Joey only grinned wider.

"Rangers suck!" A male voice boomed from the back of the crowd.

"Mom? Is that you?" Joey shaded his eyes with his hand and pretended to scan the crowd. He laughed and waved the heckler away. "Yeah, yeah. I know you all think the Rangers suck. Personally, I love them. Great guys. But in deference to your delicate Beantown sensibilities, I will give away two tickets to the next *Bruins* game." That drew a ragged cheer from the hockey fans in the crowd.

"All you gotta do to win this unbelievable one-of-a-kind prize package is come have your picture taken with me by my lovely assistant—" he looked down at the girl.

"Annaliese," she supplied.

"Annaliese. The most ridiculous photo as decided by..." he looked around and caught the security guard's eye. "That guy," he said, pointing at the guard, "wins the tickets and the poster."

The security guard stopped in front of Joey and grinned. "Yeah. Okay. But I'm gonna hafta aks you to get off the machine, please."

"No problem." Joey hopped down. "Okay. Children and single women first," he said, with the grin that had gotten him into—and out of—a lot of trouble over the years.

"You in town long?" the security guard asked. "Finally get traded to a real team?" He was a tall African-American man with graying hair who looked like he had put in his twenty with the police force before taking this job for a little extra cash on top of his pension.

Joey laughed and shook his head. "Nope. Just flying up to see my grandpa. He had a bit of a scare last night, and I had the day off, so I thought I'd try to get him to slow down a bit."

An elderly woman patted him on the arm. "You're a good boy."

"Thank you, ma'am. Okay. Who's first?"

By the time his older sister Gina swept by in a cloud of hairspray and a giant eye roll, Joey was kneeling down on the floor next to three little boys mugging at the camera. The boys' mother, looking young and exhausted in blue jeans and an Army Wife sweatshirt, smiled at Joey. "Thank you so much," she said. "We're all huge fans. My husband loves you."

The oldest of the five Luciano siblings, Gina was ten tons of pure energy packed into a five-foot-nothing body. Her big boobs, high hair, and loud voice gave her a presence way beyond the physical. At thirty-three, she still got carded at bars. She had her first kid at twenty-two, her third two years ago, and hadn't slowed done one bit.

"Don't tell him crap like that," she told the woman, her thick Boston accent comforting and familiar in Joey's ears. "His head is already big enough. Come on, Jojo. I'm paying by the minute for parking. Well, you're paying. Whatever." She flicked her long black hair out of her face.

Sensing their chance for a photo slipping away, some fans shoved closer to Joey.

"Joey! Joey!" a youngish sounding woman called from the edge of the crowd. She had bleached blonde hair, tight jeans, and a small t-shirt that pulled up to her ribcage as she pushed her way through the crowd. "Joey," she said with a breathy sigh and a flutter of her eyelashes. "Sign my chest?"

There was certainly enough room across the top of her gravity-defying breasts. They looked firm enough to handle the pen as well.

Gina yanked the woman's shirt down to cover her navel. "What's wrong with you? What are you, seventeen? Pull your shirt down. It's fucking February; you're gonna get pneumonia."

Joey bit back a smile as the woman glared at Gina. "I'll sign a piece of paper if you want," Joey said apologetically.

The blare of a klaxon heralded the return of the suitcase parade, and the crowd cheered.

It took a while, but Joey's box finally appeared. He watched it go around and around a few times as he signed autographs and posed for the last few pictures.

"Oh, please, Princess, let me," Gina said grabbing the box the next time it rolled passed them. Joey pulled a poster out of the bag and motioned the security guard over. They scrolled through the photos on Joey's phone; Gina gave a running commentary on her thoughts under her breath.

"This one," the guard said, pointing at a picture of the young woman with three sons.

"Definitely," Joey whispered, then turned to the crowd. "We have a winner!" He pointed to the wife of the soldier, and the little boys jumped up and down and clapped.

Joey gave the woman the poster and got her contact information, assuring her he would send the tickets. He made a mental note to include some swag and some extra vouchers for food and drinks for the whole family.

Gina finally got tired of inching their way through the crowd of admirers. "Fuck this," she muttered under her breath. "Hey, Joey," she said much louder than necessary. "Isn't that Tom Brady?"

Joey looked where she pointed down an empty hall. "It totally is."

The crowd around them thinned slightly as people searched for the most loved or hated man in Boston, depending on where you stood with the Patriots. Gina shoved him through the crowd with both hands on his back.

She didn't talk to him directly until she handed the parking valet her ticket. "Well, that was fun."

"Sorry," Joey said.

She scoffed. "You love it, you attention whore." She smiled and hugged him to take the edge off her words. "Maybe if you didn't dress like a fashion model just to come home, Mr. GQ, you could sneak out unrecognized.

"What's wrong with the way I dress?" He'd put on his most basic suit. A plain navy wool two-piece suit, a dark blue paisley tie, and a wool overcoat.

Gina looked pointedly at her sweatpants and parka combo. She tipped the valet and hopped into her bright red minivan, forcing her way through late afternoon Boston traffic in a hail of curses, honking, and rude hand gestures.

"Damn, Gina," Joey said, grabbing onto the door handle as she lurched around a double-parked taxicab and made disparaging remarks about the driver's parentage. Unfortunately, traffic came to a standstill immediately after that, and the driver leaped out of his cab, brandishing a small baseball bat.

"Oh my God," Joey said, eyes wide.

Gina leaned around him, rolling the passenger's side window down and leaving Joey much too close to the angry man. "Yeah? You got something to say?" she snapped.

"Jesus, Gina." He held up a placating hand to the angry man one inch from the car. "It's okay, sir. She's off her meds."

Gina snorted a laugh. The light turned green, and she rocketed the minivan through the intersection.

"Holy shit, G," Joey said with a nervous laugh. "You're a fucking maniac."

"And you're a pussy." She slapped him on the arm with the back of her hand. "You can't let jerks get away with shit."

"Easy for you to say. Last thing I need is some Twitter post saying

'Joey Luciano assaults taxi driver.' The club's already threatening to take away my phone."

"Pshaw. Not going to happen," Gina assured him. "It would say '*Sister of* Joey Luciano assaults taxi driver.' I deserve my fifteen minutes of fame as much as you."

Joey exhaled as they reached the quieter streets of their neighborhood. "Tell me the truth, how's Nonno Lollo?"

"He's okay," Gina said. "Cranky. Crankier than usual."

"Was it a heart attack?" He hadn't been able to get a straight answer from his mother.

Gina shook her head. "Nah, just some *agita* this time. But Angie got him to make a doctor's appointment next week. She's worried about his heart." Angie, the oldest of the O'Reilly kids, was a nurse and the two families' first go-to for medical issues.

"How seriously is she worried?" Joey had spent more time with Lorenzo Luciano than any other adult in his life, and Joey loved him fiercely. The thought of him dying made Joey break into a cold sweat.

"Yeah, well, he is ninety. It's not nothing," Gina admitted. "Angie said he's gotta quit smoking and stop eating so much rich food."

"He said he'd rather be dead than quit smoking." That was an exact quote.

"Well, he keeps it up, he's gonna get his wish." She pulled into the driveway separating the Luciano house from the almost identical O'Reilly house next to it. Even though Joey knew for certain that Liam, the oldest of the O'Reilly siblings and the source of all of Joey's current stress, was in Seattle working with the Thunder, he couldn't help shooting a glance in that direction.

"Looking for someone?" Gina asked.

"Nope. Just looking. Who's around anyway?" he asked as if the answer meant nothing to him.

"You talk to Liam recently?" she asked, in that scary big sister way she had of reading his mind.

"Not since Christmas day," Liam answered, without looking at her. Also known as 'The Morning After' in the privacy of Joey's head. The day that rocked Joey's world.

She snorted. He thought he heard her say *bastard* under her breath.

"Come inside. I'll feed you, and you can tell the old grouch to take better care of himself. Maybe he'll listen to you. You're his favorite."

Grabbing his bag, he followed her into the house he considered home even though he hadn't lived there since he was sixteen, nine years ago.

2

LIAM

LESLIE posted in **YOU WISH**:

 Meet your newest and cutest niece! Stella Louise Ryan-Luciano. 6lbs 2 oz, 17" long. Mom Sophia and Mom Leslie are doing fine.

LIAM: CONGRATULATIONS!

DEANO: damn soph, what is wrong with that kid?

SOPHIE: mom Sophia is NOT doing fine, I'm bleeding to death and I have stitches in places I never knew you could get stitches, and my boobs hurt

SOPHIE: She looks like her uncles

JIMMY: Congrats ladies! Enjoy never sleeping again!

DEANO: I'm just joking, I know they all look like that. She gorgeous like her mommas.

THE VIDEO REVIEW ROOM IN THE SEATTLE THUNDER FACILITIES HAD enough seats for the players and the coaching staff. Right now, however, it held only the Thunder's newest Assistant Coach, Liam O'Reilly, and his defencemen.

Liam pointed the remote at the giant video screen at the front of the room and hit pause. On screen, Joey Luciano, the New York Rangers' center, froze in the middle of splitting the Flyers' defense.

Sitting up, Liam advanced the video a couple of frames and stopped it again. "Right there." He walked to the smart board and circled the puck making sure the Thunder d-men could see exactly what he was talking about.

"Right there, he splits the D and then dangles like a motherfucker, looking like he's going to shoot the puck behind the right d-man, who is in no position to stop it, which makes this guy—" Liam circled the other defenceman. "Which makes this guy fall for it like a bass going for a fishing lure. So he breaks left to intercept the pass. But the puck's never left Luciano's stick, right?"

Liam started the video again, and Joey yanked the puck back like it was connected to his stick by a string. The camera pulled back to give them a wider shot, and Liam paused it again.

"So now who's between him and the goalie?" Liam paused long enough to let them know it wasn't a rhetorical question.

"No one," answered Paul Dyson. Paul had been called up from the Lightning, the Thunder's development team, at the beginning of

December. The twenty-two-year-old defenceman had been drafted at eighteen and spent a few years on the University of Alabama Chargers before signing a two-way contract with the Thunder.

With his blue eyes, curly blond hair, and honest-to-god cleft chin, he had the kind of face that had the media department drooling. They had him posing with kids at every hospital in a one hundred mile radius of Seattle. Luckily, he was also a great kid whose personality matched his looks.

"Exactly. Fucking no one." He restarted the video. Almost faster than the eye could follow, Joey closed the gap between him and the net, deking the puck back and forth, right and left so quickly the goalie could barely keep track of it. Joey faked a shot to his right, and the goalie committed to the stop, reaching out with his glove hand. Again, Joey yanked the puck back and shot it directly over the goalie's stick before the guy could even turn his head in that direction.

The whole thing had taken three seconds.

Robbie Rhodes, Paul's defensive partner, whistled low. Robbie had been drafted by the Thunder right after high school, and played two and a half years with Bemidji before signing. With his thick auburn hair and hazel eyes, he could have been an O'Reilly relative.

'The Boys', as everyone referred to them, had had a rough start. The first time they were on the ice together, Robbie had dropped his gloves and punched Paul's lights out. Apparently there was some history there beyond the normal Bemidji-Huntsville rivalry. What-ever it was, they'd worked it out before Liam or Andy had had to intervene.

Worked it out was putting it mildly. They'd made a miraculous turn-around. If Liam was a betting man, and he certainly was, he'd put money on the fact that they were a couple now.

"Damn," Robbie said. "He's fast. We don't have to play those guys until after the All-Star Game, right?"

The Thunder would be facing the Rangers in two weeks for the second and final time of the season. They'd lost the first game, but this time they would have the home-ice advantage. Liam was determined they would win.

But first, he had to survive the All-Star game.

The All-Star weekend was one day of skills exhibition and one day of an all-league game for the fans. Fans voted for their favorite players from each team and they competed against each other as teams and as individuals in various events. This year their starting goalie, Sergei Pergov would be representing the Thunder. Joey and Ryan McDonagh would be there representing the Rangers.

Yes. That Joey Luciano. The same Joey Luciano that had just smoked the Flyers' star goalie on screen. The kid who had grown up in the house right next to Liam's. Joey Luciano aka the Looch, the youngest of the ten O'Reilly-Luciano gang and one of hockey's rising superstars. He was also the guy Liam had slept with in his nephew's bed on Christmas Eve.

Not knowing how to handle the completely unexpected and surprisingly affecting experience, Liam had hit the road on Christmas Day, leaving as early as he could without getting too yelled at by his mother. Needless to say, it hadn't been his proudest moment.

Joey had texted a few times since then, but sometime between his first and second Christmas-Eve orgasms, Liam had lost the ability to be casual with Joey.

He'd known he owed Joey an explanation and an apology for his disappearing act, but he hadn't known what to say. What kind of flowers said *Thank you,* and *You're the hottest thing I've ever seen,* and *You terrify me*, all at the same time? He was pretty sure Hallmark didn't make a card for that.

And, of course, the longer he'd waited, the harder it had become to start talking at all. Joey's texts had been equally stilted as if he didn't know how to be normal anymore either.

Now it was almost All-Star weekend, and Joey and Liam would both be there along with every O'Reilly and Luciano family member that could get away.

But it was okay. That was fine. Liam would find Joey, apologize, and set some kind but firm boundaries for them moving forward. Boundaries that took them back to the friendship they'd shared for fucking twenty plus years. A friendship where Liam's nightly jerk-off fantasies didn't involve the kid who'd grown up next door.

"So what do we do, Coach?" Sven Anderson asked in his Swedish-accented English. "What is our strategy for facing Luciano on the ice?"

Head coach Andy Williams stuck his head into the room. "Why don't you boys discuss it among yourselves while I borrow Coach O'Reilly here for a minute."

Liam tossed the remote to Paul. "There's a couple more plays on this video I want you guys to take a look at. Watch them, go over them, and when I come back, have some answers for me as to the best ways to defend against these guys."

———

"WHAT'S UP?" Liam asked. "Is everything okay?"

"Everything's fine," Andy replied. "I like what you're doing with the boys in there. They like you and respond well to your coaching."

Andy Williams and Liam's friendship had started when Liam was sixteen. Andy had been a development coach at Shattuck-St. Mary's, the Minnesota boarding school Liam had attended. All six hockey players in the Luciano and O'Reilly families, boys and girls alike, had gone to St. Mary's.

By the time Sophia Luciano and Jimmy O'Reilly had gotten there, Liam had graduated from Harvard and was a rookie with the Laval Rockets, the AHL development league team for the Montréal Canadiens.

Liam's brother Patrick, his sister Natalie, Joey, and Joey's older brother, Deano, had all been in the school at the same time. People still told stories about the pranks they had pulled and the trouble they had gotten into.

Though he was the youngest, and the last to graduate, Joey had more than upheld the family legacy by getting signed directly to the L.A. Kings at eighteen, before he'd even officially graduated.

Photographs and newspaper clippings from Andy's illustrious career lined the walls of his office. There were pictures of Andy with past, current, and future Hockey Hall of Fame inductees, years of team pictures, pictures of Andy with various famous athletes, and most numerous of all, pictures of Andy's family. He had a beautiful wife, Cindy, and two grown children, a boy and a girl, who looked more like their French-Canadian mother than their father.

Liam had none of those things.

It hadn't mattered when he'd been an active player. Yeah, most guys got married young, but not all of them. And though he might not be

Hall of Fame material, he'd had a good, solid career that had earned him a handful of trophies and a lot of money.

Then pain he couldn't ignore led to the discovery of a torn hip labrum. Despite excellent surgeons and physical therapists, after nine months off the ice, he'd been forced to admit it was time to retire. At thirty-three, he'd been one of the older players in the league. Many of the guys he'd come up with were gone, either from injury, sickness, or simply the wear and tear of life on the road on a relationship.

It had been one of the hardest times of his life. Between parental expectations, school, college, and hockey, for his entire life he'd had goals, schedules, and clear accomplishments by which he could measure his success. And then it was gone. He had nothing specific to do, nowhere to be, and no one to answer to.

It had been awful. Despite having a career longer than most players, he'd refused to think about what came after. When he'd been forced into retirement, he'd taken a long hard look at his life and seen nothing but a middle-aged man with money in the bank, but no home, no wife, no family of his own. His personal life still looked the same as it had when he was twenty-one.

So, Liam made a plan. He'd sent out feelers for a position that would set him up for the next phase of his life. When he'd gotten the job with the Thunder, he'd bought a house and an engagement ring. Both for Michelle, the woman he'd been dating for five years.

Unfortunately, this past Christmas she'd made it one hundred percent clear that she didn't want either of those things; at least not from him.

So Liam had returned the ring but kept the house on Alki Beach. He loved being by the water, and he loved the views of the islands across the bay. He made himself a promise that he would work as hard at coaching as he had at playing, and he would be head coach of his own team by age fifty.

Andy's praise reassured him that he was on the right track.

He'd been worried when he started the job, knowing that Andy had been the one to put Liam forward and push for him despite his lack of coaching experience. If Liam screwed up, it would reflect badly on Andy, and Liam would be humiliated.

"I like them, too," Liam replied. "You've got some real talent here. I think Rhodes and Dyson have long careers ahead of them."

"Barring injuries," Andy said as he sat behind his big wooden desk. He rapped his knuckles on the top of it twice for luck. "We both know how those can fuck up a career."

Andy's own playing career had been cut short due to repeated shoulder injuries he'd been unable to fully recover from.

"So what do you need from me?" Liam asked. "Just say the word."

Andy frowned and pecked at his keyboard. He swiveled the monitor so they could see it. Joan Jett's "Bad Reputation" blared from the tinny speakers. *We heart the Looch* flashed in neon letters over a still photo of Joey's face.

The YouTube video showcased Joey and his exploits. Clips of him fighting were interspersed with shots of him skating his way through the other team like they weren't even there. A montage of his breakaways alone took up almost twenty seconds.

"Kid's got some silky mitts, eh?" Andy commented over the music.

"Yeah, he does." Liam's muttered response was a little too heartfelt. He blushed to the tips of his ears, damning his complexion, his heritage, and Joey Luciano's talented hands.

At Christmas, up in the Luciano's attic with a houseful of friends and family below them, Joey's touches had been tentative, as if he wasn't sure how to touch Liam, or if he even had the right to. But by the end of that incredible evening, his touch had been confident and strong.

Liam wished he could stop thinking about that night. He'd obsessed more over Joey in the last two months that he'd thought about Michelle in five years. *That might have been part of the problem,* his traitorous brain supplied.

He shoved that thought away and gave the fan video way more attention than it deserved.

Even on the ice, Joey played to the crowd. He made sure to throw pucks to as many little kids as he could after practice and pregame warm-ups. There was plenty of footage of Joey signing autographs for an hour after a game. Off the ice, he shone. Handsome in his perfectly tailored suits and flawless hair, he flashed an ear-to-ear grin that charmed grandmothers and babies alike no matter how tough the last game had been or whether they had won or lost.

Cartoon hearts floated up from the bottom of the screen, popping at the top with the appropriate sound effects. Picture after picture flashed across the screen like a slideshow. There were several different shots from over the years of Joey with his arm around the waists of different beautiful woman. Joey with his arm thrown casually across the shoulders of a good-looking man. The people he hung out with ranged from athletes and actors to musicians and world-renowned chefs.

Joey lived the high life and wasn't shy about keeping the world informed about it via what seemed to be every social media platform in existence. Some of which Liam hadn't even known existed.

It was hard for Liam to reconcile this dazzling, handsome, party-boy with the sweet, shy, little boy who had grown up next door to him. He picked up a pen from Andy's desk, twirling it nervously in his fingers as he watched the rest of the video. Sometimes it felt like the Joey Luciano he saw on the TV and read about in the magazines was a stranger.

Then again, Liam had moved out before Joey had turned six years old, and they'd only seen each other over the summers and winter holidays. Of course, he'd grown up and changed. But when they'd gotten together over Christmas, Joey had felt the same to Liam as he had when he was six. He had been sweet, funny, and caring. So, of course, Liam had to run away.

The video came to an end with a close-up of Joey's face surrounded by a heart-shaped frame and repetition of the assertion that the video maker did indeed heart Joey Luciano.

Andy paused the video before the next one could play automatically. "He's something, isn't he, that kid?"

Liam bristled. "He's twenty-five and been playing for the league for seven years. He's not quite a kid."

"True, true." Andy leaned back in his chair. The leather creaked underneath him as he swiveled slowly side-to-side. "The closer I get to sixty, the younger twenty-five seems. And I was two years married by that age. But, you have to admit, the boy lives large. Flashy."

Liam mirrored Andy's position in his chair, folding his arm across his chest. "That's what happens when you give eighteen-year-olds a million dollars a year. They go a little crazy."

"Yeah," Andy said with a sigh and a small shake of his head. "I remember a few ill-advised purchases with my first paychecks."

"Yeah? Like what?"

Andy laughed. "Well, let's just say I paid an amount of money no one should ever pay for a watch. I thought Cindy was going to have a heart attack. What about you? Any purchases you regret?"

Liam pictured the house on the beach that Michelle had declared 'awful' and a 'death trap' for their nonexistent children. Luckily, what she thought hardly mattered anymore. "Nope," he said. "Not one. What can I say? I like my stuff."

"Good for you. You work hard, you should enjoy it."

Liam basked in Andy's approval. He didn't need the admiration of the crowd. But he did need the respect of the people above him, people *he* admired and respected. Andy Williams had been one of those people for a long time.

"So why all the interest in Luciano?" Liam asked, though he had a pretty good idea already. The trade deadline was fast approaching and rumors were flying fast and furiously.

Andy tapped his pen on the desk. "It's on the hush-hush, of course, but we're seriously looking at picking him up."

Liam's stomach lurched at the thought. What he wouldn't give to have talent like Joey's on his team. But that would make him Joey's boss. If Joey was on the Thunder team, he'd see Joey every day and every night. Worse he'd have to see him in the locker rooms getting dressed, and they'd share hotels and the cramped quarters of team buses and planes.

It would be a personal trial for sure, but great for the team. He could handle it. He was a professional. They both were. "Do we have the cap space?"

"We will."

"What would we be giving up?" Liam asked.

"Peters and Jevpalovs, a first-round pick in 2019, and a third in 2020."

"Hmm." Liam mulled over the pros and cons of the trade. Obviously, Joey would be a great addition to their team. They were a little shallow on centers since Bryce Lowery had officially retired after Thanksgiving. They had put off replacing the big man, counting on his return after rehab for a knee injury. But then Lowery had met his Colorado farmer and hung up his skates. Love made people do unexpected things.

Sean Peters was a winger who usually played on their second line but performed well on the first on either wing when needed. He was a solid player, he and Peters hadn't seen eye-to-eye on some of the changes Liam wanted to make to the defensive style of play.

Bohdan Jevpalovs was a thirty-year-old D-man and a guy Liam knew and liked. They'd played on a few teams together over the years. The two of them hung out in Seattle trading war stories and talking about how the rookies looked younger every year.

Both men were older than Joey. Though they had some great unsigned prospects still playing for their college or Major Junior clubs, not to mention the players in development on the Lightning —including Liam's brother Patrick—they could use some new blood right now.

"Well, I'd miss Jetpack, he's a good guy, but it sounds like we'd be getting the better end of the deal. Why are the Rangers so willing to trade Joey? He's a great player. He's done a lot for them." He was offended on Joey's behalf.

Andy pointed a thumb at the screen where Joey was dancing on top of a bar with some scantily dressed women. "You know why."

"Idiots. They didn't know what they had."

"You're right," Andy said. "But you know as much as I do that team cohesion matters. He's been there, what, three years now?"

Liam nodded. "Yeah, about."

"And he's never really managed to bond with his teammates let alone his linemates, right?"

"They're jealous because he gets more attention than any six of them put together. Everybody loves Joey," Liam said, realizing as he said it how true it was. Even people who wanted to dislike Joey on general principle, found themselves smiling and shaking their heads at something he said or did. "Well, almost everybody," he amended. "I admit, there are a few outliers who don't like him at first, but eventually he wins them over."

Andy nodded slightly, acknowledging the partial truth of the situation. "Hockey players are not normally known for their sparkling personalities. But that kid, he's got a spark."

"Joey sparkles, alright," Liam said before he could censor himself.

Andy stretched his arms out, linking his fingers behind the back of his head. He stared at the ceiling as if he could see Joey's face in the off-white plaster. "So, tell me something good about Luciano. Besides his hockey skills."

Where to start? How did you sum up everything that made Joey *Joey*? Liam searched for the words. "The thing about Joey is," he started slowly, "that outside of his family, hockey is the most important thing to him. He loves it. You can see it whenever he's on the ice. He's got that stupid smile on his face that I know drives other players crazy."

"Um hmm," Andy agreed.

"He's a great guy, heart of gold, actually more shy than you would guess." Liam thought about Joey, the way he was at home surrounded by family and friends who had known him before he was the Looch. "More private. You know, it's odd that he isn't fitting in. Usually, he's great in a room. Low ego, hard working. He's funny and smart."

"He is charming, your boy," Andy said. "My wife and kids love him." He shook his head. "There's something about Luciano that makes me want to smack him upside the head and then give him a cup of cocoa or something. He's got this mouth on him..." Andy shook his head. "Gets him in trouble, I bet."

You have no idea. Liam burst out laughing. "Tell me about it. You just have to know how to take him." Liam shrugged. "We're from Boston, sarcasm is how we show love. If we're nice to you, it means we don't like you. He can be his own worst enemy. He just needs to be tempered."

Andy leaned forward with the creak of the chair, leaning his elbows on the top of the desk. He clasped his hands together, pointing his joined index fingers at Liam. "Think you can be the one to temper him?"

No. Yes. Maybe. Did he even want to be? "How so?" Liam asked, hoping his uncertainty didn't show on his face

Andy threw his arms wide. A native New Yorker, he'd never lost a habit of speaking with his hands. Their shared East Coast upbringing was only one of the things that had drawn him and Liam together despite the age difference. "Focus all that spark and energy, polish it. Grow him up without dimming him."

As soon as Andy said the words, it was all Liam wanted to do. He would polish Joey into the shining star he could so easily be. Take all that boyish charm and good looks and refine it into a devastatingly handsome, cultured man.

He'd have to keep his hands off Joey, of course. He doubted the league wanted their players hooking up with their coaches, but that wouldn't be a problem. *Lie*, his brain supplied. As if in collusion with his brain, his palms tingled with the remembered feel of Joey's skin.

With the talent and skill Joey already had, Liam honestly didn't think there was much he could teach him about hockey. But Andy could. Andy would take care of that part, honing his hockey mind, and integrating Joey into the team. He could raise all of them to a higher level.

"I think he's holding something back," Andy continued, oblivious to Liam's casting of himself as Professor Higgins and Joey as Eliza Doolittle in the *My Fair Lady*-esque fantasy he had going on in his head. (Liam had always thought his sisters were hard on poor Henry Higgins. He'd only been trying to help.)

"I think there's more to him than we see. And I worry that he's starting to spin out of control. Seems to be making fewer and fewer friends, going out more. I've known a lot of kids in my career. Seen a lot of boys turn into men. Seen a lot of them fall down under the weight of money and celebrity, and losing sight of who they really are."

"Yeah," Liam agreed. "Me too."

"So, what's your opinion? You think Joey Luciano and the Thunder could be good for each other?"

Did he? Liam gave it some serious thought. He was flattered that Andy was asking his opinion, and he didn't want to give a glib answer. Liam wasn't sure if he could do what Andy was asking of him, but damn it if he didn't want to give it his best shot.

"I think it could be great," Liam answered. "And if he screws up, you can fire me."

Andy gave him a puzzled look. "Why would I do that? Joey's a grown up. He's responsible for his own actions."

"Yeah, but I'm vouching for him." Liam's contract with the team ran out at the end of the season. So far, there hadn't been any talk about extending it. He desperately wanted to stay. He wanted to settle down for a while.

"I'd be vouching for him, too," Andy said. "And I vouched for you. Ultimately the decision is up to the front office. But I think it would be good for all of us."

Andy sat up straight, pulling the monitor back to its normal position. His hand drifted towards the mouse and his eyes looked at the monitor, signaling the end of the conversation. "He's going to be at the All-Star weekend, correct?"

Liam nodded, the butterflies in his stomach going crazy. He knew there would be no way of avoiding Joey for an entire two days, especially not after this conversation.

"Great," Andy said. "I'll keep my eye on him and report back to Semerad. Hopefully, all of us will know sooner rather than later."

Liam stood up. "That would be great. Did you need me for anything else?"

Andy was already concentrating on his next problem. "No, I think that's it. You get back to those boys. They've probably started a food fight already and are texting dick pics to their girlfriends."

Liam laughed politely and closed the door after him when he left. In the hallway, he leaned back against the wall with a sigh, closing his eyes. He didn't know if he wanted Joey to be traded to the Thunder or not. Both outcomes were equally terrifying. He stood there for a few seconds, breathing deeply and thinking of nothing, enjoying the familiar sounds and scents of the locker room.

Taking a deep breath, Liam pushed off from the wall and straightened his jacket. Either way, the outcome was out of his hands. He and Joey would just have to wait and see what the future held for them.

3

JOEY

GINA: OMFG you are NOT going to believe what your Nana just told me!!!! 😨

ANGIE: *WHAT?!*

GINA: Are you sitting down?

ANGIE: I'm at hockey practice with the kids. Where else?

GINA: Our brothers totally hooked up! 😨 😨

I caught Nana coming out of Nonno Lollo's room and she totally ratted them out!!! 🤮

ANGIE: Fuck. 🤮 Give me 30 seconds, I'll call you.

"So what are your plans for the future?" Joey's grandfather asked him, his breath fogging in the frigid air of the Murphy Memorial skating rink.

"What kind of question is that, Nonno?" Joey asked. "Gonna keep playing hockey as long as I can, what you think I'm going to do?" Joey could hear his Boston accent thickening the way it always did when he spent any length of time around his family.

They sat on the top row of the bleachers like they had so many times before. The rink stood across the street from the beach, and both places had played a big part in Joey's childhood and early teens. Somewhere in a box of memories that traveled with him from apartment to apartment, he still had his green South Boston hockey jersey with the shamrock on it.

The rink hadn't changed at all. Steel beams curved overhead giving the rink the feel of some kind of military aircraft hangar. Small kids skated tentatively across the ice either clutching the hand of a more secure skater or leaning on the blue milk crates that seemed to have been there since the dawn of time.

The watery hot chocolate they were drinking also seemed to have been there since the dawn of time. Enzo had spiked his with Irish whiskey, a habit he'd picked up from decades of friendship with the O'Reillys. Legend held it that the two families had met when Lorenzo's father had taken his family to America. Joey wasn't sure if that was one hundred percent true, but it was close enough.

When Lorenzo tried to tip his flask into the cup, Joey covered the top of his cup with his hand. "Nonno," he hissed. "I can't be seen drinking in public on a Sunday morning. There are kids around." Wouldn't the PR department love him even more than they already did if something like that got out?

Lorenzo scoffed. "No one's even looking at you, Jojo."

Well, that was just a blatant lie. Not only did Joey stand out from the rest of the parka-clad crowd in the gray suit and black wool overcoat he had put on when his grandfather had lied to him and said they were going to church, but he'd signed a bunch of auto-graphs already on the walk from their house to the rink. Joey was a hometown hero back in his hometown.

Even now, a woman with long dark hair in her early thirties, who could easily have passed for one of Joey's sisters, was making her way timidly up the stairs towards them.

A little girl who looked to be about ten years old clutched her hand. The guards on her skates made a familiar clumping sound as they climbed the bleachers. Dark, wavy braids trailed out from beneath her helmet. A pink skating skirt peeked out from below the pink Rangers' jersey she wore.

"Okay, just a little." Joey held out his cup to Enzo. "And make it quick."

Joey took a sip of his doctored drink, grimaced at the taste, and then smiled up at the woman as she stopped two levels below them. "Hi."

"Hi. Sorry to bother you, but you're Joey Luciano, right?"

The little girl stood next to her mother staring intently at Joey.

"I am."

"I told you," the girl said.

"Yes, you did honey, and you were right."

"So what's your name, sweetheart?" Joey asked.

"Molly Elizabeth Ianucci. My mom's name is Mary Elizabeth Ianucci. And you're Joseph Antonio Luciano. Number Forty-Six. Number three draft pick in 2011. You played fifty-eight games this season, with forty-one goals and twenty-eight assists for a total of sixty-nine points."

Joey shot a quick wide-eyed glance at Molly's mom. Mary had tears in her eyes and a smile on her face. "You're right, Molly," Joey said. "That's amazing. I can tell you're a hockey fan. I love your sweater."

Molly twisted so she could show him the back. "It's your jersey. But I know hockey players call them sweaters sometimes. It's not regulation but they don't make those for little kids. When I'm bigger, then I can get the real ones."

"Molly, I think you might be my biggest fan. Can I shake your hand?"

Molly looked at her mother.

"It's okay. You can do what's comfortable for you."

She turned back to Joey. "I'd rather not, thank you."

Joey nodded. This child obviously knew what she wanted. "So, how can I help you, Miss Molly?"

"Would you sign my jersey, please?"

"I would love to but I don't have the right pen."

Molly nodded sagely. "I thought that might happen."

"Mom to the rescue!" Mary dug through her very large purse and pulled out a black marker. "Taa daa!"

Joey signed her shirt to her exact specifications. She requested 'to Molly' his whole name and the date. Joey had to write carefully to fit all that on the small jersey. "All done!"

Molly pulled her shirt out to read the words. When she looked back up at Joey, her whole face transformed. She smiled broadly, her eyes shining. "Thank you, Mr. Luciano!" She turned to her mother. "Can I go skate now?"

"Go ahead. I'll be down in a minute."

All three adults watched the little girl walk carefully down the stairs.

"I hope you don't mind," Mary said when Molly was safely on the ice. "I know we interrupted your conversation."

Lorenzo patted Joey on the shoulder. "It's okay. My grandson here is just so handsome he can't keep the fans away."

From the way she hesitated between speaking with them more and leaving them alone, Joey could tell Mary either had something else to say or something to ask him. As he watched Molly stopping every person she could and showing them her shirt, he knew he had a short window of time to make his escape before word of his presence spread and he would be trapped signing autographs for an hour.

Joey adored his fans. Ninety-nine percent of the time, he loved the celebrity that came with the job, but right now, he needed some time alone to talk with his Nonno.

"I'll leave you alone in a second," Mary said. "I just wanted to tell you what a difference you've made in our lives."

"Me? How?"

Mary stepped over the bench in front of her to get closer. "Molly has autism."

"I don't know much about that," Joey confessed.

She patted his shoulder in a motherly way. "It's okay. I didn't either until I had to. But long story short, Molly's never been interested in anything. And I mean nothing. No toys, no books, no TV shows. Music a little bit."

What must that be like in that kind of a mind? Joey wondered. What was going on inside there that nothing in the outside world was worth paying attention to?

"Well, somehow, about six months ago, she learned that you, a famous hockey player, grew up in her neighborhood," Mary continued. "And all of a sudden she wanted to know everything about you, about the Rangers, about hockey in general. She even asked for skating lessons!" Mary shook her head in disbelief. "It was like having a whole different kid. Do you know, she even got a book from the library called Amazing Hockey Facts? Her first book ever. We renewed it so often; I finally just bought her a copy of her own. She tells me a new fact every day."

"That's amazing." Joey didn't know what to say. He didn't think that had much to do with him, personally. Probably if she had been a little older, she would have fixated on Liam. Or one of the girls. "I can't take credit for that personally, but I'm thrilled that hockey means that much to her. Does she know girls can play hockey?"

"She does, theoretically. But I'm not sure she believes me. She's never seen a girl hockey player."

"I can fix that. If you don't mind, give me your contact number and I'll have Nat get you some tickets to a Boston Pride game. How's that sound?"

"That sounds amazing. Who's Nat?" Mary pulled a pad of paper and a pen out of her bottomless purse.

"Natalie O'Reilly. She grew up next door to me. She's the starting goalie. If she was a guy, she'd be famous. Does Molly have any brothers or sisters? Is there anyone else who would need a ticket?"

"One sister and a dad. Thank you so much. That's great. I can't wait to tell Molly!" She handed Joey the paper. "And, please, don't feel obligated to do anything. It's not necessary. Molly will probably not take that jersey off for the next month."

"It's no problem. The girls always need more people at their games to spread the word about how awesome they are."

Mary left with a polite goodbye.

"Should we skedaddle?" Lorenzo asked when she was gone. "If you don't want to talk to anyone else, we can escape to the bar."

"Nonno. No more drinking, okay?"

Lorenzo shook his head sorrowfully. "Where did I go wrong?"

"I don't know, but maybe one of your other grandchildren will become an alcoholic. Let's go sit on the wall."

A LOW SEAWALL followed the curve of the bridge and the bay. The icy cold wind kept all but the bravest people away and Joey and his grandfather had the beach practically to themselves.

"We should go camping again one day," Joey said. The summers they had spent sailing their small boats between the many islands of Boston's Harbor and hanging out at the beach had been some of the best times of his life. The huge Nantucket compound they'd bought for the family was gorgeous, but spending summers there just wasn't the same.

"That would be fun," Lorenzo said. He patted Joey on the knee. "Tell me what's going on with you?"

"Nothing, Nonno. Nothing is going on."

Lorenzo sniffed sarcastically and rolled his eyes. "Yeah, sure. You and I, we haven't talked very much lately. As a matter of fact, we haven't really talked since Christmas when all that..." Lorenzo waved his hands in the air as he searched for the word. "All that *stuff* went down with that O'Reilly boy."

"The stuff with Liam and Michelle and Nico? That was some crazy shit, huh?"

Lorenzo waved that thought away as if Michelle getting pregnant with Nico's baby while she was dating Liam was no big deal. "No, the stuff with you and him. The—" he held his clasped hands up to his chin and made what Joey thought were supposed to be kissing sounds.

Holy crap. Despite the cold wind whipping his hair around his face and trying to burrow its way under his wool coat, Joey felt the heat burning in his cheeks and he started to sweat.

Lorenzo brushed his stuttered denial away as easily as he had the Michelle situation. "Don't even try to lie. Bridie told me."

Bridie was Brigit Dunlea, the matriarch of the O'Reilly clan. She was eighty-six years old and tough as nails. Christmas Eve, she'd caught Liam coming out of Joey's room in the wee hours of the morning. Since she'd been coming out of Lorenzo's room, she and Liam had agreed on a policy of mutual silence. It seemed Liam's grandma had gone back on her part of the bargain.

"So. What is it?" Lorenzo asked. "Are you boys dating now? Going steady? Whatever it is the kids call it these days."

"No. Definitely not." Joey tried for nonchalant but he could hear the bitterness in his voice. "There's nothing between us. It was stupid. He was drunk and upset. I was drunk."

"No, you weren't." Lorenzo shook his head and placed his hand heavily on Joey's back. "Aw, Jojo. That boy, he never could see what was right in front of him. The Irish, they're blind to love, not like us. We Italians, we live for love. It's our blessing and our curse."

"I don't love him, Nonno." A seagull screamed above his head as it flew down the beach, its cry growing fainter and somehow sadder as it went.

"Of course you love him," Lorenzo said, dismissing the subject as if Joey hadn't spent the last month or so trying to convince himself there was no way he was in love with Liam O'Reilly.

"You've been in love with him since you were eleven years old. That's too bad. If you don't love them, they can't break your heart." Lorenzo sighed like he knew the pain of heartbreak all too well.

He probably did. Lorenzo had been a widower for the last twenty years.

Did everybody know Joey was in love with Liam? Everybody but Liam, of course. It was humiliating. That was it. Joey was done thinking about Liam, worrying about him, taking him into consideration in any way, shape, or form. He clapped his hands together. "You know, let's talk about something else now. Anything else."

"Okay. All right." Lorenzo pulled the flask out of his coat pocket and took a long sip, and then he held it out to Joey.

Joey took a long sip, the cheap whiskey tasting better straight than mixed with Swiss Miss packaged hot cocoa. Maybe it just didn't go that well with mini-marshmallows.

"Tell me about your teammates. Those New York boys. Are they still giving you the cold shoulder?"

Joey shrugged halfheartedly. "Kinda. Not really." He wanted to say no. He considered some of the guys his friends, and he could usually find someone to hang out with. But the truth was, he wasn't fitting in overall with the club. He knew it was because he was loud, he was showy, and he didn't fit the League's idea of a hockey player.

As a rule, they didn't like big personalities. They were more about the team than the individual player. They would love it if everyone would be like Sidney Crosby: quiet-spoken, studious, the kind of boy you brought home to your mother.

Joey had never been quiet and soft-spoken. Mothers tended to like him, though.

Personally, he thought management should be happy with him. Where he went, the press followed. He was one of the few players even people who didn't watch hockey knew by name if not by face, and he'd been in enough magazines and newspapers and commercials that most people in the tri-state area knew his face as well. "I'm probably their best publicity. How does that make me a problem?" Joey spread his hands. "Huh? How?"

"Ehh…" Enzo gave a noncommittal shrug.

"What? You got something to say, Nonno? Just say it."

"Do you think you might be doing a little too much publicity lately? A little too much…" He mimed drinking out of his flask. "I follow you on those Instantbook things, you know. With the bottles and the beer ping pong."

Joey threw up his hands in disgust. "Jeez, make up your fu..freakin' mind, why don't you? Before you were practically begging me to drink. Now you think I'm drinking too much?" Joey jumped up and paced in the sand.

Damn it. *Damn it.* He hadn't meant for Nonno Lollo to see those pictures. Great. Yes, he had been going out more, and yes, he had been posting more photos. He had his reasons, damn it. Good reasons. But now his grandpa thought he was out of control.

Joey wanted to tell him the truth so badly. He was scared, and he needed someone to tell him everything was fine. But with Lollo's heart and everything…it wasn't a good time. The old man had his own shit to worry about.

Enzo watched him pace in silence for a moment. "Do you want to talk about it?" he asked.

"Nothing to talk about. You're right. I should go out less, drink less. I'm just trying to make some friends." He stopped pacing and sat down heavily next to his grandfather, leaning into his side.

"I think they don't like you because they don't know you. They only know the party boy Joey—that image you put out. They know the Looch." Lorenzo said Joey's nickname like he was some kind of thug.

"But that *is* the real me. You know me. I'm loud, I like to go out. That's all I am, right? That's what they like. I skate fast, I hit hard, and party harder."

Lorenzo slapped Joey so hard on the back of his head; he almost knocked him off the wall.

"Hey," Joey said rubbing his head. "Concussions, remember? What the hell was that for anyway?"

"I never want to hear you talking that way about yourself again. Never again, *capisce?*"

Joey rubbed his head slowly. "You have to love me, you're my grandfather. But really, this is all I got right now. And who knows how long it could last. I could lose it all tomorrow. So I'm gonna go big. I'm gonna make my name so big and my face so well-known, they'll never forget me. Even if I'm not playing hockey."

Enzo shook his head slowly. "Jojo, no one who's ever met you could ever forget you. Whether you're playing hockey or you're a bag boy at the supermarket."

"Now that's a lie. If I wasn't the Looch...you know how many guys disappear after they retire? Hockey's all I got."

"That's bullshit, Jojo. You're a good boy. You're smart, you're funny, and you're good to your mama and your family." Lorenzo stood up and started pacing in front of Joey, his worn leather shoes sinking into the cold sand with every step.

"I don't know what happened to you, but ever since you went away, ever since you started playing big-time hockey, you've changed. I mean, you always used to be the class clown, loved getting attention, but now, in public, I see you on the TV and you're like this big blowhard guy. All noise, always with the joking, always with the drinking and the going out. And everything you say, it's... it's like a joke, funny. Like everything's a joke to you. So tell me, what happened?"

Joey ran both hands through his hair, resting his elbows on his knees. He sighed loudly then looked up at his grandfather, his chin in his hands. Maybe he should tell him what was going on.

Enzo stopped pacing and sat down heavily next to Joey. He grimaced and put his hand on his chest. Joey didn't like the way he looked, His skin was gray, and he was sweating. *No.* He didn't need to add to his grandpa's burdens.

"Come on, kiddo. You can talk to me." Enzo pulled a handkerchief from his pocket and wiped his forehead.

A cold wind blew off the water. Even through the wool overcoat, the cement wall chilled Joey's ass and the backs of his thighs. They both needed to get home and back inside. Joey had to give him something or he'd never let it go. The old man was like a dog with a bone. He decided on a partial truth.

"You don't know what it was like, Nonno, walking into that training camp that first day. I was a kid. Eighteen. Three months before that, I'd been in high school trying to pass calculus."

Joey stared up into the gray winter sky remembering how he'd felt. He'd been the shortest and the youngest person on the entire team. Some of the guys were monsters, almost a foot taller than him. Now he was still one of the shortest players in the league, but the rookies made him feel older every season.

"So, now I'm on the ice with people whose *posters* I had up on my bedroom wall. And I'm trying to keep up with them, trying to do what they pay me close to two million dollars a year to do, without fucking it up in front of fifteen thousand fans, my family, and every kid who thought they had more of a right to be there than I did."

"You were scared?" Enzo took a sip from his flask. A little of the color had come back to his face.

"Fuckin' terrified," Joey laughed. "So I figure if I can make them laugh first, make them laugh *with* me, maybe they might not laugh *at* me so much, y'know? If I just act like I'm all that and a bag of chips, maybe one day even *I* would believe I really deserve to be there. Fake it till you make it, isn't that what they say?"

"Oh, *bambino*, you've made it, you know it. You know you're good, you have the trophies to prove it. When are you gonna stop faking it?"

"I know. I don't know if I'm even faking it anymore. What if there's nothing left? What if this is it? Maybe I am nothing more than the Looch? Maybe I got nothing to offer besides hockey and a laugh?"

Lorenzo wrapped his arm around Joey's shoulder and pulled him against his side for a hug. Even at ninety, with his hair all white, his back a little bit bent, Lorenzo Luciano was still a strong man. And even at twenty-five, with his picture in the magazines and millions of dollars in the bank, Joey Luciano still needed hugs from his grandpa.

"You're still my Jojo." Lorenzo kissed the top of his head. "If anyone lucky enough to get to know the real you doesn't like it, then it's their loss. And they can just fuck off."

Joey laughed loudly even as he blinked back tears. He loved the old man fiercely and nothing scared him more than thinking about the day when he would no longer be around.

He heard running footsteps behind them. "Looch!" someone shouted. "Hey, Looch, you gonna come skate?" Two young boys with hockey sticks thrown over their shoulders ran down the path toward the rink.

Joey blinked back tears and gave the boys his best smile. "I can't," he said, spreading his hands wide and shrugging in apology. "The National Hockey League owns this body. If I damage it anywhere but on their ice, I'm in wicked trouble."

The boys groaned in disappointment but barely slowed as they passed.

The wind picked up, whitecaps darting across the bay before crashing on the shore. Joey tucked his overcoat tightly around him. Lorenzo pulled a wool hat out of his pocket and pulled it down over Joey's hair. "Come on, it's freezing out here, and your momma was making sauce when we left. If we don't get home, those animals will eat it all before we get any."

"That would be a tragedy," Joey said completely seriously. "If Gina doesn't save me some, I'm gonna buy her son his first porno magazine."

Lorenzo laughed. "Oh, you think it would be Matt's first? You just keep thinking that."

They walked quickly back to the house, the biting wind off the water pushing them down the streets. Lorenzo ran interference for the few autograph seekers attempting to stop them.

Stepping through the front door of the old four-story house, Lorenzo's glasses fogged over from the heat, and a two-year-old ran full speed into Joey, grabbing him around the knees. From the kitchen came the sound of laughter and conversation, and the delicious scent of garlic and tomato sauce that always meant home to Joey.

As he sat down the table and passed the bowl of meatballs to his nephew, Joey wondered how much longer he'd be able to keep dragging himself away from the people who meant the most to him in the world.

4

LIAM

PATRICK: how's he looking?

ANGIE: not good. 😩

ANGIE: Did Judy call him yet?

GINA: Nope 😩

DEANO: Time for operation Judy?

GINA: Yep. Alert the troops

LIAM KNEW PATRICK WAS LYING TO HIM, THAT MUCH WAS A GIVEN.
Exactly *what* he was lying about and what he hoped to accomplish
by it were the real questions.

As the youngest of the gang, Patrick was often the appointed gofer,
but the others didn't usually ask him to lie; mostly because he was

really bad at it. He also couldn't be trusted with secrets and couldn't keep a straight face if his life depended on it.

"Why didn't Gina come and get me?" Liam asked as he followed Patrick through the crowded club. "Isn't this usually her job? She's a much better liar than the rest of you."

Blasts of arctic air from the air conditioners worked fruitlessly to counteract the body heat of hundreds of athletes, fans, and pirate-costumed partygoers that combined with the hot Tampa night to turn the club into a sauna—and not the nice kind of sauna. Liam had other people's sweat on his body. Something he didn't mind in more intimate situations, or on the ice, but that lost its appeal when it wasn't from people of his choosing.

"Gina's sweet-talking some waiter into getting us a bottle of tequila," Patrick explained.

Liam groaned. Nights that started out with the gang and tequila never ended well. *Never.* "How come Carter isn't trying to talk her out of it?" Gina's husband claimed to be making an effort to rein in his wild wife, but Liam knew he secretly loved the unpredictability and fun she brought to his life.

All the Lucianos were like that. You never knew what they were going to do.

"Carter didn't come, remember? Matt's sick." Matt was Gina's eleven-year-old son.

Patrick twisted through the tightly packed dance floor, leading Liam past a gaggle of women in tiny black and red striped skirts and white bikini tops. One of the women had wrapped a red bandana around her head in lieu of a costume. He gave her a D for effort, but an A for execution. He had no problems with the whole slutty pirate look.

"Ladies," Liam said, raising his glass to them as he squeezed past close enough to touch.

"Where's your costume, honey?" One of the women shouted over the pounding music. She trailed her long fingernail down the sleeve of his white dress-shirt.

Liam's suit and tie did stand out in the crowd, but no one had seen fit to tell him that the All-Stars was going to be a pirate-themed weekend. Unsurprisingly, he hadn't brought anything appropriately piratey. Leaving his jacket back at the hotel was as casual as he could get.

"It's at the cleaners," he told the women. He smiled and shrugged as he walked backward away from them. "My parrot crapped on it."

They laughed, and then went back to dancing with each other. As dancing consisted of the grinding on each other in various combinations, Liam wasn't offended. They looked like they could go for hours. Liam checked his watch, feeling old. At thirty-five, he couldn't keep those hours anymore. If he was being totally honest, he didn't want to.

Liam lengthened his stride to catch up to his brother. Whatever was wrong with Matt must have been serious if Carter was missing the All-Star game. When one of their own was competing, it was practically a mandatory Luciano-O'Reilly family reunion. Everyone who could show up would show up. Gina, in particular, had been looking forward to escaping the cold, gray Boston winter and hitting the beaches of Tampa Bay, and she wouldn't miss an opportunity to cheer on her baby brother.

It was Liam's first time at the Games as a coach and not as a player, and it was a completely different experience. More work, fewer parties. He'd landed late in the afternoon, then he'd been busy helping Sergei get settled in. Then he'd had a meeting with Andy and the other coaches.

He hadn't planned on running into the gang tonight, either, because he hadn't planned on going to the Pirate Party. It wasn't an officially sanctioned event; it just so happened that the Gasparilla Pirate Festival had been scheduled for the same time as the game. But when Andy had slapped him on the back and asked him if he was going to the party, the only answer he could give was an enthusiastic 'of course!'

He probably would have run into Joey sometime tomorrow after the skills competition. Sergei was scheduled to be in the net for the 'anything goes' breakaway exhibition, and Joey would be participating. So, their paths would cross eventually. No need to rush things.

"What's wrong with Matt?" Liam asked when Patrick slowed down to greet a couple of players they'd both crossed paths with over the years. At this level, everyone at least knew of everyone else, having either played with or against them at some point.

"I'm not sure," Patrick answered, walking towards the back of the club. "I don't know, flu? Dropsy? Scurvy? Do kids get that?" He stopped at the entrance of the hallway to the bathrooms where two Lucianos and an O'Reilly lay in wait.

"Get what?" Natalie O'Reilly asked. *She'd* obviously gotten the pirate memo. Her long strawberry blonde hair was out of its usual ponytail, held in place by the strap of the eyepatch she wore. An off-the-shoulder fluffy white blouse, a black corset, and black leggings tucked into knee-high boots completed the outfit.

"Scurvy," Patrick said.

"Hey, Nat," Liam said kissing his younger sister on the cheek, then dragging her into a hug.

These All-Star games had to suck for her. Though she was the starting goalie for the NWHL Boston Pride, a key player for the United States women's national ice hockey team, and was better than many of the guys Liam knew, Natalie wasn't allowed to compete at the games. None of the women's teams were.

Liam hoped the women would take the gold this year in the Winter Olympics so she could shove it in some faces.

"Does anybody get scurvy anymore?" Deano Luciano asked. Deano was a perfect example of the unfairness of the system. He was twenty-six, the same age as Natalie, and he made a million a year as the backup goalie for the Tampa Bay Lightning.

Natalie made seven thousand dollars for the season.

Sophia Luciano, the oldest of the Luciano siblings, had also played hockey in college and had been on the NWHL Buffalo team. Saying that she was feeling old at almost thirty, she'd quit the year before when the league had slashed every player's contracted salary in half midway through the season. The league lost an award-winning forward, but Sophia gained a wife. They'd just had their first kid, so she had no regrets.

"Pirates used to get scurvy," Patrick answered.

"He doesn't have scurvy, you idiot," Natalie said to Patrick. "He has the flu, and Carter is worried the other two will get it. It's bad this year."

Natalie smacked Liam on the arm with the back of her hand. "If you checked the group chat every once in a while, you would know that."

"If he checked the group texts every now and then, we wouldn't have to be here right now," Patrick pointed out.

"Speaking of right now," Liam said. "What's going on? Paddy claims Sergei needed to see me about his stick. Which is the saddest attempt at a lie since Jimmy told Mom that Conrad Sincowitz had *given* him his bicycle as an early birthday present."

They exchanged a look.

Natalie sighed. "It's an idiot intervention."

"Stop calling me an idiot at work." Liam looked around quickly to make sure no one important was around.

"This is a bar," Patrick said with frustrated patience. "This isn't work."

Liam pointed to the vast, strobe-lit expanse of the club behind him. "My boss is somewhere over there. Ergo, this is work."

"Ergo, you're a douche," Gina said, pushing through the crowd with a tray of shot-glasses filled with amber liquid and a bottle of tequila.

Gina held the tray out imperiously, offering it to each person in turn. "*Salud,*" they said in ragged unison, tossing the shots back.

The tequila went down surprisingly smoothly. If Gina was shelling out for the good stuff, things must be serious.

"So why am I here?" Liam asked again, setting his glass back on the tray.

"Is the other idiot in there already?" Patrick asked, ignoring Liam and pointing at the men's room door.

Deano nodded.

"What other idiot?" Liam asked, though as soon as he asked he knew. It could only be Joey. He'd fallen into some kind of family trap. God damn it. He used to be smarter than that.

His stomach cramped at the idea of seeing Joey again. He felt so guilty over how he'd left things between them. He was older, he was supposed to be the grown up.

As the tequila warmed his veins, he opened the door on the memories he tried to keep repressed. Joey half-naked on the mattress, tattoos gleaming with sweat as Liam worked a finger into him. Joey's cock straining against the ridiculous black and neon blue briefs he'd been wearing. Red and green Christmas lights sliding over Joey's skin as they moved together in the bed. No matter how often he pushed the images away, they always came back. Usually late at night.

He should have called.

Shoulda, woulda, coulda, as his dad would say. In the privacy of his own mind, he could admit that he was scared. Scared of what Joey would say. That he would yell and curse at Liam was a given. He just hoped Joey didn't take a swing at him. Liam was taller and heavier, but now that he wasn't playing anymore, he'd let the workouts slide. Coaching didn't require the same strict routine.

Joey worked out constantly, and he had the three percent body fat and six-pack abs to prove it. Not that Liam was thinking about his body or his abs at all. There had to be a way out of this. Maybe there was a fire alarm he could pull.

Two men headed toward the bathroom, and Gina imperiously waved them away. "Closed!" she said. "Toilet's blocked up. It's really gross."

One guy wrinkled his nose and they both walked away.

"You can't monopolize the whole bathroom, G," Liam protested. Surely someone would be complaining to the staff any second now.

"Yeah, I can," Gina said. She glared at a giant drunk guy making a beeline to the door. "It's closed. Use the ladies."

Obviously, the guy had a death wish, because he pulled himself up to his full-height, grumbling something as he stepped closer to Gina.

His buddy looked at the group surrounding Gina and tugged the guy away nervously. Drunk guy shook him off.

"Sorry," the friend said to Liam and Patrick.

Liam shrugged. It wasn't them the guy should be worried about.

Gina took a step forward, coming down hard on the guy's foot with her four-inch stiletto heel. "Yeah, I know the line for the ladies' is longer. Sucks doesn't it?" She poked him in the chest. "Welcome to my world. Now get the fuck outta here. This is family business."

The guy held up his hands and let his more sober friend drag him away. "Okay, fine."

Gina turned her gaze to Liam. Despite being a foot taller than she was, he still felt like she was looking down at him. "When was the last time you spoke to my little brother? Or even texted him directly?"

Shit. She was in full big sister mode. Liam was in trouble. Joey was the baby of both families. "Um, well, I haven't spoken to him in a while," he confessed.

Gina narrowed her eyes, hands on her hips. "Define a while."

"Since Christmas," he admitted. The stunned silence that followed surprised him.

"Damn, Judy," Deano said. "You're a dick."

"Stop calling me that." He checked the people standing near them to see if anyone important was nearby.

"Stop being a dick, and we'll consider it," Natalie said, hopping onto the 'pick on Liam' bandwagon.

Liam shrugged like it was no big deal. Trying to keep his nerves from showing on his face, he looked directly into Gina's eyes. "What's the big deal? We're both busy. We've gone months not talking before."

"Yeah, but not after you fucked him," Gina said, poking Liam hard in the chest with a long acrylic fingernail.

Oh, fuck. "What? And ow, Gina. That hurt." She couldn't really know, could she? Maybe she meant it in a 'since you fucked him *over*' way.

Gina poked him again. "Don't even *try* to pretend like it didn't happen."

"Fuck." He covered his mouth with both hands, scanning the crowd again. Coach Williams was making his way across the room. He was deep in conversation with the coach from the Rangers, Joey's current team. Thankfully, he didn't seem to be heading Liam's way.

"Does everyone know?" he asked. Stupid question. Of *course* they did. What one of them knew, all ten of them knew.

Gina pointed at Natalie, Patrick, and Deano. "We know, obviously."

"I heard it from Angie," Patrick said. "And I told Jimmy."

That left only Sophia and Nico. Sophia had to know; the girls told each other everything.

"Please tell me Nico doesn't know," Liam pleaded. That would be too much, though personally, he thought Nico getting Liam's girlfriend pregnant was much worse than him sleeping with Nico's little brother.

The other four traded glances and head shakes. "I don't think so," Deano said. "I know I didn't tell him."

The jury was still out on who was the main villain in the Nico—Michelle—Liam triangle. The times when he admitted his culpability in the situation notwithstanding, Liam's vote swung evenly between Nico and Michelle. After all, it took two to tango, as his mother always said. Oh god, his mother.

Liam leaned forward and waved them closer. "Do Mom and Dad know?" His voice dropped. "Do Aunt Jeanie and Uncle Frankie know?"

Patrick and Natalie checked in with each other. Gina and Deano had a brief discussion of what, if anything, their parents were aware of.

"I don't think so," Natalie said.

"So who told who first?"

"Nana told me," Gina said.

"What? Outta nowhere? She just blurted it out over breakfast?"

Gina grimaced. "Yeah, well, I caught her sneaking out of Nonno Lollo's room late at night, and she threw you and Joey under the bus to distract me. Totally worked by the way."

"Damn it." Liam scowled. "We had a deal. I didn't rat her out. That's not fair."

"You knew about them?" Natalie asked.

Liam surveyed the crowd, searching for a way out of what was quickly becoming the most painful conversation of his life. And that included the time at Christmas when Michelle told him she was pregnant and Nico was the father. Well, not so much *told* him as screamed it across a living room crowded with all their friends and family.

"Yeah, I knew," he admitted. "I thought we had a mutual secrecy pact. Can't trust that old Irishwoman."

"I didn't believe it at first," Deano said as he poured another round. "I mean, I knew you were playing both sides of the street."

"Lovely phrasing." Liam scowled. He'd come out as bisexual more than ten years earlier in a show of support for Sophia Luciano who had come out as a lesbian. By the time Natalie came out, no one batted an eye.

"Thanks," Deano said, completely missing the sarcasm. "So, yeah, I knew about you, but I didn't know about Joey."

Liam wasn't so sure *Joey* knew about Joey. "Does *he* know you all know?" God, even he was starting to lose track of what he was saying.

"Nope," Gina said. "He thinks we think you guys are just fighting. We know this is all your fault. You broke him, you fix him. He's miserable and you're, well, more miserable than usual." She handed him two freshly-filled shot glasses. "Get in there, Tiger."

Patrick pushed the door open with one hand and shoved Liam into the bathroom.

Liam stumbled over the threshold.

5

JOEY

NAT: Comb your hair Lucy, he's coming in

JOEY: Whatever

NAT: Don't play like you don't care. Pop a breath mint, too, buddy.

"HEY," JOEY SAID, LOOKING UP FROM HIS PHONE AS LIAM FELL into the bathroom. "Took you long enough. I've been in this fucking bathroom for ten minutes. It's not that nice. One of those for me?"

"Fucking hell," Liam said.

Those were the first words he'd spoken to Joey since Christmas Day. *Jerk. Stupid gorgeous jerk.*

"Okay, then." Joey reached for one of the shot glasses and downed it, coughing a little from the tequila burn. He'd been expecting whiskey. "Tequila?" Bad things happened when they drank tequila.

Liam nodded and poured the other shot down his throat.

"Gina?"

"Who else?"

Who else but his big sister would do that? Of course, he'd known they were planning on trapping him in the bathroom. He'd also known Liam would do what they wanted, too. The O'Reilly-Luciano double-team had a ninety-five percent success rate.

He'd gone along with it because someplace, not even that deep inside, he desperately wanted to see Liam again. To see if Liam would still have the same effect on him as he had since puberty. Joey licked the last drop of alcohol off his lips, feeling a tingle of lust when Liam dropped his gaze to Joey's mouth. *Yeah. Still, the same effect. Stupid, good-looking smug bastard.*

Liam set his glass on the counter with a thud, and then closed the distance between them, forcing Joey to look up to meet his eyes. Sometimes Joey really hated being four inches shorter than him.

"Nice outfit," Liam said taking in the remains of Joey's hastily-constructed pirate costume; red and black striped nylon pants ending in a ragged cuff just below the knee, black patent-leather Doc Martin boots, and a wide gold sash tied around his waist. He'd lost his shirt somewhere in the club. The way Liam couldn't tear his eyes away from Joey's tattoos made the loss of the two hundred dollar shirt totally worth it.

Liam picked up the end of the sash, sliding the silky material through his fingers. "How come every time I see you, you're wearing some kind of costume?" Last time they'd met, Joey had been dressed as Santa.

Liam, of course, was his normal GQ self in dark trousers, a white dress shirt, and one of his vast collection of purple ties. The perfect simplicity of his clothes making everyone else look like they were trying too hard.

"How come every time I see *you*, you're overdressed?" Joey asked.

Liam ran his hand through his thick red hair. "At least I'm not wandering around half-naked, letting everybody and their brother get their eyes all over me."

Joey's jaw dropped. "Excuse me?"

Liam scowled. "It's a snake pit out there. I got groped half a dozen times walking here."

Joey leaned back against the water-splattered sink counter. He crossed his arms over his chest. "Your point is?"

Liam stepped close enough that their thighs brushed. Dropping his hand heavily on Joey's shoulder, he watched transfixed as his thumb traced the curve of Joey's collarbone. "My point *is*, that maybe I don't like the idea of you getting pawed at by a room full of drunks and puck bunnies."

Joey knocked Liam's hand away. He had to be fucking kidding. "Tough shit." Joey pushed himself upright, poking Liam in the center of his (distractingly firm) chest, hard enough to make him take a step backward. "You got no right to tell me what to do or not to do."

"Joey," Liam said, warning in his voice.

Who the fuck did he think he was? He wasn't actually Joey's big brother. "No. Screw you. Five weeks, and you couldn't pick up the fucking phone?"

"Keep your voice down."

Music throbbed through the walls, the pounding bass rattling the mirrors. Liam's hand still caressed Joey's shoulder, so he knocked it away. "Hell, no. Don't fucking touch me."

Goddamn it. He had promised himself he would be cool, calm, and collected when he saw Liam. They'd hooked up. So what? People did it all the time. All it had taken was four seconds of Liam's hands on him, and he turned into the sulky, belligerent kid Liam probably took him for.

Liam looked stunned. He rubbed his hand across his mouth. "Sorry," he said quietly.

What? It was almost enough to stop Joey's anger. Almost. "Yeah? Sorry for what?"

Liam shook his head.

"Sorry for not calling?" Joey pressed. "For walking out like I was some one night stand?"

"C'mon, Jojo." Liam reached for him again.

"No, man. I'm not doing this." He pushed past Liam and grabbed the handle of the door. He yanked hard, but it didn't budge. Someone must be holding it from the other side. "Let me out, you fuckers!" He rattled the door.

"No fucking way," Gina yelled over the laughter and catcalls of the others. "Not until you kiss and make up."

"I hate you all," Joey yelled. "I'm not staying in here with this bastard."

"Yes, you are!"

"They're going to kill each other." Patrick's voice came through the door.

"Probably not," Natalie said.

"No," Joey shouted. "I'm gonna kill him."

That caused an argument outside as to who would win in a fight, Liam or Joey.

Joey banged his head against the door.

"Aim for his bad hip, Jojo!" Natalie yelled. "I got money on you!"

"Jesus." Grabbing Joey by the shoulder, Liam pulled him away from the door. "Stop making a fucking scene."

"You should have called, you asshole." Joey looked at the floor. "It's okay if it…what we did…didn't mean anything to you." Great, now he sounded like a teenage girl after prom.

"Joey," Liam said, voice low and gravelly.

"I mean. It's not like I was sitting by the phone with… with a daisy or something." Joey mimed plucking petals from a flower. *He loves me, he loves me not.* "But damn it, Judy, you fucking disappeared." His voice rose over the club music even as his face flamed with embarrassment.

"Joey," Liam growled.

"What?" Joey snapped.

"Keep your voice down."

"Fuck you."

Liam lunged, shoving him up against the door, face first, forcing the air out of his lungs in a whoosh. The door shook with the blow, and he heard Gina gasp.

Liam reached up and slid the bolt on the door closed.

"Don't hurt him!" Gina called.

Joey wasn't sure which one of them she was more concerned about. He could barely breathe, let alone think with Liam pressed up against him, blanketing him. Joey sucked air through his clenched teeth when Liam grabbed his hair and yanked his head to the side.

He put his mouth right on Joey's ear. "Joseph. Calm down."

The way Liam said his name sent shivers down Joey's spine. The way he manhandled Joey and ordered him around sent the blood flowing to Joey's dick.

Only Liam got to him like this. Liam was so intense, so solid and *there* and definite in the way he moved through the world, and Joey had been half in love with him his whole life. Being with Liam wasn't like anything else he'd ever done. Joey tensed, waiting for Liam to yell at him, to tell him to stop being such a needy fucker.

Instead, Liam said, "I'm sorry." It sounded sincere.

Joey tried to turn his head to look Liam in the eye, but Liam kept his cheek pressed against the door. When Liam's hand slid across Joey's bare chest, he bit the inside of his cheek to stop himself from making a sound, but he couldn't hide the shiver.

Liam ground his hips against Joey's back. "I'm sorry for not calling. I'm sorry for not saying thank you for taking care of me that night. You saved my life, and I shouldn't have ignored you." He scratched a nail across Joey's nipple and flicked his tongue against Joey's earlobe. "I'm a dick. I know. I shouldn't have done a lot of things I did."

Then why are you doing them again, now? He didn't ask out loud, afraid Liam would stop. His breath was harsh as he fought to not rub off against the door.

"If what we did meant nothing to me," Liam said, hand mapping the muscles of Joey's abdomen, "I would have called. Things would have been normal." Liam let go of Joey's hair, his hands falling to his hips, his forehead resting on the back of Joey's head. "You make me crazy."

Joey laughed incredulously. "I make *you* crazy?"

Cold air rushed between them when Liam stepped back. Joey turned around. Liam's eyes were dark with arousal, pinning Joey to the door. Joey felt his gaze like a physical touch as he raked his eyes down Joey's chest to his very visible erection.

Joey took a step forward.

Liam held out a hand. "Don't." A muscle in his jaw jumped as he clenched his teeth.

Joey wished Liam had brought the entire bottle of tequila in with him. Closing his eyes, he leaned back against the door. He pressed a hand against the erection tenting his stupid pirate pants, not sure if he was trying to come or to stop himself from coming.

"Jesus, Joey," Liam forced out through his clenched teeth.

Stale bathroom air moved across his skin, and when Joey opened his eyes, Liam stood less than an inch away. Keeping his eyes locked on Joey, Liam undid the knot of his stupid, sexy purple tie and slid it from under his collar in one smooth move.

Joey's mouth went dry, and he waited for Liam to tell him what to do.

"You need to put on some clothes," Liam said. He held the tie out in both hands, and Joey ducked his head so Liam could put it around his neck.

They both kept their eyes locked on Liam's hands as he looped the silky material over and under into a perfect knot. When he pulled the knot tight against Joey's throat, Joey whimpered, his hips thrusting off the door seeking friction.

Keeping a hand on Joey's chest, Liam took a step back, holding the distance between them. "Don't."

Undoing the top buttons of his shirt with one hand, and tugging Joey by the tie with the other, Liam pulled him off the door and backed him against the counter, out of the line of sight of the door, in case one of the gang decided to mount a rescue attempt.

With a hot, angry glare, Liam reached around Joey and grabbed the shot glasses.

Joey needed to kiss him more than he needed air but he didn't dare move. Having Liam focused on him like that, making him lose his self-control, made Joey dizzy with lust. His fingers tightened around the edges of the counter.

Liam unlocked the door, pushing it open just enough to stick out the hand holding the shot glasses. He grunted in approval when someone refilled them.

"Everything okay?" Paddy asked.

"Get out of the fucking bathroom!" a man yelled.

"Hey," Gina barked back, "The guy just found out he's got rectal cancer and two months to live. Cut him some fucking slack, heah!"

Liam yanked the door shut and locked it again. Eyes on Joey, he knocked back his shot at the same time he held the second one out to Joey.

The edge of the counter had cut white lines across Joey's palm that tingled as he reached for the tequila. As soon as he'd downed the alcohol, Liam was on him. His hands held Joey's head in place as he devoured Joey's mouth, licking the taste of tequila off his lips and tongue.

Yes. This was what he needed; for Liam to take what he wanted from Joey. He moaned into Liam's mouth, his knees threatening to give out. He reached for Liam's shoulders, but Liam grabbed his wrists.

"No." He yanked Joey's hands back, pinning them to the counter. "Don't mess up my shirt." His hold on Joey's wrists tightened as he looked at where they touched. "On second thought." He released Joey, and then held out his arm, turning the wrist up so Joey could see the gold cufflink shining against the white of his shirt.

Joey fumbled with the jewelry, his hands shaking with the memory of the last time he had undressed Liam. He flashed back to a bare mattress in a dusty attic, the sound of Christmas carols and the taste of wine on his lips.

Liam chuckled, the bastard, as Joey searched for the non-existent release before realizing it was one piece of solid gold engraved with Liam's initials. Of course, it was. He removed the first cufflink and handed it to Liam. Then he carefully rolled the sleeve up to Liam's elbow.

Holding out his other arm, Liam shifted so his strong thigh pressed between Joey's legs, right against his rock-hard cock.

Joey's heart pounded against his ribcage as he repeated the process, removing the second cufflink and neatly rolling the sleeve up to Liam's elbow. Their breathing echoed harshly in the silence between them.

"Good boy," Liam said.

Joey sucked in a breath. He should have been offended. Being called a good boy shouldn't get to him the way it did.

"I shouldn't be doing this," Liam rumbled.

"Why not?" Joey had thought about them a lot in the last two months. As far as he could tell, there was no reason they shouldn't be doing whatever they were doing.

"I'm supposed to be setting a good example for you," Liam explained.

"Oh, yeah?" Joey asked, voice rough. "Says who?"

"My dear mother."

"So you think she wouldn't approve of all this." He couldn't hold back a grin as he gestured to the grimy bathroom. Poorly lit, it smelled of urine and spilled beer beneath the scent of industrial-strength cleaner. The porcelain sink was cold against Joey's back.

Liam leaned close, his beard scratching Joey's cheek. "She always said 'Be a good example for the little ones.' She said I should be a role model." Then he shoved his hand down the front of Joey's polyester pirate pants.

"Fuck!"

"Joey? Are you okay?" Deano called. The door rattled.

Eyes wide, Joey stared at Liam

"Answer him," he said, the fucker, as his hand closed over Joey's cock. *Holy shit.*

"Yeah," Joey croaked. He swallowed, tried again. "Yeah. I'm good. It's all good."

Liam leaned his mouth against Joey's neck. "Is it okay? You want me to stop, just say the word and I'll stop."

"Don't stop," Joey blurted. "Please."

Liam's hot breath blew across Joey's skin. He shuddered, cursing quietly. "Then you'd better be fucking silent and show me how fast you can come. Okay, Jojo?"

Joey turned his head so it was his mouth at Liam's ear this time. "Why don't you show me how fast you can make me come, old man?"

Liam pulled back, grinning, and he stroked Joey's cock hard and fast. "Brat." Yanking his hands out of Joey's pants, he flipped him around by the hips and pulled Joey's back against his chest.

God, they looked fucking hot. Liam, fully dressed, loomed over a half-naked Joey.

Liam reached for the pump bottle of hand lotion next to the soap and squeezed out a handful, eyes burning into Joey's. "Watch us," he ordered. He yanked Joey's pants down to his knees and grabbed his cock.

Joey bit his lip to keep from yelling.

Liam guided Joey's arms up and around his neck, his free hand tracing the lines of Joey's tattoos over and over. He kept his eyes locked on Joey's in the mirror.

"Why did you have to grow up so wickedly talented and so fucking gorgeous?" Liam whispered.

The music grew louder, the blood in Joey's ears throbbed in time with the thud of the bass. Strobe lights flashed behind his eyes as Liam pumped him hard and quick, his own cock digging into Joey's lower back.

Joey struggled to breathe.

Someone pounded on the door. "Come on guys, make up already. I'm gonna get mobbed out here," Gina called.

Joey's cock jumped in Liam's hand.

"Calm your tits," Liam shouted, even as he rubbed his thumb hard over the slit of Joey's cock. "You guys wanted this, you can fucking well wait a few more seconds."

Joey was fairly sure his sibs hadn't wanted *this* exact scenario to happen.

Liam bent Joey over the sink and rutted against his ass. His hand stripped Joey's cock hard and relentlessly in fast, hard strokes. "Come for me now," he whispered.

Helpless to disobey, Joey wedged his fist in his mouth to muffle his groans as he shot ropes of cum over the sink. Liam stroked him through it, wringing him dry. He braced himself on weak arms, legs shaking with the force of his orgasm.

Now what? Now what was he supposed to do?

When Liam turned him with a curse and shoved him to his knees, Joey went willingly, thankful the decision had been taken out of his hands. Not bothering with buttons or the zipper and belt buckle, he pulled Liam's hard cock out through the fly of his immaculately tailored dress pants.

Joey's stomach clenched with nerves. He hadn't given a guy a blowjob in a long, long time. Not since high school, and that had ended so very badly. What he and Liam had done at Christmas had been different. Joey hadn't done anything. All he'd had to do was lie there while Liam used his mouth.

Liam couldn't seem to stop running his fingers through Joey's hair. The scratch of his nails on Joey's scalp made Joey want to purr. When Joey's hand tightened around his cock, he yanked Joey's head back to look into his eyes. "Fucking gorgeous."

Joey licked his lips.

Liam ran his thumb across the bottom one. "Still okay?"

Eyes on Liam's, Joey leaned forward and licked the top of Liam's cock. Hoping he was doing it right, he took Liam into his mouth and pulled off slowly, sucking on it like it was a popsicle.

"Fuck," Liam spit out. He closed his eyes and punched the wall closest to him. When he looked at Joey again, his grin was tight, almost angry. "You've been practicing."

"No," he said simply. "No one but you."

"Jesus, Mary and fucking Joseph." His cock throbbed under Joey's hand.

Joey couldn't stop the grin spreading across his face. He could make Liam feel like this, make him lose all control.

"Do it like you did it last time?" Joey looked up at Liam from under his lashes.

Liam's eyes narrowed. "Yeah?"

"Please." He was starting to realize *please* worked on Liam the way *good boy* worked on him.

Liam slapped him lightly on the face. "Relax your jaw and hold on to my hips."

Joey barely had time to follow instructions before Liam yanked him forward, holding him in place as he fucked Joey's face.

"Joey," he moaned. He thrust hard half a dozen times, the taste of him flooding Joey's mouth as he drooled around the huge, hard head. "Such a fucking good cocksucker," he whispered angrily under his breath. "Making me—" He shuddered hard, his fingers tightening in Joey's hair, his cock growing even thicker.

"Making me do this. Such a bad. Fucking. Idea," he punctuated every word with a thrust until he shot so far down Joey's throat that Joey couldn't even taste him.

He braced himself on Joey's shoulders, panting. "Fucking hell."

Joey leaned his head against Liam's thighs, his heart still pounding. He was afraid to look up. He had no fucking idea what they were doing. What they wanted from each other beyond this. What more, if anything, there was.

Liam straightened up, and Joey tucked his dick away, zippering his pants gently and giving his fly a gentle pat.

He couldn't read Liam's expression. His mouth was set in a firm line, but the look in his eyes was soft. He placed his palm against Joey's cheek, and Joey leaned into it, eyes closed, for two peaceful breaths, and then stood up.

They stood face-to-face, chests almost touching. Liam wiped Joey's lips reverently with his thumb. "Fucking gorgeous," he said so quietly Joey wasn't sure if he was meant to hear the words. The gentle kiss he gave Joey was the most surprising thing yet.

It settled something in Joey's chest. Made him brave. "So, not to sound like the chick in a bad movie, but are you going to call me?"

Liam smiled slowly and nodded. "Yeah, Jojo. I'm gonna call you."

He nodded back. "Good." Now what were they supposed to do? Shake hands and leave? Go outside and talk to their brothers and sisters like nothing had happened?

"Guess we should…" Liam cocked his head to the door.

Looked like it was option B. *Great.* Joey had harbored a slight hope that seeing Liam again would quiet this swirling mass of confusion in his head. And it had, for the two minutes they'd gotten each other off.

Now they were back to right where they had been Christmas Day. He wanted to demand answers to questions he didn't even know how to ask. What he said instead was, "You might want to wash your hands."

Joey closed his eyes and pulled himself together. He was tired, emotionally and physically. His head hurt and the music was making his ears ring. All he wanted was to go back to his hotel suite with his brothers and sisters, order room service, and make fun of people on reality television. He missed that more than anything.

"What do you think the chances are of me convincing the gang to stay in tonight?" he asked Liam.

Liam searched in vain for paper towels, then shook the water off his hands the best he could. "Given the way Gina was pounding down the tequila? Slim to none. However..." He stepped closer to Joey. "I could be persuaded."

Joey swallowed nervously. Alone in a hotel room with Liam. Did he want that? He wanted that, right? His body did. But people would see them. Every player chosen for the All-Star game was staying there. People would know if they spent the night together. And they would draw conclusions and rumors would start, and that always led to bad things happening.

It had been different at home. Home was safe. A bathroom in a club full of hockey players, reporters, and fans was definitely not safe. What the fuck had he been thinking? Once again, Liam had short-circuited all of the logic circuits in Joey's brain, and he'd done everything Liam wanted him to. Damn it.

Well, one crisis at a time.

6

LIAM

DEANO posted in **OPERATION JUDY**:

$100 THEY'RE FUCKING 💵

PADDY: Why are you texting?

DEANO: It's loud, bro. You in or what?

ANGIE: *NO BET.*

NATALIE: c'mon, Judy would never do it in a bar bathroom. He's too uptight

GINA: I see your 💯 and raise you 💯 I'm with Nat, L has never fucked in a bathroom in his life.

DEANO: And you know this how?

PADDY: no way. Jojo's got better taste that that. I'm in for 2.

GINA: Tequila and never have I ever is a potent truth serum

LIAM WATCHED JOEY OUT OF THE CORNER OF HIS EYES AS HE washed his hands. He fought the urge to bang his head against the wall and curse. He felt Joey's confusion. What they had just done had cleared up exactly nothing. He was a moron. He couldn't keep molesting Joey every time he saw him, no matter how much the kid seemed to want it.

Though he did seem to want it a lot, Liam thought with a touch of smugness. He loved the way Joey let himself be moved and guided. The way he did whatever Liam told him to do.

In the reflection of the mirror, he saw Joey reach for the door. "Wait."

"What?" Joey said with a sigh. "Going to tell me not to tell anyone?"

Fuck. He hadn't even thought about that. He hadn't thought about a lot of things. Joey wouldn't, would he?

"Do you want people to know? Do you want me to drag you out this door and blow you on the dance floor?" Liam wasn't the only one with a career and a reputation to worry about. Joey stood to lose a lot more. Good Lord, imagine how it would look if anyone found out about them?

Joey's dark brown eyes glittered with anger. He could never hide his feelings; kid wore his heart on his sleeve, always had.

His passion was one of his best qualities. Joey Luciano never did anything by halves. What would it be like to have Joey naked in a real bed with no one else around? Have him openly, free from guilt or shame? Liam's breath caught at the thought.

"Don't be a dick," Joey said, viciously ripping paper towels from a dispenser. "You know I don't." He handed Liam a wad of rough, brown paper towels. "But there must be some place between nothing and fucking on the dance floor."

"I'm sorry."

Joey rolled his eyes. "Thanks. Knowing you regret it makes me feel so much better."

"No. Jojo. C'mon. Just give me a second."

That wasn't what he meant. Why *was* he fighting this attraction? Obviously, no matter how ludicrous it sounded and how irrational it was, there was something between him and Joey. He couldn't blame this on alcohol or on Michelle, however indirectly.

"No. Not for what we did. For making you feel bad about it last time."

"And this time." Joey wasn't giving an inch. "Doesn't matter anyway. Not like we see each other all that much. I'm in New York, you're in Seattle, and we're both on the road most of the year."

Yes. Of course. They didn't cross paths very often. This thing between them couldn't amount to anything even if Liam wanted it to. Liam should be relieved to be reminded of reality. So why did he feel worse?

Deano pounded on the door. "Time's up, dudes. Manager's on his way!"

Fuck. Liam grabbed Joey by the tie, reeling him in for a quick but thorough kiss. "I'll call you. Tonight. You come to my room, I'll come to yours, whatever. We'll talk."

"Maybe we better keep to the phone. We don't seem to get much talkin' done when we're in the same room."

Liam ran his hands down Joey's muscular arms, fingers trailing across the tattoos he seemed obsessed with. "You might have a point."

A CROWD of angry drunk men glared at Liam and Joey when they came out of the bathroom.

"Did you guys kiss and make up?" Patrick asked, ruffling Liam's hair. Liam knocked his arm away with a scowl.

"Nice tie," Gina said, tugging at the purple tied draped around Joey's neck.

"Liam!" Natalie gasped, hand clutching at an invisible pearl necklace. "No tie? Shirt sleeves rolled up? Why, you're half-naked, Judy." She cackled like a mad woman.

Liam rolled his eyes, then poked Joey in the chest. "I thought Mr. All-Star here could use some more clothing."

"Oh, sure," Deano agreed. "And that definitely helped. Hey, d'you like this tie?" he called to a group of women passing by. He waved the end of Joey's tie at them.

They answered with wolf-whistles. One scantily dressed girl who couldn't possibly be old enough to be in the club was bold enough to reach out and run her hand down the tie.

"I think it looks hot," Little Miss Underage cooed.

"So do I," a male voice purred, and a tall kid in a florescent orange mesh shirt and short-shorts draped himself over the girl's shoulders and smiled at Joey. Like a shark.

Liam narrowed his eyes and clenched his teeth.

Unbelievably, Joey threw his arms around the skank and the boy and gave them both his most charming smile. "Thank you, darlin'."

He turned that smile on Liam at the low sound of protest that forced its way between Liam's teeth.

Natalie snorted. "Down, boy."

Liam ignored it the same way he ignored the looks passing between his friends. They'd obviously been hitting the tequila while he was having a midlife crisis. "Just give me a drink. So what's the plan?"

Gina pulled Joey away from his half-dressed fan club. "The plan is for 'the Looch' here to take us out someplace fancy for a late dinner with his ill-gotten winnings."

"Hey, those were well-gotten winnings," Joey protested. "I work hard for my money."

"Oh, please," Natalie said, "you were on the ice for what, two minutes? Come on, buy us a night out with that twenty-five K you won."

"You just ate." Liam checked his watch. "Five hours ago."

"I'm starving," Natalie groaned. "I'm a growing girl."

"Why don't we go back to my room, order room service, and watch TV?" Joey suggested.

"Sounds good to me," Liam said. "Then I can go to bed. It's late and I'm old." It was the perfect solution. He wouldn't have to be alone with Joey and risk doing something stupid again, but he didn't have to think about Joey being out God knows where, doing God knows what, with God knows who.

Not that Liam was jealous, just the last thing Joey needed was more bad press. Besides, he looked tired and he'd been rubbing his head.

Knowing Joey, he'd been going nonstop all weekend. All season. Every time Liam turned around, he saw Joey being interviewed, appearing at some charity function, visiting kids in the hospital, doing stupid games for promotional videos, or a million other things. All with his gorgeous smile.

Patrick tugged his tight black t-shirt down, smoothing out the wrinkles. He wore all black a lot. Liam thought he looked like an Irish Johnny Cash. Patrick thought it made his curly red hair and green eyes stand out even more. *The ladies love a ginger*, he'd say with a smile. "Come on, Judy. Let's go out. Have a little fun. When was the last time you went out?"

Liam gestured out at the crowd, eyebrows raised as high as they could go.

"I thought you said this was work," Patrick countered.

"LOOOOOOOCH!" The bellowed word rang out over the music blasting from the speaker. A tall, well-built guy with his arms around two extremely good-looking women joined their group.

"What's up, Zee?" Joey said, trading fist bumps and bro hugs with the kid.

"These fine ladies are hungry. What do you say we take them out on the town? Some pirates told me they're headed to this club, and I heard Snoop Dogg was asking for you specifically." He rested his arms on the young ladies' shoulders.

"Snoop was looking for me?" Joey's eyes lit up for a second before flashing to Liam.

"Yeah, dude," Zee said. "So let's not keep the man waiting!"

Oh, my god," Natalie shouted, punching Joey on the arm. "I want to meet Snoop. You have to take me."

Liam finally recognized the kid as one of the younger players he didn't know personally. Was he even old enough to drink legally? Was no one checking IDs tonight? Underage drinking, just another perk of being young and rich. Listening to the introductions with half an ear, he learned the guy played for the Blue Jackets, but he didn't particularly care.

What he did care about was watching his chance of getting some private time with Joey flying out the window. "Joey, didn't you say you wanted to get a solid eight hours before the game tomorrow?"

"Sleep is for the old," Zee said.

Joey gave Liam a pleading look, almost like he was asking for Liam to tell him not to go. What would he do if Liam told him not to go? What if Liam put his arm around Joey's shoulder and announced it was time to call it a night? Would Joey let himself be led away?

Heat pooled in Liam's stomach at the image. He was so tempted to find out. A selfish part of him wanted Joey all to himself, but Joey was a grown man and could make his own decision.

Gina pushed past Liam. "Can I come, too?" she asked.

"C'mon, Looch. You can't disappoint Snoop and these *fine* looking ladies."

"These fine looking ladies are my sister and my best friend. They're used to me disappointing them."

"So, you owe us," Natalie said. She tugged on the tie around his neck. "I wanna see Snoop. Jojo, let me meet Snoop."

Again, Joey turned to Liam with an expression Liam couldn't quite decipher. "I kind of promised Liam I would hang out with him."

"Nothing's stopping Grandpa from coming with except that stick up his ass," Natalie said, levelling a challenging look in Liam's direction.

"And the rheumatism," Liam said deadpan. "It's hurtin' real bad." He pulled Joey in, ruffling his hair like he was a little kid. "Go out, have fun. We old folk need our beauty sleep more."

"Speak for yourself," One the girls in the crowd cocked her head at Natalie. "Aren't you Natalie O'Reilly from the Women's hockey team?"

"Yes, she is. The one and only. And my big sister," Patrick said, recognizing an opportunity for a party invitation when he saw one.

Natalie grinned at the woman, giving her a quick head to toe check out. From the way the woman blushed, Liam figured Natalie was definitely going out.

"Great," Zack said, clapping his hands. "So we're all going out then?"

Two more young, athletic, and good-looking men barreled into the crowd, slamming right into Joey who staggered under the hit. "Come on, dudes! What's the hold-up?"

"No hold up, we were just leaving," Gina said.

"Alright. You're Looch's sister, right?"

"I am."

"Sweet. Let's go!"

"I'll call you to give your tie back," Joey promised Liam.

"You do that."

Liam followed a few feet behind them as they headed towards the exit. It was slow going as camera phones flashed and they were stopped every few feet for pictures and autographs.

No one gave Liam a second glance. At thirty-five and a year out of the game, he was a has-been. Even at the height of his career, he hadn't been half the celebrity Joey was. Few players were.

A flicker of conversation reached Liam's ears.

"—didn't want to interrupt you making out in the bathroom with your boyfriend," one of the guys in Joey's group was saying.

Joey reached around and smacked him on the back of the head. "That's Liam O'Reilly, douchebag."

"My brother," Natalie added. "In case you forgot."

"Did he used to play for the Wild like five years ago?" Zack asked, sounding like he was trying to remember something he learned in history class. Liam hated him a little.

"I think he's hot," one of the girls said.

Her Liam liked.

"He's a total DILF," she added.

Liam sighed and then laughed at himself. He was an idiot, and it was definitely time for bed.

Joey put his arm around the woman's waist. In her high heels, she towered over his five foot nine height. "Is he hotter than me?"

She looked back to check Liam out. Liam waved at her. She waved back. "I wouldn't mind seeing you together."

"That's gross," the other guy said. "Why do girls like that?"

"Why do you like lesbian porn?" the woman walking with Natalie asked pointedly.

"She's got you there," Joey said, forcing a laugh. He slowed down, and then looked over his shoulder, catching Liam's eye.

Liam could see the uncertainty in his expression. He shook his head and silently shooed Joey out of the club. It was fine. This thing between them was a fluke. The Thunder had one more game against the Rangers, and they were flying in the night before and leaving right after the game. They would barely have time to speak. He'd be surprised if he saw Joey before the end of the season in mid-April. It would be even longer if the Rangers made the playoffs, though that wasn't looking promising. The Thunder was still in the running for the Western Division.

Shit. Now he'd jinxed it. He tried never to think past the next game. *But wouldn't it be cool*, a little voice in his head whispered, *to make the playoffs your first year coaching?*

Yeah, it would, voice.

"Liam!"

He turned to see Andy Williams waving him over.

"Hey, Coach. What's up?"

"Am I taking you away from anything?" he asked with a glance at Joey and his crowd.

Liam shook his head. "No, the kids are going out. I was going to find you, actually."

"Great. Let's talk outside. This place is a zoo."

It was marginally quieter and a few degrees cooler outside the club. Beautiful men and women walked past singly and in groups, enjoying being young and beautiful on a gorgeous evening.

Andy led them towards the Riverwalk, a broad, paved walkway the followed the Hillsborough River. Neon lights splintered into multi-colored sparkles on the dark water, while music and laughter drifted from the bars and restaurants lining the walk.

"We need to get back to Seattle." He scowled at his phone, punching the screen with his fingertip.

"What's wrong?" Liam's mind raced with possibilities, each worse than the other.

"Fred called. Or Frank. I can never tell them apart. Someone from the PR department anyway. They need to move your golden boy's press conference up a day."

"Rhodes?"

Andy nodded. "Who else?"

"What? Why? I thought they were doing it next week?"

"You and me both. Some kind of scheduling screw up. It's tomorrow or next month, and I don't want to keep the kid waiting that long."

Liam tried not to play favorites, but he felt a bond with these two boys. After they'd come out, Liam had confided that he was bisexual. When Rhodes told him he wanted to come out publicly, Liam had been equal parts impressed and trepidatious. Despite the press department and media shitting themselves over getting to wave their rainbow flags, Liam wasn't sure how much harder it was going to make Rhodes' life. Not to mention how it was going to fuck up his and Paul's relationship which already seemed to be on the rocks the last few days.

Coming from a highly conservative religious background, Dyson was deep in the closet as far as Liam knew. But if he kept hanging around with Rhodes outside of their games, he wouldn't be for long.

"Are you shitting me?" He ran his hands through his hair. "They couldn't push it back, oh, I don't know, a day?"

"You think I find this at all amusing?" Williams shrugged. "It's a Sunday, slow news day. You know PR has been chomping at the bit for this."

"Damn it." He ran his hand over the screen of his phone. "Do I have to leave tonight?"

Andy laid a hand on his shoulder. "Sorry."

Liam sighed. "No. It's okay. I want to be there for Robbie. Luckily, I haven't unpacked yet. Let me tell the clan first."

He texted Joey. *Gotta go back to Seattle. Let the gang know, okay? Watch our press conference tomorrow. Call me when you get back.*

7

JOEY

CARTER: how am I supposed to give them Tylenol if they're puking? Matt & Maria are both puking now.

GINA: Suppositories, they're in the fridge. Wear gloves. Enjoy! 🍸 🍸

CARTER: You want me to shove cold waxy medicine up our kids' asses? 😱

GINA: Isn't parenthood a beautiful thing? Take pictures! MWAH.

JOEY CLOSED HIS EYES AGAINST THE PULSING, SWINGING LIGHTS AND the pounding music, clutching the edge of the bar as the world shifted under his feet. *Oh no, not now.* He staggered into the woman standing next to him.

"Hey!" She glared at him.

"Sorry," Joey said quickly, pushing his way through the crowd to the VIP room.

If he was reading the signs right, he needed to get somewhere he could lay down as soon as possible. The awful ringing in his ears that had plagued him on and off since Thanksgiving pierced through the noise of the club. His left ear felt like it had been stuffed with cotton and the music pounding on his eardrum hurt like a physical attack.

Damn it. He'd been fine the last few weeks.

Really? You've felt fine? On top of your game? The voice in his head sounded a lot like Liam. *Fuck off*, he told the voice. *I'm just tired. It's been a long day.* He should have stayed in with Liam. Part of him kind of wished Liam had ordered him to stay in or come up with a good excuse. Though then Nat and Gina would have been disappointed, and they really had put up with so much from him over the years.

It had been a long season. After months of slamming into the ice, the boards and the other players, his body felt like one big bruise from head to toe most of the time. Luckily, he'd had a pretty easy season this year. There had been nothing broken, no operations, and no pulled anything. Just a few minor sprains and bruises, some stitches over his eye due to a high stick and more over his cheek thanks to a bouncing puck. His shoulder had gotten dislocated again a few games ago, but it had popped back in place itself, so he hadn't done much about it.

He'd played every game so far, and he would damn well play out the rest of the season. All he needed was a nice vacation somewhere for a couple of weeks. He'd spend as much time as he could at the Nantucket house over the summer. He could work out there, get in some golf, hang with the families.

"House" was a bit of an understatement. It was more like a compound with a large main house and several other buildings surrounding a giant pool and hot tub. He, Liam, Nico, and Dean had paid for most of it, with their names being on the lease equally. They had sworn never to let their parents find out how much it had cost.

Joey clutched the handrail as he moved up the three low, wide steps to the curtained-off VIP area.

"You okay, Mr. Luciano?" the security guard in a nice suit asked. A giant man who could probably bench press Joey with one hand, Trevor had a soft voice and a great smile. His best quality was his discretion. He considered each VIP to be his personal responsibility, and what happened behind the red velvet ropes, stayed behind the red velvet ropes.

"Not feeling too great, Trev," Joey admitted. "Can you find me a place to lie down?"

"Sure thing, Mr. Luciano. And I'll call your driver as well." Trevor took Joey's arm and led him through the sparsely populated main sitting area and to a smaller curtained-off room further in. Joey appreciated the support as the world lurched beneath his feet and tilted at a forty-five-degree angle.

He collapsed onto the sofa with a curse. *Fuck him.* This was some serious bullshit. He needed to get himself together.

"Should I get a doctor?" Trevor asked as he lifted Joey's feet onto the designer sofa.

Should he? Probably. Was Joey going to let him? Not in a million years. Last thing he needed was rumors getting out that he was in less than perfect condition.

There had been whispers about his being traded that he knew had as much to do with salary caps and some promising first-round prospects that were on the table for the next draft, as it did with his ongoing struggles with the team. He'd been one of those promising draftees once upon a time. Only in pro sports could you feel over the hill at twenty-five.

Joey threw an arm over his eyes to block out the light and prayed for the world to stop spinning before he had to walk to the car.

The sofa sagged as someone set down at his feet. He hoped it wasn't Snoop. The man loved hockey, and they were close to being good friends. Joey didn't want Snoop to see him like this.

"Celebrating a little too much, Looch?" a smarmy voice asked.

Damn it. Richard Masterson had found him again. He'd been hiding from the guy all night. Why couldn't it have been Snoop? He'd rather puke on the entertainer's four-hundred dollar sneakers than shake hands with the man who had just sat down.

Masterson was publicly out, twenty years older than Joey, overly tanned, overly-gymmed, and had more money than sense. He also had some kind of military grade gaydar. Bi-dar?

Maybe it was Joey's fault. Maybe he'd given off some invisible 'I've thought about sucking dick' signals. But when they'd met at some fundraiser at the beginning of the season, the guy had attached himself to Joey like a leech.

He'd seemed harmless enough at the beginning. Then Joey had made the mistake of engaging with the guy online, responding to Masterson's comments on his Instagram and Twitter posts, answered his increasingly frequent texts, and now the guy thought they were BFFs.

The few times Joey had been unavoidably trapped alone with Masterson, he'd pushed hard to get into Joey's pants. He'd blown off Joey's claims that he was straight. "Lots of men think they're straight until they meet me," he'd said. Joey had almost punched him.

When the direct route didn't work, the guy started talking endorsement deals, and no-trade clauses, as if he had any control over Joey's contract, and as if Joey even wanted to stay in New York. The only positive he'd found about living in the city was that it was close enough to his family so he could visit his Nonno easily, and the family could come to his games and he could go to Natalie's.

"Need a little hair of the dog?" Masterson asked, holding a glass under Joey's nose.

Joey felt his hand on his thigh, and the heat of Masterson's body as he leaned over Joey's chest only added to the nausea. He wished he had a shirt on so he couldn't feel Masterson's hand on his skin. Bile rose up his throat at the thought of the vodka and tonic. He coughed it back down. "No thank you, Mr. Masterson. I'm just a little tired. Been a long day."

"Joey, how many times do I have to tell you to call me Richie?" He sounded disappointed.

How about I call you Dick? Joey snorted a short laugh at his own thought. He was losing it. Where was Trevor with the car?

"What's so funny?" Masterson asked. The bastard lifted up Joey's legs as he slid under them.

Was he fucking kidding? Joey tried to sit up to push Masterson away and the sofa rolled under him, throwing back down.

Masterson laughed. "You've definitely had a few too many, gorgeous." He sounded amused by Joey's incapacitation, and his hand slid down Joey's shin.

When Liam had called him that, he'd *felt* gorgeous. When Dick said it, he felt dirty, like he needed a shower. He wished he could risk turning his head to see if Trevor was back yet.

The ringing in his ear turned to a screech, and he winced.

Mock concern on his face, Masterson reached for Joey's forehead placing one palm there, and the other one just happening to land on Joey's naked, sweat-soaked chest. "You don't have a fever. If anything, I'd say you felt chilled. Probably because you are almost naked. Not that I mind." His hand trailed down Joey's chest as he reluctantly sat back down, still beneath Joey's legs.

Fuck it. Joey struggled to push himself up to his elbows, praying that he would puke now, all over Masterson and his fugly expensive suit.

"Woah, woah." Masterson grabbed his shoulder. "Where do you think you're going?"

"Bathroom," Joey said through clenched teeth. He could do this. He swung his legs away from Douchebag and pushed himself up.

Masterson grabbed for his arm again. "Let me help you."

Joey jerked out of his reach and promptly fell to his knees.

The curtain rings jangled softly as Trevor pulled back the curtain.

"Some privacy, please," Masterson snapped, his hand going to Joey's head. *Fucker.* Joey didn't have the strength to push him off. He just needed a second to get himself under control.

The big man stepped further into the room. "Your car is here, Mr. Luciano." His voice was harder than Joey had heard it all night. Great. Now Trevor probably thought he was some kind of gay slut. On his knees in the VIP room.

Masterson waved him away. "Send the driver away. I'll make sure Mr. Luciano gets back to his hotel." He pulled his wallet out as if he were going to pay Trevor or the driver to go away.

Trevor walked over to them and wrapped his huge hands around Joey's arms. "I'm sorry, I can't do that. I promised Mr. Luciano I would get him to his car."

Joey let himself be pulled up. "Thank you, Trevor. I appreciate it." He tried not to look like he was leaning all his weight on the security guard.

Masterson started to protest loudly. Afraid for Trevor's job, Joey stopped him. "Mr. Masterson, Richie. It's fine. Thank you for the offer. But, please, stay. Enjoy the rest of the party."

"It won't be as much fun without you," Masterson said with a leer.

Trevor's hand tightened on Joey's arm, and he subtly pulled Joey behind him. With Trevor's help, Joey managed to extricate himself from Masterson's sticky hands. Trevor's arm around Joey's shoulders was the only thing keeping Joey on his feet as they made their way to the less-public back entrance.

"Thanks, man," Joey said when Trevor helped him into the car. He pulled out his wallet and tried to hand it to the other man.

"Not necessary," Trevor said, pushing his hand away.

"Trevor, take it or I'm going to puke on you. How 'bout that?"

"I'll take it if you go to the doctor."

"No need, I just had a little too much party and a not enough food."

Trevor leaned in closer. "I know you aren't drunk, Mr. Luciano. I saw you drinking water all night."

Joey leaned his head against the seat back with a sigh. "I'm fine, Trevor. I promise. Just tired."

Trevor looked skeptical. "If you say so. I'm not your daddy, I can't make you do nothing. Goodnight." He shut the door, then pounded lightly on the roof of the black SUV.

Joey slumped down in his seat and counted the minutes until he could get in his bed.

8

LIAM

DEANO: S'up little bro?

JOEY: Hanging w/strippers, sipping Dom. The usual.

DEANO: I saw those pics from Tampa, dude. Might want to slow down a bit.

JOEY: What? And disappoint the fans of the Looch? Ruin his reputation? Not gonna happen.

DEANO: yeah, well, *the looch* can be kind of a dick.

JOEY: love you, too, bro. 🌀 👆

DEANO: I'm just tryna look out for ya.

JOEY: I know. & I appreciate it. But I'm great, I promise. Gotta go. Candy and Tiffany are starting w/out me.

DEANO: 👟👟

LIAM SIGHED AND SWIVELED BACK AND FORTH ON HIS DESK CHAIR. "I don't know why you think I can make him do anything," he said to Gina's image on his computer screen.

Six other faces stared out at him from smaller boxes in the corner. What Liam had been calling 'the Joey situation' must have been getting serious if they had all managed to coordinate a time to talk to him. He glanced again at the tweet displayed on his second monitor.

The tweet had originated from some random guy, but had a few thousand retweets by the time Liam had seen it. He'd never really gotten the hang of social media—not the way the young guys did. The only reason he'd even seen this one was because every single one of the gang had sent it directly to him.

The post contained three blurry photos of Joey, all taken on the night they'd been in Tampa. Liam knew it was that night because Joey was still wearing his pirate costume.

The first one showed him next to Snoop Dogg behind a DJ setup. Glasses and bottles littered the area and scantily-clad men and woman crowded the stage. In the second one, Joey was passed out on a sofa in some red-curtained room. In the third, Joey leaned heavily against a very large African-American man in a suit. The guy practically had his arms around Joey.

"He worships the ground you walk on," Sophia said. "He always has. You're the only one he might listen to."

"What's he been saying about what's up with him?" Deano asked. Tampa was his home base. He'd told the gang that he'd heard a bunch of stories about how Joey could barely walk and had been alone with some guy in the VIP room.

Liam reached for the Joey Luciano Funko doll which Joey had given him as a joke last Christmas. The four-inch tall vinyl doll barely resembled Joey. It wore his uniform, had his name and number on the back, but without Joey's trademark smile it didn't come close to capturing the real thing. Liam stared into the toy's big blank eyes as he shook it gently back and forth, something he'd often wanted to do to the real Joey.

"He hasn't said anything to me," Liam said. "It's not like we talk that much." He knew he sounded defensive. Maybe he hadn't called Joey that often, but it wasn't as if Joey had been burning up his phone either.

"Damn Judy, that's cold," Patrick said. "Is this going to be a pattern with you? Fuck him, then ditch him?"

"I didn't—"

Every single one of them laughed before he could finish the sentence. Goddamn it, family sucked sometimes. There were no secrets, and nothing was off limits.

"Bathroom doors aren't sound-proof," Gina said with a lift of one eyebrow.

"I was going to say I didn't *ditch* him. I've texted. The phone works both ways, you know."

"Wow," Angie, the next oldest O'Reilly sibling, chimed in. "You sounded just like Dad there." She sat in her favorite chair in her comfy living room. She, Kellen, and their three kids lived in a suburb about forty minutes away (depending on traffic) from the O'Reilly ancestral home. She claimed it was the perfect distance. Close enough for visits, but not close enough to encourage unplanned drop-ins.

"Who sounds like Grandpa Bob?" a girl's voice asked. One of Angie's eight-year-old twin girls popped her head in front of the camera. "Hey, Uncle Liam!"

"Hi, Sweetie!" Liam prayed she would be satisfied with that vague greeting.

She wasn't. "Ha! You don't know which twin I am!" She laughed and pointed at the camera.

She was definitely an O'Reilly. No mistake left unmocked.

"Come closer, let me look at you."

His niece leaned closer, her face filling the entire screen. "Hmm." Liam rubbed his beard, pretending to think. He tilted his head. "Braids. Dark red hair. Still missing a baby tooth in front. I'm going to go with Saffron."

"That's not my name!" The girl rolled her eyes at him. That meant it was Jasmine. Rose, the other twin, was more shy with him and would have covered her mouth and giggled.

"Dandelion? Tulip? Geranium?"

"Uncle Liam! You know who I am."

Jazzy was starting to look upset so he took pity on her. "Of course I know you. You're my beautiful and talented niece Jasmine. How you doing, peanut?"

"Mom says you have a really nice house in Seattle. Can we come visit? Do you have a pool? Do you have a dog? Can we get a dog?"

Liam laughed. "Yes, you come and visit. Yes, I have a pool and it's right on the beach. No. No dogs. I'm not home enough to have a dog."

Angie shooed her daughter away and waited until she was out of earshot. "So will you at least talk to Joey?" she asked.

"I really don't know what you want me to say. What am I supposed to do? Yell at him? Spank him?"

Gina glowered from her small rectangle on the screen. "Sometimes I think he really could use a good spanking. I love my little brother more than anything but he can definitely be a handful."

"Any more news on the trade to the Thunder I keep hearing about?" Patrick asked. "That would be a great idea. You could really keep an eye on him then, give him that spanking." He laughed as if it were the funniest thing he'd heard in a while.

Liam sighed and scrubbed both hands through his hair. It was getting long, he barely had time for anything outside of hockey. He needed a haircut, he needed to get some things to the dry cleaners, and he needed some food in the house. He was getting tired of eating out all the time.

"Look, even if they did make the trade, something I have no control over at all, I can't be Joey's babysitter and I'm not his dad. He's a grown-up who makes his own choices, and he'll have to live with the consequences of those choices."

Liam said that, but the words coach Williams had said to him about helping Joey become the man they both knew we could be, echoed in the back of his mind.

"Yeah, no," Patrick said. "I didn't mean it like that. But, if he did get moved out to Seattle, which would be fantastic because then maybe I'd get to see him every now and then, he could live with you. You're bouncing around in that big house all by yourself. There's plenty of room."

Oh holy hell. He and Joey living together, now there was a thought. That option hadn't even crossed his mind. That was a disaster waiting to happen. "No," he said. "That's not going to work for me."

"That's a great idea, Paddy," Deano said over Liam's objections. The rest of the family agreed.

It was time to end this conversation before Liam said something that was really none of their business. "I'll do what I can, okay? I'm only the assistant coach. I'm the youngest person behind the bench and the newest on the team. I have no power to make any kind of decisions like that. If it wasn't for Andy, I wouldn't even have this job, and you guys know it. I'm hanging on by the skin of my teeth."

"Don't say that," Angie said. "Yeah, Andy is your friend, but there's no way he would have hired you if he didn't think you could do the job."

Patrick nodded as he bounced a mini hockey puck off the blade of a toy stick. "All I've been hearing is good things about you. I think half the time the guys forget you're my brother. But everybody on the Lightning who's gone up and played with you liked working with you a lot."

Hearing that made Liam feel a little bit better, but he wasn't going to put too much weight behind the words unless they came from Andy or the people above him. Let the GM make him an offer for next year, then he would believe he was doing a good job.

"Ok. I'll reach out to Joey. And I'll talk to the coach. That's the best I can do. I can't go over his head, but I'll put in a good word for Joey."

"And call him," Gina said, her broad Boston accent thickening with concern. "He's a good boy. I don't know what's going on with him right now, but I don't like it."

"I'll call him. I promise." After ten minutes of goodbyes and last-minute reminders about birthdays, anniversaries, and potential summer plans, Liam disconnected the call. He'd talk to the coach tomorrow.

AS A COACH, Liam spent more time in the locker rooms and offices than he had as a player. Since Andy liked to be at the office by seven-thirty in the morning, Liam liked to be in the office by six-thirty, so he could get in a workout and be mentally prepared for the day. He liked the quiet time alone in the exercise room.

After a quick shower, he would fire up his laptop and go over the clips the video coordinators had put together overnight. He'd view the Thunder's previous game and the games of the clubs that had been assigned to him for advance scouting.

Players started rolling in at around eight-thirty or nine for the eleven o'clock morning practice. They would eat breakfast, chat with the doctor and physical therapists, work out, maybe get a massage, or a therapeutic soak in the hot tub before getting dressed to hit the ice.

Liam liked to take the time to grab some breakfast and his third cup of coffee and talk casually with the players, get an impression how they were feeling about the upcoming game and listen to whatever concerns they had.

Andy held a team meeting each day about an hour before practice, and then the coaching staff and players split up to work on whatever individual skills and drills they had agreed on earlier. After practice, players hit the workout room again for a cooldown on the stationary bikes or whatever their preferred method was.

Andy and Liam would meet with whatever media was scheduled for that day, and then Andy would put in a call to the GM for a few minutes to talk about the lines and any injuries or call-ups that needed to be made. Though it wasn't technically his job, Andy actively encouraged Liam to sit in on these discussions. Part of the job was figuring out who would be dressing for the game later that evening.

Not all of the players on the team would be on the ice tonight. There were twenty-three players on their active roster, not counting the men on the injured reserve list. League rules said only twenty players could be dressed for games and two of those had to be goalies. So every game, three unhappy guys landed on the healthy scratch list. Being a healthy scratch basically meant being told that you weren't playing well enough and that someone better would be taking the ice in your place tonight. Deciding which players weren't going to be on the ice that night was one of the worst parts of the job, and Liam was glad that he didn't have to make that call.

It made guys feel like shit, and they skulked around the corners of the locker room and the exercise rooms in the hours before the game. The smart ones took it as a learning opportunity and worked twice as hard during those hours.

Being scratched had happened to him only twice in his career, but he remembered the exact dates and how he'd felt in vivid detail. Angry and disappointed in himself, frustrated with having to watch the game instead of skating in it.

Since they had a home game that evening, after the team lunch most of the guys had gone home for naps, and to do whatever pregame rituals they had. The coaching staff had a break as well. Liam had spent his pacing up and down the beach behind his house, trying to figure out the best way and the best time to bring up the subject of Joey Luciano.

Now seemed like a good as time as any.

Steam hissed from the cappuccino machine as Andy made two perfect lattes. He and Liam were alone in the team rooms in Seattle's Key Arena. "I should have been a barista," Andy joked.

"Thanks," Liam said as Andy handed him one of the coffee cups. "I was wondering if you'd heard any more about the possibility of Luciano coming over to us?"

Andy's long silence was not encouraging. He took a sip of his coffee and nodded his head for Liam to follow him down the hallway to the office. "Shut the door," he said. "I gotta tell you right now Semerad isn't too thrilled about the possibility."

Hank Semerad, the GM, had called Liam at Christmas to get Liam's opinion on Joey.

"Your boy's not doing himself a lot of favors right now." Andy opened up some files on his computer with the click of a mouse. One file held Joey's stats for the season. The second folder was filled with various social media posts and news articles about Joey's behavior.

Liam took a sip of his coffee, giving himself a moment to gather his thoughts. It certainly didn't look good when compiled like that, but he knew that was only part of the story. "Yeah, I know. But there's more to him than his media presence. I think something is going on with him, and I'd like to get to the bottom of it."

Andy looked skeptical.

Through the closed door, Liam could hear the rest of the coaching staff going through their prep, and the rumbling voices of the players as they filtered in. Someone was going to be looking for them any second.

"I won't take up much of your time," Liam said. "I don't know if it will make any difference, but I very strongly believe that Joey would be a great addition to this team, and I'm willing to take personal responsibility for him. If Joey screws up, you can fire me."

Andy raised his eyebrows and rubbed his ear as he stared at the screen. "You don't have a contract for next year yet, do you?"

Liam shook his head no.

"And Luciano's a restricted free agent at the end of the season?"

"Unrestricted," Liam corrected. Under the most recent collective bargaining agreement, a player was considered an unrestricted free agent when their contract expired if they were at least twenty-seven years old or had at least seven years playing. Though being an unrestricted free agent meant that Joey and his agent were free to meet with any team to discuss potential contracts, it also meant there was a minuscule possibility that Joey would not have a position by the beginning of the next season. What was more likely was that his off ice behavior and bad reputation would drive his asking price way down.

"You feel that strongly about it?" Andy swiveled in his chair to look directly at Liam. "I'm asking this as your friend, not as your boss. Do you really think Joey can pull himself together? Are you willing to risk your reputation on that belief?"

Liam took a deep breath, held it, and then met his old friend's gaze square on. "I do. I really do."

Andy searched his face for a second, then nodded, apparently satisfied with what he saw there. "Okay, then. I'll back you on this play. Next time I talk to Semerad, I'll put in a good word for Luciano."

It was the best Liam could have hoped for. "Thank you," he said. "Who knows if it will even happen?"

"You know this game, you and Luciano might find out same time I do. No one ever knows what's going on."

9

JOEY

From NBC Sports (sportsworld.nbcsports.com)

The ideal way for players to hear about the trade is from the general manager, but that's not always the case these days, says agent Anton Thun of MFive Sports.

[C]urrent Edmonton Oiler Derek Roy was with the Dallas Stars when he was dealt to the Vancouver Canucks in April 2013.

"With social media nowadays … my brother texted me and said, 'Hey, I think you got traded to Vancouver,'" recalled Roy. "I was like 'What?' I hadn't gotten a call from the GM, and it was all over Twitter, so I'm like, 'Oh, man.' Maybe like 20 minutes later I got a call from the GM saying 'yeah we traded you to Vancouver'. I was like, 'I think I knew that.' I said, 'I saw it on Twitter.'"

"I'M FINE, NONNO. I SWEAR," JOEY SAID INTO THE PHONE AS HE watched the lights of LA slide past him as he made his way from the airport to the Staples Center where the Thunder were playing their division rivals, the Kings.

He leaned his head against the cool glass. Who the hell had shown those pictures to the grandfather? The PR department had them taken down as quickly as they could, but nothing was truly ever gone from the Internet.

He listened to his grandfather lecture him about the evils of drinking, which was comical coming from a man who drank more than all of his grandkids combined. The words washed over him, yet he could clearly hear the love and concern underlying the stern tone.

"Nonno, I swear it's not what it looks like."

"Oh? Then what is it? Because you're either about to puke on that man's shoes or give him a blowjob. Which is it?"

"Jesus, Nonno!" Talk about something he never wanted to hear coming out of his grandpa's mouth. He sighed silently and put a hand on his knee to stop the jittering of his leg that had started as soon as he boarded the plane from Texas to California. He knew damn well the old man was never going to leave it alone. Lorenzo Luciano had raised too many kids and too many grandchildren to buy any of the bullshit Joey was spouting.

"If I tell you something, Nonno, will you promise to keep it to yourself?" He really shouldn't be talking about this in public, but the Town Car taking him to the arena had privacy glass between him and the driver. And from the vibrations of the music rattling the glass, he doubted the driver could hear anything anyway.

"Aw, Jojo. You know I can't promise something like that. If you're being a *stunod goomba*, I'm going to have to tell your mama."

Yeah, Joey knew, but he also knew Nonno Lollo would keep the secret for a little while anyway. Whenever he'd found out about something Joey had done, he always gave Joey time to turn himself in before ratting him out. Joey had learned quickly that the repercussions of turning himself in were much lighter than if his mother found out from someone else.

This time, he was willing to take that risk. He had no real answers, and he didn't want to worry his mother until he had more information.

"You still there?" his grandfather asked. "If you don't tell me what's going on, I'm going to sic Gina and Liam on you."

"Oh, jeez. Don't do that. They'll be worse than Mom. Okay, I'm going to tell you what's going on, but please, *please*, don't tell Mama for a little while. I promise I'll tell her soon as I have some hard information."

"Hold on. I'm going to go upstairs."

Joey listened as Lorenzo walked up the creaky stairs, greeting various members of the family as he went to his room on the top floor. Everyone had offered to give him a room on the bottom floor so didn't have to deal with the stairs, but he insisted he liked the quiet and that going up and down was good for his heart.

"Okay, *nino*, spill."

So Joey spilled it all. The gradual hearing loss in his left ear, the occasional feeling that the ear was stuffed with cotton and nothing would clear it, and, most terrifying of all, the vertigo attacks. They had been getting worse. "I haven't had one on the ice yet," he assured Lorenzo, but they both knew it was just a matter of time.

"*Madonna Mia*, Joey. That sounds serious. You can't screw around with your brain like that! You gotta talk to the doctor." He sounded more worried than Joey ever heard him sound. He almost sounded scared, and it made Joey feel like shit so he backpedaled as quickly as he could. "It's not that bad."

"Joseph Anthony Sebastian Luciano, don't you bullshit me. Get your ass down to the doctor as soon as possible, *capisce?*"

"Yes, Nonno. I will. I promise." The car slowed to a stop as close to the players' entrance as the driver could get. *Thank God.* "Hey, Nonno, I gotta go. I love you. Give my love to the family."

"Joey, I'm serious, you call and tell me you went to the doctor sooner rather than later, or I will tell Gina and your mama."

"I swear. Cross my heart and hope to die. I really gotta go. Love you. Bye." He hung up before the old man could get another word in. If he spent any more time on the phone with his grandfather, he was going to lose the tight leash he had on his fear, and, truthfully, he had enough on his mind right now. He'd worry about his defective ear later.

The driver got Joey's bag out of the trunk, held the door open for him, and Joey stepped out into the parking lot of Staples Center.

Home to the L.A. Lakers, Clippers, and Kings, the tall, oval building loomed over the parking lot. Joey seriously considered telling the driver he'd changed his mind and that he did want to go directly to the hotel after all. He'd left the Rangers in the middle of a road trip to join the Thunder in the middle of their five-day, three-game road trip. He had his pads, two pairs of underwear, one pair of workout clothes, and a suit with him. His life was so glamorous sometimes.

On the plane ride from Dallas, he'd thought it would be funny to surprise Liam and show up at the game. Given the time difference between Texas and California and the fact that Joey's game had ended right about the time Liam's had started, Liam might not even know Joey was the newest member of the Seattle Thunder. Joey himself had only found out a couple of hours ago. Outside of the GMs and the league, not a lot of people knew, but that wouldn't last much longer.

So, yeah. Liam was going to be surprised, alright. Maybe Joey should wait and meet them at the hotel. It's not like spending time at the Ritz-Carlton would be much of a hardship. His agent had assured him there was a room waiting for him.

Dragging his suitcase behind him, Joey walked up to the familiar doors. He'd started his career there as an eighteen-year-old, seven seasons ago, and it would always hold a special place in his heart. He'd also fallen in love with the City of Los Angeles, but it might have been a little more fun if he had been legal drinking age at the time.

Luckily, he had kept in touch with a bunch of the guys on the team and in security. He'd made a few quick calls, pulled a few strings, and got access to the Thunder dressing room, no questions asked. As he got closer to the locker room, he heard the echo of the team headed down the tunnel back to the locker room during the break between the second and third period.

Even if he hadn't checked the score the minute the plane hit the ground, he would have known the Thunder were ahead. Their voices held the confident tones of a team with a nice, solid lead.

To give the team a minute to get settled in, Joey stopped to greet one of the security guards he remembered and ask after the guy's family. There was a lot to do between periods: video replays, drying gloves and underwear, tending to injuries, sharpening skates, and re-taping sticks. By the time he reached the room, he could hear Liam's voice rising strongly over the general hubbub.

"...speed, strength, skill..."

Perfect timing. Joey stepped into the room and slumped nonchalantly against the doorjamb. "...and spirit," he said loudly over Liam. "But the greatest of these is spirit."

Every eye turned to him.

"Joey!" Liam said with a smile that almost instantly changed to confusion. "What the hell are you doing here? I thought you were in Dallas." His gaze traveled down Joey's body to his suitcase, and his eyes widened. He inhaled, looked up at the ceiling, and then looked back at Joey. "You gotta be fucking kidding me."

Joey spread his hands wide. "Surprise," he said with what he hoped was an apologetic smile.

Liam's expression softened slightly, and he shook his head.

"They traded Luciano?" one of the players called from where he was getting his hand taped up. Joey thought it was Gabriel Janssen. Janssen's eyes darted to a man sitting to his right.

Players traded glances across the room as they registered the implications of Joey's appearance. Peters and Jevpalovs looked anywhere but at Joey.

Fuck. He hadn't thought of that. *Fuck.* If he was on the team, that meant they were out. And they hadn't known. Obviously, the front-office had been waiting until after the game to tell them, the same as the Rangers had done.

Liam walked over to Andy and leaned in close. "Did you know about this?" he asked softly.

Andy folded his arms across his chest. "I found out about the trade before the game. I wasn't going to say anything until afterward. I was told Luciano would be meeting up with us tomorrow in Vegas." He didn't look happy.

Yeah, Joey *really* shouldn't have come. But maybe he could save this. He smiled broadly. "There's no way I would miss watching you guys bury the Kings on their own ice."

Liam said something to Andy that Joey couldn't hear. Then he motioned to Joey. "Can I see you for a minute?"

Andy nodded and had turned back to the center of the room. He pointed at Jake Donovan, the team captain. "Okay. Donny, I need…"

Joey didn't hear what the coach needed from Jake Donovan, as Liam dragged him into the small room set aside for visiting team coaches.

"What the fuck?" Liam grabbed Joey's arm. "What the hell made you think it was a good idea to show up here?" When Liam was angry, he seemed to be more than only four inches taller than Joey.

Joey wanted to come up with a snarky answer, but he was too tired, too emotional and too stressed. All he could do was tell the bald-faced truth. "I needed to see you. It was all I could think of when they told me."

Liam ran a hand through his perfect hair without managing to mess it up. It actually looked better after he was done. "Jesus, Joey. You're a professional, and you're acting like a fucking rookie. You couldn't wait for me at the hotel? Instead, you come here and shake everyone up? Now Peters knows he's going! And so does Jevpalovs!" Liam waved his arms as he paced the four steps the small room allowed.

"I'm so sorry." He got it. He'd screwed up. Fine. He didn't see how yelling was going to change anything.

"I need them at the top of their game tonight. We need every point if we're going to get that wildcard slot for the playoffs."

"I'm fucking sorry! Okay? I get it. I messed up again. Just finish yelling at me, get it over with and I'll leave."

Liam didn't say anything.

"I'll meet you in Vegas tomorrow." Joey turned to go. So much for a new start. He hadn't even suited up and his teammates already disliked him. Even for him, that was a new record.

Liam grabbed his arm. "Stop. Just wait."

Joey stopped and stood silently, waiting.

Liam shook his head and gave Joey's arm a gentle squeeze. He leaned down and moved his hand to the back of Joey's neck. A move that in no way sent goosebumps down Joey's spine.

"For the record," Liam said, "I'm glad you're on the team. And I'm glad to have you here. Okay?"

Glad to have him here for the *team* or for *himself?* Joey wasn't going to ask. True to his word, Liam had called Joey a couple of times since the episode in the bathroom, but there had been a definite lack of anything resembling flirting. They mostly talked about hockey and their family.

Joey's timid attempts at sexting had gone unreciprocated, which was humiliating, so he'd stopped trying. He was done making a fool out of himself around Liam. The way Liam was looking at him, and the feel of his hand weakened Joey's resolve. He tried to twist out of Liam's hold.

Liam's fingers tightened on his neck, and he shook Joey's head gently. "Such a brat," he said quietly. "We'll have to work on that."

Joey tilted his head to the side to get a better read on Liam's expression. He was staring intently at Joey, pupils wide and dark. That wasn't his angry look. "Yeah?" Joey gave Liam his patented '*I'm trouble and you love it*' grin.

Liam put his mouth by Joey's ear. "Yeah. If I have to beat it out of you." He straightened up. "And that face doesn't work on me. I'm immune to your charms."

Joey seriously doubted that. Inside he was celebrating, outwardly, he was calm. "Okay," he said meekly.

Liam narrowed his eyes. "That tone I don't trust at all."

Joey smiled.

Liam smacked him gently on the back of the head. "I gotta go. Remember, I want you on the team, so does Coach Williams. But, Joey, coming here? Not the brightest of moves."

Joey hung his head. "I know." He looked up at Liam through his eyelashes—his thick dark eyelashes the girls raved about.

Liam threw a quick look over his shoulder, then shoved Joey further into the room before pulling him in for a quick, hard kiss.

Immune, my ass. Joey squeezed Liam's ass just to hear him squawk. He laughed when Liam pulled away and shook his finger at him like he was Joey's grandpa. "Cut it out. Come on."

He held the door open for Joey like a gentleman. "You gonna stay here and watch the game?" Liam asked.

"I think I'll hang out on the bus. Is that okay? I don't want to talk to the press. I had to sneak away from them once already tonight."

"You got a room?"

"You guys staying at the Ritz?"

Liam nodded.

"Then I got a room."

The intermission was almost over, and Joey could tell Liam's focus was going back to the game as it should be. Right before the entered the room, Liam grabbed him in a tight side hug and gave him a real smile. "Seriously, Jojo. Welcome to the team. Good to be on the same side for once. I hated having to face off against you."

"Most people do," Joey said with a smug smile.

Liam smacked him on the arm. "Watch it. I can make you do bag skates now, you know."

Joey whistled and shook his head. "Damn. I didn't think about that. What can I do to get on your good side?"

Liam grinned down at him. "Oh, I'm sure we'll think of something."

10

LIAM

"I'd have my cock out if I scored four goals. I'd have my cock out, stroking it." – *Joe Thornton in response to rookie Tomas Hertl scoring four goals in one game. (10/10/2013)*

BACK WHEN HE HAD BEEN A PLAYER, LIAM'S PATIENCE WITH THE seemingly constant press had waxed and waned.

There were microphones in their faces post-practice, pre-game, in between periods, postgame, and on their way home. In the locker room, the hallways, next to the ice or in front of the official press backdrop—it all blended. It sucked when you lost, was only marginally better when you won. After all, there were only so many ways to say, 'They played as hard as they could, but we were better,' or 'We played like shit tonight and they kicked the crap out of us.' There had been days where he'd thought if he had to say,

'We gotta just keep getting pucks to the net,' one more time, he would scream.

Now, as a coach, he pretty much hated it. He wanted to push through the throngs of reporters and tell them to leave his fucking guys alone. They were hot, sweaty, exhausted, and had to be on the ice again in twelve hours in a different city.

The press gauntlet at the end of this particular game was more brutal than most. Liam felt no guilt in letting Williams take the brunt of the interviews concerning the trade. A few reporters, knowing of the Luciano-O'Reilly connection tried to ask Liam about it, but all he said was, "I know Mr. Semerad, the owners of the Thunder, and the coaches and guys over at the other club are doing what they feel is best for the teams." It seemed to satisfy most of them.

Besides talking to reporters, there were a million and one things going on after the game. There was usually a quick post-game review with the coaches, and the Captain had to give out the Player of the Game award. This year, the Thunder had a metal replica of Thor's hammer from one of the Marvel movies. Liam had seen everything from a plastic shovel to crowns.

Jansson got the award for scoring the winning goal on a penalty kill while they were tied near the end of the third period.

After all that, players rotated through post-game workouts, massages, medical treatments, and rehydrating to replace what they'd lost during the game. Liam used to lose five pounds or so during every game.

Even as texts flew back and forth between him and Joey, Liam told himself his impatience had nothing to do with the Italian kid waiting on the bus and everything with wanting to get some solid food in his stomach.

Jake Donovan surprised them with a little 'goodbye, thank you, and good luck' speech to Peters and Jevpalovs. Next time they all saw each other, they'd be on opposite sides of the face-off circle.

Both of the guys had rallied quickly. Once they'd gotten over the surprise, they had taken it like pros and played their hearts out. Everybody had known it was a possibility. SportsNet kept a running countdown with faces, ages, cap hits and contract status. There were no secrets in the league, except for the timing. You never knew when it was coming, and the closer the trade deadline got the faster the rumors flew. And the deadline was two days away.

There was no way around it; in most instances, being traded sucked. But it was better than being an unrestricted free agent with no offers on the table at the end of the season. An UFA spent the last part of the season wondering if the team he was on would make an offer, would someone else make an offer, or was this the last season he would ever play in the NHL?

Eventually, though, Liam and the team piled onto the bus. A quick glance showed him that Sergei had taken the seat next to Joey. Paul and Robbie, together as always, sat in the row behind them. They leaned over the back of the seats to better hear the conversation.

With a sigh, Liam dropped down heavily into the seat next to Andy.

"Long night," Andy said, not looking up from the replays he was watching on his phone.

"Ain't over yet," Liam answered. "I'll have those even-strength reports done before practice tomorrow."

Andy nodded. "Okay."

Despite the fact that it was one-thirty in the morning back on the East Coast, Liam's family was blowing up his phone with texts in the group chat. He could hear Joey's phone buzzing two rows back. He texted Joey in a private message. *The families bugging you, too?*

He heard Joey laugh out loud. *Big time* he replied. *I'm ignoring them until tomorrow.*

Good plan.

"I forgot how big you are, you freak of nature," Joey said to Sergei. At six-foot-eight, Sergei was one of the tallest players in the league; Joey was one of the shortest. It had made for interesting photo ops when they'd both played for the Kings years ago.

"Should I get you booster seat, like I get for our babies, so you can see out the window?" the big goalie asked. Sergei and his partner Alex had become instant parents to one-year-old twins the past New Years. Despite the tragedy behind it, they seemed to be adjusting well.

A small bing on his phone notified Liam that @TheLooch had posted on his Instagram. He opened the app to see a picture of Sergei resting his arm on Joey's head while Robbie and Paul grinned over the backs of the seats. *New team, new friends, old bullies #PergovSucks, #GrowthHormoneScandal,* the caption read. Joey had tagged everyone including the Thunder official account. That should keep the social media guys happy.

It was barely a five-minute ride to the hotel but somehow the family had broken their own land speed record for getting into an argument. The argument was over whether or not Joey should move in with Liam. Technically, Liam was the only one arguing. Everyone else thought it was a swell idea.

NATALIE posted in **THE ONE WITHOUT THE LOOCH**

NATALIE: *Just until he finds his own place. You're going to make him live in a hotel? All by himself? L You know he hates being alone. He always has.*

DEANO: *all hockey players hate living alone we're needy bastards*

LIAM: *I DON'T HATE IT.*

ANGIE: *Stop yelling!*

NATALIE: *right. You're perfectly fine. I am a ROCK....I am an iiiiiiiiiiii-land...*

LIAM: *i don't hate living alone. I'm too busy. I'm hard to live with, I'm particular.*

PATRICK: *yeah, particularly annoying. But i think joey can handle you.*

Joey handling him and vice versa was exactly what Liam was worried about.

LIAM: *it's a bad idea. I'm a coach on the team, it will look like I'm playing favorites.*

DEANO: *Sidney Crosby lived with Mario Lemieux for years. And he owned the team.*

LIAM: *They were teammates when he moved in. And he was a kid! 18 years old.*

GINA: *He stayed until he had a Stanley Cup!*

LIAM: *Yeah but he was still only 21*

GINA: *Still a millionaire, could afford his own place.*

JOEY: *Has anyone asked Joey what he wants to do?*

GINA: *Deano! I thought you made a fucking chat group w/out him!!!*

DEANO: *I thought I did!*

JOEY: *SURPRISE!*

LIAM FORCED himself not to look to the back of the bus. His fingers hesitated over the keyboard for a solid two seconds before he hit send on a private text. *Well, do you?*

He told himself it would be easier to keep an eye on Joey if they lived in the same house. And if they started sleeping together, whose business was it really? Who would it hurt?

JOEY: *Do you want me to?*

LIAM: *Yeah, I do.*

JOEY: *Could be a disaster. We're gonna have to set up some guidelines, boundaries.*

LIAM: *I didn't even know you knew that word.*

JOEY: *I mean I'm sure I could find another roommate if you want. I think Chebs would let me stay with him. We've shared a room before.*

LIAM: *Lucy...*

JOEY: *Judy...*

LIAM: *I don't share*

Joey's *ha!* rang out over the general chatter.

Liam looked up and met Joey's eyes in the rearview mirror. *No shit,* Joey mouthed.

PATRICK changed the name of the group to **OPERATION GET JOEY A HOME.**

PATRICK: *So what's the deal? You guys roomies?*

LIAM: *yeah I'll let him stay, as long as he behaves.*

DEANO: *so like twenty minutes right?*

JOEY: *I'm sure I'll piss him off faster than that.*

The bus pulled into the curved driveway in front of the Ritz.

JOEY: *Gotta go. Talk to you losers later. Ciao.*

GINA: *good luck in Seattle, little brother. I think it's gonna be great.*

LIAM: *I'll make sure it is.*

Joey's laughter followed Liam off the bus.

11

JOEY

From ESPN.COM – May 13, 2014

"When we get a new player, the first thing I do is call the other team's equipment manager and swap information -- what the guy wears, any special needs, etc. If it's via a trade, we exchange some equipment too. We got Marian Gaborik at the trade deadline. He wears a custom Easton glove. I didn't have it in stock, so we spray-painted his old ones black and changed the cuff rolls until we could get him some new gloves in our colors." – *Daren Granger, KA Kings' Equipment Manager*

THE CHECK-IN PROCESS WENT SMOOTHLY AS ALWAYS. ONE THING Joey could count on no matter what team he was on, was that the support staff would be amazing. They were the engines that kept the teams running. He thought there should be some kind of hall of fame for equipment managers and travel planners.

Joey took care of his reservation at the counter while room keys were handed out to the other guys. It didn't escape his notice that Paul and Robbie were assigned the same room. For some reason, he had expected them to have separate rooms. Rookies didn't have to room together anymore, but it wasn't uncommon.

He knew they had come out as a couple the weekend of the All-Star game, but he hadn't given much thought to what it would be like to be in a relationship with someone on the team on a day-to-day basis.

Watching them walk away together, knowing they were a couple, and knowing they were going to share a room, gave Joey a sense of second-hand embarrassment. Didn't it bother them that people assumed they were going to be having sex?

Even as Liam moved around the lobby, giving last-minute feedback, and chatting with the other coaching staff, Joey could still feel Liam's eyes on him.

"Hey, do you still own that place in Malibu?" Anderson Wheeler, one of the Thunder defencemen, asked Joey. Joey had golfed in a couple of charity tournaments with Wheels. They'd hit it off, and hung out a few times, but this was the first time they'd been on the same team.

"Technically. I'm renting it out. No point in selling it." Joey had got it for a bargain, fixed it up, and the value had gone up twenty-five percent since he'd bought it.

"That place was sweet," Wheels said, bumping fists with Joey. "I remember a few wild parties there when you were probably still too young to drink legally."

"My house, my rules," Joey said.

"What are you going to do with your place in New York?" he asked.

"Considering I just found out I was moving a couple of hours ago, I don't really have a firm plan. Might as well hold on to it and rent it out, too. It's a nice place and the rental market is wicked hot."

"D'you have any pictures of it?" Robbie asked.

"Yeah, sure." A text came in while Joey was showing the boys pictures of his Manhattan penthouse.

Snoop: *heard you were in town. couple parties tonight hit me up if you want to get together*

"Dude!" Robbie said, eyes wide. "Is that *Snoop*-Snoop? Like the real Snoop Dogg?"

"Yeah, he's a sweetheart and a huge hockey fan."

"You gotta go," Paul said. "Go for me. Fuck that, bring me."

Liam yanked Joey's phone out of his hand. "Jesus Christ, I can't leave you alone for a second."

"Dude!" Joey protested. "I can't leave Snoop hanging." He grinned at Liam. Not that there was any way he was really going out. It was late, he was going to eat dinner and then go right to bed. He just loved the shade of red Liam's face turned when Joey messed with him.

"No," Liam said sternly. "Food then bed. All of you. We have a game to play tomorrow." He actually shooed them away with a wave of his hands.

Joey bit his lip to keep from laughing. "Yes, Dad."

"Yes, Coach," Paul and Robbie said in unison.

———

By the time dinner was finished, Joey was swaying on his feet.

"Come on," Liam said. "Let's get you settled. What have you got with you?"

Joey held up his carry-on and pointed to his suitcase. "You're looking at it. Clothes are on the way, but I'm having them shipped to your house."

"My house? Where did you get my address?"

Joey gave him a look.

Liam shrugged. "Stupid question. My mother of course." He grabbed Joey's suitcase, leaving the small, wheeled carry-on for Joey to pull.

"Well, since I'm moving in anyway, I don't see the problem." They walked down the quiet luxurious halls of the Ritz.

"Yeah, but you didn't know that until five minutes ago."

"Where else was I supposed to have them sent?"

"The hotel the team would have put you up in?"

Joey scoffed. "Why would I stay at a hotel when you have a perfectly good house on the beach?"

Liam sighed and shoved his hands in his pockets, but Joey caught the small smile on his face. "What about your cars? What are you going to do with them?"

"I'll have the Audi shipped. But I'm thinking of selling the Lamborghini. Gina will be pissed, she loves to drive it."

"She's menace enough in a minivan. No way does she need a car that can do zero to sixty in five seconds."

"Three," Joey corrected him.

Liam shook his head. "I can't believe you still have that fucking thing. It's the most useless car I've ever seen. How often do you drive it? Twice a year?" Liam stabbed the up button on the elevator.

"What do you got, Grandpa? A Mercedes? A BMW? Some classically-understated silver sedan?"

"Yeah. A Bentley, and it's fucking nice and you'll never drive it. You drive like shit. How often do you drive anyway?"

He had a point. Joey hadn't driven a lot since living in Manhattan. But still, it wasn't like he'd forgotten how. "Hey, I'm a great driver. I drive all summer on the island."

"Whatever, Rainman." The bell dinged and the elevator doors slid open. "Do you have your room key?"

Joey rolled his eyes, held up his white plastic keycard, and followed Liam into the elevator.

"So who are you thinking of putting me on a line with?" Joey asked. He flicked his keycard with his thumbnail, until Liam snatched it out of his hand.

"Stop that." He shoved the key into his jacket pocket. "You just got here, I'm not thinking of anything."

"That's a lie. You've been thinking of it since the first time the trade became a possibility."

"Since Christmas," Liam said.

"What?"

"Hal Semerad called me on Christmas Eve to run the idea by me." Liam seemed fascinated by the poster on the wall of the elevator advertising the hotel's restaurant options.

Joey pinched the bridge of his nose. "And you didn't think to tell me?"

Liam stabbed the button for Joey's floor. "What was the point? It might have come to nothing. How would it have helped you? Plus, I kinda had a lot of other shit on my mind at Christmas, you know. What with finding out the woman I was going to ask to marry me was pregnant with your brother's baby. Remember that?"

"Yeah, I remember that."

Liam turned, and backed Joey into a corner of the elevator, trapping him with his arms. "Besides, we had better things to do than talk at Christmas, didn't we?"

Before Joey could answer, the bell dinged again and the elevator stopped.

"Is this your floor?" Liam asked.

"Yeah," Joey answered. "I guess I'll see you in the morning. What time does the bus leave?" Being around Liam made him crazy, Joey decided. He needed at least one night alone before they started spending twenty-four/seven together.

Liam shoved Joey out of the elevator. "I'm going with you to your room."

"Why? To make sure I don't slip out the window and go wild on the streets of L.A?"

"No, I want to make sure you're alright."

"I'm fine," Joey said, following Liam down the hall. "This one."

Liam pulled the keycard out of his pocket and pushed open the door.

Having Liam in his room was potentially a horrible idea. So many conflicting emotions swirled around in his head he was almost paralyzed. He wanted Liam to make a move. He wanted Liam to leave. He wanted to ask him to stay, and he wanted to tell him he wasn't interested in any more.

Fabulous. Clear as mud. Just like his thinking every time Liam was within touching distance.

"Bullshit," Liam said as he snapped on the light.

Joey dropped down on the foot of the king-sized bed. It was nice; they always were. Too bad it was all wasted on him. He'd be at the hotel for maybe eight hours total, and hopefully he'd be asleep most of that time. As long as he had a bed and a bathroom, he was happy.

"What are you talking about?" Joey asked as he took off his shoes.

Liam leaned against the dresser, two feet away from Joey, legs crossed at the ankles and hands braced behind him. His shirt pulled tight across his chest, straining the buttons. "I don't think you're fine. And neither does the family. You've been acting strange even for you."

Joey sighed deeply and focused on untying his other shoe. Liam's gaze burned on the back of his neck. "I'm fine. I swear." He sat up and smiled. At least the questioning cleared up the paralysis. He wanted Liam to leave—the sooner the better. "Besides, new team, new start. And I'll actually have friends on your team." Crap. He hadn't meant to say that. Exhaustion had *vino* beat hands down when it came to *veritas*.

"What are you talking about? You have more friends than anyone I know. The only reason you ever spent any time alone is by choice."

Joey took his time taking off his tie and unbuttoning his shirt, trying to find the words to explain how he felt. Obviously, he wasn't going to bring up his health issues. He wasn't that stupid. But there were things he wanted to talk to someone about. Maybe Liam could be that person. He stripped his shirt off and laid it on the bed next to him.

Liam uncrossed his ankles and straightened up as if he was going to close the small distance between them.

"Have you ever been alone in a crowd?" Joey asked.

Liam stopped. "How so?"

Joey rubbed his chin. He needed another shave. One of the joys of being Italian was a permanent five o'clock shadow. Sometimes he wished he could let his beard grow, like Liam did, but the few playoff beards he'd attempted to grow had looked so awful, his teammates begged him to shave.

"Have you ever looked across a room full of people and realized that you knew less than a quarter of them?" he asked. "Did you ever think that if you lost your job, your phone would stop ringing the next day?"

Liam's brow furrowed. The wrinkles in between his brows had become more pronounced over the last year. "I think you have more real friends than you know. I think they're just waiting for you to stop running around so much."

Joey shrugged. If Liam didn't understand, Joey didn't have the vocabulary or energy to try and explain. "It's late. I'm going to sleep."

Liam ignored the not-so-subtle hint that it was time for him to leave. "Are you nervous about tomorrow?" he asked, coming to sit next to Joey on the bed.

"A little. I've never joined a team at the end of the season before. Feels weird. Got any tips?"

"Don't fuck up."

Joey laughed in spite of himself. "Thanks, Coach."

Liam put his arm around Joey and pulled him in for a hug. "We got this. Just listen to me, be yourself, and play your heart out like you always do."

Joey let himself sag against Liam. He felt safe in Liam's arms. Liam was strong and competent, and Liam had said *we*.

Liam kissed the top of Joey's head. Then, with a hand to his chin, tipped Joey's head up and kissed him on the lips. That soft kiss, gentle and so different from anything they had shared before, turned Joey's stomach into knots. He sank into it for second before pulling away

"What's wrong?" Liam asked.

"I don't think this is a good idea."

"I thought that was my line." Liam released Joey's chin, but kept a hand on his back, moving it slowly in calming circles. Joey felt the warmth of it through the thin T-shirt he wore. "By *this* do you mean right now, right here? Or *this*," Liam waved a hand between them, "in general?"

Joey sat up straight, putting a bit of distance between them. "Maybe just now. Maybe in general." He stood up and walked over to the window, staring out at the lights on the Hollywood Hills while he tried to put words to feelings he could barely understand.

"If I'm going to be here, to live in your house and play on your team," he said slowly, "I can't be... distracted. You... we have a shot at a playoff spot. I know Coach Williams is counting on me."

"Do you think I'll be a distraction?" Liam asked.

Joey couldn't get a read on Liam's tone, but he didn't turn around. He wasn't sure he would be able to speak while looking Liam in the eye. If Liam crooked his finger, Joey would throw himself into his arms.

He rubbed the curtains between his thumb and finger. Professionally, Joey trusted Liam one hundred percent; Liam wouldn't steer him wrong. But could he trust him with his heart? "I think this is an amazing opportunity for me, career-wise."

"But?" This time Joey heard the strain in Liam's voice. When he turned around, Liam's hands were clenched in the comforter.

"But there's no place for you to run if things go bad between us."

"What?" Liam stood up and took a step toward Joey. "What are you talking about?"

"You run. You ran away after Christmas. You ran away after Tampa."

"I had to go back to work. I called you like I said I would."

"Emotionally." Joey turned and looked Liam in the eye. "Emotionally, you ran away. As long as it's just, you know, physical with us, you're good. But it's like I can't talk to you."

Liam shoved his hands into his pockets. "You sound like Michelle." There was a hint of bitterness in his voice.

Wisely, Joey stayed quiet. The silence stretched between them until all he could hear was Liam's breathing and the sound of his own fingers drumming against his thigh. Joey broke first, turning back to the window.

Liam sighed. "Joey."

"I'm sorry." He wasn't sure what he was apologizing for.

"Joey," Liam said softly. "Look at me. Please? I'm not mad, I promise."

Liam looked like he wanted to kiss Joey again. This softer side of Liam was messing with Joey's mind even more.

"Of course I'm not going to force you to do anything," Liam said. "I want you to be happy here. I want you to be as amazing as I know you can. I know I'm a hard person to get close to."

"No, you're not. You're amazing."

Liam laughed. "Amazingly annoying at times. Controlling, bossy. I've heard it all."

Joey gave him a lopsided grin and shrugged.

"Not going to tell me I'm not?" Liam said with a twist of his lips.

"I'm going to defer to your expertise."

"Brat," Liam said, but he was smiling.

Joey's shoulders relaxed. Maybe they'd be okay, no matter what happened.

"It's late, I'm going to go if you want me to," Liam said.

Joey nodded, not trusting what might come out of his mouth.

"Okay, then. The bus leaves for the airport at eight. Breakfast is at seven in the small ballroom. Goodnight," Liam said.

"Goodnight."

Joey waited until the door shut before falling backwards on the bed. What the hell was he doing?

JOEY WAS FINALLY DRIFTING off the sleep when he heard the door to his room open with a soft click. He sat up and fumbled for the bedside light.

"It's me," Liam said, striding into the room. He was still in his shirt and tie.

"What? How did you get in here? Did you steal my room key?"

"Nope. I told the nice lady at the desk that you locked yourself out of your room wearing nothing but a towel." Liam stood next to the bed. "So, of course you couldn't come down half-naked and get another key. I told her I would take a picture for her, if she gave me the key."

Joey pushed himself upright in the bed, the sheet and blanket slipping down to his waist. "You lied to the desk clerk?"

"Uh-huh. I did." Liam pulled his tie off with one hand.

Joey's heart pounded against his ribs as Liam started to unbutton his shirt. The look in Liam's eyes dried the moisture from his mouth. This was what he had come to expect between them. This predatory look, and the way Liam took control.

"Why?" he asked.

Liam sat on the edge of the bed and ran his hand across Joey's chest, tracing the tattoos as if he couldn't help himself.

Joey shivered, nipples tightening into hard peaks. "Why?"

"Two reasons, really. Number one, I thought about what you said about being alone in a crowd."

"Yeah?"

"And I remembered last year when I was doing rehab for my hip. I hated it. I was lonely. And you sent me a postcard twice a week.

Not an email, not a text. But an actual postcard." Liam smiled, his incongruously blue eyes catching the low light. He ran his fingers through Joey's hair. Joey leaned into the touch.

"I know how much rehab sucks," Joey said. Everyone had to deal with it at one point or another, usually multiple times over the course of a career.

"Some of the guys tried to stay in touch, but you know how it is. So, yeah, I was lonely. And I realized that nothing made me as happy as getting those stupid postcards."

"I'm glad they helped. So what's the second reason?"

Liam's hand slipped down to the back of Joey's neck, fingers tightening. He leaned his mouth against Joey's temple. "The second reason is because I think you're wrong."

"Shocking. About what exactly?"

Liam slid his hand up Joey's neck, caressing his cheek and running his thumb across the stubble. "This. I think *this* is a very good idea. You make me lose my mind, and I don't even know why. I'm not going to force you, but I am going to promise you that I won't run." He ran his thumb across Joey's lips, and his mouth opened involuntarily. "Honestly? I don't think I could."

Liam slid the tip of his thumb into Joey's mouth, his eyes locked on Joey's face. "I think you know what's best for you. I think you're confused, and a little lost, and you want somebody to tell you what to do."

Joey's eyes closed and he shuddered. God that sounded like heaven. On the ice, he knew exactly what to do, exactly who he was. But off it, he floundered, not knowing who to trust to go to for advice.

"Do you trust me?" Liam asked, as if he could read Joey's mind.

"Yes," he answered immediately. "I trust you."

"Good." Liam stood up and started undressing.

Joey watched in silence as Liam stripped down completely.

Holy shit. He'd felt Liam's body naked against his when they'd shared a bed on Christmas Eve, but hadn't seen it.

Dark, red hair dusted the ivory skin of his muscled chest, and narrowed to a happy trail ending in the thick bush of auburn curls surrounding a thick, half-hard cock. His thighs were thick with muscle. Liam cupped his cock as if he were half-covering, and half-fondling himself. "Going to let me in?" he asked.

Joey froze, his eyes darting up to Liam.

Liam laughed. "In the bed. Are you going to let me in the bed?"

Joey slid over, and Liam pulled the covers down. He lay on his side, propping himself up on one elbow. He rubbed a hand across Joey's chest. "Your skin is so soft." As always happened any time they were close, Liam's fingertips slid across Joey's skin, but instead of tracing his tattoos this time, his fingers found all the scars from the stitches and injuries Joey had taken over the years. He kissed every one, and Joey found it hard to breathe. He gently probed a new fist-sized bruise on Joey's hip. "Hit the boards tonight?" he asked.

"Yeah. Those Texas boys hit hard."

"And I know you're not one to shy away from it."

"No, I'm not."

Liam's fingers trailed down to the top of Joey's tiny black and bright blue briefs. "Are these the same damn pair you were wearing at Christmas?"

Joey nodded.

"Did you wear them for me?" Liam pressed his hard cock against Joey's side.

"Yes," Joey admitted, barely able to process anything beyond the feel of Liam's body plastered to his.

Liam's hand slipped beneath the waistband of the small Armani briefs, scratching through the dark curls there. Joey's breath sped up, and his cock twitched, thickening under Liam's hand.

"I think you like this," Liam said. "So we're doing this."

"Okay."

"How it's going to work is, you're going to listen to me. If you're not sure what to do, ask me. If you're worried an idea is stupid, ask me. And I won't run. I'll be there for you."

Joey rolled onto his side, "Promise?"

Liam pulled their bodies together. "Promise. And I'm going to kiss you now, if that's okay?"

"Oh, thank God, I thought you were going to talk all night," Joey said.

Liam slapped Joey's thigh hard enough for the sound to fill the room. "No backtalk. There's no one from the team on this floor. I could spank you and no one would hear it."

Joey couldn't control his shudder at Liam's words.

"Hmm," Liam said, grabbing Joey's ass hard. "Maybe I should. Would you like that?"

Joey thrust against Liam, rubbing his cloth covered cock against the other man's bare skin. "Jesus, are you going to tease me all fucking night?"

Liam gripped Joey's hips, holding him in place, and touched his mouth to Joey's. "Maybe." He dragged his tongue across Joey's lips.

"Liam," Joey said desperately, trying to pull away from Liam's hold so he could move.

"What? What do you want?" He slid his hand down the back of Joey's underwear and pulled it out slowly, nails scratching his skin on the way back up.

"Liam, fuck," Joey said through clenched teeth. How could he have forgotten what a fucking cock tease Liam was? How he got off on making Joey beg?

Liam nipped at Joey's lips.

Okay, fine. Begging was good. Joey could beg. "Liam, fucking touch me, blow me. Let me blow you, something, anything."

Liam pushed Joey's last piece of clothing down his legs as far as he could. "I have a better idea." He pushed Joey down onto his back and rolled on top of him, straddling Joey's hips. He rolled his body down, sliding his cock slowly, tortuously against Joey's as he kissed the breath out of his lungs.

And he kept on doing it. Sliding, grinding, and rubbing slowly. Pushing up on his hands, he licked his palm and wrapped it around their cocks and squeezed.

Joey gasped as his cock throbbed.

"Help me," Liam said breathlessly. "Give me your hand."

Licking his palm, Joey did as he was told. "Fuck," he shouted at the feel of their hands and cocks together. "Fuck, fuck, fuck."

Liam's hand clamped down on Joey's shoulder. Joey wanted desperately to spread his legs, but the tiny underwear bound his thighs together. All he could do was lie there and let Liam fuck up against him.

Liam grunted with each thrust of his hips, his breath hot against Joey's cheeks, and his thighs trembling. As their moans grew more desperate, their harsh breathing and the slap of flesh on flesh grew louder, Joey's brain finally, mercifully, shut down. He gave himself over totally to the pleasure surging through his body.

"Shit," Liam cursed, body tensing. "Oh, fuck." He sucked in a deep breath and clamped his legs around Joey's hips as he came.

The space between grew hot and slick and Liam jerked them harder and faster. Joey came with a yell, his fingernails digging into Liam's back. Liam's strokes slowed but he didn't stop until it almost hurt.

Giving Joey a quick, hard kiss, Liam flopped down onto the bed, breathing hard. "So, did I make the right call?"

Joey nodded as he tried to get his breath back.

"Still worried about tomorrow?"

Joey shook his head, and then punched Liam weakly on the arm. "Thanks for the pep talk, Coach. I feel like I might need more one-on-one coaching another day, though."

"I think that can be arranged." Liam ran his fingers through the mess on his stomach. "Sticky." Groaning, he sat up.

Joey fell asleep to the sounds of Liam getting ready for bed. The warmth of the washcloth as Liam wiped him off roused him halfway.

"Go to sleep," Liam whispered. "I got you." He clicked off the light and slipped into bed, pulling Joey into his arms.

12

LIAM

From the Toronto Sun, March 17, 2015

"I was shocked when I came into the hockey world and would see my husband's much younger teammates, at 23, 24, married, and then with two or three children by 26, 27.

"Perhaps having someone with them when they're in and out of hotels, and after games, gives them a sense of comfort," DeWulf said. "A lot of the women in their lives, they've known since they were in high school. They really need stability. These guys are regimented. They need habits. Not having stability doesn't work for their mentality. Also, professional sports makes you feel like you're aging at a very rapid pace. I think that's in a lot of their minds, that 30 is so old. That's the age when your job's done." – *Noureen DeWulf, wife of Vancouver Canucks goaltender Ryan Mille on why NHL players marry young.*

LIAM DIDN'T BOTHER KNOCKING BEFORE HE WALKED INTO THE ROOM Joey had chosen. It was Liam's favorite room and he kind of wished he had staked it out first instead of taking the master bedroom. Michelle would have hated it though. She didn't like any stray streaks of light to sneak past the blackout curtains she had installed in her bedrooms.

Glass panels separated by thick white beams made up one wall and the entire ceiling of this room. A telescope pointed towards the water and let a person get a nice view of the islands. Liam had spent quite a bit of time looking through it.

Joey was passed out on top of the blankets. He slept naked, because of course he did, and Liam took a minute to admire the view. Joey must have put some kind of a spell on him, because Liam couldn't keep his hands off a naked Joey if his life depended on it.

He sat down gently on the bed, wanting to enjoy Joey, warm and cozy and beautiful in bed. Like a magnet, the black swirls of ink on Joey's back and shoulders drew Liam's fingertips. He lightly traced them, then spread his hand flat and ran his palm down the sun-warmed valley of his spine. Joey shivered, but didn't open his eyes.

The bruises from last night's game on Joey's hips and side attracted his attention. Joey probably didn't even know they were there. Liam hadn't noticed his until he'd stopped playing hockey and palm-sized bruising stopped being an everyday occurrence.

Hockey players in general had great asses, but Joey's belonged in a museum somewhere. The combination of Italian genes and skating had given him a perfect bubble butt. Liam knew he had to have his pants specially tailored to fit.

There was only one thing to do with an ass like that. Liam lifted his hand and smacked it hard enough to leave a handprint.

"Don't start something you aren't going to finish, old man," Joey murmured.

"Wake up, princess."

"What time is it?"

"Eight."

"Ugh." Joey turned his head to look at Liam, resting his cheek on his arm. "What are you doing home?"

"I ran home to pick up some stuff. Figured we could ride back together."

Joey started to turn over. Liam placed a hand on his back. "Don't turn over. Talk about starting things we don't have time to finish."

Joey grinned like he knew he had Liam wrapped around his, well, let's just say his little finger. He was right. Ignoring Liam's hand on him, Joey rolled onto his back. Liam's hand followed the rolling motion around his side, coming to a stop right above his navel.

Liam dipped his pinky into the small depression. "Brat. No game tonight so we're free after lunch."

Joey stretched, arms reaching over his head, his back arching off the bed. "Not me. I have that media thing, remember?"

"Can't you ditch it? When was the last time you had an afternoon off?"

"It's fine. It will be easy. I just have to smile and play nice and do whatever they tell me. But I'd rather do whatever *you* tell me to do." Joey batted his eyelashes.

It should have been ridiculous but it wasn't. It was adorable. "Yeah?" Liam cocked one eyebrow.

"Promise."

He smacked Joey hard on the stomach. "Then get dressed and get your ass downstairs. I gotta get back."

"You suck."

"Not right now I don't. Hurry," he called over his shoulder as he left the room. If he stayed in the bedroom a second longer, he was going to have to come up with a really good excuse for why they were late.

"WHEELS! Head up, stick on the ice!" Liam yelled at his d-man. "This is pee-wee-level stuff!"

Joey sped towards them, turned an unnecessarily flashy spin-o-rama past Rhodie, sent the puck between Wheels' legs and underneath his fucking stick—which was, of course, not on the fucking ice—and after a downright *filthy* dangle, sent the puck top-shelf over Sergei's glove hand.

He hooted and pumped his fists and he did a one-legged celly around the rink. "Eat it, Pergs!"

Wheels watched him with a mixture of disgust and respect. The kid wasn't a bad defenceman really, just needed to dig deeper, find that little bit extra, and he could stop spending time in a suit as a healthy scratch and maybe get some ice time.

"Have I mentioned how happy I am that I don't have to play against you for this season?" Robbie said as Joey skidded to a stop in a flurry of ice shavings.

"You have, but don't let that stop you from saying it again."

"Stop flirting with my boys, Lucy," Liam yelled. "Whatever he's telling you, don't listen. He's a bad influence. Show some hustle. Set it up again. After last night's shitshow, you're lucky you're not all doing bag skates. You, too, Luciano," he added when Joey laughed. "Don't think I can't make you. Now get the fuck outta here and leave my boys alone!"

"So, you and Coach O'Reilly really are friends?" Paul asked, hopping over the boards to take his turn in the drill.

"Not on the ice we're not," Liam said. "And soon, not off the ice if you don't get out of my face."

"Not related. Grew up next door to each other." Joey answered as if Liam hadn't said anything at all.

"Has he always been so… intense?" Robbie asked bouncing the puck up and down off the blade of his stick.

Joey snorted in response. "Judy? Nah, he's all bark and no bite."

Liam closed his eyes and prayed for the strength to survive Joey on his team.

"Seriously, though," Joey added, skating lazy backwards circles on one foot, "you guys are lucky to have him. I always knew he'd make a great coach. He taught me how to see the game, how to understand it, know what I mean?"

Joey winked at Liam as he skated away. Liam shook his head. He had a feeling he'd be doing that a lot the next few months.

JAKE DONOVAN CAUGHT Liam in his office right before the afternoon media show.

"Hey, Coach, got a second?"

"Yeah, of course. Always time for you." Liam and Jake had come up a few years apart in the league, but he'd never heard a bad thing about the man.

"It's about Luciano." Donovan shut the door behind him.

Liam leaned back in his chair, toying with a pencil. "What about him?"

"How's he working out?" Jake leaned against the four-drawer file cabinet.

Liam spread his hands wide. "I should be asking you that. You're the captain. What do you think?"

"From a technical perspective? He's great. The way he skates the puck through the neutral zone is fucking incredible. And we needed that. He's strong and his edge work is better than mine. The guy can play keepaway in the corner for fifteen seconds without any backup."

"But?"

Jake frowned and pushed away from the file cabinet. "I see him hanging out with Rhodes and Dyson and some of the younger guys. I think they look up to him." He sat on the arm of the chair near Liam's desk.

"I'm still not seeing the problem."

"I'm worried that he's going to be a distraction. On the ice, and off it. Seems like they're always hanging around laughing."

"That's not a bad thing, is it?"

"No, just..." Jake shrugged and looked a little sheepish, but he didn't back down.

Liam leaned forward. "Just you're the captain and your job is to watch over your guys. I get it. And I admire it. I promise I'll take your feedback very seriously, and I know Andy will, too. But you do me a favor?"

"Yes, of course."

"The next practice or next game whenever you're around him listen to exactly what Joey is saying without prejudice. I actually like him hanging around with some of the younger guys. I think they're good influences on him, particularly Robbie and Paul."

"Oh? How so? And why them in particular? Does it have anything to do with their press conference?"

"Yeah, but not in the way you're thinking." That was a bit of a lie, but it had nothing to do with this conversation. "Around Paul and Robbie he doesn't have to be all macho. He is more himself with them than with anybody I've ever seen outside the family. I think he's actually trying to make a good impression on them. He wants them to like him."

"He does seem very comfortable with them and with Sergei. I noticed he spends more time with them than the guys on his line."

Liam didn't pay as much attention to the forwards as he did to his boys obviously, but he hadn't noticed any tension in the lines. Maybe he should start playing closer attention. "Is there a problem? You're trying him out with Anderson and Jansson, right?"

Jake nodded. When Bryce Lowery retired, Jake had moved up to the first line center to take his place, but the second line of Daniel Lipe, Alex Huberdeau, and Jake had been a powerhouse line. They hadn't been able to recreate that magic. They'd tried rotating people through those first and second lines, couldn't quite find the right combination. If Joey could handle the first line, that would put Jake, Lipe, and Hubs back together, giving the Thunder a lot of depth.

"Again, not technically. They played great together, I think it's gonna work out well. They don't seem to hang out very much together."

"Well, it's only been a week. And Ders and Gabe both have partners and kids, right?"

"True. True." He stood up. "I guess I'm worried about nothing. And you're right, even though you didn't say it, I've been judging him on his past press, and that's not fair."

"He's a good kid, a good man. Give him a chance, he'll grow on you."

"You think?" Jake looked skeptical.

"I bet you fifty bucks by the end of the regular season you'll be the biggest Luciano fan on the team."

"Yeah? You're on." Donovan pulled his wallet out of his pocket and took out three bills and handed them to Liam. "Biggest fan, right? Not just like I like the guy or he's okay?"

Liam took fifty out his wallet and slid the bills into the top drawer of his desk. "Biggest fan. You can't avoid it; you might as well give in to it."

Jake laughed and shook his head and left the office. Checking the clock, Liam realized Joey would be in the middle of his PR thing. He wasn't sure exactly what Joey would be doing but it was always fun to watch. He slipped his jacket back on and went to go find the crew.

Coach Williams stopped him in the hall. "You gonna watch Luciano?" Liam nodded. "Got some news for you before you go."

"Good or bad?"

"I don't know, you tell me. Wings just pulled a fucking muscle in the weight room, so we are moving Petes up to the third line and calling your brother up from the Lightning."

Liam made a face.

"Something I should know?"

"No. I'm just thinking of having Paddy and Joey in the same house. Pray for me."

"Can't the kid just stay in the hotel?" Andy asked. "Get some room service, use the minibar?"

Liam shook his head. "You don't know my family. I'd get bombarded with calls and texts asking how could I let 'poor little Paddy' stay all by himself in some cold and lonely hotel when I had an extra bedroom?"

"Well good luck. Try not to let them stay up too late watching cartoons or playing video games."

"That'll be easy because I don't have a video game console."

Andy raised his eyebrows in surprise. "And you call yourself a hockey player, son?"

"Not anymore, Coach," Liam said with a smile.

"Damn right, Coach." Andy patted him on the shoulder.

LIAM WALKED into the media room where they'd set up a tall table in front of a wall decorated with the Thunder logo. Multiple blond, bearded, and helmeted cartoon Vikings leered down at them.

Joey stood on one side of the table across from Hubs. At nineteen, Hubs was the youngest player on the team, but he'd already been with them a year and was holding his own on their strong second line. The blond Canadian was one of the friendliest people Liam had ever met and reminded Liam of a golden retriever with his big open smile and friendly manner. Apparently they were reading bad jokes to each other.

"What do you call a person who walks back and forth screaming one minute, then sits down weeping uncontrollably the next?" Joey asked Hubs as Liam walked in.

Hubs screwed up his face as he thought, then shook his head. "I don't know. A lunatic?"

"Ooh, so close," Joey said. "The correct answer is Coach." He winked at Liam over the other man's shoulder. "Okay, your turn."

Hubs looked down at this sheet of paper in his hand and read woodenly from it. "Why didn't the lousy hockey team have a website?"

"I don't know?" Joey answered. "Why didn't they?"

"They couldn't string three W's together." They both laughed at that, and the small crowd around them groaned.

"Who writes these things?" Joey asked. "These are terrible."

"You can do better?" Hubs asked.

"Sure." Joey looked up, contemplating the ceiling while he thought. "Okay. Try this. Did you hear about the restaurant on the moon?"

Liam couldn't hold back the groan. He knew what was coming.

Joey's eyes twinkled as he looked at Liam.

"No," Hubs said.

"Great food," Joey answered, "but no atmosphere."

"That is not even close to better," Liam said. The cameraman turned the camera to him, and a person Liam assumed was the director waved him closer to the table. He shook his head. He wasn't going anywhere.

"I think you taught me that one," Joey said.

"Not me. That was a Natalie favorite."

"Oh, right. You liked puns." Joey rolled his eyes.

Liam shrugged. "I still like puns. They're clever. Not like knock knock jokes."

Joey laughed surprisingly loud. "Oh man, I'd forgotten about that! When I was a kid I used to torture Liam with knock knock jokes," he explained. "I was like, what, five?"

"Yeah, because I hadn't left for school yet, so I was fifteen?"

"Tell us some," the director ordered.

"I don't remember any specifically, just that they were really bad and he told them over and over. Half the time, he would be laughing too hard to even finish."

"Whaddya talkin' about?" Joey said pulling out all the stops on his Southie accent. "Those jokes were classics. Classics! Watch. Knock knock."

Liam shook his head. Hubs grabbed his arm and pulled him to the table. "Come on, Coach. Say hi to the people."

It wasn't 'the people' Liam was worried about, it was his bosses, the GM, the owner. Telling kids' knock knock jokes wasn't very dignified.

"C'mon," Joey said with a quirk of his upper lip, giving Liam the puppy dog eyes. "You know you wanna."

"No." Liam crossed his arms over his chest, and bit his lip to keep from smiling.

"Don't you trust me?"

"Not as far as I can throw you."

"You're no fun." Joey batted his stupidly long, thick eyelashes. "Please, Judy? For me?"

"Judy?" Hubs asked.

Great. Joey had done that on purpose. Liam needed to draw attention away from the old nickname or they'd be calling him that until he retired.

"Liam's the oldest of the kids, right?" Joey offered before Liam could change the subject. "So, kind of bossy. I know. It's shocking."

Liam glared at Joey, hoping his expression convened his imminent death.

If it did, Joey chose to ignore. "Anyway, one day his sister Nat— Natalie O'Reilly, Goalie for the Boston Pride, just won a gold medal at the Olympics, you might have heard of her. If you haven't, check her out. Anyway, Liam was being…Liamy…and Nat accused him of being 'Judge Judy and Executioner. And it just kinda stuck."

Liam hung his head as the room laughed. He wasn't getting out of this with his dignity intact, was he?

"Fine. *Lucy*," he said pointedly, stepping up to the table. Mentally, he banged his head against an imaginary wall. Why did he always let Joey talk him into things?

Then Joey flashed him a genuine smile, eyes lighting up with joy as if Liam had given him the pony he'd always wanted for Christmas.

Oh, yeah, that was why. Liam couldn't look away from his face and smiled helplessly in return.

Joey always had been the only one able to talk him into something. His sibs had complained that he was way easier on Joey than he was on them. He was beginning to think they may have had a legitimate complaint.

The cameraman changed positions and some guy in jean shorts shifted a light.

"Okay, I got one," Joey said. "Ready?"

Liam waved him on. "Give me your best shot."

"Knock knock," Joey said.

"Who's there?"

"Radio."

"Radio who," Liam asked without enthusiasm.

"Radio or not, here I come!" Joey was the only one who laughed.

"That was horrible." Liam looked at the camera and hoped that the GM wasn't watching.

"You have no sense of humor. Okay, your turn."

"I don't remember any." Liam didn't. It was like his brain had shut off.

"Yes, you do. Think real hard."

By now, Robbie, Paul, and Sergei had joined the group, and the room was starting to feel crowded. "Come on, Coach," Sergei boomed from across the room. "Tell us the joke!"

"Okay fine. Let me think." What was that one Joey always used to laugh his fool head off when he told? Oh, yeah. "Knock knock."

"Who's there?" Paul, Robbie, Sergei, and Joey asked in unison.

"Interrupting cow."

"MOO!" Liam shouted over Paul and Robbie's "Interrupting cow who?" Joey couldn't say anything, he was laughing too hard.

"I think my little nephew told me that last time I was home," Paul commented.

"That's because your little nephew and Lucy here have a lot in common." Liam was two seconds away from sticking his tongue out at Joey.

Joey waved everyone quiet. "Okay, okay. I got it. You love this one."

"Doubtful."

"Shut up. Knock knock."

Liam gave a fake put-upon sigh. Truthfully, he was having fun. He couldn't remember the last time he'd done something so ridiculous. And he'd never done anything close at work. "Who's there?"

"Ether."

Oh god, not this one. "No."

"Yes." Joey reached across the table and poked him in the chest. "Say it."

"No." And there he was again, acting like a five-year-old. It was amazing he hadn't told Joey he wasn't the boss of him. "You can't make me."

"Sure I can." Uh-oh. Joey's grin promised trouble. "Say it, and I'll find a way to make it worth your while."

Liam's eyes widened slightly, and he remembered the smack he'd given Joey on the ass earlier. A completely-inappropriate-for-work twinge of lust tightened his groin. Oh, Joey was going to have to pay for that. He narrowed his eyes, hoping Joey could read his intentions. "Fine. Ether who?"

"Ether bunny!" Paul and Joey yelled, then cracked up laughing.

The director check the time on his watch, then looked over at John, one of the club's media team.

"Oh, he's not done yet," Liam said to them both. "Give him a second."

They did, and Joey pulled himself together. "Knock knock."

"Who's there," Liam asked resignedly.

"Cargo."

"Cargo who?"

"Car go beep and kill the Ether Bunny!"

Sergei gasped like he truly hadn't been expecting that. He had to be the only one in the room who hadn't heard that joke a hundred times before they turned ten. He leaned over to Paul and whispered loudly. "Dead bunny is funny in English?"

Joey laughed so hard there were tears in his eyes. Liam felt the smile spreading across his face in response. It wasn't that anything was particularly funny, but Joey's total honest enjoyment of his stupid jokes was infectious. He was so genuine in his reactions right now, so different from the guarded, too-cool image he'd been cultivating.

Liam banged his knuckles on the table. "Get it over with, Luciano, civilizations are rising and falling while we wait for you."

"There is more about Easter bunny?" Sergei asked, which set Joey off again, and they had to wait while he got himself under control.

"Okay, okay," he wheezed, holding his arm across his stomach. "Knock knock."

"Who's there?" Liam asked through a grin. This always had been Joey's favorite part.

"Boo!" he forced out with a laugh.

"Boo hoo?"

"Don't cry, Ether bunny be back next year!"

There were completely over the top cheers and whistles. Joey took a bow, accepting the applause.

"That's a wrap," the director yelled. Most of the crowd had cleared out, headed home for lunch and naps.

Liam sagged, resting his elbows on the table, his shoulders shaking with silent laughter.

Joey ran over and draped himself over Liam's back, clapping his hands on his shoulders. "Still love me?"

Still laughing, Liam shook his head. "No."

The table rocked as Robbie slammed into it. "That was awesome, Coach!"

"Rhodie," Liam said, pushing himself up. "I'm going to need you to get that tape. Kill the cameraman if you have to."

Robbie snapped to attention, saluting smartly. "I'm on it."

"What are we on?" Paul asked, slamming into Robbie and making the table rock again.

"Muuuuurder," Robbie said, drawing out the syllables with a terrible attempt at a British accent.

"Cool. Can we do it after we eat?" Paul gave a Joey-worthy sad-puppy look, his sky blue eyes wide and pleading.

Liam straightened up. "Get the fuck away from me, both of you. Go play video games or whatever you kids do when you don't have to work." He regretted the words as soon as they came out of his mouth. He chose to ignore the lascivious look they shared.

Joey snorted.

"You. Stay," Liam said. A few short minutes later they were alone in the room.

"So what's the plan now?" Joey asked, standing as close as he dared in public.

"Now you go home, and think about how you're going to make it up to me."

"And what will you be doing?"

"I've got a couple more hours' work."

Joey groaned. "Can't get out of it?"

"No, I can't get out of it. We're one game out of that wildcard spot. Enjoy this time off, might be the last you have for a while." He stepped closer, sweeping the room with a glance. No one was around, and he really wanted to kiss Joey goodbye.

Joey smirked, stopping him with a hand to his chest. "Not at work, big boy."

Liam shoved him gently. "Go home."

Joey blew him a kiss as he left.

13

JOEY

JOEY: I can't find canned San Marzano tomatoes. What should I do?

MOM: Use the Redpack canned plum tomatoes, I like them better anyway.

JOEY: Gasp! 😮 Don't let Nonno Lollo hear you.

MOM: The old man is so deaf he wouldn't hear me if I yelled. Plus if he don't like it, he can cook himself. You got the pig feet?

JOEY: I got the feet. And the veal.

MOM: Good. Now be careful with the lid, okay?

JOEY: Ma, I know. I gotta go. Love you. 💜

MOM: Love you, too, baby. 💜 Tell me how it comes out.

JOEY JUMPED BACK AS A BUBBLE OF HOT TOMATO SAUCE ROSE TO the top of the pot and burst, splattering the counter and just missing scarring his naked chest.

"Might want to wear a shirt there, buddy," Patrick said. "I don't think your sweat is adding much to the flavor."

"You don't have to worry about it, because you aren't getting any." Joey gave the sauce a stir, put the lid slightly askew so the steam had some place to go, and turned the heat down. He wiped the counter. It was hard to make tomato sauce without getting some red somewhere, but any mess felt so out of place in Liam's pristine kitchen.

Patrick took a swig of the beer he held cradled in his hands and grimaced. "Jojo, I'm hurt. I'm crushed. You would deny me Aunt Jeannie's sauce? I'm going to call and tell her."

Joey heard the faint swoosh of the elevator doors opening followed by the slap of leather soles on the tile. Perfect timing. Liam was going to be so happy. Joey's cooking wasn't quite as good as his mother's, but he was getting close. Give him a few years.

Liam strode through the kitchen, looking like some kind of old-school Irish mob boss in a dark blue suit and the gray wool topcoat he hadn't bothered to remove. Both the set of his shoulders and the clench of his jaw telegraphed his irritation. Arousal and nervousness collided inside Joey's gut, stealing his breath.

Wearing nothing but an old pair of basketball shorts, Joey felt like the frat boy he'd never been. "Hey."

Without pausing, Liam grunted what might have been a greeting and headed for the large butler's pantry. There was a sucking sound of a fridge door opening and the rattle of glass beer bottles.

Liam came back into the kitchen scowling and holding a dark beer bottle. "What are you doing here?" he asked Patrick. He reached above Joey, opening a cabinet and pulling out a rounded glass with a heavy stem, all without touching Joey or looking him in the eye.

"Looking for a beer. But all you got is fancy shit," Patrick complained.

"This is a Trappistes Rochefort 10, you heathen. The monks at this monastery have been brewing beer since the fifteen hundreds." He turned the glass so they could read the gold Trappistes Rochefort logo engraved on its side.

"I just wanted a Guinness, not a lecture." Patrick tried to pull the glass out of Liam's hand for a taste, but Liam held it away from him.

"I'm sure they have some at the hotel. You know, the one you're *supposed* to be staying at."

Patrick rolled his eyes. "I didn't think you'd mind if I stayed here. I want to hang out with Jojo. But you're, like, extra cranky even for you. What crawled up your ass?"

"Coach Williams." Liam's voice was flat.

Uh oh. "Coach Williams?" Joey echoed.

Oh. Now that made Liam look at him. "Upstairs," Liam said, striding out of the room without a backwards glance, confident that Joey would follow.

"Uh oh, Dad's mad," Patrick said, "What did you do now?"

"Nothing that I can think of." What in the world could have happened in a few short hours?

Patrick shook his head sorrowfully and drained his beer. "Be careful," he said, followed by a large belch. "Looks like you're going to get a spanking."

Joey stumbled on the threshold of the kitchen remembering the sharp slap Liam had delivered to his ass that morning. He'd gotten a wooden spoon swatted on his ass in passing, and plenty of slaps upside the back of his head from all kinds of family members, but that was almost an expression of love. But he'd never been spanked as punishment in his life, and he was fine with that.

Now *sexy* spanking, on the other hand... He could admit it, he was intrigued.

"Ew," Patrick said with a shudder.

"What?"

"Now I'm thinking about Judy spanking you. Gross. I need brain bleach."

Joey glared at him. "Just shut the sauce off. And don't pick out all the sausages."

THOUGH THE REST of the house was showroom perfect, tastefully decorated with classically elegant furniture, a modest display of Liam's trophies and awards, and striking pieces of art Liam had accumulated over the years, Liam let his personality show through in his office.

His office, like his bedroom as a child, was his sanctuary. A glimpse into the parts of himself that he didn't let most people see.

Liam's back was to Joey and the sound of last night's hockey game came from his laptop. He'd taken off his overcoat and tossed it on the leather armchair in the corner. As he crossed the room, Joey trailed his finger across the spines of the books on Liam's shelves.

Books on coaching, motivational and leadership books, bios of hockey players and other prominent people throughout history, shared shelf space with the large collection of dog-eared thrillers Liam loved to read.

Pictures of friends, past teammates, and a multitude of O'Reillys and Lucianos lined the walls and covered most of the available flat surfaces. Joey picked up a framed photo of a much younger Gina wearing a flower costume at one of the dance recitals she'd loved so much.

"Gina said she found a new studio to dance at," he said to the tight angry line of Liam's back.

"Good for her." He kept his eyes locked on the game.

"Now that Pookie's bigger she's thinking of going back to work. They are going to let her teach a class. Like an audition."

Liam shook his head, thick red hair picking up the lowlights and looking so soft that Joey had to clench his hands into fists to keep from running his fingers through it. "Does that kid even have a real name?" Liam asked.

"It's Lorenzo, after Nonno Lollo." Joey answered as he silently willed Liam to look at him.

"Why did I never know that?" Liam clicked the mouse and the Thunder's last game paused then rewound on the screen of his laptop.

Joey watched over Liam's shoulder as his penalty kill team executed a play that had number 22, Robbie Rhodes, screaming down the ice towards the Cane's net on a breakaway. The kid was fast, really fast, and he sent the puck through the tendie's five-hole with a beautiful wrister. The rush watching it on the screen was almost as strong as it had been at the time. "That kid is fucking amazing. If he keeps improving like that, he's got a shot at the Norris." The James Norris trophy was awarded to the to the defenceman who demonstrated throughout the season the greatest all-round ability in the position.

Liam grunted something that might have been agreement.

Okay. That hadn't worked. Enough was enough. Joey walked right up into Liam's space, leaning his butt against the edge of his desk. He smiled at the plastic Joey complete with uniform and hockey stick that he'd given Liam for Christmas keeping watch on his desk.

Leaning across Liam's computer to reach it, Joey spun the plastic figure between his fingers. "You should get a Nintendo. If you got a Switch, we could play on the plane."

"Jesus. You think I have time for games? I spend the entire plane ride reviewing video and finalizing rosters and lines with Andy. Besides, why don't you post something on your Instagram about it? It could get seventeen thousand likes and the company would probably send you one for free. Plus you're fucking rich, stop sulking and go buy one."

Joey sat the toy back on the desk and rolled his eyes. "Yes, Dad."

14

LIAM

If only he had been. Maybe then he'd be able to knock some sense into the kid. Mr. Luciano had never laid a hand on his kids, even when, in Liam's opinion, a little smack on the ass was called for. Now, Mrs. L, she had no problem swatting out with her wooden spoon or delivering a warning smack upside the back of someone's head.

Liam turned his chair so he could look Joey directly in the eye. "If I *were* your dad, I'd take a wooden spoon to that perfect ass you seem so anxious to share with the world."

"What the fuck are you talking about?"

"You really have no idea?"

Joey shook his head. "I really don't."

Unbelievable. He probably didn't know. And wasn't that emblematic of the whole problem. Joey lived in la-la land, he acted without thinking. Liam picked his cell phone up off the desk and scrolled down the screen. "Maybe this will spark something." He turned the screen so Joey could see.

Huh. Well, that certainly was him. He took the phone from Liam to look at it more closely. Oh, and that was *definitely* his ass. It was all coming back to him.

He'd mooned Sergei on his way out of the parking lot, slapping his own ass and saying something incredibly crude in Russian. (One of the disadvantages of learning a language from hockey players was that you didn't often get a chance to use what they taught you in polite company.)

Joey laughed. Someone had caught the exchange with their cell phone and posted it on Twitter. He watched it again. "Hey, where's the part where Sergei mooned me back? That's not fair."

"It's not funny." Liam took the phone back.

"It's a little funny."

"Coach Williams didn't think it was funny."

Joey frowned and walked away casually, giving Liam a great look at the tattoos on his muscular back. Liam hadn't thought he had a thing for tattoos. Christmas had taught him otherwise.

Joey ran his fingers over the edge of Liam's books. "Well, he didn't say anything to me."

Liam rotated in his chair, following Joey's slow circuit of the room. "Because you're my responsibility."

Joey stopped pacing in front of Liam's trophy case. Liam liked having them in his office, it reminded him that hockey was his job as well as his passion, and he didn't have the luxury of resting on his laurels.

"I'm your responsibility?"

"I vouched for you, said you'd be a great addition to the team, and that I could keep you in line."

Joey crossed his arms over his still-naked chest.

Despite his annoyance, Liam couldn't help but appreciate the way the movement made Joey's tattoos ripple over his muscles. The way the ink followed the contours of his hipbone and trailed underneath the waistband of his pants was very distracting. Maybe after the fight they were about to have, they could have make-up sex.

"Like I'm a *child?*" Joey's voice rose on the last word.

"If you act like a child, you're going to get treated like one." Liam braced his hands on the arm of the chair, ready to deliver the speech he'd been practicing in his head the entire trip home.

Joey inhaled deeply and clasped his hands behind his head. His loose basketball shorts slipped even lower on his hips, exposing the vee of his abs and bringing his six-pack into sharp definition. He was making it very hard for Liam to stay angry with him.

"It's not that big a deal. It's just a blurry video from across the parking lot with a two-second shot of my butt."

Liam rubbed his temples. And right on schedule, he was irritated again. "And cursing."

"In Russian!" He threw his arms up in the air. "Jesus, what's the big fucking deal?"

Liam stood up. "Don't you get it?" he asked in a voice that had quieted several locker rooms in the past.

Joey took a step closer to Liam, jaw set. "I get that you all obviously think I'm a *moron* who doesn't know how to behave in public!"

"There is no 'you all'. It's just me."

"So it's just *you* who thinks I'm a moron? That's much better. Fuck you," he spat out, shoving Liam away from him with both hands.

Liam grabbed Joey's forearm as he stumbled back, yanking Joey against him. Gripping a handful of the hair on the back of Joey's head, Liam pulled down, forcing Joey to look up at him. Both of them breathing hard, their bodies pressed together. Fire shot from Joey's eyes as he struggled against Liam's grip.

He might have been younger and stronger than Liam, but Liam had five inches on him and wasn't above fighting dirty. A well-placed kick on the back of his ankle and a perfectly timed shove and hair pull combination had Joey tumbling backward.

"Fucker!" Joey exclaimed as he grabbed Liam's tie, taking Liam with him as he hit the floor.

His hand on the back of Joey's head saved him from an off-ice concussion. Liam landed hard on his knees and his free hand. "Stop it," he hissed.

Joey, the asshole, shook with laughter beneath him. "Hair pulling, Judy? Party foul, man." Twisting wildly, he tried to shove Liam off of him.

Liam grabbed his wrists and leaned forward quickly, trapping Joey's hands over his head. Their faces were inches apart.

Anger warred with desire in Joey's eyes, igniting the same in Liam. Fuck or fight. Why was it always one or the other between them? "You make me insane."

"Get in line." Joey breathed hard, chest rising and falling as he tested Liam's grip on his wrists.

Liam's body betrayed him as it usually did around Joey, his knees sliding on the slick wood floor and dropping him hard onto Joey's hips.

Joey's jaw jumped as he clenched his teeth, nostrils flaring. Joey rolled his body, rubbing his half-hard cock against Liam.

Fuck. Liam's thigh muscles tightened as he fought the urge to grind back against it and see how quickly he could get Joey fully hard. "You gotta stop doing that kind of shit. You gotta start using the wicked smart brain I *know* you have inside that fucking thick skull."

Joey's eyes blazed and he jutted his chin out. "Make me."

Liam's fingers tightened on Joey's wrist. He felt the bones and tendons shifting beneath his grip. "I should. If I can't get it through your head, I can beat it into your ass."

Joey licked his lips. His eyes darkening almost to black as he searched Liam's face trying to judge how serious he was. "I'd like to see you try."

In a flash, Liam yanked Joey's arm across his body at the same time as he shoved his hip with his knee and flipped Joey onto his stomach. Keeping Joey's hands trapped, Liam leaned over his back and whispered harshly into his ear. "It's time to grow up the fuck up, Jojo."

"Oh yeah?" Joey asked breathlessly.

"Yes. And since you won't do it by yourself, I'm going to have to help you. Make you a better man, the man I know you can be."

"How?" On screen, a horn blared and the crowd screamed. "Goal!" bellowed the announcer.

"By telling you when you're being an ass. Every time you get the urge to say something funny, I want you to think 'what would Liam say?' before any words come out of your mouth. If you have a decision to make and you have the urge to do anything even *remotely* stupid, I want you to call me. As long as you're on my team, you're going to behave."

"And what if I don't?"

Ignoring the pain in his hip, Liam sat back on his heels, straddling Joey's thighs. "I'll see how much of your ass my hand can cover."

Joey inhaled sharply. He flexed his fingers, working out the numbness from Liam's hold. It would be easy for him to throw Liam off now. Liam wouldn't even fight him. There was nothing else to say.

"You don't have the balls," Joey smirked.

Before he could think too much about what he was doing, Liam yanked Joey's shorts down below the curve of his ass and lifted his hand.

The sharp crack of flesh on flesh was surprisingly loud, and the stinging of his palm took Liam by surprise.

Pink flared on Joey's skin, and he twitched, inhaling through his nose.

Liam spanked his other cheek, feeling the strong muscle shake. The pink handprint on the first side was fading quickly so Liam brought his hand down again, a quick one-two on each side.

The muscles in Joey's back tightened and he pillowed his head on his arms, neck bowed.

"You. Will. Listen." Liam punctuated each word with a hard smack. Part of his brain was screaming at him to stop, but he pushed it aside. His focus narrowed to his hand and Joey's body.

Four more slaps and Joey's skin warmed under his hand. The pink had shaded to red and was lasting longer between each slap.

Joey grunted with each hit, twisting underneath Liam. Liam's kneecaps pressed painfully into the floor as he balanced precariously on the back of Joey's shins.

Breathing hard, he wiped the sweat off his forehead with the sleeve of his dress shirt. "Enough?" he asked as he unbuttoned his sleeves and rolled them up to his elbows.

Joey trembled beneath him, breathing harder than Liam. "Yeah," he said, voice shaky yet somehow still managing to sound pissed off. "Sure."

That earned him two quick, hard slaps.

He yelped in surprise.

"Stop fucking around in public."

"I'm not!"

"You're better than that."

Joey shook his head in denial. "Get off me."

Liam smacked his ass hard. Joey's foot kicked out and he cursed. The spanking had to be hurting him. Liam's hand was stinging and slightly swollen. "Yes, you fucking are."

"Let me go," Joey yelled.

"You're better than that!" Damn it. What the hell was the kid playing at? Did he just want to be smacked around more? Liam didn't know if he could do that.

"What if I'm not?" Joey said loudly, breaking through Liam's concern. "What if I'm not?" he repeated under his breath. He struggled under Liam in a half-hearted attempt at escape.

Somehow Liam knew this was it. This was the key moment, the thing he'd been searching for without knowing.

"Let me up."

"No. Not until you say it." Another smack and Joey shuddered.

"No. I'm not anything. I'm just another jock."

Smack, smack. Joey's ass burned red, marks in the shape of Liam's palm blossoming on his skin.

"No, you're not. You're special."

"No! I'm not!"

Jesus fucking Christ. Why was Joey fighting this so hard? Liam was trying to give him a compliment. What was he so afraid of?

"Jesus, Joey," Liam whispered. He let his hands drop, and rubbed Joey's ass gently, feeling the heat of Joey's skin against his palm. "You are. You really are. You gotta start acting like it."

"What if I can't?" He shuddered, his muscles so taut Liam was afraid he was going to pull something. "What if this is all I can be? You should let me go. I'm not worth it."

Good god. Was this really how Joey saw himself? Is this what he *thought* of himself? This had to stop. "You are. You are. You're worth everything."

Joey shook his head.

Mary and all the saints give him the strength to deal with this thick-headed idiot. Liam channeled his inner big brother and gave Joey a stinging slap with the tips of his fingers. Before Joey could draw breath to yell, Liam leaned over him, putting his mouth right by Joey's ear. He gripped Joey's hair tightly, forcing his head up.

"You are fucking worth it," he said firmly. "Do you think I'd do *this* for just anyone? For anyone else on this whole fucking *planet*? Do you think I have *time* to waste? I'm fucking here for you. And if I have to beat that bullshit out of you every night, I fucking will. And do you know why?"

Joey took a shuddering breath and let it out. "No," he said softly as if he were confessing a sin.

Liam reached for Joey's ass, grabbed a handful of hot flesh and squeezed. "You know why. Tell me. Let me hear it."

Joey cried silently, his shoulders shaking.

Liam sighed. Kissing the side of Joey's head, he sat back on his heels. Carding his fingers gently through Joey's hair, he tried to figure out what else he could try to do to make Joey see himself the way Liam saw him.

Joey shuddered as Liam's fingers combed his scalp, then suddenly he surrendered completely, his muscles lax, all the fight gone out of him. He drew in a sobbing breath.

Hallelujah. "Come on, Jojo. You know why I'm here. You can say it."

Joey took a deep breath. "Because I'm worth it," he mumbled into his crossed arms.

Liam exhaled from what felt like the soles of his feet. *Thank Christ.* He was shaking, adrenaline coursing through his veins and sweat staining his undershirt. Stifling a groan, he moved painfully off of Joey and stretched out next to him on the floor, resting on his side. He ran his fingers through Joey's thick dark hair and then continued down the gorgeous valley of his spine. "Hey," he said with a kiss. "Are you okay?"

Joey nodded and sniffled.

Liam kissed every part of Joey's shoulders he could reach and caressed his back, his fingers tracing the black lines of his tattoos as always, while Joey pulled himself together.

He didn't get it. How could such an amazing man see himself so twisted? But they'd made progress, broken through a wall Liam hadn't even realized Joey had built.

"You want to get up now? I'm too old to lie on the floor."

Joey kept his head turned away, but he huffed a laugh, so Liam took it as a good sign.

"I need to take a shower," Liam was oddly shy and nervous now that the heat of the moment had passed. "Do you, uh, want to come with me?"

"I don't think so," Joey whispered. "I... I need a minute."

Liam nodded. "Okay. Okay. But first I'm putting some arnica on that... on your ass."

Liam got to his feet as gracefully as he could, then reached a hand down for Joey. After Joey pulled up his shorts, Liam pulled him in for a hug, tipping his chin up. "Hey, look at me." He wiped the tears from under Joey's eyes, then kissed him gently. Joey clung to him. "I mean it. I'm here for you, I'm looking out for you not because I think you're a moron, but because you don't take yourself seriously. You don't see yourself as a professional, as a grown up. So I'm going to do it for you until you understand how amazing you are." He smiled. "If it kills both of us."

He let Joey go. Joey took a step back and winced in pain.

"Come on." Liam led Joey into the master bedroom that was right off the office and guided him to the big soft bed. "Lay down, I'll be right back."

Liam's hands shook as he wrung out a warm washrag, filled up a glass of cool water, and got the arnica out of the medicine cabinet.

What the hell had he done? What the hell had he been thinking? This could have fucked up everything. What if Joey hated him? What if he could never look Joey in the eye again?

Joey lay face down on the bed fully naked, his shorts on the floor.

Looking at his bright red ass, Liam felt a combination of pride, affection, fear, and lust that did nothing to calm the worries in his mind. What kind of person looked at their handprints on someone's skin and felt proud? What kind of person looked at someone they cared about who had been through the emotional wringer and got hard?

Scrubbing his hand through his beard, he steeled himself for rejection and went into the room. He handed Joey the washrag. "And I got you a glass of water. I'll put it on the nightstand." He sat on the edge of the bed closest to Joey. "This might be a little cold."

"I hope it is," Joey said with a watery smile. He hissed as the cool gel landed on his skin. Liam rubbed it in with all the care and attention he usually gave to his game, covering every inch of red, abused skin. He could actually feel the indentations from his fingers in the swollen skin.

Joey's breathing grew softer and steady. Liam's hand slowed until he was gently caressing Joey's ass. He squashed down the little shiver of arousal it caused. This wasn't about sex. That wasn't what Joey needed right now, though it might make Liam feel better, feel like he'd made the right call. But this wasn't about him. It wasn't for him.

"I meant it, you know."

"I know," Joey answered.

"Do you believe me?"

Joey breathed silently in and out a few times before answering. "I guess I believe *you* believe it. And you don't lie. You're kind of an asshole sometimes, but you don't lie."

"That's a start at least. Luckily, I can believe in you strong enough for both of us." He placed a gentle kiss between Joey's shoulder blades. "I need to take a shower. Are you sure you're okay?"

"I'm sure." Joey's breaths lengthened and his eyes fluttered shut.

"Okay." Liam stood up, shoving his hands in his pockets, brow furrowed as he looked at Joey. He turned to go.

Joey rolled a little to his side and held out a hand. "Hey."

"Yeah?"

Joey wiggled his fingers impatiently, and Liam smiled and reached for his hand. "Give me a kiss," Joey ordered.

Liam kissed him gently, careful not to push Joey onto his back.

"Thank you," Joey whispered.

What could he say to that? Liam squeezed his hand in answer. "Go to sleep. I'll be right here."

By the time he finished showering and changing, Joey was asleep.

15

JOEY

LIAM: I think your sauce is burnt. I shut it off.

JOEY: How burnt?

LIAM: I don't know. How do you tell?

JOEY: Taste it. From the top. Don't stir it.

LIAM: Oops.

JOEY: Did you stir it already?

LIAM: Only a little. I thought that's what you did with sauce!

JOEY: Leave it alone. I'll be down in a few.

LIAM RESTED HIS HANDS ON JOEY'S SHOULDERS AS HE FROWNED AT

the saucepan full of semi-scorched tomato sauce. "Can you save it, doc?" he asked.

"I think so. Do you have another big pot?"

"Let me check." He gave Joey's shoulders a squeeze and dropped a kiss on his head before starting his search of the many cabinets in the large kitchen.

"Where's Patrick anyway?" Joey asked. "I told him to turn the heat off under the pot."

"He texted, said he was running to the liquor store for 'real' beer. Philistine." Metal clanged as Liam rummaged through the cabinets nearest the stove. "Aha!" He straightened up, holding a large pot aloft in triumph.

"Put it in the sink, please." Joey carried the hot pot over to the sink. "This is some high-end stuff," he commented. "All-clad?"

Liam shrugged. "I just got what the gal at the store recommended. I bought them for... you know."

Joey knew. He'd furnished the kitchen for Michelle. Joey poured most of the sauce into the new pot, careful not to let the meatballs and sausages splatter sauce everywhere.

He wondered if Liam expected Joey to feel jealous, or maybe guilty when he talked about the woman he'd spent five years of his life with. Mostly Joey just felt bad for her.

He knew what it was like to want all of Liam O'Reilly's attention and not get it. To have the appearance of having him, but knowing you weren't first in his heart was painful. Liam was a professional at keeping people at a distance. Everyone in the family had watched Michelle investing more and more of her time and energy into a relationship with a man who didn't seem to care whether she came or went

Liam certainly cared where Joey went and what he did. Joey had the stinging ass to prove it. He tried not to feel smug about it. Their relationship might be a little messed up, unconventional, but no one could say it wasn't passionate, for better or worse. Still, he wasn't going to assume it was anything that existed outside the house.

"You have a lot of kitchen stuff for a guy who doesn't even cook." Joey set the burnt pot to one side to soak and tasted the sauce. "A little more sugar and one more can of tomatoes and it should be fine."

"I cook." Liam lifted the pot with the saved sauce out of the sink and set it back on the stove.

"What can you cook? Name three things."

"Steak. On the grill. Broiled chicken breast. Scrambled eggs." Pulling a fork from a drawer, Liam aimed it at a particularly plump meatball hovering near the top.

"Leave it," Joey said warningly, taking the fork away from him. "Your scrambled eggs are terrible. I've had them." He pushed Liam gently towards the table. "Just sit. You take care of me, I'll take care of you, deal?"

"Yeah?" Liam crowded against Joey's back, his breath curling around Joey's ear. "You like it when I take care of you?"

Hah. Joey fucking loved it. Loved all Liam's intensity focused on him, loved having Liam O'Reilly, of all people, thinking him special enough to care about.

Shouldn't he have been embarrassed about that? He was a grown ass man who should be able to take care of himself, right? But the way Liam said it, it sounded like a good thing. Sounded like something Liam wanted to do.

"Is that what it was?" He stared intently into the pot, spearing the pieces of meat and shoving them under the surface.

Liam's hand rested on the back of Joey's neck and squeezed gently. "Yeah, that's what it was. I'm going to take care of you even if you don't take care of yourself."

"Well, then yeah," he said, staring into the swirl of hot tomatoes. "I like it."

"Good."

Joey pulled his neck out of Liam's grasp. "Now grab some pasta bowls and sit down at the table. You take care of me, and I'll take care of you. Deal?"

"Deal. But when I get fat, remember it's your fault."

"OH MY GOD. SO GOOD," Liam moaned around a mouthful of meatball. "That's so fucking good."

Joey's dick stirred at the sexy sounds coming from Liam's mouth, while his soul basked in the praise. "You like it?"

"I fucking love it. Tastes just like your mom's. I haven't had it in forever. The meatballs, where did you get the stuff for them?"

"Italian butcher shop in the market. I called up and ordered it."

"Order whatever you want, if this is the result. Charge it to me."

"Does that offer extend to me?" Patrick asked from the doorway.

"No," Liam said.

"Is it safe to come in?" Patrick asked. "Is the yelling over? Oh, fuck, the sauce. I forgot to shut it off. I was playing video games with Vicky."

Patrick pulled out a chair and dropped heavily down into it. The same age as Joey, Patrick looked a lot like a leaner version of his brother. In ten years, he might match Liam in width. His copper-penny hair blazed bright enough to be seen across a dark field.

"Vicky?" Liam asked. "Our Vicky, the goalie? I thought you were going to get beer."

"I was. Then Vicky called and invited me over to play. So I took the beer to him. He appreciated it, unlike some people." Patrick helped himself to a giant bowl of pasta. "He's a good guy. A little odd, but cool. So, how did Lucy fuck up today?"

"Shut up, dick," Joey said. "It was nothing."

"Joey mooned Sergei in the parking lot, then said some rude things in Russian, and some bozo caught it on camera and posted it online," Liam explained.

"Dang," Patrick said with a laugh. "What did Pergs do back?"

"He told me to go fuck a cow," Joey said. "Of course that didn't make it to the internet. It's so fucking frustrating, I can't pick my nose without seventeen people posting about it." He thought he'd have a little more anonymity in Seattle, but the city had embraced its expansion team with a fever. A year before the franchise had officially opened, the rights to buy season tickets had sold out ten minutes after they'd gone on sale. He'd forgotten how insane Pacific Division fans could be.

Patrick scoffed. "Oh, yeah, that must be so tough. Let me wipe my pity tears with your piles of money."

And that was why Joey never complained about anything to anyone. Part of him agreed with Patrick. What right did he have to bitch about his life?

Surprisingly, it was Liam who answered. "Come on, Paddy. That's not fair. Sometimes it would be nice to go shopping without having to take a selfie with ten people. It's part of the job, though," he added.

Patrick waved Joey over. "Sit down, bro. Plenty of room."

That wasn't going to happen until tomorrow. "I'm good. I feel like standing. It's easier to pace and rant than sit and rant." He set his bowl down on the counter he was leaning against. "So, you're saying because I make a lot of money doing something I've been working at since I was four years old, I'm not entitled to a private life."

"Joey," Liam said, a warning in his voice. "Nobody is saying that. Stop exaggerating."

Okay, maybe he was being a little whiny and exaggerating, but he wasn't that far wrong.

"You are entitled to a private life. The operative word being private. The parking lot of the arena is not private."

Sometimes it felt like nowhere was private. "If people could get cameras into my bedroom, they would."

"And wouldn't they be surprised," Liam said straight-faced.

Joey shuddered. "God forbid." That would be a nightmare.

"When you're out in public, you're representing the team, not just yourself."

"I know," Joey said. "Play for the name on the front of the sweater, not the one on the back. I know."

"Everything you do reflects on the team, and you know damn well everyone has a cell phone today."

How long was Liam going to keep repeating the obvious? Did he think Joey didn't know all this?

"Yeah, the Looch can't fart without someone tweeting about it." Patrick shoved half a sausage into his mouth. "Guess that would get old," he mumbled. "Good thing you don't care what people think about you. Fuck 'em, right?"

"You're wrong," Joey said, surprising himself. "I care a lot." Until he talked to his grandfather about it, Joey had never admitted this out loud. Now it seemed like he was blurting it out every time he got an opening.

"Really?" Patrick said skeptically. "Because from the outside, it looks like you just do what you want to do and screw anyone who doesn't like it."

Joey shook his head and looked down at the countertop. He traced the grain in the black marble with his fingertips. "Well, yeah. That's part of the act."

"Huh," Patrick said.

Liam's silence unnerved Joey. When he dared to look up, the other man was staring at him like he had never considered that Joey was doing the things he did deliberately. Joey moved restlessly around the kitchen, stacking dishes and randomly moving things.

Liam leaned away from the table, throwing an arm over the back of his chair and watching Joey as he paced. "And how's that working for you? Do you like being 'the Looch'?" he asked shooting straight for Joey's weakest point.

How should he answer that? Which answer made him look less like an idiot? Saying yeah he loved it and hoped one day he'd grow into that image, or admit that no, he disliked a lot of it but he didn't know how to stop being that person?

But Liam had said he would take care of Joey, right? That he would help Joey become the man Liam knew he could be. If Joey wanted that, and he did, he'd have to be completely honest with Liam.

Well, maybe not completely honest. But really, it would be stupid to say anything about whatever the hell was going on in his head before he had some answers. No point worrying everybody unnecessarily. It was probably just stress. Besides, that was different. It had nothing to do with what they were talking about.

"Joey," Liam said. "I asked you a question, do you like this image you've created?"

"Not all of it. I mean it's not totally an act. But it would be nice to be able to tone it down a bit. I'm getting tired."

Liam's laugh had an edge of bitterness. "This game can wear you out fast if you're not careful."

The words poured out of Joey like they'd been waiting for an outlet. "I feel so constrained all the time," he said, pacing rapidly across the long kitchen. He had to move. "It's like I can't be all of me. I have to think about everything I say and do all the time and it's exhausting."

"So stop doing it," Liam said.

As if it was that easy.

Joey rolled his eyes. "But the fans love it. They love the public me.

What if…" He trailed off. "You guys done with the pasta?" he asked. "Should I clean up?"

"You should finish your thought," Liam said. He stood up from the table and picked up his and Patrick's plates.

Joey reached for them as he got closer. "Let me get those."

Liam ignored him and sat the dishes down on the counter. "Finish your sentence." He punctuated his command with a light tap to Joey's butt that reminded him he'd promised to listen to Liam.

To his surprise, the reminder was comforting. He didn't have to decide what or how much to tell Liam. All he had to do was answer the question honestly.

"What if they don't like the real me? What if they stop caring about me?" Standing this close to Liam, Joey had to crane his neck to look him in the eye. He could see Liam giving his questions serious consideration. God, he loved that.

"Of course they're gonna still love you," Patrick said, slamming into the counter next to Joey, who had almost forgotten he was still in the room. "You're Joey. Everyone loves you. Old ladies name their cats after you."

"That's not true," Joey said.

"The people who matter will like the real you better," Liam said firmly, with no room for argument.

"Was Coach Williams really angry?"

"He wasn't happy when I went in to talk to him."

"I'm sorry. I promise it won't happen again."

"I believe you. What's more important is the drinking and partying. It has to stop or it's both our jobs."

"What partying?" He couldn't even remember the last time he'd had a drink. This close to the end of the season, it was all work, all the time. If they were lucky, they'd have time to go out to dinner when they weren't on the road. And Liam worked longer hours than he did.

"Tampa." Liam reminded him. "And the times before that."

"Oh, Tampa. With Snoop. I wasn't drunk in Tampa," Joey said without thinking.

"No? Then what was it?"

Shit. He had to think of something quick. He turned back to the pot in the sink and started scrubbing at the burnt remainder of sauce on the bottom. "I think I got food poisoning or something. It just hit me all of a sudden."

He didn't have to turn around to know Liam had his arms crossed and was scowling at him. "Why didn't you say anything?"

"I didn't think it mattered. People are gonna think what they want to think, regardless of what I say."

"Which is it, Jojo? Does it matter what people think or does it not matter?"

"Both?"

"You guys wanna catch some Top Chef?" Patrick asked. "And is there any dessert?"

"You know there is. You watched me make those peanut butter bars," Joey said.

"Yeah, so pull them out, Lucy, and let's get our cheffing on."

16

LIAM

"This is something that goes above and beyond stats. 99.9% of the time, Joey makes the right decision with the puck. As a player, I can't tell you how hard it is to have that kind of vision. You see what he does on TV, and he makes it look so simple. But when you're at ice level, things are really chaotic. Everything's moving so fast around you. Maybe there're ruts in the ice. Maybe there's a defenceman stepping up on you, or you're getting hacked from behind. You're looking down at the puck in your periphery. You're trying to process where your teammates are. And you're trying to do all this at full-speed. To be able to make the right decision every time like Luciano does, your brain has to be a supercomputer." *Daniel Lipe – Seattle Thunder*

"OH, COME ON," JOEY YELLED AT THE TELEVISION. "YOU'RE cooking for high rollers. *Think* people."

"I can't believe no one went for the caviar and Wagyu beef," Patrick added. "It's sitting right there!"

"Did you ever have the Wagyu at the Palace Arms in Denver?" Liam asked. "Fucking brilliant."

"At the hotel? Oh, yeah. It's great. Best food I ever had, though, was on that boat with PK, remember? When we cruised the Med?"

Joey sat on the couch, next to Patrick. Liam had claimed the large overstuffed chair over to the side.

"I remember that," Paddy said. "Wasn't that the same year Deano and his boys beat your ass in game seven?"

Joey gave him the finger without looking.

Speaking of beating Joey's ass, Liam figured he hadn't done any permanent damage to it, but from the way Joey squirmed on the couch, he wouldn't be forgetting about it any time soon.

A spot of pink touched Joey's cheekbones each time he shifted on the couch. Liam's cock twitched when he did, and he had to fight the urge to slide his hand between Joey's legs. He also wasn't beyond accidentally on purpose leaning heavily on Joey's shoulder at every opportunity. Frankly, he was impressed that Joey could concentrate on the show at all. Every time Joey glanced his way, their gazes locked, and Joey would lick his lips.

He couldn't wait to get Joey upstairs and naked.

He felt light, more relaxed than he had in a while. Some of the tension had left Joey's face, too. For such an easy-going seeiming guy, Joey carried a surprising amount of anxiety. Joey worried about everything he did, which made his slip-ups even more surprising. The problem was, he agonized over the wrong things in Liam's mind. It didn't matter what the unwashed masses thought, but it mattered what the owners, GM, and coaches thought. What your teammates thought.

"One more episode?" Joey asked when the losing contestant had been told to pack up her knives and leave.

"I'm going to bed," Liam said. "I've got one more quick thing to take care of, and I have to be at the rink by seven-thirty."

"Just me and you Joe," Patrick said, slapping Joey on the shoulder.

"Oh, uh, okay," Joey said. "I guess I can do one more."

From where he stood, Liam could see both their expressions. Joey looked torn. Patrick was smirking.

"Jesus. I'm just fucking with you," Patrick said, rolling his eyes. "Both of you get the fuck out of here and... fuck. The sexual tension is killing me. I'm going to have to watch porn and jerk off just to deal with it."

Joey's eyes opened wide, and he looked back and forth between Patrick and Joey. Liam wasn't going to deny it. He didn't care if Patrick knew they were fucking.

"Um," Joey said. "Paddy, we're not..."

Patrick laughed right in his face.

"Dick," Joey said, punching him on the arm. It only made him laugh harder.

"Seriously, though. Are you okay with this?"

Patrick made a face. "No. I'm disgusted."

Joey looked stricken, but Liam knew his brother was an asshole. (It was a family trait.) So he waited.

"Disgusted with your taste in *men*, Lucy. I mean, I get why Liam would, you know, wanna hit *that*," he pointed at Joey's ass. "You're hot as fuck, dude. But what could you possibly see in *his* cranky old ass?"

Liam smacked Patrick on the back of his head. "Show some respect for your elders, Sonny Boy."

"He's not old," Joey said defensively.

"But he is cranky."

Joey nodded, conceding the point. "Do you really want me to tell you what I see in him?"

"No!" Paddy put his hands over his ears. "I can't hear you!" He sighed. "I wish to *god* I couldn't hear you." He hurried out of the room.

"There's always the hotel," Liam called to his retreating back.

Patrick twirled around and gave him the finger and a broad smile.

Liam took the stairs two at a time, practically whistling under his breath. If he didn't get his hands on Joey soon, he was going to explode. Joey followed more sedately behind. Liam assumed the aches and pains of the day were catching up to him.

"Hurry up, old man," he said, throwing a grin over his shoulder. "I have plans for you."

Joey smiled with a little less enthusiasm than Liam had been hoping for.

Liam waited until they were in the bedroom with the door shut to say anything. Joey stood in the large room as if he wasn't sure what he was doing there.

"What's wrong?" Liam asked. "Did I not thank you enough for cooking? Because thank you. That was delicious."

"Cooking's easy. It's everything else I'm worried about."

"What are you talking about? What else?"

Joey shrugged and looked at something over Liam's shoulder. "Everything."

What? Hadn't they just talked about this very subject? He really didn't know this insecure Joey Luciano at all. He had always known there was more to Joey than he showed the rest of the world, but he hadn't had an inkling of the self-doubt that plagued him.

Liam felt every one of the ten years between them.

Joey always had felt everything deeply. There was no middle ground in his world; everything was either fabulous or horrible. He took the maxim that there was no such thing as second place, only first loser, a little too seriously.

It would be foolish to think that one conversation, one spanking, would erase such a deep-seated misbelief. So more than anything else, more than getting Joey to think before he acted in public, his mission was to replace the critical voices in Joey's head with his own kinder, more supportive voice.

He could do that. Pulling Joey close to him, he tilted the man's chin up to make sure Joey saw the sincerity in his eyes.

"Joey. It's not about *me* being disappointed." He searched for the words. This was way out of his comfort zone and he wasn't usually one for self-reflection. He'd always known what people expected of him, what the world demanded of him, and he simply did it to the best of his ability. "It's about you being disappointed in yourself. You are, aren't you?"

"I could do better in a bunch of things, probably."

"You can do anything. You have it all. You are capable of more. And I want you to get there. You're talented and you work hard. You deserve better than what you're doing to yourself."

"I know I'm not even close to the brightest one in the family."

"What? Are you fucking cracked in the head?"

Joey yanked his head out of Liam's grip and took a step back. He raised his chin confrontationally. "C'mon I have a high school diploma, and I needed a tutor to get that. Don't act like I'm something I'm not. You went to fucking *Harvard* for chrissake. No one even talked to me about where I wanted to go to college."

Liam closed his eyes, pinched the bridge of his nose, and counted to ten. He was going to shake the idiot until his teeth rattled in his head. He'd spank him more, but his ass was probably still sore from the first one.

"No one asked you because everyone knew you were going to make it to the show as soon as you could. If they could have signed you as a sixteen-year-old, they would have! You are a *better hockey player* than the rest of us put together."

"Really?" Joey gave him a suspicious look.

"Do I strike you as the kind of person to give you - or anyone really, but especially you specifically - compliments just to make you feel better? Build up your delicate millennial self-esteem? You can go count your trophies if you need that."

"No. But that's not the same as being smart."

"You want to go to fucking college, go to college when you're my age. There's no age limit. But we both know hockey is a young man's game. You had to grab it with both hands as soon as you could. You know what I have to show for my 'Harvard education?' A fourteen-year-old business degree!'"

"But you're a coach!" Joey flung his arms wide, his voice rising.

"Ten years ago I wasn't!" Liam yelled.

What had he been ten years ago? Focusing, working harder than anyone around him to make up for his limitations and impress his coaches. If anyone should feel inadequate, it was him. Joey had been a stronger player at fifteen than Liam had ever been.

Ten years was a long time. A lifetime. He had to remember that Joey was still so young and though his experience was deep in the hockey world, it was very narrow when it game to everyday life. There was so much he hadn't experienced yet.

"I know you've been surrounded by people who say what they think you want to hear, say what they need to in order to get the best performance out of you. I'm not them. I know you've got the hockey skills. You got that? What I'm concerned about is the man beneath the name. And he's fucking incredible. You know I'm not a yes man."

Joey snorted.

"If I'm going to be the boss of you..." Liam said with a smile. "That is what you want?"

"Yes," Joey replied quickly. His eyes flicked to the floor. It was what he did when he couldn't physically escape a conversation or situation he wanted to get out of. "Please."

"If I'm going to be the boss of you, then you have to listen to me. Do you trust me to only do what's best for you?"

"I do," he answered quickly.

"And you want me to tell you? To reward you when you're good and punish you when you're bad?" Liam felt a little ridiculous spelling it out like that. But he had to be sure they were on the same page, and things between them were as clear as they could be.

Joey swallowed, eyes wide. "I do," he whispered. "Is that bad? Is it weird?"

"It is bad that I want to do that for you? That I want to mold you, to teach you? To make you listen for your own good?"

"I don't think so," Joey said.

"Then we want the same thing. And how can that be weird or wrong? It's nobody's business but our own. In here, behind closed doors, it's only us. Only you and me. Out there, in the world, you're Joey Luciano. Someone I am proud of, proud to coach, proud to call a friend. And I would never embarrass you in public."

"Intentionally." Joey's mouth quirked in a half-smile.

"Intentionally."

"And in private? Who am I then?" Joey sagged like he thought his private self was nowhere near as good as his public persona.

"Still amazing. Still someone I'm proud of. But the real Joey. The whole Joey. Not the Looch. Not the kid with all the answers."

"You'll still treat me like any other player, right? Be your normal loud cranky self?"

"On the ice, you *are* any other player. And if you give me a reason to yell at you, you bet your ass I will. But, Jojo-"

"Yeah?"

"You never do. What did I tell you before?"

Joey searched his memory, every emotion visible on his face. He shook his head. "That the sauce was burned?"

Grabbing his upper arms, Liam whirled Joey around and slapped his ass hard enough to spark Joey's memory. Joey gasped and shuddered.

When Liam turned him back, his eyes were wide and his mouth hung open. Liam ran his finger across Joey's plush lower lip. "What did I tell you?"

"That I'm worth it?" he said softly.

"You're worth it. You had one thing to remember and you forgot already, didn't you?" Liam took a step closer to Joey, backing him up against a wall. He bracketed Joey's body with his arms. Joey's throat moved as he swallowed. The energy in the room shifted, the air between them warming. Joey's body softened and his pupils dilated.

"I did."

"Obviously you need another lesson." He reached between Joey's legs, squeezing gently.

Joey shuddered and sucked in a breath. "Um, okay. Yes." His eyes were locked on Liam's. "What do you want me to do?"

"We start by you getting naked, and then I'm going to tell you exactly how you can make it up to me."

"Will you be naked, too?"

"When I decide you've earned it."

With a hand to his shoulder, he guided Joey to the floor to kneel between his legs. Without taking off his belt, he unzipped his pants and pulled his cock out. "Blow me."

He had never spoken so crudely before, never this direct. It shocked him how easy it was to do it with Jojo and how hard it made both of them.

Sitting back on his heels, his hands resting on his thighs, Joey looked up at Liam with those big brown eyes. A thrill slid down Liam's spine when he realized that the gorgeous man was waiting for instructions.

Now he knew exactly how he was going to keep Joey off-balance. He would make Joey ask for everything he wanted. Make him understand that everything that happened to him from here on in was something he had specifically asked for. Joey reached for his cock, and Liam stopped him with a hand on his head. "Do you want this?"

Joey nodded.

"Then ask for it. Tell me what you want."

Joey's face flushed bright red, and he made a strangled sound. Oh, this was going to be good.

"Nothing?" Liam shrugged. "Oh, okay." He took a step back and started to zip his pants back up. Joey look stricken, and Liam bit his lip to keep from laughing.

"Wait!" Joey said.

Liam stopped, raising one eyebrow, and waited.

"I want…" He licked his dry lips, then turned away with a whispered curse.

"I'm sorry, I didn't hear that."

Joey looked back, fire in his eyes. "I said 'asshole'."

There he was. There was the Joey Liam knew was there.

"Is that what you want? My asshole?"

Joey actually rocked back on his heels. "No!"

Holy shit. He hadn't known Joey could get quite that shade of red.

"No?" He'd said it like he meant it, but his cock seemed extremely interested.

"No! I mean," Joey's brow furrowed, "you'd do that? Let me do that?"

Hmm. *Interesting*. "I would. If you were very good and if you asked for it nicely."

Joey blinked, his mouth opening and closing. Well, what do you know? A speechless Joey Luciano. Who even knew that was possible? "But not tonight. What do you want tonight?" He slid his hand slowly up and down his cock, feeling decadent and more turned on that he'd ever been in his life. Nothing in his life had prepared him for this.

Joey's eyes followed Liam's hand up and down. "I want to suck your dick."

"What are you waiting for?"

"Well, I've never…" Joey blushed deliciously. "I'm not sure what to do?"

"Oh, I seem to remember my cock in your mouth plenty of times."

"But usually you're, you know, in charge."

Liam's balls clenched tight when he realized what Joey was implying. "You mean, I'm usually fucking your face, and you're loving it."

"Yeah. I guess." Joey blushed a rosy glow touching his olive skin.

"You guess you like it? Hmm. I guess I'll have to stop doing it until you're sure."

"No! I like it. Okay? I love it."

"You love what?" God, watching Joey blush and squirm was delicious. Did that make him some kind of sadist? Well, if it did, fuck it. He could live with that. Joey was a big boy and he was free to walk away any time he wanted to.

Joey mumbled and looked at the carpet, sitting back down on his heels. He looked ashamed but his cock was still hard.

"Jojo. Look at me. We don't have to do this. We can go back downstairs and watch TV. We can lie in bed and read or just go to sleep."

"No, please. I want this. Please."

Jesus. His knees wobbled. Time for a small change of plans. He backed up and sat at the foot of the bed, spreading his legs wide. "Then prove it." Liam leaned back on his hands. "Suck my dick like you love it. So you can't even lie to yourself that it was out of your hands, that you had no control. That I was just using you."

"I want this." To Liam's grateful surprise, Joey knee-walked over to the bed, put a hand on both of Liam's thighs and licked Liam's cock like a lollipop.

Sweet baby Jesus, Joey had a fucking amazing mouth. Liam couldn't lie, he did love fucking it. Joey took it so well and looked so amazing when he did. But Liam needed to rid himself of the lingering worry that he was forcing Joey.

Even though Joey was a grown, successful man, there were still power dynamics at work. Joey was younger, and Liam was Joey's coach with real, if limited, influence over his future and standing on the team. There was no room for error.

Luckily, Joey wasn't making any.

While he still had use of most of his brain cells, Liam gave Joey directions, telling him exactly how he liked to have his cock sucked.

Faster, slower, use your hand. Touch my balls.

Not that he needed the instruction. Watching Joey concentrating, studying Liam's dick like there was going to be a test, was almost enough to get Liam off all by itself.

Joey forced himself onto Liam's cock, gagging as it pushed into the back of his throat.

Goddamn. Liam groaned and pushed Joey away. He looked wrecked, eyes wet and wide, mouth red and swollen. Fuck it. He stood up, shoved his fingers into Joey's mouth and pushed his jaw down. Then he fucked Joey's face hard and fast.

Joey's eyes fluttered shut like he was in ecstasy. He reached down for his own cock, apparently content to come from jerking off while he deep-throated Liam.

"Get your hand off that cock," Liam ordered. Curving his hands around Joey's skull, he shoved in as far as he could. Joey gagged, chest heaving as he struggled to breathe around the fat cock filling his throat.

When Liam tried to pull out slowly, Joey's hands flew to Liam's hips, holding him in place. He whined when Liam shoved him off. "Fuck, Judy," He croaked, throat sore and full with spit and precome. "Don't fucking stop."

"Have you learned your lesson?"

"Yes." He reached for Liam again, and Liam stopped him.

"And it was?"

"I'm worth it."

"Yes. And I want you to remember one more thing."

"What?" Joey's hand drifted to his cock like it had a mind of its own. Liam let him get away with it because he looked so pretty doing it. "What else? I'll do it."

"No more ass pictures on the internet."

"No more ass pictures on the internet."

"And why not?" Liam traced Joey's mouth with the tip of his cock. "And why not?"

Joey stuck out his tongue and licked around the head of Liam's cock. "Because it's immature and unclassy. And I'm classy."

He was something, all right, on his knees, cock shiny, mouth swollen and pupils blown.

"And?"

Joey couldn't answer, so Liam wrapped a hand around his cock and guided him to his feet. "And why else?" He grabbed Joey's ass with both hands, squeezing the still-tender flesh hard.

Joey moaned. "Because you don't like it when I do."

"And why don't I like it?" He pressed his fingers between Joey's ass cheeks, rubbing against his opening. Joey squirmed like it felt good and he wanted it more but was embarrassed about wanting it. Interesting, he'd certainly liked it well enough at Christmas.

Joey whined and bucked against Liam's hand.

"Why won't I like it?" he asked again, stroking Joey's cock loosely, barely touching it and rubbing his finger across the sensitive head.

Joey broke. "I don't fucking know why. Just let me touch you for fuck's sake. Touch me. Let me come."

Liam pushed the tip of his finger hard against Joey's hole. "I won't like it because this ass is mine. Nobody else's. No one gets to see it but me. Alright?"

"God, yes. Yes. No one." He rutted against any part of Liam's clothed body he could find.

Liam pushed him away and back down to his knees. "Blow me. Make it good and maybe I'll let you come."

Joey made it good.

Between Joey's gorgeous, hot mouth, on his cock, and the rough skin of the strong hand on his balls, Liam's knees gave out. Moaning and cursing loud enough for Patrick to hear, he gripped Joey's shoulders hard, trying and failing to care about the marks he might be leaving. His balls pulled up so tightly they hurt and he yelled with every pulse of the orgasm he shot directly down Joey's throat. He was still coming as he pulled out, the last drops hitting Joey on his face as Liam stripped his cock as quickly as he could.

Yanking Joey against him, Liam sealed their mouths together. Even kissing Joey was miles away from anything he'd felt before. Something about Joey touched this wild part of him, stripping away all thoughts of what sex should be, what Liam should like, and replacing it with raw passion. He pushed Joey back on the bed and crawled over him. "Head on the pillow," he growled. Joey's instant compliance put a feral grin on his face. "Do you want to come?" he asked, hand tracing the dips and rises of Joey's perfect abs.

"Fuck yes," Joey said through clenched teeth. "Keep looking at me like that, and it's gonna happen whether you want it to or not."

"Oh, I don't think so. Hold on to that headboard, and don't let go."

"I hate you," Joey said as he complied. "I fucking hate you."

"I know."

By the time Liam finished torturing Joey, bringing him to the edge again and again with his hand and mouth and then cutting off his orgasm, they were both covered in sweat, and Joey had moved beyond cursing and moaning to gasping for air with tears leaking from his eyes and rolling down the sides of his face.

Liam jerked Joey's cock so fast, he could feel the ache in his arm. Joey's body jerked up, his hands clenched on the wooden headboard. "Come on, baby," Liam whispered. "Come for me now. Let it go."

Joey sobbed a deep breath and his hand flew off the headboard to cover Liam's on his cock. His hips thrust off the bed, fucking into the joined hands, and he came so hard, Liam could see every gorgeous muscled outline perfectly under his skin.

Keeping his hand working on Joey's cock, Liam kneeled up and used his free hand to jerk off all over Joey's chest. He shuddered through his second orgasm, flinching at the touch on his painfully sensitive cock. "Holy fucking shit." He collapsed down onto the bed, panting and shuddering with aftershocks. "Holy shit."

Joey stared at the ceiling fan, leg and abdominal muscles twitching, and his skin shiny with their mingled releases.

"You okay?" Liam asked after a few long seconds of silence. It felt like a stupid question, but Liam didn't know what Joey was thinking. Maybe he was regretting all the choices he'd made that had led to this moment. "Jojo?" Liam pushed himself up onto one elbow. "You good?"

"No," Joey croaked. "You fucking killed me. Put it on my tombstone. 'Tortured to death by fucking Liam O'Reilly'."

"Do I have to put up with the cursing? I don't think your mother would like it."

"Yes, you have to put up with the fucking fucking since you killed me with your fucking." The smile he turned to Liam was blinding.

Liam laughed in relief and kissed him long and hard. "We good?" he asked when they finally separated.

"Yeah, we're good. We're great. But I could use a shower."

"Me, too. In a minute, when I can feel my legs again."

THEY'D HAD to hold each other up in the shower. It had been a long, draining day, emotionally and physically. Liam should have been sleeping. He had to be up in less than six hours. But instead, he was sitting up against the headboard and watching Joey sleep the sleep of the just. Even Liam's fingers carding through his hair didn't draw so much as a blink in response.

The kid always had slept like the dead. A baby in a house full of siblings, friends, and kids running wild didn't get the luxury of having a quiet house to sleep in. If they didn't learn to sleep through chaos, they would never sleep at all. Getting a chance to watch Joey sleep always felt like a special gift to Liam. Awake, Joey was always in motion: talking, walking, or joking. Even when he was sitting, something on his body was moving even if was just his eyes as thoughts flew through that wicked smart brain of his.

Here in the dark, in his bed and in the sanctuary of his mind, Liam felt safe enough to let some of his own insecurities out to rattle around his mind. Was he doing everything he should be doing? Was he doing it right? School had been easy. You took a test, handed in a paper, you got a grade. Bam. Hockey was easy too; you played, you won or you lost. Black and white.

But coaching was more abstract. If you were lucky, you were building a legacy, not only by what you accomplished personally but what the kids you coached accomplished, how their lives went. The ripples could spread over years. Liam still remembered each coach, each teacher, who had taught him, mentored him, and helped turn him into the player and the man he had become.

And now he was taking on that role for other people. For Robbie and Paul.

And most importantly, for Joey.

In here, he could admit he was scared he was going to fuck it up. He had this precious thing, this man who only grew more fascinating, more interesting, with each new layer Liam unwrapped. Part of him worried that he didn't deserve to have Joey. Here he was, pretending he had all the answers when really he was only making it up as he went along.

Even though he did want the world to see the Joey he was privileged to see—the sensitive, caring man who loved with every atom of himself—part of him wanted to tuck Joey away and keep him to himself. Joey was hiding something, Liam knew it, and it was something that Joey was scared of. And that scared Liam. What could it be? Was it the drinking? Was it worse than Liam even knew?

He wished there was someone he could turn to who would tell him what to do, someone to share his burdens with, but that wasn't the way life worked. He was the oldest, he was the responsible one, the one the others turned to.

With a sigh, he slid down into the bed. He reached for Joey, pulling his body against him and letting the warmth of his skin and his familiar musky, spicy scent lull him to sleep.

17

JOEY

GINA posted in **YOU WISH**:

Guys help me out. Angie thinks Vin Diesel is hotter than the Rock. Tell her she's wrong.

SOPHIA: The Rock is way hotter 🔥 🔥

ANGIE: Lesbians don't get a vote!

NATALIE: That's homophobic. I'm telling mom.

GINA: Would you sleep with him?

LIAM: Channing Tatum is hotter than both of them. 🔥

NATALIE: With the Rock? Hell yeah.

PATRICK: Gasp, he texts!

SOPHIA: It's true. I'd sleep with Channing Tatum.

208 | A. E. WASP

PATRICK: Yeah, I might, too. You know, desert island, etc etc.

JEAN: I'd sleep with him. 🔥 Or Rhianna. 🔥🔥

PATRICK: Aunt Jeanie!!! Gross @!@!!! Who let her in?!

LESLIE: I'd share Rhianna with you.

PATRICK has left the discussion.

WITH BOTH PATRICK AND JOEY LIVING IN THE HOUSE, LIAM'S living room had sprouted a few improvements. Fluffy pillows and fleece blankets softened the edges of the designer furniture, a large television replaced a triptych of abstract paintings on the wall, and controllers for a brand new PS4 sat on a coffee table built to withstand the abuse of a houseful of hockey players.

Liam was still holding firm in the face of Patrick's attempts to get him to change out the suite of furniture for a giant leather sectional.

"It's the traditional furnishings of our people!" Patrick had argued.

"Your people think a beer can pyramid is a perfectly good decoration."

In the meantime, Paul and Robbie shared the normal-sized couch while Joey occupied Liam's favorite armchair.

"I miss Shangela," Paul said. "She totally got robbed season three."

"Hmm," Robbie answered noncommittally, his eyes closed. "They brought her back for All-Stars."

Burrowing deeper into the couch, Paul grumbled deep in his chest. "What about you? Looch. Who's your favorite?"

"Oh, ah…" Joey hadn't been paying much attention to the contestants of the current season on Ru Paul's Drag Race. The outrageously dressed drag queens lip-synching for their lives paled in comparison to Paul's head resting on Robbie's thigh, and the drowsy smile on Robbie's face as he carded his fingers through Paul's messy blond curls.

They radiated joy and contentment, and Joey couldn't look away. If only he knew for sure if the twisting feeling in his stomach was homophobia or jealousy. Could that completely innocent display of affection be making him uncomfortable, or did he ache to have it for himself?

Ooh! Ooh! I know the answer to this one! his heart screamed. His brain told it to STFU.

Assuming Liam would be fine with Joey sprawling all over him like that in public, would Joey want to do it? It was one thing to come out as gay—Joey had mad respect for the boys in doing that—but it was another to rub people's noses in it.

Listen to yourself, man, his brain said. *You're a dick.* This time, his heart was in total agreement.

Robbie and Paul weren't in public. Joey should be thrilled that the guys were comfortable enough around him to be themselves. Paul and Robbie actually *liked* Joey, they sought his company out. It was a far cry from his situation a month ago.

Joey was the only other one in the house at the moment. Liam was still at work, and Patrick had gone right to McVicker's house from the airport last night.

Apparently, those two were BFFs now. If Joey hadn't been so wrapped up in what was going on with him and Liam, he might have been insulted at being dumped. Instead, he was just happy that

Patrick had found something, or someone, to keep him busy. Patrick could be… a lot to take.

Someone on the television sashayed away, and Joey couldn't help comparing them to the two men in front of him. How could they all have this huge thing in common? Wanting to have sex with other men, falling in love with other men.

Paul and Robbie made it look so possible. So normal. Like something Joey could maybe one day actually have without everyone hating him.

God. His leg jittered and he wished he could go for a run down the beach. He loved the sound of the waves and the feel of the hard-packed sand under his feet. Falling in love with the Seattle coast had taken him by surprise. He even loved the gray mornings and the sound of the ferry horns in the fog.

Sophie, Leslie, and Natalie would smack the crap out of him if they could read his mind.

His whole life, he'd listened to them rant about how you couldn't tell a person's sexuality from their appearance, and how you shouldn't make assumptions, etcetera. He'd nodded and agreed with them to keep the peace, but inside he'd thought they were full of shit.

He'd have to find a way to apologize without getting yelled at for being an idiot.

What did people see when they looked at him? Could they tell he was having sex with a guy? Probably not. He looked as normal as Paul and Robbie. And he wasn't *gay* gay. If anything, he was bisexual, like Liam. He'd like to say it was only Liam who did it for him, but some of the fantasies he'd found drifting through his head lately proved that was a lie.

You could have knocked Joey over with a feather when he'd found out Alex and Sergei were a *couple* couple. Like a 'we're-in-love and probably-have-sex' kind of couple. He found himself watching them together and picturing them having sex. He really needed to stop doing that, but he couldn't seem to.

Sergei, man. He was just so *big*. And Alex was so petite. Damn, they must be so hot together.

"You okay, there, Lucy?" Paul asked. "You seem a little wound up?"

"What? No. Just got a lot on my mind. End of the season, you know how it is."

"Oh, yeah," Robbie agreed.

The last few weeks of the regular season were grueling. They'd been made even worse, in Joey's opinion, since the league had instituted a bye week; a mandatory five-day break every team took in the second half of the season.

It sounded good on paper, but in practice, it meant the same number of games had to be packed into a shorter schedule. Five days didn't seem like a long time, but it was long enough to lose a lot of momentum. The first year it had been implemented, nearly every team had lost their first game back by a wide margin.

"Fuck, yes." Paul flopped onto his back and pulled Robbie's arm down over his chest. "I'm beat. I think my stitches are getting infected." A rogue puck had popped up under his mask the night before, opening up an inch-long cut on his cheek. It hadn't been serious. Paul hadn't lost any teeth, and the doc had sewn him up in the locker room. He'd been back on the ice ten minutes later.

"Aw, poor baby," Robbie cooed. "Did that mean old puck hurt you?"

"Yes," Paul said with an exaggerated pout. "And I've been disfigured. Do you still think I'm hot?"

"*Still* hot?" Robbie asked. "That would imply that you *were* hot at some point. What do you think, Joey, is he hot?"

Paul fluttered his eyelashes at Joey, and to his mortification, Joey blushed. "Oh, um, yeah. He's your boyfriend, I wouldn't look at him, I mean, I haven't really thought about it."

Paul laughed. "Told you."

Told him what? Joey wasn't sure he wanted to know.

"Whatever," Robbie said. "The internet says I'm hot. Besides, Lucy only has eyes for a certain angry red-headed DILF."

DILF?

"Dad I'd like to…" Robbie explained at Paul and Joey's blank looks.

"Are you talking about *Liam*?" Joey asked. Were other guys looking at Liam and thinking things about him? Sex-related things? Joey frowned. Liam was his.

"Are you dating another angry sexy redhead?" Robbie asked.

"Dating?" Joey's jaw dropped.

Paul punched Robbie's thigh hard. "We talked about this, you fucking idiot."

"Ow!" Robbie said, flicking Paul on the forehead. "Jerk."

"Sorry for my idiot boyfriend," Paul said to Joey. "I told him to mind his own business."

"No. It's okay." Joey stood up. "I'm going to get a drink of water, anyone want anything?"

"Water, please," Robbie said.

"Want us to pause the show?" Paul asked. "There's a great fight coming up."

"Yeah, sure."

"If you have any snacks, I wouldn't say no," Robbie called.

Joey contemplated his options as he filled some water glasses and rummaged through the cabinets for some kind of snack. He either had to admit to his thing with Liam or deny it.

Dumping some nuts into a bowl and pulling out some cheese from the fridge, he added up the pros and cons of coming clean.

Pro – Robbie and Paul didn't seem angry at the thought of him and Liam hooking up. They kind of seemed into it. Weird, but supportive.

Pro – he'd have someone to talk to about what was going on with him. People he could trust not to out them to the press.

Con – he'd have to tell Liam that Robbie and Paul knew.

Con – he'd have to stop lying to himself about what was going on between him and Liam. If he said it to someone else, it was real. He was in a *relationship* with Liam. They were, for want of a better word, dating. *Boyfriends*. Jesus.

Fuck it. He refilled his glass and walked back to the living room. Robbie sat up, shoulders slumped. Paul glared at him. Robbie jumped up when he saw Joey.

"Hey, man. I'm sorry. I didn't mean…like, we like Coach O'Reilly. And you. So. Together. I mean. It's just you guys fight. Like, a lot. So." He trailed off, shrugging at Paul.

Under pressure, Robbie's brain had a habit of jumbling all his words together so they came out in varying degrees of coherence. Paul played translator; sometimes literally when Robbie got so frustrated he turned to the sign language he'd learned to help organize his thoughts.

"We thought you were together," Paul said, "because of how you guys are around each other. You're always up in each other's spaces, either yelling about hockey or arguing about stupid shit."

"And the chemistry, *woah*," Robbie chimed in. "A man could get fried standing between you two. Before our press conference, Coach told us he was bi. Which was really cool, by the way, and then, well, he looks at you like…"

"Jesus, Rhodes." Paul rolled his eyes. "Shut up."

"Oh fuck," Robbie covered his mouth, eyes wide. "You knew that, right? I mean, he didn't say it was a secret." His cheeks flamed red.

"It's okay." He handed Robbie the water. "Liam came out to the family over ten years ago when my sister Sophie, who is his age, came out as a lesbian. And then Liam's little sister Natalie did, too. It's no secret to us."

"Oh, thank god," Robbie collapsed down into the couch. "It's really, really not good to out people without them saying it's okay."

"Yeah? That's good to know. So, you guys wouldn't, like, tell anybody else if you knew about someone." *Oh, smooth, Looch, they'll never figure out what you're talking about.*

Robbie sat up straight. "No." He exchanged a look with Paul. "Absolutely not."

Paul rolled his eyes but gave Robbie a sweet smile. "You're adork-able," he told his boyfriend.

"And you're just a dork. Let the man talk." He turned to Joey. "You were going to talk, weren't you?"

Joey nodded. "Yeah, okay. But it doesn't leave this room, *capisce?*"

"Cross my heart," Robbie said, crossing his heart.

"Liam and I are… together I guess. I don't know what to call it."

"Yes!" Robbie gave a fist pump and then pointed a finger at Paul. "You owe me a hundred bucks!"

"You still owe me two hundred for being able to catch ten peanut M&Ms in a row in my mouth."

"Then now I only owe you a hundred. Put it on my tab. So, Joseph, tell us everything about you and the frightening yet sexy Coach O'Reilly. Don't leave out any details."

Joey laughed out loud. "Oh, I'm leaving out all of the details. You'll just have to use your imagination."

"He already does," Paul said. "Trust me."

Did he just imply Robbie had been thinking about him and Liam having sex?

"Oh, please. Like you haven't spent a few showers wondering about Sergei and his giant dick."

"That thing is fucking huge," popped out of Joey's mouth without his permission. Was that a normal thing to say? He'd just admitted to looking at Sergei's dick in the showers. Did all gay guys talk about other guys the way straight guys talked about women? That kind of literal locker room talk had always made Joey uncomfortable. He'd done it just enough not to draw attention to his lack of participation.

So why did talking about *guys* like that feel different?

He wasn't sure how he felt about knowing people might be looking at him 'that way' in the locker rooms and showers. Somehow he'd convinced himself he was the only one, and he'd perfected the art of not looking while trying not to look like he was *deliberately* not looking.

"I know," Paul said through a mouthful of cheese. "And Alex is so tiny. And we know for sure that Sergei can lift him with one hand."

"We do?" Joey asked.

"He showed us at our Christmas party," Robbie confirmed. "Just lifted him up on the palm of his hand like he was a cheerleader." He demonstrated with a couch pillow.

"Damn."

"I know. The mind boggles at the implications." Paul swung his feet up onto Robbie's lap. "I feel like we should get to see it. For science."

Joey nodded absently, lost in thought.

"Coach O'Reilly is big. Tall," Robbie stammered.

"Judy? Yeah, he is."

"You're not tall," Robbie said, blushing.

"What he's trying to say is," Paul translated from his prone position, "that he would like to see some inappropriate player contact between you and Coach O'Reilly."

Robbie's jaw dropped and he punched his boyfriend hard on the upper arm. "Ow! That's my jerking off arm!"

"Ooh, and you're going to need that this week, too. Pity."

Paul's hands moved as he said something to Robbie in sign language.

"Fuck yeah." Robbie patted Paul on the legs. "Get up."

"Where are you goin'? Show's not over." Joey wasn't ready for them to leave. He wanted to talk about him and Liam some more. He had no idea what he wanted to say, but there was so much he didn't know about being with a guy. Hidden minefields he didn't even know to ask about.

"We have to… go do… a thing." Robbie made vague hand gestures.

"Is that thing fuck like bunnies?" Joey asked bluntly but with a smile.

"Maybe," Robbie admitted. "How do bunnies fuck anyway?"

"Based on my sister's rabbits, they have really fast sex, two weeks later they have babies, and then they eat them," Paul answered. Even his sexy Alabama drawl couldn't make that any less gross.

Robbie scrunched up his nose and started to sit back down. "Okay. I've changed my mind. That was a boner killer."

"Robbie." Paul made a gesture with his hand that even Joey with his non-existent knowledge of sign language could understand.

"You make a persuasive argument," Robbie said.

Before they could put their plan into action, the sound of the back door opening and closing echoed through the house. "Hey, Loo-cy, I'm home," Liam called from the kitchen.

All three of them jumped. Paul started the show again, the music loud in the sudden silence.

Liam draped his jacket over the back of a kitchen chair and entered the room rolling up the sleeves of his pin-striped lilac dress shirt.

"Hey," he said to Joey with the smile he saved only for him. Like he was surprised and happy to find Joey waiting for him in his home. "Hey, boys," he said noticing Paul and Robbie. "I thought that was your car." Paul's 1967 Corvette was easy to spot.

"Hey, Coach," they said in ragged unison, looking as guilty as Joey felt.

Liam stuck his hands in his pockets and looked among the three of them. He shook his head. "I'm not even going to ask what those expressions mean. I'm going to change and come back down. Did you guys eat dinner?"

"No, sir," Paul said, answering for all them. "But we were just leaving."

"Don't leave on my account."

The door opened and slammed closed again as Patrick and McVicker barged into the house. "Who's leaving?" Paddy yelled, opening the refrigerator door.

"Rhodie and Bama," McVicker answered, greeting them each with a one-armed hug and a thump to the back. Joey liked the young backup goalie. He was never in a bad mood, never complained about not getting enough ice time, and was genuinely the most laid-back professional athlete Joey had ever met.

"Tell 'em to stay," Patrick said, as if it was his house. "There's like half a cow in here. Joey can grill up some steaks."

"Why me?" Joey asked.

"Because you're the best cook," Liam said, laying a hand on Joey's shoulder and squeezing. It felt almost like a kiss.

Joey stood up. "Flattery will get you dinner."

Joey hummed under his breath along with the music streaming from his phone as he loaded the last of the plates into the dishwasher. Paul and Robbie had offered to help clean up, but Liam had overruled them, telling Patrick since he had invited the guests, he was on cleanup duty. McVicker's contribution had been to quote all the dirty limericks he could think of. For a young guy, he knew an awful lot of them.

Of course, Patrick had grabbed McVicker and disappeared as soon as Liam had headed up to his office to take a last look at the video for tomorrow.

Liam strolled into the kitchen in sweatpants and a Harvard Crimsons hoodie that was beginning to fray at the wrists.

"All done?" Joey asked.

"For now, I'm starting to see double. Want to get some fresh air?"

"Sure. The beach?"

Liam nodded.

Joey's breath streamed into the still night air as they walked to the low wall separating the sand from Liam's back lawn. He didn't know where he'd gotten the idea that Seattle was warm in the winter. Sure it wasn't as frigid as a Boston March, but he should have grabbed a sweatshirt. The wind off the water added to the chill and Joey rubbed his arms for warmth.

"Cold?" Liam asked stepping over the wall.

"A little."

"Sit here. I'll be right back."

Joey sat on the wooden bench seat pushed up against the stone, figuring it would be warmer on his butt.

Liam ran into the glass-walled building that held the hot tub and an outdoor shower room. He rummaged through a closet, coming up with an armful of fabric that turned out to be an old quilt Joey remembered from the O'Reilly's living room.

"Does Aunt Kathleen know you stole her quilt?" Joey asked.

"Considering I took it when I left for high school, I think she's had time to adjust to the idea. Come here." Liam draped the bedcover over Joey's shoulders and arranged it until they sat with Joey's back to Liam's chest.

Liam wrapped his arms around him, and Joey sighed in contentment.

"Better?"

"Perfect." Stars blazed in the clear moonless sky, breaking up into pinpoints of diamonds on the black water.

"Thanks for cooking tonight," Liam said.

"You know I like it."

"It was fun having the guys over for dinner. I think that's the first time."

"You haven't had them over before?"

"I'm not sure how to act now that I'm a coach, you know? Where the boundaries are."

"I'm pretty sure cuddling on the beach with one of your players is crossing some kind of boundary."

Liam was quiet for so long, Joey was afraid *he* had crossed a boundary. Maybe they weren't supposed to be talking about it. He was going to say he had just been joking when Liam spoke.

"It might be. There's no rule against coaches and players dating that I could find." His arms tightened around Joey's chest.

"You looked."

"I looked. And my lawyer looked."

"You *looked?*"

"Why do you sound so surprised?"

Joey couldn't catch his breath.

"Hey, what's wrong?" Liam turned Joey's head up so he could see his face.

"It's just... why? Dating? Are we dating?"

To his surprise, Liam laughed. "Fucked if I know. Can you date someone you've known their entire life? Can you date someone you're already living with? I have a feeling there isn't a word in English for what we're doing."

"Crazy?" Joey suggested.

"Probably. Definitely." He turned Joey around, pulling him against his chest.

"And what if you'd found a rule against it? Then what?"

Liam sighed. "I don't know. As much as I hate to admit it, I would probably have tried to hide it until after the season. Then started talking to a whole lot of people."

"You would do that? For me?"

"Well, I like to think I have a vested interest in it, too."

"But why?"

Liam grabbed Joey's chin and turned his head back. "You know why."

"Because I'm worth it," Joey said breathlessly.

Liam kissed him hard, bruising his lips against his tongue. Joey was panting when he pulled away. "Yeah, because you're worth it. Now, let's go back inside. It's a school night and it's past your bedtime."

18

LIAM

MICHELLE: I miss him. Is that normal?

ANGIE: Yeah

MICHELLE: I don't deserve to miss him. I'm a cheating ho. I can't stop crying.

ANGIE: Are you watching Lifetime TV again?

MICHELLE: Maybe. Being pregnant sucks. I can't breathe, I have to pee constantly, and I'm hungry all the time.

ANGIE: Come to the kitchen. I'll feed you.

MICHELLE: I don't deserve you either. I was bitch to you in high school

ANGIE: Water under the bridge. Come, let me feed you. I

have a genetic condition where I need to make people eat. It's a sickness.

THE USUAL ON-THE-ROAD ROUTINE WAS AN EXHAUSTING progression directly from the ice to bus to plane to hotel to another bus, another rink, and then yet another bus ride to another airport. The Thunder had traveled almost fifty thousand miles during the previous twenty-seven week season on road trips lasting anywhere from two to six days. They'd clocked ninety hours in the air, eight hours longer than regulation game time for the entire season, and on fourteen occasions they'd played back-to-back games.

But tonight was special. Not only did they have the luxury of sleeping at the hotel a second night rather than heading directly to the airport after the game, but also, with the victory over the Arizona Coyotes, they'd secured themselves a wild card spot in the Western Conference playoffs. It was the first step on the path to The Cup, and the first time that Thunder had made it into the playoffs in their four-year history.

Even though it was late on a Wednesday night, the bar at the Phoenix hotel was packed and the celebration was headed towards rowdy. Besides the players and the team staff, there were the usual husband- and boyfriend-hunting puck bunnies with their miniskirts and Louis Vuitton purses, a handful of local Thunder fans, random guests who'd had no idea what they were in for, and several hotel employees who'd stuck around after their shifts to congratulate the guys. Liam had been at this hotel more times than he could count and had grown to know some of the staff well.

From the relative quiet of his corner booth, Liam sipped his beer while he watched Joey working the room, shining in the dim lighting like the star he was.

He had killed it in the game. Andy had been experimenting with the lines; moving Joey to the first line, and Jake to the second to work with the two younger wingers there. Both lines had worked together like well-oiled machines, racking up six goals and nine assists among the six of them.

The post-game press had been even more insane than usual, and Liam's phone buzzed like a beehive with congratulatory texts from family and friends.

Meanwhile, the texts were still pouring in, hours after the game. The family group chat in particular was buzzing. Deano's team, the Tampa Bay Lightning, had a spot in the Eastern Conference, making things that much more interesting. It wouldn't be the first time they'd met in the playoffs. They'd faced off in 2015, when the Rangers lost to Tampa Bay in game seven. There had been epic celebrating at the Nantucket house that summer.

GINA: *Hey Jojo, how many playoffs in a row is that now?*

JOEY: *Ten, if you count high school. Which I do.*

LIAM: *He's been in at least the first round every year of his career.*

PATRICK: *Aw, dad's proud!*

NATALIE: *I won a gold medal this year, in case you've forgotten. Jus sayin' First one for the US Women in 20 years? Anyone remember that?*

GINA: *Nat we all know you play better than any of them. Except maybe Jojo.*

NATALIE: *Hey, what happened to sisters before misters?*

GINA: *Baby brother trumps friend. Sorry.*

NATALIE: *Fair*

PATRICK: *Does that mean you love me best nat?*

NATALIE: *dream on little man*

Fuck yes, Liam was proud. Proud of his team, proud of his fellow coaches, and proud of Joey. Watching Joey play at the top of his game was fucking sexy.

Joey in action was lightning in a bottle, and one of the reasons Liam had barricaded himself at a table with Andy, Jake Donovan, and a few of the older guys, was to stop himself from grabbing Joey and dragging him upstairs to his room. They were all a little drunk. Even Andy was feeling no pain. Tomorrow the even harder work of playoff prep would start, so they were giving themselves the night off. Liam's phone vibrated across the tabletop.

"Jesus, O'Reilly," Jake Donovan said, grabbing the phone. "You got a fan club or something?"

"I got a big family. A big, loud, nosey, loving family." He couldn't wipe the grin off his face at the thought of them all.

Jake's eyebrows rose. "Ooh, it's the ex!" He turned the phone so Liam could see Michelle's name on the screen.

It felt like a blow to the heart. Liam grabbed the phone away from him.

"She still texts you?" Donovan said.

MICHELLE: *Congratulations! I knew you'd be a great*

coach. And I know how much this means to you. You worked so hard for it, you always do. Looks like that old-school Red Army style is working for you. Good thing you traded Peters for Jojo. He would have hated that. Congrats again.

Liam blinked away inexplicable tears. That was such a Michelle thing to do. She always had been the thoughtful and kind half of them. If it had been Liam's responsibility, no one in his family would have ever gotten a card or a phone call for their birthday, let alone the special gifts Michelle picked out for them. It must have been hard for her to reach out, but she'd done it. She was the bigger person. He hadn't spoken to her since Christmas.

"You're still talking to that harpy?" Donovan said. "She's got some nerve."

One of the few non-hockey guys at the table was Aditya Om, floor manager at the Marriott. Adi had been at the Marriott for as long as Liam had been coming to Phoenix. He'd worked his way up from housekeeping to floor manager and knew enough secrets about celebrities and athletes to make him a rich man if he'd had fewer scruples. Luckily, Adi was as tight-lipped as a priest. "Is it true she is pregnant by Nino Luciano?" he asked.

"Yeah, it's true," Liam said absently as he stared at the phone.

"That's cold, man," Jake said. "I can't believe you can even look at Luciano, let alone have him on the team."

"It's not Joey's fault."

"Yeah," agreed Hannu Kaarela. "It's her fault."

Liam glared at the big man. It was Liam's first time working with

228 | A. E. WASP

the forth-line wingman. They weren't close enough friends for Hands to be making comments like that.

A drunk brunette perched on the arm of Donovan's chair and pointed a manicured finger at Liam. "Yeah, it was that slut. Nino Luciano's on the Rockies, right? Baseball pays like twice as much as hockey, right?" Liam thought he recognized her from other games. Her name was something like Ruby or Diamond. Some expensive rock. She shook her head. "Damn, I can't wait for Spring Training to start. God bless the Cactus league." She raised her glass in a toast to baseball.

"No," Liam said forcefully, surprising himself. "That's not fair. You can't blame her. It's my fault." Liam didn't really want to talk about his relationship, but given that hockey players as a rule were huge gossips, he was surprised they'd waited this long to bring it up.

"I was a shitty boyfriend. I loved hockey more than I loved her." Man, saying that out loud hurt. Joey had been right, Michelle had been right. Everyone who'd told him he was a shitty boyfriend-which had pretty much been every female in both families-had been right.

He'd had a smart, gorgeous, understanding girlfriend who was everything you could ever want in a wife, and he'd taken her horribly for granted. Worst of all, when push came to shove, he simply hadn't loved her enough to fight for her. He loved her like a sister. There was just something fundamental missing between them.

"She gave up her career, her family, everything to follow me around the country, and I took it for granted."

The brunette snorted. "Not like she was suffering."

"That's not true, Emerald" Andy said. "Outside of military spouses, our wives are some of the strongest women you'll ever meet. Yeah, they get money, maybe, if their husband doesn't get injured in his first year. But they're alone a lot. They have to move at the drop of a hat, taking care of everything—kids, selling the house, buying the new one, everything—all by themselves."

Jake nodded reluctantly. "Yeah. I never thought she was right for you, but this life is hell on relationships. Why do you think I'm single? I'm a fucking catch."

The brunette put her arm around his shoulder. "Yeah, you are, baby." There was a good chance she'd end up in his room tonight. "So what are you looking for now, Liam?" Emerald asked. "What have you learned?"

That was something he'd thought about a lot the last few months. Something he thought about whenever he looked at Joey. There was no comparison between the way he'd felt about Michelle and the way he'd felt about Joey. Joey brought out a possessive, caring side of Liam he hadn't known he'd had.

Joey claimed Liam 'glowered' at anyone who was friendly to him, and 'growled' when he spoke to them. Liam wouldn't go that far, but he could admit he didn't like watching everyone and their mother flirting with Joey non-stop. He didn't like the way Joey made himself available to every Tom, Dick, and Harriet who wanted him.

"I learned that I need to be with someone I can't stop thinking about. Someone who makes me want to be with them more than I want to be away." Someone who he was with because he wanted to be with them, come hell or high water, rather than being with them because they fit some imaginary checklist of the perfect partner he'd had in his head.

"So?" she pushed. "Got anyone in mind?"

It took all of Liam's willpower not to look for Joey, and he couldn't stop the secretive smile stretching his lips.

"Ooh," Em said, pointing a finger at Liam. "I know that smile! There is someone." She scanned the room but didn't find any likely candidates. "Who's the lucky girl? She's probably back in Seattle, right?"

"I promise you, there's no woman," he said with a laugh.

A girl who looked barely old enough to drink slid tentatively up to their group. She wore a loose-fitting Thunder t-shirt and jeans. Emerald gave her a quick once over and, dismissing her as competition, smiled at her. "Hey, honey. Don't be scared of the boys, they don't bite."

"Well..." Donovan said, and she smacked him on the back of the head.

"Hi," the girl said in a wavering voice. "I'm sorry to bother you, but I was wondering if I could get your autographs? The bartender said you wouldn't mind."

"We don't mind at all, honey," Jake said, waving her over. "What's your name and what do you want us to sign?"

It turned out her name was Eloise, she was Seattle born and bred and living in Arizona for physical therapy school. Her family had gotten season tickets for the Thunder the first day they'd gone on sale.

Liam was a little drunker than he should be. He shouldn't be sitting here, shouldn't be wasting time. There was so much to do to get ready. He excused himself and stood up from the table with a vague notion of doing 'Something Useful.' "Eloise, want to meet some of the boys?"

"Yes, please!" she said, lighting up.

Catching sight of his brother was easy enough. There weren't a lot of people with hair that bright red. Eloise followed him to the table where he sat with McVicker and some of the younger players on the team, including Robbie and Paul. Seeing them all together like that made Liam feel ancient, and a little wistful for his long-gone twenties.

"Boys," Liam said.

"My, aren't we paternal tonight," Patrick said.

"Oh, I'm sorry. Boys and punk-ass, I meant to say."

"Who's your friend?" Patrick asked with a grin at Eloise.

Liam put his hand on her shoulder. "This is Eloise. She's in PT school, and for some reason she's a big fan of ours. I thought I'd bring her over here and introduce her to some nice young players. Patrick, you don't talk to her."

He turned to Eloise and introducing each player in turn. "This is James McVicker, Robbie Rhoads, Paul Dyson, Alex Huberdeau, and Devin DiDiomete."

"Hi," she said with a small wave and big eyes.

"Call me Triple D," Devin said. "And please, have a seat." A nineteen-year-old from Long Island, he reminded Liam of Joey at that age but without the brilliance. Not that he would ever say that to anyone but Andy.

"What am I? Chopped liver?" Patrick said with a smile.

"Eloise, that person is my little brother Patrick. Don't listen to a word he says and keep a hand on your wallet at all times. For your own safety, stick with Dyson, he's a gentleman, or Vicky, he's a goalie."

"I know," she said squeezing in between Paul and Robbie. "Thank you Mr. O'Reilly."

Patrick snorted. "Mister. We were just talking about the future with the rookies. Got any words of wisdom?"

Liam looked at the table. Hubs and Triple D were nineteen years old, lord help him. He could almost be their father. Paul and Robbie, were twenty-one and twenty-two, not much older.

"Yeah, I do. First, Hubs, D, what are you drinking?"

"Coke," they answered in unison.

"Good job. Okay, here are Liam O'Reilly's tips for a long, healthy life. Life, not career." He held up a finger. "Number one, can anyone tell me the average length of a career in the NHL?"

"Three years," Hubs said.

"Three years. You could be out of here before your friends back home have graduated college. But you won't have the benefit of a college degree."

"But we'll have money," D said with a laugh.

"It beats working for a living, that's true. But if you're lucky, you'll live for another sixty-years. That's a long time and you aren't going to make enough money to cover that. What are you going to do with those years?" From the looks on their faces, he was bringing the party down for sure. "Look, if you're smart, you'll be fine. Think about it, talk about it with your family and partners. Don't pretend it won't happen."

"Number two, don't do anything you would want your grandmother to read about."

Patrick raised one eyebrow. "Do you tell Nana everything?".

"Yeah, Paddy. She knows everything." Liam smiled. "My grandmother is worse than the cops," he explained to the boys. "She finds out everything. If you admit it first, you'll get off with a lighter sentence."

Andy Williams joined them, clapping both hands on Liam's shoulder. "Hey, boys. Excellent game tonight. I'm proud of you."

There was a ragged round of 'thank you coach' from everyone. That wasn't the first time he'd praised them, obviously, but you could never say it too much.

"Mind if I borrow my colleague here for a moment?"

"Please take him," Patrick said. "He's cramping my style."

"What style?" Vicky asked.

"I'll have you know I am wicked charming," Patrick said with the broadest Boston accent he could manage.

Andy shook his head and led Liam into a quieter corner. "That right there?" he asked. "That's one of the reasons I hired you. These babies need someone to talk to them. Most of them come from a decent middle-class background. Their parents probably aren't bad with money, but who listens to their parents at that age? I know I didn't. You tell them something, they're more likely to listen. After all, you've been in their shoes." Andy ordered whiskey for both of them from a passing server.

"I came home to a house full of kids yesterday," Liam said. "Rhodes, Dyson, McVicker, and of course Paddy and Joey," Liam said. "It's like being a camp counselor."

"They're all good kids. What were they doing?"

"Watching TV. Sprawled all over my furniture. Eating my food." He sipped thoughtfully. "Maybe Rhoades and Dyson have the right idea. Date someone in the league."

Andy barked a laugh. "I have a feeling that's not a helpful option for most of the boys. Most," he said, at Liam's look. "You and I both know those boys aren't the first teammates to be knocking boots. They're not the first and won't be the last."

Andy looked around the room, taking in the happy chatter and various levels of flirting going on around the room. "I swear there's so much testosterone in that locker room you can smell it. I'm surprised I haven't caught anyone fucking in there. You see how Rhoades and Dyson look at each other when they make one of those fucking stupendous plays of theirs? Jesus, I feel dirty just watching it. I have to call my wife after. I keep expecting those two assholes to do it on the ice one day. God help us if we ever win the Cup."

Liam fought to keep from laughing. He'd forgotten how talkative Andy got when he drank.

"Oh, go ahead and smirk," Andy said, pointing at Liam with his glass. "I took on Luciano because I knew you could handle him. And you are. I don't want to know how. I'm not asking, and you're not telling, but you might want to find a way to make the yelling seem more like you're actually angry and less like foreplay."

"Um, ah," Liam stammered and blushed.

Andy ignored it and ran right over him verbally. "I've lost too many kids like him. He's one of the best players I've seen in my career, I don't want him to blow it and regret it for the rest of his life. The Rangers' front office wasn't doing shit for him. Practically pushed him into the spotlight, encouraged the behavior until it got out of their control. Then they were just ready to toss him away as a liability. 'Play our kind of game?' the fuck? So he's not the biggest body out there. So what? He plays a head game. Like you did. I hired you because of that hockey mind. You see all the pieces, should have been a goalie."

"I like to skate too much to stand still in the goal for sixty."

"I hear that." Coach Williams had been a star forward in his day, switching from right to left wing. "So, yeah, O'Reilly. You're new, you're green. But I got an eye for talent."

That he did. Andy starting scouting kids in junior high school. He had a reputation for finding the hidden gems, the boys who were going to bloom later. He had a habit of acting as a surrogate dad to the youngest players; often letting them bunk with him. Both Hubs and Triple D were living with him this season. Mrs. Williams loved it. When they moved out or got traded, they might lose touch with Andy, but no one forgot Deborah. She got more Mother's Day cards than an Irish grandmother.

"The way I see it, I got you at a bargain. One day clubs are gonna be fighting over you for head coach. After I'm dead of course. So I'm a narcissist. I want to put my stamp on your coaching style now, while I still can. I want people to say, oh yeah, he's the best. He trained with Old Man Williams." He spread his arms, waving them as he spoke.

"No one calls you Old Man Williams," Liam said with a laugh.

"They will one day," he said portentously as if he were looking forward to the day.

"You're what fifty-two? You have decades of coaching left."

He shrugged, growing more serious. "Maybe. Maybe I do. But I got grandchildren, you know? I missed a ton of my kids' lives. I kind of want to be there for this."

"Where do your kids live? "

"The youngest is in Seattle, headed for U-Dub. My middle boy is backpacking around Europe or Southeast Asia or Africa somewhere, digging wells, planting schools, whatever. And my oldest daughter lives in Colorado on some land."

"She's a farmer?"

"Rancher. They raise llamas. No, what are the little ones?"

"Goats?"

"No. the little ones. Like llamas but smaller."

Joey snuck up next to them, resting a butt cheek on Liam's chair. "Alpacas?"

"Yeah. Alpacas. That's it. Cute buggers," Andy said.

"Why are you talking about alpacas?" Joey took a sip of Liam's whiskey. "Mm. Nice."

"Coach's daughter and her…?"

"Wife," Andy supplied. "The girls raise alpacas somewhere in Colorado. Matter of fact, I think it's near where Lowery and his farmer live. I should get up to see both of them over the summer. Be nice to check up on the boys."

"I wanna come," Joey said. "I wanna see the alpacas. Can we see the alpacas? I wanna pet one. I've heard they're really soft. Please? Please dad?" He batted his eyelashes at Liam.

To his surprise, Liam found himself wanting to promise Joey he could pet an alpaca. From the smirk on Joey's face, he was well aware of his effect on Liam.

Andy laughed at both of them. "Tell you what, you help us win the Campbell Bowl, I'll get her to send you a blanket. Have her dye it in Thunder colors and everything. Deal?"

"Deal. But I still want to visit. I wanna see Lowery. Thank him for giving me a job."

Liam shoved him away before he pushed him up against a wall and kissed the laughter right out of his mouth. "Be right back, Andy. I've got a message for the Looch here from his mom. She wanted to make sure he got it."

Andy raised his glass at them. "I'll be here. Holding up the wall."

Liam pulled Joey into a relatively quiet corner.

"What did my mom have to say?" Joey asked.

"Nothing, I lied. But if she were here, she'd probably tell you to go to bed. You look tired."

"She'd be right," he admitted to Liam's surprise.

"Why don't you go upstairs, take off the suit and lie down. I'll be up in a little while." Officially they had separate rooms, but they always seemed to be assigned to adjoining rooms, often with a connecting door.

"Maybe. The guys are so pumped though. And there are still fans hanging around."

"Joey." Liam took his chin in his hand. "Go to bed."

Joey closed his eyes and sighed wearily. "Yeah. Okay. One more round so I can say goodnight. See you up there?"

"Soon."

"Okay." They shared an intense look until Liam grinned. "I'm not gonna kiss you goodnight."

"You want to, though." Joey smiled wickedly at him.

"Yeah, I do, brat. Now go to bed."

"Yessir," Joey said with a salute.

Liam shook his head and went back to Coach Williams.

.

19

JOEY

On the Town LA - JUNE 21, 2012

Kicking it Kings' Style

The party continued over the weekend for the Stanley Cup champion Kings, who tore it up at Dazzle Saturday night.

When all was said and done, the team racked up a four-hour bar tab that totaled $156,679.74, and included the now-famous $100,000.00 bottle of Ace of Spades "Midas" champagne, which was a gift according to Kings Player Joey Luciano. Already on his second season with the Kings at nineteen years old, the Looch, as he is known by his legion of mostly female fans, isn't old enough to legally partake of the bubbly, but seemed to enjoy himself nonetheless.

No one kicked it as hard as the Looch and his unnamed friend who spent much of the night on top of the bar, shirtless, and spritzing the crowd with champagne. They were occasionally joined by teammates, some of whom seem to be using these postseason parties to perfect their Dougie, the dance made famous by Lil' Wil.

The tab also lists a built-in tip of $24,869.80 for Danielle (the server whose name is on top of the tab below), which we imagine she had to split up with a few other servers at Dazzle.

DANG. ALPACAS. HOW AWESOME WOULD THAT BE? MAYBE THEY could get some? Maybe they should start small, with a cat. Then he remembered how traumatized he'd been when his rats had died. Maybe he should get a goldfish. Maybe he should have stopped at one vodka tonic.

Nah. They were celebrating. Getting a spot in the playoffs never lost its thrill. He'd make his rounds, say goodnight, and then head upstairs. And maybe have one more drink. He hadn't had a vertigo attack or even a headache in a while. Maybe he was getting better.

A selection of classic rock and current country music fought to be heard over the sound of the replay of their game on repeat on the TVs scattered around the bar.

Paul and Robbie waved him over to their table. They were stoked. First year in the show, first playoff spot. He remembered that feeling well.

Joey threaded his way through the gauntlet of scantily-dressed women clogging the floor between him and the boys. He wished the team could just go somewhere and celebrate alone.

Fans were one thing, but some of these professional husband-seekers got on his nerves.

He'd loved going out at the beginning. Who wouldn't? He was young, rich, and good-looking. Why wouldn't he enjoy it? Why shouldn't he?

Back then, he could drink anything, stay out all night and not have it affect his game the next day. He'd never gotten arrested or caught doing anything he shouldn't be, and he'd never used any drugs, beyond the league-approved painkillers they were always shooting into him. And maybe a few anxiety meds for a few months. But he was past that.

Lately, though, the scene was starting to get old. He watched Anderson Wheeler, one of the older D-men, leave with his arm around a giggling mini-skirted blonde. Wheels was one of those guys who had a wife and two kids in Seattle and a girl in every other city. He'd better be saving his money for those future alimony and child support payments.

At least he wasn't sleeping with a teammate's wife. That was a disaster.

Local hopeful hockey boys with stars in their eyes hovered near the players, trying to be casual. Joey's cynical thought was that if they were old enough to be drinking and they were any good, he would have already heard of them. By twenty-one, you knew where you ranked.

Tourists had no idea who all these big rowdy guys in suits were, but they were happy enough to accept the rounds being bought for them.

The bartender caught Joey's eye as he pushed through the rowdy crowd. He made his way to the less crowded end of the bar.

"*¿Qué pedo?*" Matty asked with a fist bump. "Need another?"

"Nah. I'm good."

"See anyone you like out there?" Matty asked. Matteo was a seri-ously good-looking Mexican guy who always seemed to be on duty when Joey came through. He was funny and smart and Joey liked hanging with him.

A tiny waitress with skin tanned dark brown from a lifetime of Arizona, nudged his arm as she slid her empty tray back on the counter. "I get off at two," she said with a wink. "Just let me call my husband, he won't mind."

Joey and Matty laughed. "Get lost, Lea. You'd break the boy," Matty said.

Even pushing fifty, Lea was a knockout with a great smile and laugh lines around her eyes. "I'll be gentle," she said taking fresh drinks from Matty. "Will it be your first time, honey?"

"Virgin as the first snow of the season." Joey fluttered his eyelashes at her

She laughed again, flashing bright white teeth, then kissed him on his cheek with a loud '*mwah*' "I got bunions older than you, baby. I swear you boys get younger every year. I had to card those three boys over there." She shook her head. "Babies all dressed up in suits like they're going to the prom. That blondie with the accent though. That smile. What a charmer. If I was twenty years younger I'd let him *yes ma'am* me all night."

Joey burst out laughing. He couldn't wait to tell Paul he had a cougar fan club. Though he probably already knew.

"Go take a cold shower," Matty said, snapping his bar rag at her. "Or go home and make Barry a happy man."

She turned her back to them with a sniff. "Barry is just happy I put up with his lazy ass all these years."

As he watched her move expertly through the room, tray held over her head, Joey caught Liam's eye. Oh the promises in that man's eyes. They were going to have a good night for sure.

Matty looked over Joey's shoulder at where Liam sat. His eyebrows raised and he gave Joey a penetrating look. "I think Lea's barking up the wrong tree anyway. Isn't that blond kid the one who came out this year? Dyson? And the other guy is his boyfriend, right?"

Shit. He couldn't read Matty's expression. Was there going to be trouble? He seriously doubted Matty would start anything physical at work, but Joey had been having a good time and he liked Matty. He didn't want to get into an argument with him.

Not that it was a secret that Robbie and Paul were dating. There had even been a few nasty signs in the audience during the game and a few Coyotes players had had to be taught a lesson in acceptable chirping on the ice. Joey's confirming it wouldn't be gossip.

"Yeah. Got a problem with it?" He felt protective of those boys, and he wondered if this was what it was like to have a younger brother.

Matty looked at Joey like he was crazy. "*Órale*, man. I'm just bummed that two hottie hockey players are off the market before I even knew they were on it."

"Oh." *Oh!*

Matty smiled. "Yeah. *Oh.* Your gaydar is totally broken, isn't it?"

Joey froze. It suddenly occurred to him that Matty had been subtly flirting with him all night. And probably every other time he'd been there.

"At least now I know why you never took me up on my many, many offers." Matty laughed. "And here I thought you were flirting with me cuz I'm so cute. You're just like that with every one, no?"

Even with his back to the room, Joey felt Liam's gaze on him. He resisted the urge to look back. If he drew his attention to Liam, Matty would know something was up in a second.

Joey sipped at the melted ice in his glass. Matty shook his head and poured a new vodka tonic with a twist of lime and slipped it to Joey.

"On the house, *amigo*." He leaned over the bar, waving Joey closer. "Imma help you out because you're not that bright. That redhead over there?" Matty grabbed Joey's chin, keeping his head still. "Don't look. The hot one with the beard who's scowling at me like I'm touching his candy?"

Joey nodded.

"Uh-huh. You know who I mean. That *papi chulo* wants to do things to you that would make *me* blush." He released Joey's chin and straightened up, casually wiping a glass without meeting Joey's eyes. "Just in case you didn't know. And if you're not interested, send him my way." Matty laughed at the look on Joey's face. "Now you're scowling at me, too." He pushed Joey away. "Go get your man, *mijo*"

"Matty…"

"Don't worry. I won't say anything. But you might want to tell him to take it down a notch."

It took Joey for-freakin'-ever to get across the bar. He kept getting trapped in conversations he had no interest in. Mostly stories about his past that started with variations of "Aren't you the guy who…?"

"Didn't I see a picture of you with Heidi Klum recently?"

"That was for an episode of Project Runway. They were doing clothes for athletes. It's hard to fit these butts you know."

"Remember that Sports Illustrated swimsuit issue party in Vegas? Damn. I can't believe no pictures of that got out."

"You should have seen him Jell-o wrestling down in Cancun. What were you, like 20? Second year?"

"Could you even drink legally?"

"In Mexico he could. The drinking age is white."

He breathed a sigh of relief when he reached his friends. "Hey, you guys want to go back to my room? I'm so over this."

THEY ENDED up in Paul and Robbie's room simply because it was closer to the elevator than Alex's or Joey's room. Joey still had a hard time believing that the couples shared rooms in public. Sure, he and Liam spend most nights in the same room, but they always booked separately.

Then again, those guys were out as a couple, and Joey wasn't out to anyone outside of a few family members and the people in this room. *Technically*, he hadn't even told his parents about him and Liam, but he figured they knew. They'd probably known before he had.

Alex didn't usually come on the road trips. As their figure skating coach, they could probably benefit from having him around more, but he and Sergei didn't like to be away from the babies at the same time. The work he'd been doing with Joey and his line had been paying off in speed and maneuverability, and Coach Williams had wanted them to keep up with it.

Paul poured them all strong rum and Cokes without asking. They were all tipsy, headed for flat-out drunk. God help them if they ever won the cup. Joey hadn't been sober for three entire days the year the Kings had won. Then he'd been hungover for four.

"You're a brave man, Joseph. Coach O'Reilly scares me a little. He's a yeller." Alex was saying. He had the cutest French-Canadian accent. Joey could listen to him talk all day, though since moving in with Sergei, he'd started adding Russian words and phrases into the mix. The more excited he got, the less English he spoke.

"Dude, don't even worry about him," Joey assured him. "Liam thinks you're so pretty, that if your boyfriend wasn't six eight of solid muscle, he'd be asking you out."

"Really?" Alex asked.

"Yes, you really are pretty," Joey assured him.

Alex waved him away. "No, I know that. But are you telling me that crazy Irish man is gay?"

"He's bi," Joey said.

"How did I miss that? I mean, with you..." he gestured at Joey, "it was obvious."

What? Joey almost spit out his drink.

"It's hard to see around Pergov's dick," Robbie said, making Joey choke on his drink. Robbie almost never made crude jokes like that. Maybe it was time to cut him off.

"Plus, he only has eyes for Lucy over here," Paul added, flopping onto the bed and dragging his tipsy boyfriend down with him. "Not that you can blame him. Have you seen his ass?" He aimed a foot a Joey's butt, missing by a mile.

Robbie slapped a hand over Paul's mouth. "Okay. No more for you, Bama. You're cut off."

"Does he really think I'm pretty?" Alex asked with a smile.

"Everyone thinks you're pretty, Pookie," Robbie said.

"Pookie? Don't make me make you do inside edge drills for an hour."

"That hot bartender sure thought you were pretty," Paul added.

"Oh, please," Alex said, popping open the bottle of champagne he'd grabbed on their way out of the bar. "That bartender is totally a bottom."

"Really?" Joey blurted out. "You think? But Matty's so macho."

"And?" Alex asked, lowering the champagne bottle and staring at Joey.

If Joey had been more sober, he would have heard the warning in Alex's voice. But he wasn't, so he didn't. "I don't know. I didn't think he would...I just thought that was what guys, you know, more like you, did."

Alex's jaw dropped, and silence descended on the room.

"Oh, shit," Paul whispered.

"Paul and I switch," Robbie blurted out.

"I'd kind of wondered," Joey admitted.

Paul groaned, covering his face with his hands. He rolled out of bed. "Ooh-kay. I need way more alcohol for this. Hand over the bubbles, blondie."

After filling a glass for himself, Alex passed Paul the bottle of champagne. "So, Joey, tell me more about your theory of bottoming." He held out a hand to stop Joey from answering. "But first, have you ever had sex with a man? Top or bottom?"

"What? No. I mean, not like *real* sex."

Robbie snorted. "He sounds like you did six months ago," he whispered loudly to Paul.

Alex appeared unimpressed with Joey's lack of experience. *"T'es don' ben con.* And what would you say if I told you that Sergei liked to bottom on occasion?"

"No way. I didn't think Sergei would, you know…"

"Well, he does 'you know' sometimes. And in the TMI spirit of the mildly-drunk, let me add that we don't often have, as you call it, 'real sex'."

"Why not?" Paul asked.

Robbie snorted. "You've seen the size of Sergei's dick, right?"

"Good point." He took Robbie's empty glass and filled it with champagne. "We're fancy now. Drink your champagne."

"Wouldn't Sergei be mad if he knew you were telling people that?" Joey asked.

Paul groaned again. "Lucy, man, I love you, but shut the hell up before you dig yourself a bigger hole."

"Because it's not masculine to be the bottom?" Alex asked bitingly. "To be the one who takes it up the ass?"

Between the alcohol and the way his fantasies about Sergei and Alex were morphing in his mind, Joey was having a little trouble keeping up with the conversation. "Um, yeah?"

"And you would be embarrassed if people knew you did that. That you liked it." It wasn't a question.

Joey heard a slap from the bed and Robbie hissed loudly, "Paul

Stonewall Dyson, Jr., you put that cell phone away right this second or so help me..." Paul choked on a laugh.

"Well, yeah." His mouth went dry as the memory of Liam's fingers and the discovery of his prostate cascaded down his spine. What would it feel like to have something...bigger...up there? "You're a figure skater, you're all pretty."

"You mean I'm an *effeminate* figure skater so it's okay if people assume I'm on the bottom. But it's not okay for you because bottoming makes you less of a man?" Alex stated flatly. *"Ok, là, j't'en tabarnak."*

By now the warning sirens in his brain were loud enough to penetrate Joey's alcohol fog. Red lights spun and flashed behind his eyes. DANGER! DANGER! *Fuck.*

"Ostie de crisse." Alex advanced on Joey, brandishing his champagne flute like a weapon. Joey reached for the nearest glass and downed it, gagging on the taste of warm, watery rum and Coke.

"Let me tell you something, you *beau cave.* Anything you do is something a 'man' would do," Alex said, looming over him. Joey always forgot how tall the other man was because he was so slender and so often standing next to Sergei who was a giant, but Alex had a good three inches on Joey and right now he was using every one of them.

"Because you are a *man* and *ergo* anything you do is 'something men do!' Men cry, wear nail polish, are stay at home dads, show emotions, *et oui,* even sometimes take it up the ass. And not just men flying the rainbow flag. Plenty of straight men enjoy getting pegged by their girlfriends."

"I like to get spanked!" Joey blurted out, desperately fishing for a way to redeem himself.

With that announcement, the discussion was over.

Alex collapsed down onto his chair, and dropped his head into his hands. Robbie and Paul laughed so hard, they fell off the bed, gasping for air. Paul ran to the bathroom before he pissed his pants.

"Holy fuck, I love you," Robbie said when he could speak again, grabbing Joey around the neck and pulling him down onto the bed.

After the laughs had died down to the occasional chuckle, giggle, and joke about Joey being a bad boy, they ordered steaks from room service and another bottle of champagne. Wearing real clothes had gotten old in the meantime, so they'd raided Paul and Robbie's meager travel wardrobe for comfy clothes.

Paul wore a green and white Bemidji State Beavers t-shirt and a pair of black boxer briefs. Robbie had a brand new pair of boxer briefs that apparently came with a lecture on sweatshops and overseas labor. Joey didn't pay much attention, pulling on a pair of Thunder sweatpants and rolling up the legs. He'd opted for the shirtless look. He could have gone to his room and gotten his own clothes, but it seemed so far away.

Alex had simply stripped down to his underwear, somehow making it look elegant. Pouring the last of the champagne into his glass, he leaned back in the desk chair he had commandeered and crossing his legs at the ankles, rested his feet on the bed Joey lay on. "So, young Joseph…"

"Dude, we're the same age."

Alex waved the objection away. "Age is a state of mind. And you, my friend are a baby gay dealing with internalized homophobia. Which seems odd given the general level of homo- and bi-sexuality present in the Luciano-O'Reilly clan."

"Dude, I'm not homophobic. I mean, shit, I can't be. I've…I

mean…we've…" He trailed off, finding the bottom of the wine glass fascinating.

"We know *you've,*" he said, waggling his eyebrows. "Well, we'd assumed. Now we know for sure."

"We knew!" Paul called from the bed. "Joey told us first."

Joey wished he wasn't trying to have this conversation while he was drunk, though there was a lot to be said for the tongue-loosening effects of alcohol. "It's just, I don't know anything about being gay," he confessed. "I don't know how to do it. I mean, my sister is gay, and Liam's sister. But they're girls, it doesn't…"

Alex kicked his leg hard. "If you say it doesn't count, I am going to tell Sergei that you said Davy and Tanya were the ugliest babies you'd ever seen."

Joey went pale. "Please don't do that."

"First things first, do you consider yourself gay?" Alex asked. Paul and Robbie looked on with obvious curiosity.

Did he? Probably. "Well, yeah. I mean, I like Liam. I've always been in love with him."

"Awww," Robbie said from the bed. "That's so romantic."

"It is," Alex agreed. "But you could be bisexual, like Coach O'Reilly, or some other thing."

"There are more things?" Paul asked before Joey could.

"Let's table that discussion for Sexuality 201," Alex suggested. "Have you had any kind of sexual encounter with other men besides Tall, Red, and Angry?"

The room heater kicked on with a hiss while Joey searched his memory. "Yes?"

"Is that a question?" Alex said.

"Well, does-"

"Let me stop you right there. Everything 'counts'. So that's a yes, then."

"Yes, in high school."

Paul started making *bowchikawowow* sounds from the bed. Alex quieted him with a glare.

"And you have had similar experiences with the fairer sex, *oui?*"

Joey rolled his eyes. "Not as much as my reputation would suggest, but, yeah. Some."

"Did you like it?" Alex asked.

Joey shrugged. "It's not terrible or anything. I mean, I haven't done it too many times. I'm busy, and you never know if..."

"Gay," Alex said, cutting him off.

Robbie sat propped up against the headboard, with Paul's head in his lap. It seemed to be a favorite position of theirs. Drunk Joey could admit he really wanted to lie with his head in Liam's lap.

Joey sighed. "Yeah."

"You don't have to say anything to anyone else if you don't want to," Paul said. "But let me tell you, eventually you're going to meet someone who makes you want to shout it from the rooftops." He smiled at Robbie.

"Is it worth it?" Joey asked. "I know how much shit you get from people, how much time you spend talking about your sex life instead of hockey."

"You're scared what will happen if people find out?"

Joey nodded.

"I totally get it," Robbie said. "I'm sure we all do. We still get scared."

Much to Joey's surprise, Alex nodded his agreement. "You'd be surprised how homophobic the ice-skating world can be. It's brutal. Ask Sergei about his first boyfriend."

"What about him?"

"It's not my story to tell, but ask him. He likes you a lot, he'll talk to you. Come over one night, meet the babies, pet the cats, and bring him a bottle of vodka. We'll talk."

"I will. I'd like that." Tears pricked behind Joey's eyelids. It had been a long, emotional day, and finding real friends on his team after feeling so alone for so long was going to push him over the edge. Another drink should help.

Paul spoke up from his position in Robbie's lap. "You gotta think long and hard about who you are, what you believe and what makes you happy. There are people whose opinions matter, and people whose opinions don't matter one whit."

"You can't worry about the fans, or even the league. It only matters what the people who love you think. And it doesn't sound like your family will have any problem with you and Coach O'Reilly being together."

That was true. "They won't." They'd get endless shit from their families. Endless. Until they were dead. And then their children would do it, but they wouldn't be mad. "Besides, I think they know. I think they set us up in Tampa."

"Lucky you," Paul said with a trace of bitterness. There had to be a story there; Joey would ask him about it one day. "So, to answer your question, is it worth it? Hell yeah, to be with Robbie, it is."

"Besides," Robbie added, "It's a lot bigger than just me and Paul. It makes a difference to so many kids. I can't even tell you how many letters, emails, and DMs we get from all kinds of kids, telling us how our coming out made them feel better about themselves. Gave them hope. If I, we, can save one kid from suicide, it's worth a million haters."

Room service arrived and after giving the guy a generous tip and some signatures, they dug into the steaks and potatoes and a bottle of complimentary red wine.

"So," Alex said, waiting until Joey had a mouthful of beef. "Tell us more about the spankings."

20

LIAM

LIAM HAD GOTTEN TRAPPED IN A CONVERSATION WITH AN equipment manager from the Coyotes, and it had taken him longer to escape the bar than he'd hoped. Then when he'd gone up to his room, Joey wasn't there.

He either had to be in the boys' room or Pergov's room. He'd started with the boys' because it was closer to the elevator. As he got closer, he could hear the boys laughing from down the hallway and it made him smile. He loved these guys. He loved his job. He loved everyone in this damn hotel.

Laughing at his semi-drunken mental love fest, he found the room. The door was ajar, so he walked in to find Joey coughing on a mouthful of something, and Paul slapping him hard on the back. Alex smirked over the edge of his champagne flute, looking rakish even in his underwear. Tears ran down Robbie's cheeks from laughter. Liam estimated the pink in his cheeks was half laughter, half alcohol.

"Why do you always look guilty when I find you together?" Liam asked. "Are you trying to kill my star forward?" He pulled Joey toward him. A little bit of searching turned up a semi-clean glass, and he filled it with water from the bathroom sink.

"Not after that game," Paul assured him. He'd gotten the assist on one of Joey's goals.

"You all look cozy," Liam said, handing Joey the glass. "Quite the party you guys were having, sorry I missed it."

"Oh, me, too," Alex said sincerely.

Liam picked at the still-warm French fries on Joey's plate. "Alex, Sergei said to come home."

"I was just leaving." Grabbing the half-empty wine bottle, Alex kissed everyone goodnight, including Liam, to his surprise. "I think you're pretty, too," he said with a pat on Liam's cheek. Then he swooped out of the room with a flick of his long hair.

Liam turned and glared. "That's it. I'm officially never leaving you three alone again. From now on, you need a chaperone."

Robbie and Paul looked like they weren't sure if he was really angry or not, so he smiled at them. "Excellent game tonight, boys. You hit it out of the park, couldn't have asked for better."

"Thanks Coach," they replied together.

"Now give me back my player, and I'll make sure he gets to bed safely."

"Yeah," Robbie said with a drunken giggle. He whispered something to Paul, and they both cracked up.

Joey draped his arms over Liam's shoulders and looked at him with a dreamy smile on his face. "You are pretty."

Robbie and Paul laughed harder. Obviously he wasn't going to get any useful conversation out of them.

"Okay," he said, with a pat on Joey's cheek. "Bed time. Goodnight boys. Bus leaves at nine, try to be on it."

"Yes, Coach."

"Got your room key?" he asked Joey.

Joey slapped at his pockets, a look of consternation on his face. Then he smiled, pulling it out of his pocket. "Yes, Coach."

"Good. Go." He swatted Joey's butt as he passed by and Robbie giggled.

THEY NEVER MADE it to Joey's room. Not wanting at all to be alone tonight, Liam steered them to his room. They didn't run into anyone, didn't have to hide from anyone. In a way, it was a little disappointing. He wanted to show off the ridiculous, adorable, insanely talented man next to him and say yeah, he's hot, he's young, he's a superstar, and he's mine.

Exhaustion and alcohol had caught up with Joey, and he was half asleep by the time Liam poured him into bed. He'd refused to wear anything to sleep in and insisted that Liam take off all his clothes, too.

"Fine, you lunatic." He climbed into bed, and Joey rolled into him, wrapping Liam in his arms and draping a leg over his. Liam hummed in appreciation.

"See? Naked is good," Joey said smiling, his eyes closed.

His dark eyelashes almost reached the top of his cheekbones. Liam ran a fingertip gently across them. "Yes, naked is good." He placed a feather-light kiss on Joey's lips.

"Mmm, feels good. Do it again."

Liam did, and they kissed without urgency. Liam slid his hands across as much of Joey's soft warm skin as he could, skimming gently over tonight's batch of bruises and small cuts. His fingers found a knot under Joey's shoulder blade, and he pressed hard against it.

Joey's moaned in a mix of pleasure and pain, and he arched into the touch. He carded his fingers lazily through Liam's wavy hair. "We should fool around," he said through a yawn.

Liam chuckled softly. "We should sleep."

"I could just do you quick," he offered. "I don't want to disappoint you."

"You could never." Liam kissed his eyelids, mentally shaking his head in disbelief at the sappy gesture. What was it about Joey that brought that out in him? Michelle would have killed for that small gesture of affection, but it had always felt so forced. For the millionth time he made a note to call her and apologize for not loving her enough.

Joey's breathing evened out, his chest rising and falling slowly against Liam's. Eventually, they'd have to separate or Liam's arms and legs would go numb. But not yet.

"Do you think Paul and Robbie are in love?" Joey asked just as Liam thought he was sound asleep.

"I do."

"Did you," he yawned again, his words slurred with sleep, "did you love Michelle?"

Liam rolled onto his back, taking Joey with him so that Joey laid with his head pressing against Liam's heart. He ran his fingers through Joey's hair as he searched for an answer that would be both kind and truthful.

"I did. I think I still love her as much and in the same way as I ever did. It just wasn't the way she needed me to love her." Heart fluttering like hummingbird wings, he waited for Joey to ask the obvious follow-up question.

"Do you," he stared before cutting himself off with an even larger yawn. His eyes fluttered shut and his head grew heavier on Liam's chest.

"Do I what?" Liam asked after a few long seconds. He was so ready to answer the question.

"Do you know that Sergei likes to bottom?"

"I—what?"

No answer.

"Jojo?" A soft snore was his only response.

He hadn't known that. Hadn't ever needed to know that. Pinching the bridge of his nose with his fingers, he vowed seriously to never leave those four alone again.

Laughing at the unpredictable thing his life had turned into, he kissed the man responsible for the wonderful chaos in his head.

I do love you, he said silently.

21

LIAM

Transcript from ESPN.com video of interview between Joey Luciano (Thunder center) and William (Ders) Anderson (Thunder right winger):

Ders: Would you say you spend your money wisely?

Joey: Yes.

Ders: Is it true you are in the midst of trying to buy a Rolls Royce?

Joey: No. You're probably thinking of Coach O'Reilly.

(laughter)

Ders: You wouldn't lie on ESPN.com would you?

Joey: No.

(*cut*)

Ders: Name any two people you would go to dinner with.

Joey: Wayne Gretzky and Barack Obama

Ders: Do you not like girls? (*laughter, pause*) You got to meet him when he was President, right?

Joey: With the Kings when we won the Cup.

Ders: Are you single?

Joey: I am.

Ders: who is your favorite ninja turtle?

Joey: Michelangelo

Ders: Do you like horses?

Joey: I like stallions more

Ders: Would you go horseback riding with me?

Joey: No, too much time with you.

Ders: Are we not the bestest of friends already? (*laughter*)

APRIL WAS CERTAINLY THE CRUELEST MONTH IN THE HOCKEY world. By April, the teams were facing one of two scenarios. Half the league was out of the running for the Cup. Players on those teams had to deal with the disappointment of not making the play-offs while staring down the barrel of a post-season summer that seemed to get shorter every year.

By the end of the season, everyone was exhausted. Some guys had been playing injured for the last month or so and would have surgery and recovery to look forward to while they tried to fit in a years' worth of family obligations into two months. Summer was when they had to make up for every wedding, birthday, holiday, and major family event they'd missed during the season.

The players on the sixteen teams headed into the playoffs had to ramp into an even higher gear at the end of a season that had already been long and grueling.

The race to the Cup was an endurance contest for sure. To make it to the final slot and play that best-of-seven series, a team had to grind through two months of extremely intense, emotionally exciting, and physically draining hockey. In playoff hockey, the hits got harder, the fights got more serious, and the plays got more intense.

And the ice got more crowded at practice as the clubs started calling up guys from their AHL teams to bulk up their roster for the playoffs. Some of the guys would be sticking around for next season, some would go back and forth between the clubs, and some would never get ice time in the NHL at all. That was the way it went for AHL players.

Liam hoped Patrick would be one of the players sticking around. He fit in well with the team, and was a solid player with flashes of brilliance that would come more frequently the longer he played.

Liam played with the zipper on his sweatshirt, pulling it up and down as he put the new guys through drills in order to evaluate where they could best fill in for injuries on the main lines and the special teams. As a defensive coach, the penalty kill lineups were his responsibility.

Sergei and Vicky were both in the net on opposite ends of the ice. When Liam blew the whistle for a line change, Alex skated up to his boyfriend. Sergei pushed the helmet back on his head and shot water into his mouth as he laughed at something Alex said. Alex leaned an arm on the crossbar and stood up on the toes of his skates to whisper into Sergei's ear. Sergei laughed loudly enough for Liam to hear him across the rink, then turned and saluted Liam with his water bottle.

Liam blushed and turned away, pretending to find his clipboard totally absorbing. *Damn Joey.* Why had he said that thing about Sergs bottoming? Now Liam couldn't stop staring at Sergei and Alex any time they were together even as he tried desperately to repress the images flashing behind his eyeballs. Not only were they inappropriate, they were fucking distracting.

With the soft scrape of a skate blade and a flurry of snow, Alex skidded to a stop next to Liam. "You keep staring. Is there something wrong with my hair?" he asked.

"No, of course not." Liam answered without making eye contact. Realizing that might seem odd, he lifted his head and gave what he hoped was a normal grin. "You look great as always."

Alex narrowed his eyes suspiciously. "Did Joey say anything to you about the conversation we had last night at the hotel?"

"What? No? Of course not. What conversation? Hotel?" Liam's cheeks heated and he barely resisted hitting himself in the face with the clipboard. *Very smooth, O'Reilly, completely not suspicious at all.*

The laughter that sparkled in Alex's eyes was at odds with his serious expression. "So, he *didn't* mentioned how shocked he was to find out that Sergei likes to bottom every now and then?"

Heat crawled up to Liam's temples, and groaning, he covered his face with the clipboard.

Alex's laugh rang over the sounds of pucks and bodies hitting the boards and the players shouting encouragement to each other. "I'll take that as a yes."

Liam sighed and lowered the clipboard. "In his defense, he was pretty drunk. Despite his reputation, Joey's not really much of a drinker."

"I noticed that." Alex pushed off from the wall, turned a few graceful one-footed figure eights, and skated back to Liam. "Your boy has some issues."

"Don't we all?"

They stood side-by-side against the rail watching the boys skate. Liam used his clipboard for its intended purpose and wrote down any suggestions Alex offered on which improvements each player could use in their skating skills.

When Coach Williams blew his whistle, calling for them to huddle up, Alex turned to Liam with a smile. "Joey also said you thought I was pretty."

"I'm going to kill him," Liam growled.

The look Alex gave him was so wide-eyed and innocent that Liam braced himself for whatever was coming next.

"Don't kill him," Alex said, fighting a smile. "We need him for the playoffs. Maybe just...a spanking." He snorted a laugh before clapping his hands to his mouth.

Oh, he was getting a spanking for sure. Picturing that, combined with his previous mental images of Sergei and Alex, diverted some of the blood in Liam's body down to his dick. He slid the incredibly useful clipboard in front of his groin. This situation had definitely *not* been covered in any of the coaching seminars he'd attended.

"Is it true? Do you think I'm pretty?" Alex fluttered his eyelashes at Liam.

It was more effective when Joey did it, Liam thought uncharitably.

Alex's blond lashes and light blue eyes didn't make half the impression as Joey's thick fan of dark lashes and his big brown eyes did. *God, he had it bad.*

Time to get control of this conversation. There was no way he was going to let a twenty-something figure skater throw him off. Liam had been playing more than one game a lot longer than Alex had.

Throwing a look over his shoulder to make sure Sergei wasn't standing behind him, Liam skated right into Alex's personal space bubble, the toes of their skates overlapping. He'd been told more than once that his stare was intimidating and he wasn't above using it to his advantage.

He didn't touch the other man, but still Alex lifted his chin as if Liam had tapped it with his finger. Making sure he had Alex's full attention, Liam stared into his eyes, then dropped his gaze and gave Alex a slow once-over from head to toe, ending up back at his eyes, which had widened considerably.

"Yes, I think you are very pretty. And if you hadn't started dating my goalie, who is the size of a small mountain, I may have said something about it eventually."

Two small spots of pink appeared on Alex's sharp cheekbones, and his jaw slackened.

Liam grinned.

The sound of someone very large skating very quickly came from behind him. Sergei raced up from behind them and scooped up Alex as if he weighed nothing. "Mine!" he yelled, lifting Alex over his head with both hands.

Smiling wide, Alex stretched out his arms and legs and bent back into a graceful arch. His hair spilled from its messy bun and flowed behind him as Sergei skated around the rink to the wolf whistles and applause of his teammates.

The shrill scream of Andy's whistle split the air. "Alright, alright. Back to work. Flirt on your own time, men. We have games to win!"

Liam shook his head. Back to work for real. He searched the ice for Joey, and he found him in a group with some of the new guys, at least two of whom Liam knew didn't speak much English. They were laughing at Joey as he bounced a puck off the blade of his stick and tried to learn words in Russian and Finnish. They were probably more curse words, but everyone had to start somewhere.

Liam didn't even try to hold back his smile. Yep, he had it bad.

"LUCY, I'M HOME!" Liam called as he walked in the door. Something smelled delicious. "Joey?" He followed the scent to a roasted chicken dinner in the kitchen being kept warm under aluminum foil. The familiar sounds of a hockey game led him to the living room to find Joey lying on the couch watching the last period of the Rangers away-game in Denver. They were down three to one with five minutes left in the third period.

"Hey," Joey said.

"Hey, yourself." Liam bent over the back of the couch for a kiss. He froze for a second at the comfortable domesticity of the whole scene. Were they an old married couple already? Hadn't they skipped a few hundred steps? "Where's Paddy?"

"Vicky's. Where else?"

Liam leaned his forearms on the couch back. "Do you think there's something going on with them?"

Joey paused the game. "I don't know. I hadn't considered it, but now I'm curious. You hungry?"

"Nothing that can't wait until after the game." He shrugged out of his jacket and pulled off his tie. Walking around to the front of the couch, he tapped Joey on the shoulder. "Sit up."

"But I'm comfy," Joey said, burrowing deeper into the wide sofa.

Liam lifted Joey's head with both hands and slid underneath him. "There," he said, letting it fall into his lap. Joey tensed. He ran his fingers through Joey's hair, and Joey relaxed, head heavy against Liam's thighs. "Still comfy?"

"Better," he said with a smile.

Liam bent down as best as he could to kiss him again. "It pays to listen to me. Now start the game. Let's watch the Avs hand the idiots who let you get away their asses."

"GO PUT ON SOMETHING COMFORTABLE," Joey suggested after the Rangers suffered a satisfying defeat at the hands of the Colorado Avalanche. He tried to sit up, but Liam pulled him back down.

"I don't want to move," Liam said. "I'm too tired. Just leave me here to die. Tell my mother I love her."

"Just your mom? Not your father? Grandmother?"

"I like to keep the rest of them guessing," Liam said.

"Hmm," Joey commented.

Should he say it? He'd always loved Joey. He was family. It was a given. But should he tell Joey he was *in love* with him?

Liam twirled strands of Joey's hair around his fingers, pulling gently as he imagined how the conversation would play out. As ridiculous as the idea was, he had to admit to himself that he was in love with the infuriating, stubborn, gorgeous, charming boy next door.

He'd thought he'd been in love with Michelle. This thing between him and Joey was a million times harder and more exciting than what he'd had with her. So it had to be love, right?

Joey sat up, and this time Liam let him go, his hair sliding like knotted silk through Liam's fingers. "Go change. I'm hungry, and I was waiting for you."

"Bossy." Liam closed his eyes and let his head fall back. "I'm so tired. Feed me?"

Joey slapped him hard on the thigh. "Get up, put on some sweats, and I'll make you a plate. If you don't come back down, I'm eating it all myself."

"Fine." Liam groaned as he stood. He really was exhausted. His days grew longer and longer as the playoffs approached. He was looking forward to the few days off they had before the first post-season game. He was going to sleep for twenty-four hours straight.

Promising to do an extra five minutes on the bike in the morning, he took the seldom-used elevator to his second floor bedroom. He quickly stripped, throwing his shirt and suit pants onto the ever growing pile of clothing that needed to go to the dry cleaners. The two overflowing laundry hampers held most of his sweats and t-shirts.

Digging deep into the recesses of the shelves in his walk-in closet, he found an old *Kiss me I'm Irish* t-shirt and a pair of old sweat-pants with bleach stains on them. He made a mental note to talk to the housekeeping agency about keeping a better eye on the laundry.

Downstairs, Joey had plates full of chicken and vegetables set up for them on the kitchen island. "Did you make all this?" Liam asked.

"Hell, no. I'm way too exhausted to cook. I asked Clara to make something super healthy and delicious. Guaranteed playoff fuel." Clara was the team's nutritionist. Her services extended to providing players with meals at home if they wanted them.

"That is the sexiest thing I've ever heard." He grabbed Joey and pulled him in for a quick kiss and grope.

Joey twisted out his grasp. "And even better?"

"Better than food?" Liam slid into one of the stools at the counter.

"I hired a house manager."

"A what?"

"A house manager. She'll take care of, you know, things." Joey shoveled chicken into his mouth.

"Things?"

"Like drying cleaning your suits, throwing out the moldy stuff in the fridge. Making sure the bills are paid, mail taken in, house-keepers taken care of, etc., etc." Joey punctuated his conversation with waves of his fork, like he was conducting an orchestra. "If we got a dog, she'd make sure it got walked and stuff when we're on the road."

Liam frowned. "I don't know. That sounds so pretentious."

Joey put the fork down. "Let's be realistic. I own two places, neither of which I live in. Plus we have the Nantucket place. And we manage both of our parents' homes. Right? And what do you have? There's the house in Scottsdale."

"Man, I miss that place," Liam mused. "It had the best pool. And it was right on the golf course."

"I miss the sex bathroom," Joey said spearing a piece of broccoli off Liam's plate.

"The one with the giant shower with the bench and the free standing three person hot tub?"

Joey nodded. "That's the one."

"Please tell me you didn't have sex in my shower."

Joey raised one eyebrow, then laughed at the expression on Liam's face. "No, I didn't have sex in that bathroom. But I thought about it. Imagine how much use we could get out of it now."

Liam did for one pleasant moment, then returned to reality. "Yeah, so I still own the Scottsdale house. The apartment in St. Paul is on the market."

"Anything in Montreal?" Liam had purchased a nice condo after his first game with the Canadiens.

"No, I sold that one. It was too hard to deal with internationally."

None of the kids talked about it in public, but between the Lucianos and the O'Reillys, they were building quite the real estate empire.

Growing up, their parents had regaled them with horror stories about professional athletes who had gone bankrupt a few short years after retiring. Based on the astronomical rise in the value of the Boston homes since their purchase at the turn of the century, their families had pounded it into their heads to invest in real estate.

Besides the properties he and Joey owned, Jimmy, Nino, and Deano had property in places they had lived. Jimmy owned a home in Brazil and an apartment in Sweden. Even Patrick had purchased a nice house in Bakersfield.

"Between us, we have three cars that need to be kept registered and insured," Joey continued. "There are just so many little things that have to be done, and we need someone to handle it."

Liam still wasn't convinced. It sounded ridiculous to have to pay someone to run their lives. Didn't they have enough people doing that already? "We already have lawyers, business managers, agents, and a housekeeper."

"Yes," Joey said. "And now Antoinette will deal with them for us. Imagine it. One person who knows everything. 'Hey, Antoinette, did my mother get a birthday present?' 'Yes, Mr. Luciano, I sent her a lovely purse.' 'Antoinette, did the Nantucket house get winterized?'"

"How come you call her Antoinette but she has to call you Mr. Luciano?"

Joey rolled his eyes. "I don't care if she calls me butthead as long as someone knows what's going on. You know we don't have time, especially during playoffs."

Liam sighed "I know. You're right. It was easier when…" He trailed off.

"When you had Michelle," Joey finished for him.

Liam shrugged apologetically. "It sounds bad when you put it that way. I didn't realize how much she had been taking care of until she was gone. I'd forgotten."

"I get it," Joey said. "I swear that's half the reason so many guys get married young. Someone has to run your life during the season. Agents can work deals, but they can't get your car serviced. Dealing with all of this by yourself sucks. And we've twice the work now with no one to help. So, I hired us some." Joey shifted in his chair. "What? Why are you looking at me like that?"

"Because you're amazing," Liam answered honestly. Competent adult Joey was as sexy as the Looch on a breakaway.

Joey rolled his eyes.

"No. I'm really impressed with everything you did tonight."

"You mean everything I paid someone else to do," Joey said with a hint of self-deprecation.

"No. You saw a problem and took care of it, competently and efficiently. I didn't do it. It didn't even occur to me. Without you, I would have lived with chaos. Thank you. Thank you for dinner, too."

Joey blushed and looked down at his plate with a smile.

"Want to take some wine down to the hot tub?"

Joey's bright smile was answer enough.

22

LIAM

"FUCK," JOEY SAID AS HE SUNK DEEPER INTO THE HOT TUB. "MY everything hurts."

"I remember that feeling." Liam lowered himself into the water. They were going in *au natural*. If any passersby had a problem with it, they could just keep passing by. Though anyone getting a glimpse of Joey naked would be more likely to come closer than complain.

The hot tub lived inside a glass-walled cabaña right on top of the seawall at the bottom of his property. Liam would be the first to admit it was one of the main reasons he'd bought the place. Besides housing a six-person hot tub, the cabaña had a sleeping loft tucked under its peaked roof and a full bathroom.

Liam had spent hours in the hot tub, watching pods of orcas gliding majestically past him on their journey up the Puget Sound.

Sitting there with Joey, Liam felt extraordinarily lucky. A line from a poem he'd had to memorize in high school floated through his head. *For thy sweet love remembered such wealth brings, that then I scorn to change my state with kings.*

God, he was turning into such a sap. Next thing you knew he'd be carving *L.O.+ J.L. 4Eva* on a tree somewhere. Maybe he was having a midlife crisis. A has-been hockey player on the downhill slide to forty falling in love with a Lamborghini-driving hotshot ten years younger than he was. A midlife crisis two-fer. Buy the boyfriend, get the sports car for free!

It didn't feel like it though. Truthfully, being with Joey felt so right it scared him.

"My agent called," Joey said jolting Liam out of his self-reflection.

"And?"

"And the Thunder made an offer."

"Really? Already?"

"You didn't know?"

"I had no idea. Was it good?" They had turned the inside lights off, the better to see the night sky and moonlight reflecting off the water, so Joey's face was shadowed. Liam couldn't gauge his emotions from the flat tone of his voice.

"Yeah, it was good."

Liam took a long sip of his wine to buy some time. "You going to take it, or wait to see the other offers?" There was no doubt there would be more offers.

"What do you think I should do?" Joey asked.

Liam pulled himself up to sit on the tiled edge of the tub, his feet dangling in the water. "I think you should do what's best for you. What did Bartlett say?" Toby Bartlett was Joey's and Liam's agent.

Joey slid over to Liam and leaned against his knee. "I thought you were the one who knew what was best for me?"

"I did say that, didn't I?" He wrapped his hand around the back of Joey's neck, gently massaging the tight muscles with his fingertips. "In this case, I know what I think. But I can't make this decision for you. No one can. It's too important. Besides, you don't need any help when it comes to professional decisions."

Joey pushed back against his hand. "God, that feels good. Can you at least give me your opinion?"

Liam tugged at the hair on the back of Joey's neck, pulling it straight and watching it bounce back up. The little pieces got so curly in the humidity. "All I can tell you is what I want, and you have to know I'm far from neutral about this."

Joey ran his hand up and down Liam's leg under the water. He was quiet for so long, Liam wondered what he was thinking. Did he have any doubt that Liam wanted him to stay?

"Tell me what you want," he asked finally, watching his hand as it moved over Liam's skin.

Liam slid back into the water and pulled Joey onto his lap. He wanted to make sure Joey heard what he was saying without filtering it through a lens of insecurity. "I want you to stay. I'm too old to play games, to dance around this. I want you here, on my team, in my house, and in my bed. Live with me. Do this with me."

Joey's hands tightened on Liam's shoulders, and his eyes widened. "Really? You want me to stay? As what? A...a...couple?"

"As in *I'm in love with you and I can hear the universe laughing at me for it*. Or maybe that's just our brothers and sisters laughing. I don't care how or why it happened, but it did. Stay with me. Be with me."

Normally, Liam could read Joey like a book, but his expression was unreadable. Liam's heart skipped a beat. Had he read the whole situation wrong?

"Do we have to tell anyone?" He asked finally.

Okay. That wasn't quite the reaction Liam had been expecting to his confession. He ran his hand through his hair, then smoothed his beard. "You don't even have to say yes. You're free to go anywhere." Maybe Joey didn't love him back. He hadn't even considered that. Maybe he *was* the arrogant prick his siblings accused him of being.

"No! No. I want to. I do. I...I love you, too. Not in a I've known you my whole life and I love you like a brother way. But like, the real thing. I think."

"You think?" Liam ran his hands up and down Joey's back. He leaned forward to lick some of the water off the tattoo on Joey's chest, and Joey wiggled. Combined with a lapful of naked Joey, Liam like that response a lot, so he did it again.

"Don't mock me," Joey said wrapping his arms around Liam. "I've never said it to anyone before, idiot. And this might sound weird, but I feel the same way about you that I have for a long time. So either I've been in love with you for as long as I can remember, or I'm not in love with you now and I'm just delirious."

"Now this decision I can make for you." Liam slid his hands around Joey's firm ass cheeks. "You are in love with me."

Joey pulled far enough back to look him in the eye. "Oh, really, Mr. Smug. You're that confident?"

"I am." He kissed his way over Joey's collarbone and up his neck, his beard leaving light pink scratches on Joey's skin in its wake.

Joey cursed and ground down against Liam's lap. *Perfect*. "Do you believe me?" Liam asked.

"That I'm in love with you or that you're in love with me?"

"Both."

Joey smiled from ear to ear. "Yeah, I almost believe you. You should probably try to convince me more."

"Really?" Before Joey could answer, Liam gripped his ass tightly, and stood up with Joey in his arms. He turned them, and sat Joey down on the edge of the hot tub. "I can do that," he said sinking to his knees. With a hand on each knee, he spread Joey's legs.

"Fuck." Joey reached for Liam, his cock starting to perk up.

It only took a few strokes of his hand for Joey to get hard.

Liam wasted no time in getting Joey into his mouth. Sliding his mouth rapidly up and down Joey's cock, he wrapped a hand around the base and stroked hard like he was going for a land-speed blowjob record. They were a little too exposed for him to draw it out the way he loved to. It reminded him of the rushed awkward blowjobs of his teens behind bedroom and locker room doors. It was kind of hot.

Joey's fingers tightened in Liam's hair and his hips jerked, strong thighs shoving his cock deep into Liam's mouth. "Oh shit," he whispered. One shove pushed his cock against the back of Liam's throat and he coughed.

"Oh, fuck, sorry!" Joey pushed Liam's head off of him. "I'm sorry."

Liam shook his head and sunk deeper in the pool. He tilted Joey's cock down, changing the angle. "Do it," he said, wrapping his mouth around the head.

"Oh, fuck." Joey touched Liam's face reverently as he slowly pushed in.

It had been a long time since Liam had done this. He tried to relax his jaw and throat against the intrusion. The desperate whimpers spilling from Joey's mouth, and the way his harsh breaths echoed off the walls of the cabana were worth the tears forming at the corner of Liam's eyes.

The drag of Joey's cock across his tongue as he slowly slid in deep, blocking Liam's breathing for a half-second before pulling out just as slowly was driving Liam mad. His cock bounced in the water. Sweat and steam dripped from his temples and down his back.

"Faster, Jojo," he said when Joey pulled out. "We ain't got all night." Joey's eyes glittered almost black in the moonlight and his nostrils flared wide as he sucked in air.

"Fuck." He leaned back, resting his weight on one arm, and gripped Liam's hair with his free hand. Another whispered fuck was the only warning he got before Joey's hips pistoned off the tile, shoving his cock in and out of Liam's mouth until he could barely breathe around it.

Liam's world narrowed to the slap of water against the tile, the sounds of Joey's moans, and the feel of him filling up Liam's mouth. He'd forgotten how fucking good this could feel. He moaned around the cock in his mouth, fingernails digging into Joey's thighs.

Joey's back arched one final time and his muscles locked up, thighs clamping shut around Liam's head as he came hard. Liam coughed and swallowed and willed himself not to come. He had plans for the rest of the night.

"Holy shit," Joey said with a shudder as Liam sucked on his over-sensitive dick. From his prone position on the wet tile, he pushed weakly at Liam's shoulder. "Stop. I can't. Fuck."

Liam let Joey's cock slip out of his mouth, and kissed his inner thigh before pushing himself up on the edge of the hot tub. "Now do you believe me?"

Joey nodded. "You're probably going to have to remind me in the future. The very near future."

"Let's go inside and I'll remind you in a way you won't be able to forget for a while."

"Excellent."

23

JOEY

THEY WALKED BACK TO THE HOUSE IN THEIR BATHROBES. AS THEY hit the flagstone patio Joey stopped Liam with a hand on his arm. "We don't have to tell anybody about us, right? Not officially?" Worry put a line between his eyebrows.

"We don't have to announce it to the society pages or anything," Liam assured him.

"Coach Williams?"

"Pretty sure he already knows. He told me he has a strict don't ask, don't tell policy. If you want to keep it private we can."

"It's just I think the timing is bad. With the playoffs and everything, the last thing we need is something like this. More gay guys on the Thunder. People are going to be mad. People are going to yell for you to be fired, they're going to think...well all kinds of things about you and me."

When the public found out about them, there would be a backlash. There would probably be a backlash with the league, too.

"I know. But, Joey, listen to me." Liam tugged Joey to him by the ties on his robe. "When we are ready to go public, I'll deal with it. I'll protect you. And people can think whatever they want. Do you know why?" He cupped Joey's chin in his hand and tilted his head up.

"Because I'm worth it," Joey said seriously.

"Damn straight." They shared a sweet and lazy exploration of lips and tongues. Then Joey slid his hands into Liam's robe. Liam's hands tightened on Joey's arms. "Upstairs," he growled.

"I love when you get growly," Joey said with a laugh. Dropping his robe, he strolled stark naked past Liam.

Liam swatted him on the ass. "You'd better hope Paddy isn't home or you'll scar him for life."

"Like he hasn't seen me naked before. Besides, he's gone for the night."

"So how much does Semerad think you're worth?" Liam asked as he managed to climb the stairs and grope Joey's ass at the same time.

Joey made him wait until they got to the office at the top of the stairs to answer. Why waste a good reveal? Turning around, he leaned against the doorjamb with a feigned nonchalance and a shit-eating grin. "Five million a year, with a five million dollar signing bonus. For six years."

Liam shouted. "Fuck yeah!" He picked Joey up and swung him around like a girl in a romantic comedy. Sometimes Joey didn't mind being shorter.

"Did you sign it?"

"Not yet, they're taking care of it tomorrow or the next day."

Liam crowded Joey against a bookcase, his arms on either side of him trapping him in place; not that he had anywhere else he wanted to be. "You are so fucking sexy," Liam said, voice deep and gravelly.

Joey pulled the sash on Liam's bathrobe. "I knew it. You just love me for my money."

"No," Liam said as he pressed himself full length against Joey. "I only love you for your body. And your brain. And your spirit. And your heart." He splayed his hand over Joey's chest.

Said heart was beating so hard, Liam had to be feeling it in his palm. Joey swallowed, breath coming faster. "Really?"

Liam grabbed his ass cheek hard and squeezed. "Do I really have to prove it to you again?"

Though he had had an orgasm not five minutes ago, Joey's cock jumped at Liam's words. Of course, Liam noticed, what with plastering himself all over Joey. He smirked. "I guess I do. Go upstairs to your room. I want to look at the stars tonight. I'm going to run by my bedroom and I'll be right up. Be naked."

JOEY SAT PROPPED up against the headboard in his boxer shorts, arms crossed behind his head. Liam walked in, his strong body gloriously nude, and his arms full of clothes. He raised one eyebrow when he saw Joey. "I thought I told you to be naked?"

Joey raised an eyebrow back at him. "So you did. What are you going to do about it?"

Liam's eyes narrowed, and he dropped the clothes on the nearest flat surface. Joey winced as his dick stirred at the look on his face as he stalked toward the bed. Liam crawled over the foot of the bed and straddled Joey's shins. With one swift move, he dragged the offending boxer shorts down Joey's legs.

"What?" He stared at Joey's dick, then burst out laughing. "What the fuck?" He flicked at the bright green ring with two huge google eyes Joey had wrapped around himself. His cock hung out between the eyeballs like an elephant's trunk. "Where did you get that?" He could barely speak over laughing.

"Found it in the stadium." He clenched his muscles, making his eyeball-topped dick bounce up and down. "Like it?"

Liam laughed long and loud, in a way Joey hadn't heard him do in years. He doubled over, tears slipping from the sides of his eyes for the second time that evening. "Oh my god. Only you, Jojo. Only fucking you."

With a few deep breaths, he got himself under control. Grabbing Joey behind the knees, he dragged Joey down until he lay flat on the bed. The look in Liam's eyes as he kneeled over Joey took his breath away.

It also thickened his cock. "Ow! Ouch!"

Liam's eyes widened in alarm, as Joey reached for the toy on his cock, and he started laughing again.

"Don't laugh, you dick, it fucking hurts." It took him both hands to pry the ring apart and off his dick. Joey tossed it across the room. "Worth it though."

Liam shook his head and lowered himself until they were pressed together head to toe and breathing each other's breath. "I love you," he said.

Oh god. He did. This was really real. It was happening. Joey's focus narrowed like it did when he was headed toward the crease during a shootout. All he could see was Liam's face. "I love you, too," he whispered. "It's terrifying."

Liam smiled softly. "I know." Then he kissed Joey.

It was the best kiss of Joey's life. For about six seconds until his mind starting throwing crap at him.

Liam loved him. Astounding. But what did that mean? Did it change things? Was it forever? No, that would be ridiculous. Could he tell Gina? Should he tell Gina?

Liam pulled away. "I'm sorry, am I boring you?"

Joey grabbed his shoulders. "No, god, no. I'm sorry. It's my brain. It won't shut up."

Liam kissed Joey on the forehead. "I remember you saying that as a kid. My brain won't shut up. What's it yelling about now?"

"It's worried that everything is going to change."

Liam rolled to his side and tucked Joey up under his arm, Joey's head resting against his chest. "Nothing is going to change. We don't have to say anything we don't want to and it's nobody's business. When Sergei and Alex got together, they didn't make a big deal about it, right?"

"No. But Robbie and Paul…" Joey ran his fingers through the curly hair on Liam's chest.

Liam rubbed soothing circles on Joey's back. "You weren't here, so you don't know what was going on behind the scene. The boys actually weren't together when Robbie planned his press conference. He told me he was doing it for all the gay kids who were thinking they had to choose between playing hockey and being true to themselves. Paul chose to join Robbie up there for his own reasons."

"Wow. They really are brave guys."

"Yeah, they really are. And somehow they already know about us. And Alex and Sergei know. As a matter of fact..." Liam's tone changed to something a little more playful but with a hint of danger in it that made the hair on the back of Joey's neck stand up. "As a matter of fact, they know a little bit more about us than they should. I wonder how that happened?"

Distracting Joey with a completely unfair combination of kissing Joey on the neck and fondling his cock—which was very quick to get back on board the let's have sex train—Liam maneuvered him onto his stomach.

Liam ran his hand down the curve of Joey's spine, making a detour to trace the black lines of Joey's tattoos as he always did. Goosebumps sprang up on Joey's skin from the feather-light touch. He felt Liam skim gently over the bruises littering his body. The recent ones were deep red and blue, the older ones turning ugly shades of green and yellow as they faded.

"God, your fucking ass is perfect," Liam growled against Joey's ear as his palm slid over the curve of Joey's ass. He reached down to cup Joey's balls, and he whimpered, spreading his legs wider.

Liam wound the fingers of his free hand through Joey's hair and nipped at his earlobe. His grip on Joey's balls tightened. "How do you think that happened?" he asked.

"Wha...?" Joey's brain was rapidly going offline. "How? What?"

"Pay attention." Liam yanked his hand from between Joey's legs and laid a sharp, stinging slap on Joey's right cheek.

"Ow!" Joey jerked up at the unexpected pain. Or he tried to, but Liam's grip on his hair jerked him back down to the bed. "Fuck" he muttered into the pillow.

"I had a very interesting conversation with Alex today," he said conversationally as he caressed Joey's skin, soothing a bit of the pain.

"Oh." Joey did not like the direction this was going in. Well, his brain didn't. His cock was all for it, and he couldn't help grinding as unobtrusively as he could against the mattress.

Liam's fingers skimmed down the crack of Joey's ass, ghosting over his hole. Joey shivered, the hairs on his arms standing up stiff, his muscles tense.

"What do you think we talked about?"

"I don't know," he answered, though he was terrified he did. Again, his cock transmuted the tiny frission of fear into arousal and he felt it growing harder beneath him.

Liam slapped him again, the crack loud in the quiet room. "Think harder."

"Skating?" Joey's back tensed in anticipation of the next slap.

Liam didn't disappoint, giving him two quick smacks on the other ass cheek. Joey couldn't hold back a moan, and Liam chuckled.

"One more chance." He flicked his fingers against the tender skin. "Think real hard."

Joey gasped, grinding into the bed, the pain and the anticipation and Liam's intense focus only stoking the fires of his arousal. "About me?"

"Very good." Liam kissed his shoulder. "About this ass, specifically.

What you like having done to it." He spanked Joey, fingers spread, hand flat. "And what you don't." He dragged a finger up the crack of Joey's ass again, this time stopping directly on his hole and rubbing gently, almost imperceptible.

Joey's breathing was loud and harsh in his ears.

"That is not the kind of information I appreciate anyone else knowing. This ass is mine, and you do *not* need to be talking to anyone else about what I do or don't do with it."

"I'm sorry!" Joey cried. "I was drunk!"

"Yes, you were." Liam sat up. "I told you to go to bed, remember? Not go hang with the boys and get drunk and talk about your sex life. That was bad decision number one." He grabbed the pillows from the top of the bed and tapped Joey on the hip. "Lift up."

When he did, Liam slid the pillows under Joey's hips so his back was arched and his ass on full display.

Oh god. Joey's fingers scratched on the sheets.

Liam spread Joey's legs and positioned himself between them. "I counted three instances of poor decision making. One, not listening when I told you to go to bed; two, making ignorant comments about something you have never experienced; and three, telling personal details about my life to my players. Did I miss anything?" He ran his hands up and down Joey's thighs, squeezing them hard. "Fuck, I love your legs," he muttered. "Did I miss anything?"

"No," Joey answered quickly, squirming against the pillows. "That's it. I swear."

"You know there are consequences for your poor choices. What should you have done?"

"Talked to you first."

"True." Slowly, he slid his hands all the way up Joey's back until they rested on the bed on either side of his head. His hard cock pressed tight and insistent against Joey's ass, and he rocked his hips against Joey. "I'm thinking you need another spanking to remember. Though, I'm not sure it's punishment enough seeing as how you told half the team how much you enjoy it."

"No!"

"No, you don't enjoy it? Or no, you don't deserve it?"

The slow glide of Liam's dick against the crack of his ass was driving Joey crazy. His hips kept making these jerky thrusts into the pressure and then back against the not-nearly-firm enough surfaces of the pillows. "Oh, god," he groaned.

His fingers bit into the sheets, and Liam covered Joey's hands with his, gripping them tightly. He thrust against Joey in a parody of fucking until all rational thought fled from his mind. His breath blew hot against Joey's ear and the bed creaked softly in rhythm with his thrusts.

"Fuck." Joey's grip on Liam's hand tightened and he pressed back hard against his cock, seeking friction anywhere. The feeling was maddening, driving him close to the edge without ever being enough to push him over. "Liam, please."

Abruptly, Liam sat up, straddling Joey's thighs. His cock rested gently against Joey's ass. Joey shivered with the rush of cold air on his sweat-covered skin.

"Please what?" He grabbed one of Joey's cheeks in each hand and spread his ass open. With a grunt of approval, he thrust forward, dragging the full length of his cock across Joey's opening.

Joey's inhale was deep and shaky. "Oh god. Let me come. Please. Make me come."

"Consequences first. You willing to be spanked so you'll remember to think before you speak?"

"Yes. Please. God yes."

"Good boy." His gave Joey's cheeks an approving squeeze. Then he cursed softly and did it again, kneading the flesh as if lost in the sensation.

Every movement drove Joey's cock into the pillows beneath his hips, and he bit down on his forearm to keep from making any sound that might make Liam stop.

He couldn't stop his chest from expanding with the force of his breaths, or the trembling of his legs.

"Okay," Liam said a little breathlessly. "Six each side. That sound fair?"

That sounded like he was getting off easy, pun certainly intended. "Yes. Do it."

"Ask me nicely."

"Please."

The mattress rocked slightly as Liam shifted his weight. "Count carefully. I might lose track."

Joey nodded and reached for the headboard, holding onto the curved iron bars.

Liam's hand came down on one side and then immediately on the other, the sound of flesh on flesh loud and unmistakable but the impact itself not too hard.

"One," Joey gasped out

Two and three followed swiftly, with no breaks in between. Sweat beaded on Joey's forehead and his back. His chest heaved as he breathed heavily through his nose. Liam rubbed his ass, somehow soothing the pain and turning it into something that sat warm and heavy in his groin.

"Okay?" Liam asked.

Joey nodded.

"Three more. Ready?"

"Yeah." He was. This time was completely different than the last time in the library. There were definitely going to be orgasms after this. A little more force in the right direction and there might be one *during*.

He wriggled, trying to stretch out the muscles he'd been clenching. He may have paid more attention to his lower back muscles than strictly necessary.

Liam's hand came down sharply on the top of his thigh. "Stop that."

"Ow, you fucker." That one hurt.

"I know what you're doing, and cut it out. You don't come until and unless I say you can. You take these next three like a good boy and I might let you."

"You dick," Joey said with a breathy laugh. "Get a fucking move on then."

Liam sat back on his heels. "I'm sorry. What was that?" He did not sound amused.

Oh, shit. "Nothing. I'm sorry. Please don't stop."

"I don't think you're taking this seriously. You embarrassed me in front of players I am responsible for. Risking my effectiveness as a coach at a very important time."

Joey stilled. He had, hadn't he? The things he'd said could have undermined Liam's authority as a coach, made the guys take him less seriously. Not that he thought Paul or Robbie would, but stuff had a way of getting out. "I'm sorry. Really. I am."

"Prove it. "

"How?" Joey asked. He'd do anything.

"I'm sure you'll think of something." Liam rolled onto his back and crossed his arms behind his head, his body laid out like a feast.

Oh damn. Joey sat on his knees next to Liam, trying to figure out where to start. He was bad at sex, really didn't know what to do. He slid his hands up and down the body until Liam took pity on him.

"I'll give you a hint. Start with that gorgeous mouth."

Okay, Joey could do that. He kissed Liam on the mouth gently. Liam didn't move his hands from behind his head. "Sorry," Joey repeated and then began kissing his way down Liam's body. When he kissed over Liam's nipple, Liam shuddered. Joey had never done that before to Liam; probably only once or twice to a girl. He flicked at the nub of flesh with his tongue, tentatively biting gently until it hardened. Liam seemed to enjoy it so he kissed his way across his chest and repeated the action on the other side. "Like that?" Joey asked.

"I like a lot of things," Liam said. "And I expect you to find them all. Eventually. Keep going."

"I'm sorry," Joey said as he kissed his way down Liam's legs, avoiding his cock completely. He made his way to the top of Liam's foot and then kissed his way up the other leg. Liam's hard cock brushed against his chin.

"Joey," Liam said warningly. Joey grinned against Liam's skin, and then, taking hold of his cock, licked his way back up to the top, swirling around it like it was a lollipop.

"Yeah," Liam said. "Good boy."

Joey was growing very addicted to the feel of Liam's cock in his mouth, not something he'd ever thought he say. He loved how much Liam loved it. He got so turned on hearing Liam's moans and grunted words of praise. He explored different techniques, cataloging the way Liam responded to each nip, lick, and suck. Feeling brazen, he pushed Liam's legs apart and bent down to lick at his nuts.

"Oh fuck," Liam said. "That's perfect." So Joey did it again keeping a hand on Liam's inner thigh to keep his legs spread. He dragged his tongue back up slowly to the tip of Liam's cock then took it in his mouth, sliding down on it as far as he could, which wasn't very far yet. Still, Liam moaned like he was loving it.

Reaching down, he pulled Joey up by his hair, tugging until Joey straddled his waist.

Joey winced slightly as Liam's hair rubbed against the tender skin of his ass. "Do you believe that I'm really sorry yet?"

"Maybe." He slid his hands around Joey's hips, feeling the heat of his skin. "You feeling okay?" he asked. "Not too bad?"

"A little tender," Joey confessed.

Liam grinned and stroked Joey's cock. "Doesn't seem to be affecting certain parts of your body now."

Joey arched forward, pushing into Liam's hand with a pleased moan, and then hissed as he sat back down.

"Turn around," Liam said with a slap to Joey's ass. "And try not to kick me in the face when you do."

"I'm fucking graceful as a gazelle, dude," Joey said, executing the tricky maneuver without damage to either of them.

"Head down, baby," Liam said, guiding him with a hand between Joey's shoulder blades.

Oh, fuck, that was hot. Joey let himself be maneuvered until his mouth hovered over Liam's cock, and his ass was embarrassingly near Liam's face.

"Hmm," Liam said. His finger traced a pattern on Joey's cheek. "I can see my handprint. I like that. You could get a new tattoo. 'Property of Liam O'Reilly'," he said.

Joey laid his head on Liam's hip. "Oh, that would go over great in the locker room."

"Hold on," Liam said. He wrapped an arm around Joey's hips and rolled them both on their sides.

"What are you doing?" Joey said through his laughter as Liam stretched his arm as far as he could and yanked the nightstand drawer open.

"Fuckin'," Liam muttered, his hand flailing blindly. He tossed a bottle of lube onto the bed but kept searching. Joey was one second away from distracting him with another lick to his cock when he gave a triumphant *aha*! and rolled them back to their original position.

Joey couldn't see what he had.

"Hold still," Liam said.

"Bossy tonight," Joey said, sliding his hands up and down Liam's legs, enjoying the feel of his soft hair tickling his palms. Something wet and cold touched his ass cheek, and he jumped up.

"Just tonight?" Liam spanked his butt lightly. "I said hold still."

Joey held still while Liam wrote something on his ass. "What the heck are you doing?"

"Marking my territory, babe. Making sure you remember from now on." There was a click as Liam presumably put the cap back on the marker. He tossed it on the floor.

"I think you need to get back to showing me how sorry you are. While I remind you of how much you liked certain things on Christmas Eve." He dragged his finger over Joey's hole. "I seem to recall you begging me to fuck you."

"Oh shit." He shuddered. "You remember that?"

"I remember every second with you, Jojo," he said, voice rumbling in his chest. "Less talking, more blowing."

Joey got to work, and Liam slipped his hands into the creases of Joey's thighs and pulled him gently back and down.

Then his beard scratched against Joey's cheeks and his tongue flicked against his hole.

He pulled off Liam's cock, gasping. "Oh, my god."

Liam chuckled against Joey's body, and Joey shuddered. "You can't..." he started. But apparently, Liam could. His tongue did amazing - possibly illegal - things to Joey's ass. Joey had never expected to have this done to him, it sounded disgusting. But it felt fucking amazing.

"Oh shit." He gasped and moaned as Liam rimmed him, completely abandoning his blowjob. "Oh, fuck, Liam. Fuck." He found himself grinding back against Liam's face, no matter how hard he tried not to.

When his brain came back on line, he would make a note to be embarrassed by the whines and whimpers coming out of his mouth, and the way he writhed against Liam's incredibly talented mouth. He ground his rock hard cock against Liam's chest. "God, Liam. Fuck, I need...ugh." He panted for breath. "God. I need more. Something."

"Yeah?" Liam rubbed his ass firmly with one hand and reached for something with his other. There was the flick of a cap, and cold lube dripped down Joey's ass crack. Oh, shit.

A whine got caught in his throat as Liam slowly pushed the tip of his finger in. "Good?"

Joey mumbled something incomprehensible and pushed back against the probing finger. "More. Please." God, it felt so good.

"Uh huh." Liam slid his finger out and Joey whined with the loss. He exhaled on a moan, resting his head against Liam's hip again as Liam slid what felt like two fingers in torturously slow. "Oh, fuck. Oh, god."

"Have you changed your mind about bottoming?"

"Yes. God." He wanted it. He was ninety-five percent sure. "I'm sorry. I was an idiot," he gasped out between Liam's thrusts. "Fuck me, please."

"Are you sure? It's not too unmanly for a macho hockey player?" He spread his fingers and stuck his tongue in between them as far as he could go.

Holy Jesus and all the saints. That was it. When Joey felt that cool slick intrusion he was done.

He grabbed Liam's cock and jerked it fast and hard. Liam's head thumped back onto the pillow and he shouted.

"I will beat you to death with Sergei's twig if you don't fuck me right now."

Liam moaned and slapped at Joey's hip. "Turn around. Fuck, baby, turn around."

Joey turned around much less gracefully than he had last time. Liam locked his arms around Joey and pulled him down, kissing him within an inch of his life. His legs clamped against Joey's hips, and he pushed his tongue past Joey's lips before Joey could protest.

With one of Liam's arms wrapped around his waist like an iron band, and the other holding Joey's' head still, Joey could find nothing to complain about.

They gasped into each other's mouths, sliding their cocks together, trapped between their bodies. Joey's heart pounded as Liam rolled them over so Joey was on his back.

Liam smoothed Joey's sweaty hair back from his forehead, looking at him with so much love in his eyes, it drove any remaining doubt out of Joey's mind. "I'm going to make it so good for you, Jojo, you'll cry for all the years you wasted not getting fucked." He kissed him again, and Joey clutched at his shoulders, fingers pressing in hard.

"C-condoms?" Joey stuttered.

"I don't need them. You? Clean bill of health?"

"Yeah, yeah, of course."

"Do you want them?"

Did he? No. He needed to feel all of Liam. "No."

"Okay. Roll over," Liam said gently.

Joey shook his head quickly. "No. Like this. I want to see you. I need to see you."

"It'll be easier."

Joey locked his legs around Liam's hips. "No."

"Okay, okay." He kneeled up, propping one of Joey's legs on his shoulder and then reverently kissing his ankle.

Liam squeezed more lube onto his fingers and over Joey's opening. Two fingers slid in with a squelch that would have made Joey laugh if he had any air left in his lungs.

Three fingers took a bit more effort, but no pain, just an intense stretch that had Joey gasping and moaning.

Liam pumped his fingers hard, pushing them in deep. Every time Joey's muscles tightened up and he got close to orgasm, Liam slapped him on his tender skin. A sweaty trembling mess reduced to begging and babbling, Joey clutched any part of Liam he could reach.

Breathing heavily, Liam lowered Joey's leg to the bed, and sat back on his heels stroking his cock. "Fuck, Jojo. I'm going to come just from hearing you beg. I should fucking record it."

"Please, please. Please." It was all he could say.

"Okay, okay." He dragged a pillow towards them, and lifting both of Joey's legs to his shoulders, slipped the pillows under his hips and shuffled forward until his cock rested against Joey's hole. "Ready, baby?"

"Please."

"I love you," Liam said staring into Joey's eyes.

"I love you, too." The words caught in his throat as Liam pushed forward slowly. "Oh. Fuck," he whispered.

His legs trembled and he was grateful he didn't have to support his own weight. Oh god, it was so much. It felt so big. So intense. *Oh, fuck, oh, fuck* he chanted silently. He had no breath left to even moan.

Slowly, Liam slid almost all the way out. "Okay?'

Joey nodded, not trusting his voice.

"Yeah?" Liam's breathing was harsh and strained.

"Yeah. Yeah. More."

Liam pushed forward, rolling Joey's hips up even more. "That's it, baby," he said in low soothing tones. "That's it. God, so good. You're so good for me."

The words sunk into Joey's soul at the same time as Liam's cock pressed its way into his body.

His groin flush against Joey's body, Liam held himself up with one shaking arm. He was inside Joey as deep as he could be. Joey's ass clenched around the intrusion, sending shockwaves of pleasure through his groin.

Liam groaned, his hips shuddering forward in short, sharp thrusts. "Fuck, Jojo." Each move pressing his cock against Joey's prostate and pushing a yell out of him.

"Move. Move," he begged. "More."

Liam shifted his grip on Joey's leg, searching for more leverage, and they both gasped. He slid out and slammed back in hard and fast. Joey shouted and his eyes rolled back in his head. "Oh, god. Oh. Fuck. Yeah."

Joey's arms flailed, yanking the sheets off the corners of the bed, grabbing at the headboard and scratching over Liam's skin as he searched for something to ground him while Liam pounded him into the mattress.

There were only the sounds of flesh slapping against flesh, moans and shouts of pleasure, and the blood pounding against Joey's eardrums; the whole scene not so much different than earlier, when Liam had paddled his ass. Liam was taking care of him again. Always.

"So close," he moaned. "Need to come." His legs were bent almost to his shoulders, making it hard to breathe, but the loss of oxygen only added to the painful pleasure building in his entire body.

He felt the orgasm pounding everywhere; his balls, the base of his spine, the back of his throat, the pit of his stomach, and in his palms.

Liam dropped down, bracing himself on his forearms, his hands tangled in Joey's hair.

Joey wrapped his arms and legs around him, feeling him trembling. His cock reached deep inside Joey in this position, and he ground himself hard against his body.

"Joey," he whispered. "God." He pulled back slowly, dragging a groan out of Joey. "Touch yourself, baby. Come for me." One arm collapsed as he pushed back in just as slowly.

Joey wanted to grab his cock, but he couldn't seem to let go of Liam. Liam would have bruises tomorrow for sure. Joey's heart pounded.

"Oh, Joey," Liam breathed reverently. "Joey." He rested his forehead against Joey's. "Joey."

Joey came with a cry, Liam's name on his lips.

He couldn't breathe; muscles locked up, hips arching off the bed, and his legs clamped around Liam. He was vaguely aware of Liam pounding into him, forcing out burst after burst of come as his fingers dug bruises in Joey's thighs.

When he finally stopped coming, brain nothing but white noise, muscles boneless and not under his control at all, Joey felt Liam go rigid above him, caught in his orgasm.

Liam shot deep inside, filling him up, and nothing had ever felt so right.

Liam collapsed down on him with a muffled curse. He thrust erratically into Joey, giving him aftershocks so big they almost qualified as separate orgasms. Joey yelled with every thrust.

Eventually, he grew soft and slid out, but neither one of them moved. They held each other, trembling and gasping, for a long time.

JOEY TWISTED AROUND to see his ass in the mirror. Water from the shower dripped down his back and over the very obvious handprint on his ass. That in itself was bad enough, but what really put the cherry on the sundae was the 'property of Liam O'Reilly' scrawled across his ass in black marker.

"How do I get Sharpie off skin?" Liam asked his phone. It was his third attempt to get the sentence out without dissolving into laughter. "I like it. I think you should keep it,' he said while the phone did its job.

"Shut up, Judy," Joey said with a scowl. "It's not coming off! Not going to be so funny tomorrow in the locker room."

"I'm sorry! I thought it was the dry erase!" Liam sat on the bed scrolling desperately through his phone. "Okay, the internet says to get Sharpie off of skin - nail polish remover, rubbing alcohol, or hairspray."

"Do you have any of those things?"

"No. But the Safeway up the road is open twenty-four hours. What was Antoinette's phone number?"

"I'm going to kill you."

"I'm going, you big baby."

"Come over here and let me paddle your ass red and see how you feel."

"I think you feel pretty good," Liam said with a smirk. "It sounded like you were enjoying yourself."

Joey laughed. "I admit it. I feel fucking great. But I think I'll stay pantless for a while."

"Good, that's how I like you best."

"Perv."

"That's how you like me best." He gave Joey a quick kiss between the shoulder blades and left whistling under his breath.

Smug bastard. Thought he was all that just because he gave Joey amazing orgasms. Joey grinned with the memory of the last two, maybe Liam had a small point.

THE DOOR to the bedroom opened, rousing Joey from his doze. "That was quick," he said, pushing up on his elbows and turning to look over his shoulder at Liam.

It wasn't Liam. "Holy shit," Patrick said with a laugh. "Oh my god." He whipped out his cell phone.

Joey had been lying on his stomach on the bed in nothing but a t-shirt. He was chilly and his butt still stung. "Fuck!" He grabbed for a blanket, a pillow, anything to cover him.

"Oh damn." Patrick snapped a few pictures then ran from the room, Joey hot on his heels.

"I'm going to fucking kill you!" Joey shouted as he pounded down the stairs, cock flapping in the wind. "Delete those fucking photos!"

"No way, Lucy," Patrick called over his shoulder. "This is blackmail material for *life*."

"You fucker." Joey stopped running and listened for a hint where Patrick was hiding. His voice had come from the back of the house, he better not be headed outside. Sneaking quietly around the big square pillar separating the kitchen from the den, Joey almost caught Patrick as he jogged through the room. "Fuck!" he yelled as Patrick's shirt slipped through his fingers.

"Too slow!" Patrick called right before he slammed his foot into the side of the couch. "Oh, fuck me!"

Joey tackled him to the couch and tried to pry the phone out of his hands.

"Get your naked ass off me!" Patrick yelled, stretching out his arm to keep the phone away from Joey.

"Give me that fucking phone," Joey grunted, poking his fingers hard into Patrick's ribs. The entire O'Reilly family was incredibly ticklish. It was their Achilles' heel.

"Not fair!" Patrick curled into a ball to protect his ribs. They struggled, neither one able to get the upper hand. The front door slammed and they froze.

"Oh fuck," Patrick said, still laughing. He shoved Joey, and they fell to the floor, Patrick landing on top of Joey and knocking the breath out of his lungs. Joey closed his eyes, waiting for Liam to lose it on his brother.

Instead, Liam walked calmly over to them, a plastic bag hanging from his hand. "Patrick," he said in a low voice, "what have I told you about touching things that belong to me?"

"Don't do it?"

"Don't do it."

"And what does it say on Joey's ass?"

"Property of Liam O'Reilly," he snickered.

"Exactly." Liam hauled Patrick up by the back of his collar. "So hands off." He kept his hand twisted in the shirt as he turned Patrick to face him. With an expression that promised death, he shook Patrick. "And there had better not be any pictures on that phone."

"Or what?"

"Or I'll tell mom that you were the one who stole the bottle of wine she and dad had gotten on their honeymoon and were saving for their fiftieth wedding anniversary."

Patrick paled, and Joey sucked in a breath. That was the deepest secret the kids had ever kept. They had known the penalty would be severe – breaking Jeanie's heart.

"You weren't even in the house! How do you know it was me?"

"I have my ways." He released Patrick, who staggered a step away, then he reached down for Joey's hand. "Now no pictures, right?"

Patrick crossed his heart. "There aren't. There won't be. I'll delete them. I swear."

"Good." He put his arm around Joey, who was caught somewhere between mortification and awe that Liam had, well, basically claimed him so publicly. It was only Patrick, who knew they were fooling around, but it counted.

He couldn't help but wonder how it would feel to tell the whole world. Maybe he should start with the team.

After the playoffs.

24

JOEY

PADDY posted in **QUICK QUESTION**

VICKY: Dude, did you mean to send this to me?

PADDY: isn't it hilarious. That's what I came home to last night.

VICKER: Did you mean to send it to everyone in your family, too?

JIMMY changed the name of the chat to **PADDY'S WAKE**:

Dude, you are so fucking dead, I can't even say how dead you are.

NAT: Should we wear black?

EMAIL FROM VOICEMAIL: You have 10 new voicemails.

Transcription 1: hahaaahahahaahahhahha

Transcription 2: oh my fucking god you <unintelligible> unbelievable <laughter>

Delete voicemail

Delete voicemail

Delete voicemail

SWEAT DRIPPING DOWN HIS FACE, JOEY JOGGED TO CATCH UP TO Robbie on their way off the ice after practice. "Hey, Rhodes, hold up."

Robbie stopped halfway down the tunnel. "S'up?"

"Just wanted to say sorry again." He'd been so caught up in the play, he hadn't heard the coach's whistle blow to end the scrimmage, and he'd caught Robbie completely unaware, hitting him smack on the numbers and sending him sprawling on the ice.

"It's okay. I know it was an accident. Actually, there's something I've been wanting to ask you." They were alone in the tunnel, most of the guys were still on the ice.

"What?" Joey asked.

"Are you having problems hearing lately?"

Shit. Joey hadn't counted on anybody else noticing. He'd thought he was covering it pretty well. He'd been expecting some hockey-related question or something about how to handle public appearances and endorsement offers. Paul and Robbie had been getting a bunch of those from companies trying to promote their inclusivity. Subaru had been the first.

Robbie's cheeks turned pink like he was embarrassed to be asking such an invasive question, but he powered on. "It's just that I noticed that you turn your right ear to people when they're talking."

Joey tried to look confused as if he had no idea what Robbie was talking about. "Really? I do that?"

Robbie nodded. "And, and, in like crowds. You mostly just kind of like nod and smile."

"I'm a happy guy," Joey said with a grin.

Robbie pulled off his helmet and wiped his forehead, pushing his auburn hair back from his face. He really was a cute kid. Joey was glad he had Paul, they made a good couple. But damn, he was perceptive.

And brave, because he didn't drop the subject when Joey frowned. Robbie waved at Hubs and Triple D as they jogged down the tunnel, waiting until they were out of sight to turn back to Joey. "Look, I'm not trying to put you on the spot. You might not even notice that you're doing it. But I have a lot of hard of hearing friends, and I just notice stuff, you know."

Joey's best plan was to bluff, pretend the whole thing was news to him. "Huh. You're right. I hadn't noticed. It's just so loud when everyone's around, you know? I probably just spaced out. I have a little cold; my ears are probably just clogged up. I'll ask the doc for something to clear them out."

He was talking too much, he knew it, but he couldn't seem to stop himself. Robbie looked like he was going to say something when they heard Patrick bellowing down the hall. Moving as quickly as they could in skates on dry land, they headed towards the locker room.

"What the fuck? Who did this?" Patrick was yelling. "Who put this here?" A torn piece of paper with hockey tape trailing from the corners fluttered in his hand as he stormed out of the shower room. Hubs and Triple D snickered in the corner, elbowing each other as they got dressed and looking extremely amused with themselves.

He would not want to be them right now. Patrick was about to go nuclear on their asses. What the hell could be on that paper?

"Hubs? D? It had to be one of you fuckers."

Joey grabbed the paper out of Paddy's hand as he stalked towards the two. When he saw the picture, the blood ran from his face. He felt light-headed and grabbed onto Robbie for support.

Robbie turned Joey's hand so he could see the page for himself. "Oh damn," he whispered, eyes wide.

Joey's red ass stared out at him in glorious Technicolor; Liam's name clearly legible on it. Patrick had managed to get Joey's face in the photo, too, so there was no doubt who was on the bed. Someone had printed the picture out and taped it to the shower room wall with a caption reading *'Have you seen this ass? If found, please return to Coach O'Reilly. Reward'*.

Joey couldn't breathe. Patrick was still yelling at the top of his lungs and everyone from everywhere was running into the locker room, including Liam and Coach Williams.

Joey's knees actually gave out, and Robbie grabbed him, holding him up.

"What the hell is going on here?" Andy bellowed. "And don't tell me nothing." Everyone froze.

Patrick whipped his head around to stare at Liam. He had the front of DiDiomete's jersey gripped in his fist. Joey caught Liam's gaze, of course, and Liam eyebrows lifted in alarm. He must look like shit.

"I got him," Robbie said, hustling Joey past Liam. As he did, he slipped the piece of paper into Liam's hand. "Here," he said quietly.

"O'Reilly," Andy yelled. Both Liam and Patrick turned. "Both of you, out of here."

Joey wanted to ask Robbie where they were going, but he couldn't seem to get enough air into his lungs to breathe, let alone speak. His thoughts fragmented, splintering in a thousand different directions. Liam would hate him. Everybody knew. It was over. He had to run, had to get away. His heart raced, pounding in his chest until he thought he must be having a heart attack. Fear burned through him, making his body sweat and his vision blur. His legs trembled, threatening to drop him to the ground. Only Robbie's arms kept him upright.

"Paul!" Robbie yelled down the hallway. "Help me."

A shrill tone rang inside Joey's ears, the loudest and most painful attack yet, and the ground lurched under his feet as a wave of vertigo crashed over him.

Sheer willpower was the only thing keeping him conscious. If he passed out now, they would send him to the hospital for sure and then everything would be over.

His fear-soaked brain fixated on two thoughts: everyone hated him, and he wasn't going to the hospital. If he did, the story would be all over the internet before he got discharged.

Joey felt himself being pushed down onto a bed and his stomach lurched. Without warning, he leaned over and vomited on to the floor. He was sweating rivers of salt, oceans of sweat. He was going to drown.

Hands pulled at his clothing, tugging off his shirt, his pads, and he shivered in pain and let them toss and turn him like a rag doll.

Oddly enough, the nauseating vertigo and deafening ringing in his left ear cut through the chaos in his brain, bringing a little clarity in its wake.

He wasn't dying; he was having a panic attack. It had been so long since the last one, he'd forgotten how truly awful they were. He'd thought they were gone forever.

"Joey. Joey. Can you hear me?" the doctor asked.

He nodded, and his stomach lurched under another wave of nausea. He closed his eyes and tried to take deep breaths like the therapist had suggested. Anything to physically calm down his body.

"What happened to him?" the doc asked Robbie.

"I don't know. There was some...something...a fight. In the locker room. Paled. He got pale and then started shaking. Like, like those little dogs and there was yelling and Coach Williams yelled."

"Panic attack," Joey forced out, not really concerned about anyone finding out about his problem. Anxiety was so far down the list of things to be embarrassed about now. He lay back on the bed, throwing his arm across his eyes to block out the light. He inhaled deeply, shuddering, and counted. *One-two-three-four*. He let it out through clenched teeth. *Four-three-two-one. I'm okay, I'm okay*, he repeated mentally. *I'm safe, everything is okay.*

No, it fucking isn't, another part of his mind yelled. *It's fucked to hell and back.* His laugh sounded crazed even to him.

"Panic attack?" The doctor asked. "You've had them before?"

Joey nodded. "Not…not in a long time…years. Five?" *Breathe in, hold it, breathe out.* "Six?"

"Can you take a Xanax? Vicodin?"

"Not…not Vicodin." He pushed out through chattering teeth. "Itches."

The doctor laughed, like seeing a player break down in the locker room was an everyday occurrence. Maybe it was. God knew Joey had seen it more than once. "That's pretty common. Xanax, then?"

Joey didn't want to. He didn't like the way it made him feel, or maybe he liked it too much. Then he heard Liam's voice above the general clamor. "Where is he? Where's Joey?"

"Yes. Please," Joey said. He was swallowing the pill when Liam barged into the treatment room.

"What's wrong?" Liam asked to the room as a whole.

"Panic attack," Paul said. "He's fine. Going to be fine. Right?" He directed that to the doctor.

"Absolutely. He'll probably sleep soon, though. I'll keep him here for a while. Keep an eye on his heart rate, blood pressure. He could go to the hospital for testing if he wants."

"No," Joey said adamantly. "No hospital. I'll be fine. Just give me, give me an hour."

"Everyone out," Liam said firmly. "Now."

Paul and Robbie hightailed it out. The doctor looked at Liam. "Please, I need a minute," Liam told him.

"Fine. I'll be back in a few to check on him." He shut the door behind him as he left.

Joey braced himself for the yelling. He turned his head, not wanting to see whatever was in Liam's eyes.

"Hey," Liam said softly, sitting down on the bed and putting his arm around Joey.

Joey jerked away. "No! They'll know. They…we can't."

"I think that cat is way *way* out of the bag," he said completely seriously, but he stood up anyway, sticking his hands in his pockets as if it was the only way to keep himself from touching Joey.

"I'm sorry," Joey said.

"It's not your fault. It's fucking Paddy's fault. I'm going to kill him." Liam's voice dripped with rage. Joey had never seen him so angry. "This could fuck up…" he trailed off. "Sorry. I'm sorry. Jojo. Jesus, you just had a panic attack, and here I am—"

"Everything. It could fuck up everything."

"We'll handle it."

Joey steamrolled him. "We, we have to conduct ourselves," he took a deep breath. It felt good, so he did it again. He listened to the ringing in his ear, high and piercing and he realized he'd been hearing and ignoring it for weeks.

"Jojo? Babe?" Liam sat down next to him and put a hand on his head. "Are you sure you're alright?"

Joey let himself enjoy Liam's hand on him for what might be the last time. "We have to conduct ourselves 'on and off the rink'... really good. Moral, honest, all that Boy Scout shit. And 'refrain from conduct detrimental to the best interest of the Club, the League, or professional hockey generally.'" He closed his eyes.

"You memorized that?"

Joey nodded.

"Joey, that's just...they aren't talking about your personal life... what we did...do...That's between us, it doesn't affect the team at all."

The drugs slid their calming, warming tendrils into his brain and bloodstream, and he welcomed the calmness they promised. He hoped it would put him to sleep. But Liam was wrong. "No? No effect? So this is nothing? Andy's not waiting to read us the riot act? No one is, is, *talking* about us? The team, the equipment manager? The Zamboni guy? Security? No one?"

"Fuck, Joey. I don't care about that. I only care about you."

Joey laughed bitterly. "But I care," he admitted, keeping his eyes closed so he didn't have to see Liam's expression. He shivered as the adrenaline drained out of his body as the attack tapered off. Thank God it had been a short one. His muscles would ache later, and his head was already pounding, but that was okay. The Xanax wouldn't let him worry about that.

"You really don't care at all that everyone knows we're fucking," he asked Liam. "And that I let you spank my ass until it's red and then write on it like a drunk frat boy?"

Liam sucked in a breath and paced the room. Joey opened his eyes and watching him stalked back and forth like an angry tiger. Liam exhaled, ran both hands through his hair, and then yelled up at the ceiling. "Fuck!" he roared.

"That's what I thought," Joey said when Liam finished yelling.

"Fuck," Liam repeated softly.

Joey picked nervously at the blanket, staring at the thin cotton as if it were the most fascinating thing he'd ever seen. "I think, maybe, we should really think if us being together, like that, is a good idea." Saying it made him want to throw up, but he had to say it.

He heard Liam's sharp inhale. "What? Like, at all?"

Joey was spared having to answer by a sharp knock on the door.

Andy walked in without waiting for an answer. "Joey, how are you doing?" he asked. His expression was compassionate, but Joey could read tenseness and anger in the tightness of his mouth and the wrinkles on his forehead.

"I'm okay, Coach."

"No, he's not," Liam said.

Andy turned a glare on Liam. "I need to talk to you in my office."

Liam turned pale, but his mouth thinned with determination. He stuck his hands in his pockets and nodded.

"Now, get out of here, so I can talk to Luciano alone."

"Sir."

"Out O'Reilly. My office. Be there. Grab us some coffee. And if you have anything stronger in a desk drawer, bring that too."

Joey laughed, surprising himself. "You'd get along with my Nonno Lollo," he told Andy. The drugs must really be kicking in now. It was probably the best time for Coach to scream at him.

"I've met Lorenzo many times, remember?" Andy said. "He's a great guy. Loves you, all of you, very much."

Liam made a sound and Andy rubbed his forehead. "Out. Now."

Liam left.

Joey closed his eyes with a sigh and waited. He heard the scrape of a chair as Andy pulled one over and sat down next to the bed. "How are you really feelin' kid?"

"Fine, Coach."

Andy made an exasperated sound. "Fuck *fine*. Me and the whole team just saw your red ass with O'Reilly's name on it. Something I never needed to see. Wanna try again?"

Fuck it. He'd asked, so Joey would give him the truth. "You wanna know? Scared. Like a total moron. Fucking humiliated and I want to puke again. If I could find a way, I'd never leave this room again."

"Good."

Joey snorted and opened his eyes. "Good?"

Andy leaned back in the chair and closed his eyes. "At least it's what you really feel. You're always managing things, controlling what people see of you. Always got this mask on, Joey, this wall between the world and the real you."

Oh fuck. A tear slid from the corner of his eye. *Goddamn it.* He hadn't been prepared for that. Andy waited quietly, giving him space, but Joey had no response.

Andy sighed and stood up. "And Liam." He shook his head. "Always so worried what people think of him. Both of you are so fucking smart and talented and so goddamn insecure in your own special fucked-up ways. Come to think of it, you're probably perfect for each other. No one else could put up with either of you."

To Joey's horror, the laugh he reached for turned into a sob.

Andy patted him on the shoulder. "It's okay, son. We'll figure it out. It's going to be okay, you hear?"

Joey nodded.

"And do you believe me?" Andy pressed.

Joey's mouth opened and shut. He didn't. Not really.

"That's okay. 'Hear me now; believe me later'," he quoted in some horrible fake accent. "Get some sleep, and I'll find someone to take you home."

Joey pushed himself up on his elbows. "No, Coach. I'm fine. I'll be fine."

"Yeah. I don't think so. You're benched tonight. I'm scratching you for tonight. The doc will check up on you tomorrow, but you rest up over the break." Today was the last game of the regular season. They had four days before the first playoff game in Seattle. Thank god for small favors.

"Yes, Coach." It was all he could say.

The doctor came back into the room and after a brief consultation with Andy, cleared Joey to go. He handed Joey a pill bottle with some more Xanax in it. "I'm not letting you drive home, though."

"I'll find someone to take him home and stay with him," Andy offered.

"Jesus, Andy. I'm fine. I swear. I'll just sleep, no need for a babysitter."

Joey rested his head against the window of Alex's red minivan. Alex hadn't turned the radio on and the silence stretched uncomfortably between them.

Two car seats were strapped to the middle row of chairs, and general baby detritus littered the floor. It reminded Joey of being a kid and being wedged in the middle of the third-row seat because he was the youngest. He was hit with a wave of homesickness like he hadn't experienced since his first year in L.A.

"Do you want to get something to eat?" Alex asked as he pulled onto the highway. "I can stop somewhere?"

He should be hungry. There were leftovers in the fridge and he could probably whip up a protein shake or something, but it all seemed like so much effort. He thought about the empty house waiting for him, and the empty hours stretched before him while he sat out a game and waited for Liam to come home and tell him he had to move out.

"Can I stay with you and Sergei tonight?" he asked Alex. "I know it's an imposition, but I don't want to be at Liam's house, and I don't want to be alone."

"It's not an imposition at all. Really. We'd love to have you. You can see the babies."

Joey smiled. The kids were damn cute. They were at the roly-poly pudgy baby stage and laughed at everything. "As long as I don't have to pet those creepy cats of yours." They had no hair, it was just weird, and they stared at Joey like they were peering into his soul.

"Torvil loves you. I can't be responsible for her snuggling."

"Fine."

"Want to go by the house and pick up some clothes? Toothbrush? Any extra sauce you might have lying around?"

Joey laughed softly, glad for Alex's company. "I think you're the one who is hungry."

"*La*, that sauce is *incroyable*."

"I think I have some in the freezer. It's the least I can do. You're letting me crash at your house."

"It's going to be okay," Alex said as he pulled into the driveway of Liam's beach house.

Joey shook his head and opened the door. Everyone kept saying that, but he didn't see how that was going to happen.

25

LIAM

From The Detroit News April 17, 2018

Detroit – The Detroit Red Wings will not bring back assistant coach John Torchetti next season.

Torchetti, 53, oversaw the power play and forwards. His two-year contract expired after the season.

The power play ranked 24th in the NHL (17.5 percent), a mild improvement over the 2016-17 season (27th, 15.1 percent).

The Red Wings finished 28th overall in goals (2.59 per game) this past season.

HOW THE FUCK WAS HE SUPPOSED TO FIX THIS? LIAM SCRUBBED AT his forehead as he walked down the hallway. He didn't actually have a headache, but it felt like he should. He'd spent so much time in the locker rooms and hallways of rinks of all sizes, he barely noticed his surroundings anymore, but right now it felt like all his senses were on high alert. He couldn't block out the scent of too many sweaty men in too small of a place, the faint smell of ice, laundry detergent, and rubber mats.

His hearing picked up every squeak, thud, and whispered voice. Like the two coming from around the corner of the corridor.

"It's real. I'm telling you it's a real photo," D was saying in a loud whisper.

"No way," Hubs said emphatically in the same tone. "It's Photoshopped. No way Coach would do that. The Looch is a player. Plus the Looch ain't gay."

Liam slowed down to listen, a greasy ball of anxiety forming in his stomach.

"Coach is bi though," D argued. "Maybe he changed Looch's mind?"

"I don't think it works that way, moron."

"Maybe." Hubs sounded unconvinced.

"Is there a male cougar?" D asked, voice fading as they walked away. "Coach ain't the sugar daddy 'cause you know Looch makes way more money."

Liam sighed and leaned against the wall, gently banging his head against the concrete blocks.

Someone was coming down the hall. Time to put his game face on. He opened his eyes bracing for whatever might come. It was Patrick. Guilt was written all over his face."

Liam pushed off the wall, grabbing his brother's arm. "I'm going to fucking kill you." He shoved Patrick. "My office. Now."

It was hard to wait until the door was closed to yell.

"What the fuck, Paddy?" His voice was hoarse from the effort it took not to yell.

Patrick held his hands up in the face of Liam's anger. "I am so fucking sorry. I sent it by accident! I posted it on the wrong thread. I thought I was only sending it to James. I'm so sorry."

"James?"

"McVicker. That's his first name."

"Whatever." Liam paced as much as he could in the small room, trying to get his temper under control. "Well, you didn't. So what are you going to do about it?"

"I don't know. What are you going to do about it?"

"I don't know. Some kind of damage control. It's a fucking mess, Paddy." He knew Patrick hadn't meant to send the picture, but that didn't undo the damage. His reputation had already taken a blow with Joey's way-too-detailed conversation but at least that had just been with Robbie and Paul. Two guys he knew would keep their mouths shut. Way more people had seen this photo. At least one guy he'd heard spewing some homophobic bullshit to a friend when he'd thought no one was around.

"You gotta come clean," Patrick said. "You gotta own up to it."

"No." Liam shook his head in a vehement denial. "No way."

"Why not? Are you embarrassed?" Patrick crossed his arms over his chest and leveled a glare at Liam.

"Yeah, I'm fucking embarrassed!" What a fucking stupid question. Who wouldn't be?

Patrick's eyes narrowed. "That's low, Judy. Just fucking like you. Joey's good enough to fuck in private but—"

With two steps, Liam shoved him against the four-drawer file cabinet. "Not that way, you asshole. I'm embarrassed by myself! He makes me fucking crazy. When I'm with him, I do shit I would never do. I can't think right when I'm around him. I haven't been careful. And he's been telling me to the whole time."

He let go of Patrick's shirt, turning his back and pacing more. A small metal trash can got in his way and he kicked it hard. It hit the wall with a satisfying clang. "If anyone should be embarrassed by the relationship, it's Joey. He could do way better than me. Way better." Blowing air out of his cheeks, he walked over and righted the trash can. "You know," said without making eye contact as he picked up the paper that had spilled out of the can. "He's not exactly pushing to go public either. Last night he made me promise not to tell anyone." He said the last part like a confession.

"I'm sorry," Patrick said with something close to pity in his voice. Great. Just what Liam needed. "I'm sure he's just trying to figure stuff out. I mean, no one even knew he was into guys until, well, you know."

"He knew," Liam muttered unkindly.

"Did he? Really?"

Liam bit back a *fuck you*, knowing Joey's hesitance to embrace this new part of himself wasn't Patrick's fault.

"But it's going to come out," Patrick said. "It always does. Better you control the message."

"Damn it, don't you think I know that? He just wanted to wait until after the season. Besides, it won't come out if there's nothing to say," he said bitterly. Now that the first rush of shock and anger were passing, hard reality was making itself known. This setback had probably scared Joey so far back into the closet, Liam wouldn't be surprised if he got married to some puck bunny next weekend. Hopefully, they didn't have any Vegas games on the schedule.

He'd be lucky if Joey made eye contact with him from now on, let alone stayed with him. "I'm going to get fired, too," he said.

"If the Coach asked if you were in a relationship with Joey, would you say yes?"

"Right now I don't fucking know, Paddy! It's a big fucking deal, okay? It could fuck up both of our entire careers."

"You know what I think?" Patrick got right up into Liam's space, poking him in the chest hard. "I think you're a fucking coward whose priorities are fucked up. Paul and Robbie came out in public and they're kids!"

"No one cares about them!" Liam yelled. "They're rookies!"

The door to his office swung open, and Andy shoved his way in. "Both of you, shut up and calm the fuck down." He shut the door.

Patrick and Liam backed up, unconsciously standing side by side. Andy pointed at Patrick. "You, butthead, I assume, without knowing anything, that this clusterfuck is your fault?"

"Well, it's not like I was…" He trailed off in the face of Andy's withering glare. "Yes, sir. I accidentally sent that picture out to the wrong people."

"Why the fuck would you send it to *anyone*? Why in the fuck would you even take it? Liam's kinky sex life is none of your fucking business!" he roared.

"I know, sir. I just…"

"I don't want to hear it. Just go out there, and act like it was a joke, okay? Tell Hubs and DiDiomete and whoever else that it was a fake. Can you do that?"

"Yes, sir."

"Okay, now, give me twenty minutes with my assistant coach here and we'll get this day back on track."

"Yessir." Patrick scurried out without a backwards glance.

"Let's go get a cup of coffee," Andy said after Patrick had gone. "Show your face, act like nothing's wrong."

Liam nodded. "Okay."

Walking into the players' lounge felt like he imagined walking into a junior high locker room with a kick me sign taped to his back would. His shoulders ached with tension as he waited for the coffee machine to fill his cup.

Players moved in and out of the lounge looking for food or to kill some time between PT and massage appointments and workouts. He nodded and smiled at every 'hey Coach" tossed his way and prayed he looked normal.

A few of the guys looked at him twice, and he heard one quick whispered conversation, but no one said anything directly to him.

"Let's talk in my office," Andy said.

Liam followed obediently.

Andy shut the door behind him and motioned Liam to a chair.

"Nothing's out, you know." He said "No one outside this arena knows anything. Not yet."

Liam placed his coffee cup carefully on Andy's desk. "They will, though. Someone will leak it. Not everyone on this team is happy with Robbie and Paul you know. It's not all sunshine and roses."

Andy's expression was sympathetic. "Only a few people saw it. It was in the players' bathroom, not even in the main locker room. Truthfully, if you and Patrick had only kept your heads, it could have been passed off as a joke. A badly Photoshopped joke. Which is what Hubs and D thought it was."

"So I heard."

"From what I was able to get out of them, only they and McVicker got the original photo. And only a handful of players saw the poster those morons put up. Now, I am going to have to address the team soon."

"What are you going to tell them?"

"That's what we're deciding right now, you and I." Andy pulled some sugar out of a desk drawer and dumped it in his coffee.

"What do you think I should do?"

"About this situation or about you and Luciano in general?" Andy looked up at the ceiling, exhaled, and looked back at Liam, running his fingers through his hair. "So close. We were so close to the end of the season."

Liam waited for Andy to say something else.

"Think you and Luciano can keep quiet for the rest of the season?"

That had been the plan, but for some reason hearing the coach say it was like sandpaper on Liam's already shot nerves. He was so tired of hiding. "So if someone asks me if I'm in a relationship with Joey, I say no?"

Andy leaned forward, staring Liam in the eye. "If someone asks you if you are *fucking* one of your *players*, you say no!" He leaned back and took a deep breath. "I'm going to work very hard to make sure no one asks that question. No one on the team, no one in this building and definitely no press."

"Am I going to have to lie about this until one or both of us retire?" Liam took a sip of his coffee to stop himself from speaking.

"How serious is this thing?" Andy asked.

How to answer that? Liam could feel his every cell of his body telling him to go be with Joey right now. "Very serious."

"Of course it is. Nothing with both of you involved would ever be anything but intense. Why did I even ask? I can't believe I even have to be having this conversation. Oh, and for the record, I did not see that photo. I made damn sure of that."

"Oh, thank god," Liam said, shoulders slumping. They drank their coffee in silence for a couple of seconds. "I don't know what to do," Liam admitted. "I love him."

Andy's eyebrows rose to his hairline. "I should fucking hope so. I would hate to think all this trouble is just for some fling."

"Okay, okay. Let's break it down. The Boys just came out in a press conference. Sergei and Alex didn't; they don't make a big deal of it, but they don't hide it. No one's business but their own, but they aren't going to deny it. But you and Joey aren't them."

"That's what I told Patrick."

"Joey is already a publicity lightning rod. Half the fans want to fuck him, half want to punch him. Little old ladies love him and men tell their boys to be like him. When he comes out, if he comes out, and admits to being in a relationship with his coach, all that's going to change."

"I know. Don't you think I know? And he knows it best of all."

"What does he want to do? Have you talked?"

"He wants to wait until after playoffs to say anything. Do we even have to tell people?"

"You're going to have to tell Semerad, and the lawyers and the PR team at the bare minimum. And eventually, if you guys stay together, it's going to come out. This problem isn't going to go away."

"Sometimes I think he'd stay underground until he retired," Liam said bitterly.

Andy looked sympathetic. "That's something you guys are going to have to work out. As your boss, I'll say you have to decide what is right for you. As your friend, I say, say nothing. Act like nothing happened. Lay low until we're done this season, okay? Just, try to reel it back a little. I'll do damage control here. You can tell whoever you want the truth. And you can tell the world for all I care, after."

"What about my job if I do? What do you think will happen? "

"I don't know. Luciano's already signed his contract. You haven't."

"I didn't know I had one."

"Well, you do. I was going to talk to you about it later. I knew you'd want to read it over, maybe negotiate, make a counteroffer. Have your lawyer and manager or whoever look it over, but I suggest you sign it right away." Andy pulled a stack of papers out of his desk for Liam to sign. He handed Liam the contract and a pen.

"Will it hold?" Liam asked flipping through the pages.

"I don't know." Andy rocked back in his chair, toying with a pen. "They might question your judgment, your morals. Say you're too young to coach. But I don't know if the brass will care if we win the fucking cup, eh? Or at least the conference finals, so how about we concentrate on that and shelve this shit for later, okay?"

"Yeah okay." Liam would be happy if they never had to speak about it again.

Andy stood up, shoving his hands in his pockets. They both had work to do. Club business didn't wait for any personal crisis, no matter how embarrassing. "I sent Luciano home," Andy told him. "Alex drove him. We got a game to win tonight, so I need you to go and be a coach and we'll pull this team back together." Andy opened the door for Liam. "Liam, say something to Hubs and D, okay? Those kids are shitting their pants. It's like their dad is mad at them."

"I'll make 'em do some bag skates, clean out the toilets or something," Liam promised. "I heard the guys already fined them five hundred in the court." The kangaroo court was a self-imposed series of fines for various infractions, both serious and non-serious. The money usually ended up being divided into bonuses for the staff at the end of the season. "I'll fix this."

26

JOEY

PATRICK posted in **SAVE MY BACON**:

ALERT 🔥 *ALERT* 🔥 *ALL AVAILABLE PEOPLE GET YOUR ASSES OUT HERE ASAP.*

JOEY SAT ON THE TOILET BOWL AND WATCHED ALEX BATHE TWO wiggly babies like he'd been doing it his whole life. The twins sat in warm water up to their tiny butts, and were held in place by the same circular plastic tub seats Joey remembered his sister using.

Dean, Alex's black hairless cat, sat in the water as well, calmly supervising the proceedings. Every now and then he would place a paw on Alex's hand and Alex would obligingly soap him up and pour a little water over his head. The babies thought it was hilarious and giggled their heads off every time.

It was hard to hold on to a bad mood around them, but Joey gave it his best shot.

Torvill, the white cat, sat on Joey's lap, purring and kneading his thighs with her needle-sharp claws. Every time Joey stopped petting her, she would turn her enormous green eyes on him, skewering him with her glare. He'd been squeamish about petting her when he'd first seen the cats; their naked skin gave him the heebie-jeebies. But they actually felt pretty cool. Besides, Torvill loved him no matter what; as long as he didn't stop petting her.

"I'm not used to seeing your cats naked," Joey commented. The cats had a bigger wardrobe than Joey, with matching outfits for every occasion.

"Do you take baths in your clothing?" Alex asked.

"Not if I can help it."

"Well it's bath time for everyone in the Pergov-Staunton household, right kidlets?"

"Baa!" David said, slapping his hand on the water. Tanya was too busy chewing on a rubber duckie to respond.

"So much easier to tell them apart when they're naked," Joey observed. "The babies, not the cats. You sure you don't need any help?"

"Not right this second, but when I'm done with Davka, I'll hand him out to you."

Jealousy sat heavily in Joey's chest as he watched Alex and the babies. He had everything Joey wanted. Real love, a family, and someone who believed in him totally. Things money couldn't buy.

Joey picked Torvill up and looked into her face. "Your daddies are lucky men," he told her.

"That is true," Alex said. "Though I often find you have to work hard for luck."

"It seemed so easy for you and Sergei. Outside of, you know." Joey pointed at the babies.

Alex's laugh had an edge of bitterness. He lifted David out of the tub and laid him down on the towel he had set up. "None of it was easy. Except loving *Seryozha*. It feels like I've been in love with him my whole life."

"Oh, I know that feeling."

"Yes, you do," Alex said in a singsong tone as he dried David off. He lifted the baby up and kissed him on the top of his head. "Hold this," he told Joey, passing the baby over.

"Sorry," Joey said to Torvill as he gently encouraged her to jump off his lap. He took David gratefully, cuddling the boy against him, and inhaling his sweet clean baby smell. "So how did it work with the team? Were they weird around you?"

Alex lifted Tanya out of her bath ring and laid her down on her own towel. He dried her off, laughing and giggling with her, telling her she was beautiful in three different languages.

"You're beautiful, too," Joey said to David, not wanting him to feel left out. David smiled and reached for Joey's fingers.

"Hold this, too." Joey shifted David to his left arm and took Tanya, balancing her on his free leg. "Hi, sunshine," he said to her. "You smell delicious, too."

"I'm sure there was some grumbling from the team," Alex said answering the question Joey had almost forgotten he'd asked. "But everyone loves Sergei, and you know him. He wouldn't give a fuck what they had to say anyway. He's probably going to retire next year when his contract is up." Alex looked up from the wet cat. "Don't tell anyone I said that."

"I won't."

Alex stood up, holding a wet cat. Grabbing a towel, he wrapped it around the animal. "Follow me. Bring the babies."

"Like I was going to leave them in the bathroom," Joey called to his retreating back.

"Can you dress them?" Alex said when Joey came into the kid's room. "I have to dry off Dean. They catch cold easier than the babies."

"No problem," Joey assured him. "Point me to the jammies. Diapers first," he added quickly, realizing he was carrying two un-potty-trained humans.

"Diapers are on the changing table. Pjs, top drawer of the white dresser. They always wear the Thunder ones on game days."

"You two wait here," Joey said to the babies as he placed them gently into one of the cribs. Torvill jumped up, landing almost soundlessly on the mattress. The twins sat and watched her, gurgling happily and petting her with surprising gentleness when-ever she got close enough for them to reach her.

Alex plugged a hair dryer into a wall outlet and sat on the floor with Dean between his legs. "So you and Liam are...what now?"

"I don't know," Joey confessed, laying David down on the changing table. He made quick work of the diapering, remembering just how far boy babies could shoot their pee. "We're something. He told me he loved me, last night."

Alex smiled. "Really? But that is good, no?"

"I guess so," Joey said, wrestling David into the blue and white pajamas with Sergei's name and number on the back. "It's just so surreal. I spent so many years pining, knowing it would never happen. *We* would never happen. And then it kind of did at Christmas."

Dean had a look of utter contentment on his feline face as Alex dried and pampered him. "*Vrainment?* I didn't hear this story. Come, tell Uncle Lyosha everything. Don't leave out any of the good parts."

Joey covered David's ears with his hands. "In front of the *babies*?"

"They're not even one yet, and they're learning French, English, and Russian. They have no idea what we're talking about. *Ne tak li, zvezda moya?"* he said to Tanya and he blew her a kiss. "Now spill. Was it magical? Did he kiss you under the mistletoe?"

Joey put David in the crib and lifted Tanya out, grateful to see she hadn't peed the mattress. "He was shit-faced," Joey admitted. "And he kissed me in the attic of my parent's house. He'd just found out Michelle was pregnant with Nino's baby and they'd had a screaming match in a living room full of half-drunk relatives. I snuck him up to the attic and he, well, you can imagine."

"Oh, *oui*. I can imagine very well, *la*." Joey scowled at him, and he snickered.

"It was fucking amazing, okay? And then he left as fast as he could." Joey snapped up Tanya's outfit with more force than it needed, and her eyes grew big. "Sorry," he said. He picked her up, bouncing her gently as he talked.

"But it's not really real, you know? It kind of feels like something that can only exist in our house. It can't survive in the real world. It was just a dream."

"It doesn't have to be," Alex said softly. Joey had to look away from the pity in his eyes.

"I don't know if I'm strong enough," Joey confessed in a whisper.

Alex let that lie, keeping up a stream of inconsequential chatter as they finished getting the babies ready for bed. Joey was thrilled to see the cats had matching Thunder pajamas with their names on them.

Joey found himself sitting with David tucked against him in the world's most comfortable rocking chair as he read "Goodnight Moon" to the sleepy baby.

"Goodnight stars. Goodnight air. Goodnight noises everywhere," he recited quietly. David's weight seemed to double as sleep claimed him. He was a warm soft bundle in Joey's arms, radiating peace and contentment. Joey blinked back tears, emotionally and physically exhausted from the events of the last twenty-four hours.

Alex laid a gentle hand on Joey's shoulder. "They're sleeping. Let's put them down."

"Do they always share a crib?" Joey whispered as Alex shut the light off and closed the door.

"Only way they'll sleep, ever since Elena died. I'm sure they'll grow out of it."

They stopped in the kitchen to grab a snack and some tea on their way to the den. Alex collapsed down onto the giant ugly sofa with a sigh.

"That was exhausting," Joey said. "Do you do that every night?"

"Sometimes me alone, sometimes Allie alone. Sometimes me and Serhoya, sometimes me and Allie. You get used to it."

Joey settled on the far side of the couch from Alex. "I'm sorry I said those things about, you know, bottoming," he apologized sheepishly. "I was wrong."

Alex dug through the clutter on top of the coffee table, searching for the TV remote. "Yeah, well, don't knock it until you've tried it, *mon chum*.

When Joey didn't respond, Alex turned to look at him, eyes narrowed knowingly. "You did, didn't you?"

Joey blushed. "I…"

"Oh my god. Tell me everything."

"No!" Joey said, holding up a finger. "I can't. This is why Liam doesn't want us being alone together anymore."

"You have to talk to someone about these things, *mon beau*. Who better than I, your personal gaysexlopedia."

"You're a bad influence," Joey said with a smile.

"Tu m'aimes," Alex replied, blowing him a kiss.

Joey pretended to knock it out of the air. "No, *Sergei* loves you. I like you, but I don't *like you* like you."

Alex harrumphed but didn't push Joey. Joey was finding himself more and more comfortable around the other man. He was kind and perceptive. "You know, Alex," he said. "I think this could be the beginning of a beautiful friendship. That is, assuming I don't get fired and sued for breach of contract."

Alex sighed and stretched far across the long couch to pull Joey into a side hug. "It's going to be okay," he said. "I promise."

How exactly was it going to be okay, Joey wondered for the thousandth time that day.

"Should we watch the game?" Alex asked, settling back down on his side of the sofa.

Joey checked his watch, surprised to find it was only eight-thirty. It felt closer to midnight. What a fucking day. After an amazing night. No wonder he had emotional whiplash.

Did he want to watch the game? Watching your team play when you couldn't be on the ice was always an exercise in frustration, but not watching was worse. "Yeah, put it on," he said.

While Alex called up the game on the huge television hanging over the fireplace, Joey leaned his head back against the padded arm of the couch and closed his eyes.

When he opened them again, the room was dark, he was alone, and he was covered in a crocheted afghan that looked like someone's mother had made it. He also had to pee like a racehorse.

Checking the time, he saw that it was three-thirty seven a.m. Man, he had gone down hard. He swung his legs off the couch and rubbed his eyes, trying to get his bearings in the unfamiliar room.

It took him a second to find a bathroom in the dark, and after he'd taken care of business and splashed some water on his face, he knew there would be no getting back to sleep.

Restless, he wandered through the big house, comparing their distant view of the bay with Liam's beachfront property and finding it lacking. He checked the score on his phone, disappointed but not surprised to find they had lost by two points. That was his fault.

Passing through the kitchen, a note with his name on it taped to the fridge caught his attention. *I brought your car back*, Sergei had written. *The keys are by the back door. Thanks for letting me drive it. It was awesome. You can drive my Mercedes one day.*

Perfect. That was just what he needed. He scribbled a quick reply that he'd gone for a drive and would see them in the morning, and headed for the garage.

JOEY'S metallic-blue Lamborghini hugged the curves at fifteen miles over the speed limit. What was the point of having a sports car and money if you couldn't drive fast every now and then?

He'd taken the Five north until he hit a road that cut west to the coast. Trees lined the two-lane road and there were few signs of humanity visible. It would probably be beautiful in the daytime; at night it was dark and empty, just what he wanted.

God, he loved this car. It was gorgeous inside and out and drove like a dream. His family had given him all kinds of shit about it, but it was one of the first things he'd bought for himself after he'd signed his first multimillion-dollar contract.

Seeing that deposit hit his bank account had been unreal. It still felt unreal. The numbers on his contract with the Thunder were beyond anything he'd ever expected. He was a bonafide one-percenter. It was crazy. Insane. He was just a kid from Southie who loved to play hockey. He'd played hockey, done what his coaches had told him to, and here he was. A superstar.

And he loved it. He loved everything about hockey. He loved being able to take care of his family financially, loved how happy his teams made the fans and how excited little kids were to meet the player; but most of all, he loved playing the game at the highest possible level.

His opponents were the best of the best, and he was pushed to the limits of his talent and skill every time he hit the ice.

Slowing down, he cut left at the Kayak Point County Park sign.

The weird thing about his life, besides the ridiculous money, was that he couldn't pinpoint a time when he had actually made a decision to play hockey. It was as if he'd been born with a hockey stick in his hand. His earliest memories included plastic hockey sticks and foam pucks.

Sometimes he felt like his entire life had been pre-planned for him, and he just went with the flow. .

The small drive led to a parking lot. According to the sign at the payment box it was technically closed at night, but Joey shoved twenty bucks into an envelope and parked anyway. He pulled his coat tighter around him against the chilly wind and headed to the beach. As he walked, he tried to remember if there had even been a time where he'd had to make a choice about something; if he'd ever had the opportunity to choose.

Most of the time there hadn't been a question as to what was the right thing to do in any given situation. Was he supposed to have turned down an opportunity to play on the IIHF World Championship team? Should he have said no to the Kings when the offered him an entry-level-contract right out of high school?

His brothers and sisters had gone to Shattuck-St. Mary's, one of the best high schools for hockey in the country, so he went to Shattuck-St. Mary's. His parents told him to invest in real estate, so he invested in real estate. His only responsibility was to keep his body in tip-top shape and show up and play hockey. Other people handled every part of his life, from buying his groceries to managing his career. Sometimes he felt like he and the other players were no more than pampered thoroughbred races horses who only existed to make the owners money.

He walked to the edge of the water and stared up at the sky. Dramatic, maybe, but it felt right. Looking up at the vastness of space and thinking about the thousands of miles of ocean stretching out from the coast, definitely gave him perspective.

He had to face some hard truths about himself. Sure, he'd worked hard, extremely hard, to get where he was, but he'd been treating his life like it was a movie. Something he watched, but had no control over, where his actions had no consequences. Like he was a child.

It was time to stop letting life happen to him. It was time to grow up.

There were only two things in life that he had chosen for himself. Two things he had looked at and said 'That. I want that.'

His damn car and Liam O'Reilly.

He loved Liam. Liam made him happy, made him want to be a better person. Let the whole world give him shit about it. He didn't care.

He had to stop running and deal with everything like a man. And that meant *everything*, including the headaches and the vertigo. There was a chance he could lose both his career and Liam by admitting he'd been hiding a potentially serious medical issue from his coaches, but he had to face the fact that there was something wrong with him.

If it was a brain tumor…His mind shuddered at the concept, his thoughts trying to skitter away to another subject, anything but that. He forced them back on track, taking deep breaths and listening to the waves lap at the shore. The last thing he needed was a panic attack on a deserted beach.

If it *was* a brain tumor, and he didn't get it treated in time, he could die. And he desperately wanted to live.

There was a disturbance in the water, and a whale breached the surface, gray against the black of the night. It rose up to inhale life-sustaining oxygen and then splashed back down under the water.

Joey walked back to the picnic area and sat on a bench, his back resting against the table. If he had to recreate himself, he would. Where there was life, there was hope. Though he was more than just 'the Looch,' that persona was a part of him. Confident, strong, like-able, charming, the Looch could do whatever he wanted.

If he did end up being forced to quit hockey, either for medical or personal reasons, he had options. He could try to get a job as a talking head on ESPN. Maybe coach like Liam. Heck, he could dive full-on into real estate investing or buy a boat and sail around the world.

He could go college. Maybe he would become a sports psychologist. Those docs were amazing. Did psychologists have to go to medical school? Was he smart enough for medical school? He'd start with community college and worry about that later.

Before he traded in his skates for some textbooks, there were a couple of calls he needed to make, and more than a few people he needed to talk to. Starting with Andy and Liam.

It was just a little after four a.m., way too early to be making phone calls. He sent a text to the coach, asking him to call Joey as soon as he could, and assuring him that although it was urgent, it wasn't an emergency.

Liam wouldn't care if he called and woke him up, but he wasn't quite ready for that conversation yet. He wanted to get at least one duck in a row before he did. He also wasn't quite ready to get back to Sergei and Alex's domestic bliss. Walking back to his car, he pulled up his map app and looked for someplace to get breakfast. There was a Denny's a few miles away. Sounded perfect.

27

LIAM

How the hell was he supposed to fix this?

No one had been less surprised than Liam when they lost the game. Everyone was distracted, even the coaches. For the first time in his life, the game couldn't end fast enough for Liam.

But whatever magic Andy and Patrick had used for damage control seemed to have worked. There was an undercurrent of curiosity from the staff and the players, but Paul, Robbie, Patrick, and Sergei seemed to be quashing any gossip before it could gain traction. It had died down to a wild rumor that someone had photoshopped Liam and Joey's heads on to a screencap from a gay porno.

Joey had texted Liam hours ago to let him know he needed some time alone. He was safe at Sergei's, and he might be out of touch the next day.

Liam was full of nervous energy with no outlet. He practically vibrated with the need to *do* something, but he couldn't figure out what to do.

His calls to Joey had gone right to voicemail; his texts remained unread. He hadn't expected any different, but still. He didn't know where they were, *what* they were to each other, and it was driving him crazy.

The phone rang as he was crossing the West Seattle Bridge, the Seattle Skyline shining to the north and the lights of the port blazing beneath him. It was a Boston number he didn't recognize. It was almost three in the morning in Boston; this couldn't be good. Heart in his throat, he pressed the button on the steering wheel to answer the call. "Hello?"

"Liam?" Lorenzo Luciano asked.

"Nonno? What's wrong? Whose phone is this?"

"Yes, yes. Nothing is wrong here, and I'm calling on my new cell phone. Sophia got it for me. Do you know you can play games on these things? Watch movies. It's crazy. Like Star Trek."

"I know, Nonno. They are very cool."

"Too bad they are crappy phones. When I was your age, you called someone, they were home, they answered the phone. Now you kids got your freakin' phones on you twenty-four seven, and I can't get a holda nobody."

"You got me."

"Yeah, well, I'm tryin' to reach Jojo. He didn't play tonight. The announcer said he was out with an 'upper-body injury,' whatever the hell that means. And he didn't answer the phone when I called."

"Maybe he didn't know it was you. If this is a new phone number, he might not have recognized it."

"I called him three days ago. He has the number. Made a big deal about putting my name in his phone. Told me how to do his. So why isn't he answering? And all his brothers and sisters are in some kind of a tizzy, running around like crazy people, but they won't tell me what's going on. I'm worried. I can't sleep until I know he's okay."

Oh crap. His brothers and sisters must have seen the picture. Which meant his Joey's family had seen it, too. Patrick must have sent it to them as well as his idiot teammates, or he'd called them after it all went down. Either way, Liam was surprised his phone wasn't blowing up. The silence was unsettling. What the fuck were they up to?

"Liam? You still there? Can you hear me?" His voiced faded away and then came back. "Fucking tiny phones," he muttered.

"Yeah, I'm here, Nonno. Sorry. Got lost in thought. Joey's okay, I promise you." How much detail should he tell Lorenzo? "He, well, he had a panic attack. And the doc recommended he sit this one out."

Lorenzo breathed a sigh of relief. "Ah, poor Jojo. He hasn't had one of those in a long time. Do you know what set him off?" He sounded old and tired, and Liam really wanted to tell him everything. Joey always had been his grandfather's favorite, and the two of them had a special bond. If anyone could give him insight into Joey's brain, it would Lorenzo.

He took the Harbor Avenue exit and came to a decision. "It was me. Us. Our...relationship. A, um, picture of us, together, got out. We're...we're together."

"Everyone knows that. Why is that such a big deal?" He sounded genuinely confused. "That wouldn't have Gina and Sophia flopping around like chickens with no head." He didn't sound convinced. Lorenzo might be old, but he was still sharp. Not much got past him.

"Maybe they didn't know?" Liam hedged.

Enzo dismissed that idea with a loud scoff. "Bah. You kids always were meant for each other. I been waiting for you two get your heads out of your asses."

Liam laughed, something he hadn't thought would be possible tonight. "I can't speak for Joey's head, but I'm ten years older than he is, in case you'd forgotten." Both grandparents tended to lump all the kids together as being the same age, especially now that they were in their twenties and thirties. Hell, even Liam had a hard time keeping track of everyone's ages. "I kind of had to wait for him to grow up, don't you think?"

"Yeah, yeah, sure, there's that. But why wait so long? He's twenty-three, right?"

"Twenty-five. Twenty-six this June."

"Pfft. Past old enough. By the time *I* was twenty-five, I was married five years and had three *bambinos*."

Liam followed the road north around Duwamish Head, grateful as always that he had found the house on Alki Beach. Worlds away from Downtown and the industrial areas, it was worth every second of the commute.

"I gotta go, they're telling me. Tell Joey to call me, when you get home?" Lorenzo asked. "I don't care what time it is."

"He's not home, not at my house. He's staying with a friend tonight." Liam sighed. "We sort of had a fight," he confessed. God that sounded so juvenile. And misleading. Fight didn't accurately convey what they'd said to each other.

"What did you do?"

"Why do you assume it was my fault?"

"You can be…difficult," Lorenzo said. "Joey likes to keep people happy, needs everyone to like him all the time. He spends half his energy keeping everyone around him happy, happy with him in particular. Even if it costs him."

"That's what I told him!" Thank god someone else noticed Joey working himself too hard. Liam wasn't crazy. "He doesn't take care of himself."

"And you like to take care of people. That's why you are perfect for each other," Lorenzo said, as if it were obvious, and not an earth-shaking revelation that made Liam slow down to twenty-five miles an hour while the words echoed in his heart.

"He left, Nonno," he confessed. "What do I do? Should I go get him and drag him home?"

"Give him his night," Enzo said. "Let him have some space and some time. And you, you take some time too. Really think about what it means to love him. The good and the bad. And what it will cost him to love you."

Liam pulled into his driveway but left the car running. "When I am as old as you, will I be so smart?"

"Maybe. If you're lucky."

"I hope I will be. Thank you."

"So, Jojo. Has he gone to the doctor yet?" Lorenzo asked. "That's another thing I'm worried about."

"What?"

Liam sat in the car while Lorenzo filled him in on all the problems

Joey had been keeping from him. He didn't hang up until he'd wrung every ounce of information he could from the man. Only the fact that Sergei and Alex had sleeping babies kept Liam from driving directly to their house and demanding to see Joey.

28

LIAM

LIAM'S HOUSE HAD NEVER FELT SO DEAD AND EMPTY BEFORE.

An empty house felt different than a house with people in it, even if the people, or person, was sound asleep in a dark room.

Built into a slight bluff, the street level of the house was actually the top floor; the same level Joey's room was on.

Liam walked slowly down the stairs to the master bedroom. Stripping off his coat and tie, he dropped heavily on to the foot on the bed.

He was exhausted, but sleep would be a long time coming. Was he really that hard to love? Would it be better for Joey if Liam just…let him go? They both stood to face serious career repercussions if they came out as a couple.

But if they weren't together, who else would make sure Joey took care of himself? Who else could tell when Joey was hiding something important?

Well, apparently not him, he realized, remembering what Lorenzo had told him about Joey's vertigo attacks and headaches. Goddamn it. Whatever was causing them could be serious. Not to mention that if he'd been having vertigo attacks bad enough to make him pass out, he should not be driving. He was literally a danger to himself and others.

God, Liam hated feeling powerless, helpless. He wanted to do something, to fix it. To make things right. But he had no idea how to do it.

Suddenly, he was hit by the desire to talk to Michelle. Until Christmas, she'd always been the one he turned to when he needed to talk a problem out. They'd been together for five years and friends even longer than that. No one knew him as well as she did, not even Joey. For all the connection and history between them, in the grand scheme of things, he and Joey hadn't spent a lot of time together since they were children.

Liam pulled out his phone and texted Michelle. *Are you awake?* It would be a miracle if she saw it and answered it.

While he waiting for a response that would probably never come, he unclipped his cufflinks, running his fingers over the cabochon ruby. It was the pair Joey had removed with shaking hands on Christmas Eve. Happy and content after their intimate night, he'd worn them out of sentiment.

Christ, had it really been less than twenty-four hours since he'd told Joey he loved him?

His phone buzzed.

I am now. I had to pee for the 17th time tonight. Michelle wrote.

Liam's fingers hovered over the screen. It was late, he was

emotional, and it probably wasn't the best time for a serious discussion. There was no telling what he might say.

Then again, maybe that made it the best time to talk. He responded to her before he changed his mind. *Do you have time to call?*

His phone rang by the time he'd taken off his shoes and pants. "Hey," he said feeling foolish.

"Hey yourself," Michelle responded. She sounded the same. Why had he expected her to sound different somehow?

"Thanks for calling. I know it's late and I'm probably the last person you want to talk to."

"Why would you say that? I haven't called you because I figured you wouldn't want to talk to me," Michelle said. "I probably wouldn't want to talk to me, if I were you. I'm a lying cheater, remember?"

"I haven't called you because I didn't know what to say. I'm not gonna lie and say I was thrilled you were sleeping with Nico, but we both know I wasn't the easiest person to be with." He put the phone on speaker as he stripped the rest of his clothes off.

"Oh, we do?" Michelle asked, sounding surprised. Liam would bet she was dying for a cigarette. She'd never smoked very much, but every now and then, when she was up late, she liked to sit on the balcony and think and smoke. "It sounds like you've been doing some soul-searching. I know how much you love that."

"It's about time, don't you think?"

"Well, it's a little late for me, personally, but I'm glad for you."

"I'm sorry…" He didn't know how to finish that sentence.

"Sorry for what?"

"A lot of things. The way I treated you.

The way it ended." He took a deep breath and closed his eyes. "I'm sorry I couldn't love you enough. I'm sorry I hurt you." His voice broke on that. He may not have loved her the way she needed, the way she deserved, but he did love her. He'd never wanted to hurt her, but he'd ended up doing it anyway.

There was silence and then sniffles on Michelle's end of the conversation. "Bastard," she said, voice thick. "You can't spring shit like that on me in the middle of the night. I'm a mess of fucking hormones. I cried at a fucking dog food commercial yesterday."

"Sorry."

She sniffled some more and then cleared her throat. "Yeah, well, thanks. And I'm sorry for not womaning up and leaving when I realized what was going on with Nino. I don't know what I was thinking."

"Where are you?" he asked. "Still living with my parents?"

"Yeah. Right now, I'm sitting on that death-trap of a fire escape of theirs and wishing I could have a cigarette."

"I knew it. Hold on, I'll join you in spirit." He grabbed the nearest pair of sweatpants he could find and an old hoodie he had thrown on the floor.

"You have a fire escape out there?" Her voice was so clear. She sounded like she was in the next room; like he could turn a corner and see her.

"I miss you," he confessed. He really did. Somehow, without him truly noticing, she had become his only friend.

She sighed heavily into the phone. "I miss you, too. And I'm sorry for the way shit went down, too."

Liam opened the double doors to the balcony and sat on the chair he'd put there to watch the whales as they migrated.

"So, we all know what I did. What are you sorry for?" Michelle asked.

He leaned forward, resting his elbows on the cold metal railing. "Everything, I guess. I still don't know why we couldn't make it work. On paper, we were great."

"Yeah, on paper, we were." She took a deep breath as if she were smoking that imaginary cigarette. "And we looked damn good together."

"You were perfect."

"No. I wasn't then and I'm not now. What I *was,* was good at playing the role you wanted me to play. Until I couldn't. You've always had this vision of what life should be like, your life, and anything that didn't fit the box, you didn't see, didn't acknowledge."

"That's not true," he protested automatically.

"Keep telling yourself that. Do you think I just started being with Nico for no reason? Because I was bored? Do you really not remember the many conversations we had, or rather I attempted to have with you, about our relationship?"

"I guess you're right." She had been his entire emotional support system, listening to his problems, advising him, and he had barely listened to her. He'd been a dick.

Maybe he was still being a dick. Had he really listened when Joey had been sharing his fears of being out, his concerns for his future and both their careers?

Change had to start somewhere, and he should start with Michelle.

He owed her that. "I'm sorry. I didn't know." He tried to pick his words carefully. How could he put words to the guilt and regrets he'd been feeling? How could he explain how being with Joey had shown him what love really was without hurting her more?

"You still there?" she asked.

"Yeah, just thinking."

"Sounds like you've been doing a lot of that lately."

"I have. And it sucks. For the record, I really did think that what we had was enough. That it was what grown-up relationships were supposed to be like. Calm and predictable. Easy."

She laughed. "Wouldn't that be nice? But you'd never really been in love before? I mean, in love-love with someone who made you crazy. Who challenged you and your entire world?"

"I thought I had been."

"Uh-huh. But now you know it wasn't for real, right? Because of Jojo? Because he gets to you."

"Yeah," he confessed quietly. "How crazy is the whole thing. I mean, it's ridiculous. I never saw this coming. You have to know that. I swear I wasn't pining for him or anything when we were together."

"Don't apologize. I know you weren't. I remember saying something like that to you at Christmas. Do you remember?"

He thought back. Most of his memories of that night revolved around Joey. He'd been drunk for the majority of his conversation with Michelle. He'd started drinking immediately after she'd told him she was pregnant and leaving him. He still felt that was an appropriate reaction.

"In your parents' bedroom?" she prompted after he had been silent too long.

"The Dr. Pepper?"

"The Dr. Pepper."

"You told me you were hanging out with Nico one day, and when you got up to get a drink, there was a case of Dr. Pepper in the fridge."

"And why was that important?"

"Because Nico doesn't like Dr. Pepper. He had bought it specifically for you, without you even having to ask for it. And that was when…"

"When I knew he loved me," she finished for him.

Wow, did he get it now, even more than he had that night. He thought about the PlayStation 4 and the two Nintendo Switches he'd ordered for their upcoming birthdays. Born four days and ten years apart, they'd celebrated birthdays together their whole lives. This one was going to have been special.

He thought about the email he'd sent to Andy's daughter asking if he and Joey could visit sometime over the summer and pet a damn alpaca. That's what relationships were supposed to be like. And he hadn't understood until Joey.

He'd never done anything like that for Michelle. He'd bought her everything she'd asked for, given her free rein with the money, but he'd never seen something and thought *Michelle would love that. I should get it for her.*

And what did she have to show for all those years she'd wasted being with him? Nothing. Not even alimony, since he'd never asked her to marry him, and she wasn't the type to ask first. She hadn't asked for any money when she left.

She'd sacrificed her career for his. That's what Coach Williams had meant when he'd said that the hockey spouses were some of the strongest women he knew. He owed her. "I'm sorry I took you away from your career, and I ruined your life for all those years."

"Liam, only you could apologize for 'ruining someone's life,' and still manage to make it about you."

Offended, he sat up straight. "What?"

"Don't give yourself so much credit," she explained. "You never had the power to ruin my life. I wasn't a child when we started dating. I was thirty, and I knew what I was getting into. I had just gotten out of a long, hard relationship that ended ugly. I was Head Teller at the bank I'd started working for in high school. There wasn't much to ruin." She sounded oddly calm. "God, I wish I could have a cigarette," she said with a short laugh.

"Me, too," Liam agreed. "Or just a drink."

"You could have a drink. As a matter of fact, you should have one for me, since I can't do that either. Stupid kid's not even here yet and she's ruining my life." He could hear the smile in her voice.

"It's a girl?" he asked, his voice catching and his eyes suddenly, unexpectedly, filling with tears.

"Yeah," she said softly as if she heard something sad in his voice.

"I always assumed we'd have one together someday day," he confessed.

"I'm not sure that would have been a good idea."

"What? You think I'd be a bad father?" Man, she really must have been unhappy with him. How hadn't he noticed?

Michelle chose her words carefully, speaking slowly. "I think you have the potential to be a controlling father. One who might have a hard time letting a kid be who they want to be without trying to turn them into who you think they should be. I don't know how well you would have handled the unpredictability of children."

"Was I controlling to you?" The thought horrified him. "I never meant to be."

The pause was a little too long for Liam's comfort. "No, you didn't need to control me."

"Oh, thank god." At least he hadn't been a total shit.

"With you, that's not really a good thing. You didn't try to control me, because you didn't really care what I was doing."

Ouch. "That's not fair," he said. "I cared about you."

"I didn't say you didn't care about me," she clarified. "I said you didn't care what I did with my time, with my life, as long as it didn't reflect badly on you and how our relationship looked from the outside."

"A fat lot of good it did me anyway. Somehow I turned around and it feels like everything is behind me. Career, family, friends." He'd lost it all, almost in one night. "And if I stay with Joey, and it comes out, I stand to lose the new career I've started to build, and the respect of everyone in the League."

"So?"

"What do you mean so? It's a big deal, Michelle. My career, my reputation."

"You reputation? Please." He could practically hear the eye roll. "You know what your problem is, Liam O'Reilly, you've never had to risk anything to get what you wanted. You never had to say fuck it and jump off that cliff, take a chance of losing everything to get something better!

"Shooting for a career in hockey was risky," he said defensively.

No, it was a long-shot, for real, but you trying to make it work? Not a risk at all. If you didn't make it into the pros, what was the worse you came out with? A degree from Harvard with no student loans? A family that loves and supports you? Oh poor you. Your life would have been so hard."

"I could have ended up skating for chump change in the SPHL!"

The Southern Professional Hockey League was a tiny semi-professional league based in the South. Players made on average a couple of hundred dollars a week.

"You wouldn't have. You never would have made the decision to do that, not in a million years. You would have gone on to some other professional function in the league, manager, agent, or, oh, I don't know, *coach*? You're risk averse, Liam. You always have been.

"But…"

Michelle was on a roll. There was no stopping her now. Her voice rose with each sentence. "You want to talk hard? You want to talk risk? Your family and Nico's family are as close to me as my own. We both risked losing all of that by admitting our affair. I wouldn't have been surprised if they'd kicked us both to the streets. Instead, they've been better to me than my real family. My own mother called me a *putana*."

He heard metal clanging as she paced back and forth on the tiny landing. "I didn't have to do it, you know. I could have gotten rid of it."

"You wouldn't. Not in a million years," he said echoing her earlier comment.

"I could have. Without anyone ever knowing. I could have told him it was over, it was a mistake and just gone on living my life with you. But Liam, for the chance to have a love like I sensed I could have with him, I was willing to risk everything. It was worth it."

Worth it. How many times had he told Joey he was worth it? He'd literally tried to beat it into him. And now here he was acting like he still had a choice to let Joey walk away.

"You have to decide what the most important thing to you is," Michelle said. "It sure as fuck wasn't me. You didn't fight for me."

"I did! At Christmas."

"No, you screamed at me, accused me of getting with Nico for his money and called me a slut. Not once then or since then, did you ever say anything like, 'Come back, 'Chelle. We can fix this.' You didn't even try."

Oh. Fuck. That was the part of Christmas Eve he preferred not to dwell on, but he couldn't deny it had happened. "I'm sorry," he repeated for the hundredth time. He was starting to realize how little that mattered in the face of her pain.

"I know you were angry and hurt. And shit-faced," she said, giving him an out even as she accused him of not caring enough.

"No," he said. "That wasn't it."

"Excuse me?"

"Yes, I was drunk, and I was furious. I mean, you dumped that all on me like a brick, you gotta give me that."

She sighed. "Yeah, I know. My timing sucked. In my defense, I'd been trying to get up the nerve to tell you for a month. It wasn't easy."

That night, he'd imagined that she and Nico had been laughing at him the whole time they'd been screwing around behind his back. That she had been gleefully waiting for the worst time she could find to drop her bombshell. Now with time and distance and his recent revelations, he realized it must have been very difficult for her. "You know what my first reaction was when you told me?" he asked.

"That I was a slut?"

"That people would think I was an idiot. Then when the news got out, I would be humiliated. I was angry because I was embarrassed. It was all about me."

"Yeah," she said voice hard. "That tracks." She sighed again. "Why did you call? What do you want from me, Liam? Absolution? My blessing?"

"I don't know. Both?" he joked weakly.

"I can't give you either of those things. But I can finally be open and honest with you. I'll give you advice if you want, but you have to be willing to actually hear what I'm saying."

He could picture her clearly; the wry smile on her face as she shook her head. Her blonde hair curling around her chin. "If you're going to be a maudlin Irishman, you might as well be drinking some whiskey," she said.

"Go inside, you're probably freezing, and pour some of the good stuff. We'll walk down memory lane a bit, apologize to each other a couple more times, and figure out what you're going to do about Jojo."

"I really am sorry for everything," he said. He realized that he was, in fact, cold. He shut the doors behind him and headed for the liquor cabinet in the living room.

He stood in the living room, taking in the view from the twenty-foot high windows. He really loved this house. Of all the places he had lived, this was his favorite. He hoped he got to stay there for a while.

Grabbing a tumbler from the dry bar, he opened the liquor cabinet and took stock of his options.

"I hear bottles clanking," Michelle said. "What are you drinking?"

"It's a choice between Jameson twelve-year-old Special Reserve…"

"A classic," she said.

"And a new one one of the boys got me after we made the play-offs." He pulled the aqua-capped bottle out to read the label. "Tullamore D.E.W. Irish Whiskey. Says it's got a Caribbean rum cask finish."

"Ooh, try that one. I love rum."

"Okay. On ice or straight up?"

"Hm, on ice."

"For you, I will." He poured a generous three fingers, figuring he deserved it after today.

"Now where are you sitting?" Michelle asked.

"Living room. Hold on." He snapped a picture of the room. She'd only seen the house once, and it was before he decorated. He sent her the photo.

"Oh, it looks beautiful," she said. "You did a good job."

"The designer did a good job."

"Either way." Metal clanged as she made her way off the fire escape. Mid-April in Boston still felt like winter at night.

"I do."

She breathed heavily into the phone. "Jesus Christ, I'm like a barge. I think this baby is sitting on my lungs." She huffed and puffed, and then sighed. "Much better. I'm back inside.

Remembering how she'd accused him of not listening to what people were trying to tell him if he didn't want to hear it, he took a minute to reflect on everything they'd talked about. It hurt to hear how she'd felt all those years, but she wasn't wrong. "You're right. I was a dick. And I am truly sorry."

"Stop apologizing. I could've walked away, Liam," she said, surprising him again. "I'm a grown-ass woman, and I knew what you were like. You didn't keep me trapped. And it's not like I pushed very hard for much more either. I didn't even know what was missing. I didn't even recognize that I was falling in love with Nico until it was too late."

Liam laughed. "Now I know exactly what that feels like. It's weird how just sneaks up on you, isn't it?"

"Life is weird. Sometimes awful, sometimes wonderful, sometimes both at the same time."

"What's going on in Massachusetts? Is everyone in Boston a philosopher all of a sudden?"

"We're a very wise, ancient people. How's the whiskey?"

"Delicious. You'd love it."

"Good. Send me some when the baby is born. I can't stand champagne."

"I promise." The entire conversation had gone better then he'd imagined it would, better than he had ever dared to hope. "I don't deserve you in my life," he told her.

"I know. But you've got me. We're going to be kind of family. Is that a thing?"

"I don't know. But can we be friends, too?"

"It's all we ever should have been. I think that's what we're best at. Now drink up. Pour a second glass and tell me what's going on with you and Jojo. I heard something about a picture, but no one would show me."

"Oh fuckin' holy hell," Liam said. "Hold on." He slammed down the rest of his drink and poured a second round. Then he told her everything, sparing no detail. He was on drink number three when she interrupted him, laughing so hard she could barely catch her breath.

"Wait, back up. You...you spanked him?" She sounded like she was choking on something.

"Yes," he sighed wearily. "And then I wrote property of Liam O'Reilly on his ass in permanent marker."

She laughed so long and loudly, he had to pull the phone away from his ear. "Say that again," she demanded. "Louder."

"I fucking wrote Property of fucking Liam O'Reilly on his fucking ass! Happy now?"

She was laughing too hard to speak, and he found himself laughing as well. She was probably the only person in the world who could have made him laugh at that, laugh at himself.

"Oh my god. Shit," she said when she finally got herself under control. "You can't make a pregnant woman laugh that hard. I peed my pants. I'm going to get contractions."

Liam reached desperately for any remaining shred of dignity. "Chelle, this is my career, my job. I was mortified."

"Oh, my God. I have to see this picture. I'm going to make it my phone background."

"Do that, and pregnant or not, I will kill you."

She took a few deep breaths, exhaling slowly. "I know. I know how important your image is to you. You're right. It's very serious."

"Thank you." He paused. "It is kind of funny, though."

"Liam O'Reilly, is that really you?" she said in mock shock.

"People can grow," he said, a tiny bit annoyed at the disbelief in her voice.

"Yeah, they can." She yawned. "It's really late, Lee. And not to sound like a girl in a rom-com, but I'm not the person you should be talking to."

"Joey asked for some space," he admitted. "Said we needed to decide if we thought it was a good idea to stay together. Besides, I called him ten times. He's not picking up."

"Aw, I'm sorry, hon. Sounds like you've had a shit day. I saw you guys lost tonight, too."

"Yeah, thanks for bringing that up. You're funny." He walked to the kitchen to wash his glass. "Can I ask you a favor?"

"Sure. I'm not promising I can do it, but ask away."

"As my newest, and probably only, friend, will you tell me when I'm being a dick from now on? Tell me straight up when I'm wrong?"

"I would think you had enough people horning in on your life. You don't need me."

"Yes, but my brothers and sisters are horrible people. They do things just to make me look bad. You, I trust."

"I'm honored. I promise. I will tell you if you're being an ass."

"Thank you."

"Liam?" she said.

"Yes?"

"You're being an ass."

The front door slammed open. Patrick must finally be home. He'd gone out with some of the guys after the game. With his arrival, most of Liam's good mood disappeared.

"Fuck, Patrick's home. I have to go. But I'm going to call you tomorrow and ask you what you meant by that."

"I think you'll have figured it out for yourself by then. Goodnight, Liam. Keep me posted, okay? I think things will look different tomorrow."

"I will. Keep me posted about the baby. Goodnight. Get some sleep."

He heard Patrick coming down the stairs. If Liam ran for the seldom-used elevator, he might be able to avoid talking to him. He hesitated a minute too long.

"You're still awake?" Patrick asked catching sight of him.

"Just headed to bed now. Goodnight."

Patrick grabbed his arm as he tried to walk past him. "You're an idiot, you know that?" His breath smelled like he'd been drinking, and Liam narrowly avoided asking him if he'd driven home.

"*I'm* the idiot? I'm not the one who 'accidentally' sent a picture he never should have taken to half of North America." He shook Patrick's arm off.

"Yeah, you're a fucking idiot." He poked Liam in the chest. "Man, if I had someone who loved me like Joey loves you, I would never let them go. But nothing's ever perfect enough for you, Judy, is it? Now you've lost *two* amazing people who were crazy enough to put up with your cranky ass."

Oh, that was enough. "Michelle left me!" he roared. "I'm not the one who ran out and got pregnant. And I didn't push Joey away. He *left*! He walked out on his own two feet. He's the one that won't see me!"

"That's bullshit," Patrick said. "You're older than he is. You're supposed to be protecting him from himself! But you can't because you're too scared. Who's protecting him from your bad choices, huh?"

Liam was stunned. Jesus, why had everyone in his life waited until now to shower him with their wisdom?

They hadn't, a voice in his head that sounded a lot like his mother whispered. *You just never listened before.*

Patrick took advantage of Liam's stunned silence to push past him. "I'm going to bed," he announced.

"'Night," Liam said absently.

So that was what Michelle had meant. He was an idiot for letting Joey think he could just leave like that. He needed to let Joey know he wasn't letting him go without a fight.

Patrick was right, something Liam didn't admit very often. He was supposed to be taking care of Joey, stopping him from making stupid decisions. And breaking up with Liam without talking about everything was one of them.

First thing tomorrow, he was heading over to Sergei's house whether Joey wanted him there or not.

29

JOEY

JOEY PULLED HIS CAR UP TO THE BACK DRIVEWAY OF SERGEI'S house. He'd forgotten to take a garage door opener when he'd left. An unfamiliar minivan occupied the second spot. Eight in the morning was early to have company. It probably belonged to Allie, the nanny. He hadn't met her yet, but Alex raved about her.

As soon as he opened the back door, Torvill came running across the kitchen so fast, she skidded on the tile and overshot his legs. "Woah, cat. Leave the ice skating to your human namesake." Risking life and limb, he picked her up. She went willingly, climbing up and hanging her front paws over his shoulder.

He heard voices coming from the great room on the other side of the big kitchen, so he headed that direction, calling to Alex as he did. "Hey, Alex, look what I got. I think this makes me a full-fledged member of your—" He stopped dead. "Family." The living room was full of his family.

"What the fuck?"

"Oh, you she likes," Gina said, looking up from the bagels she was pulling out of a brown paper bag. Poppy seeds rolled around on the table top, bumping into containers of cream cheese from a bagel shop in Boston. The two cardboard boxes of coffee were from a local Seattle shop.

Torvill's claws dug into Joey's back at the sound of Gina's voice. He didn't blame her one bit.

"She took one look at me and ran the other way," Gina said, glaring at the cat.

"Smart cat," Joey said walking into the room like he was walking into an ambush. Which he was, he had no doubt about that.

"Hey, dude," Deano said. "This house is gorgeous, and the view is amazing. No wonder there are more windows than walls. Damn. I didn't even know Seattle had hills. You should get something like this."

"Liam's house is on the beach," Joey said absently as he took stock of what he was up against. All the girls were there. Gina, Angie, Sophia, and Natalie. Patrick was there, not a surprise, but somehow Deano had managed to fly across the country, too. At least they had the decency to look exhausted from the overnight flight. Served them right. He figured Jimmy was still out of the country, and Nico couldn't get away from baseball.

"So, what's going here? It's like a party without the fun."

"We were worried about you," someone said from the sofa across the room.

"Nonno?" Joey's voice cracked, his hands tightening on Torvill. She howled in complaint and scrambled down his back.

"Hey, Jojo. Come over here and hug me. I'm too tired to get up." Lorenzo sounded exhausted and there were dark circles under his eyes, but his smile was as bright as ever, and Joey couldn't remember ever being happier to see anyone in his life.

He ran over, not seeing anything else, and dropped down to his knees. Then he laid his head in his grandpa's lap and cried. Lorenzo let him cry, running his hands through Joey's hair the same way he had when Joey had fallen off his bicycle. Or when he'd been angry and frustrated about the 'big kids' leaving him out of something again.

His family gave him what privacy they could, moving quietly around the room, getting food and coffee and heading out to the wide deck wrapping around the entire house.

"Are we good?" Sergei asked coming up behind Joey. "You want I send them away? Is my house. I can do it."

Joey laughed through his tears. "No. Don't bother. They'll just come back. They're like locusts. They are insane, but they love me. They mean well. Thank you for letting them invade. It must have been quite a surprise."

"Da." Sergei's eyes widened and he nodded.

"Where are the babies and Alex?" Joey asked, pushing himself slowly to his feet. He wiped his eyes.

"There are babies?" Sophia mumbled through a mouthful of bagel. She had come back in for another cup of coffee.

"Twins," Sergei said proudly. "David and Tatyana. My babies."

"I want to see them!" She looked at Joey with a pleading expression.

"Don't look at me, they're not my kids."

"I will get them." Sergei was thrilled at getting to show off his babies. "Too many people for Allie and the little house." He practically jogged out of the house.

"That is one damn big man," Gina said. "I want to climb him like a tree." The family had given up the pretense of not listening and come back into the room.

"I think his fiancé would be a little pissed." Sergei and Alex had gotten engaged at the babies' first birthday party before Joey had joined the team. Apparently, it had been quite the scene.

Gina shrugged. "A girl can dream. Now come on, eat. You don't want to get yelled at on an empty stomach, do you?"

"I ate already. Denny's. How did you get bagels in the middle of the night anyway?"

"What? I called Mrs. Schwartz. She had a bunch of day olds from the store at home. So eat. I woke an old lady up in the middle for the night for you." Gina put cream cheese on a salt bagel and handed it to him.

Even though he'd just eaten, he was tempted. Two things he missed from New York, bagels and pizza. But he'd already demolished his diet enough for one day. "The carbs, Gina."

"Stuff it, Lucy," she said. "You can't have a family crisis on keto. Idiot interventions call for comfort food or tequila. And it's too early for tequila, so bagels it is. And coffee."

"We have food," Alex said as he came in holding Tanya. "You didn't have to bring your own." Sergei followed close behind, David looking small in his arms.

"Like I'm gonna show up empty-handed at your doorstep with this mob? I'm not a freakin' barbarian. Jeez. We got presents, too."

David saw Joey, and he babbled happily, reaching out for Joey.

"Oh, the baby likes you, too," Gina said. "Of course."

"Everyone loves Joey," Liam said.

Joey hadn't even heard him come in. In hindsight, he should have expected it.

"Everyone?" Joey asked.

"Yeah, everyone." Liam smiled tiredly, then he caught sight of Lorenzo. "Nonno Lollo, what are you doing here? Did you call me from a plane last night?" He went over and gave the old man a big hug and a kiss on the cheek.

Lollo reached into his sports coat, pulled out his phone, and waved it at Liam. "Nifty gadgets."

"He called you?" Joey asked, alarmed.

Liam shot him a look. "Yeah. We had an interesting talk, didn't we, Nonno? Neither of us is too happy with you right now. We need to talk. Alone."

The look he gave Joey let him know that all his secrets were out of the bag. He wasn't looking forward to that talk, but at least he didn't have to talk about it in front of the entire family.

"Well, duh," Angie said, walking over to hug Liam. "Why do you think we're here?"

"To interfere in my life?" Liam suggested.

"Nah, that's just a bonus. We're here to make sure you talk."

"How'd you get off work?" Liam asked. As an emergency room nurse with three kids, Angie didn't have a lot of free time. Of all of them, she looked the most like their father. Tall and broad, with a head of wild red hair she tried to keep back in a ponytail.

"Family emergency I told them." She hugged him. "You know I'm always here for both of you."

"Very sneaky. I assume this was all Patrick's idea?" Liam addressed the question to the room as a whole.

"It was," Patrick admitted. "But Nico's the one who pulled it off. Got someone connected to his club to loan them a private plane."

"Nice to have connections." Liam said. "Oh, bagels."

Joey could only watch as Liam made his way across the room, kissing brothers and sisters and O'Reillys and babies. This was nothing like how he'd expected today to go, though, really, when had his family ever kept their noses out of his business?

He had to admit, it felt kind of good, seeing how much everyone cared. And knowing that Liam hadn't been able to stay away gave him a little thrill.

Sophia dropped down onto the sofa with a sigh. "Someone bring me more coffee," she ordered.

Joey sat down next to her and put his arm around her. "Soph, I can't believe you left the baby and flew here in the middle of the night."

She kissed him on the cheek. "Best sleep I've had since I was six months pregnant. I'm a zombie, stupid baby doesn't sleep through the night. My wife is a cop who's gone a lot and every time she is, I worry that she's gonna get shot. I'm a cranky, sleep-deprived, over-caffeinated thirty-year-old mom of a two-month-old. So, Judy, get your ass over here so I don't have to yell. I'm only going to say this once."

"Soph!" Gina complained. She was holding Tanya in her arms. "We had a plan! A script."

"We did," Natalie said. She was sitting on a chair, having a conversation with David. He was babbling, and she was nodding.

Sophia waved Gina's objections away. "I don't have the patience to be nice." She stood up and pointed to the spot next to Joey. "Sit," she told Liam.

She paced in front of them, with the other kids in a half-circle behind her like a jury. "So, the way I see it, you two are together, right?"

They nodded.

"And my idiot brother outted your kinky escapades to the team, and now you think you have to break up because of, I don't know why, exactly."

"Soph," Joey said. "It's complicated. Being gay in the league. Liam's a coach. It's going to be hard, messy." He looked at Liam for support. To Joey's surprise, he was smiling. He leaned over and whispered in Joey's ear. "Don't go there, dude. It doesn't end well. Trust me."

"Can it, Lucy. I don't want to hear your whining," Sophia said, shutting him up with a glare.

"Told you," Liam whispered. "I talked to Michelle last night."

Joey turned to him in surprise. "Really?"

Sophia snapped her fingers at them. "Hey, hey. Eyes up here. Pay attention. We talked a lot about it on the plane, and we decided that's bullshit."

"Big time," Patrick said. "I'm on the team, I know how it is." He took David from Natalie.

"Hey," she said. "I wasn't done with him."

"Go find one of the weird cats to play with," Patrick told her. "You have Sophia's baby at home to hold."

"Look," Sophia said. "It's not that hard. You know what's hard? Pushing a watermelon out your vagina."

"Ugh, Soph," Joey groaned, wincing. Alex and Natalie were right there with him.

"Did you know you can rip? From pussy to asshole. Did you know that?" She made a graphic tearing sound. "And even if you manage to avoid that, you're bleeding for the next six weeks and you have to wear a fucking diaper so you don't get blood everywhere."

"Sophia," Nonno Lollo said firmly. "I think you've gone off the track."

"Fine. Sorry." She took a sip of her coffee and got herself together. "Anyway, my point is, you're both rich white men. You can pretty much do what you want, and if someone in the league has a problem with it, you tell them to fuck off."

"But my contract," Joey said. "And Liam doesn't even have one yet."

"I do, actually,' Liam said. "Andy had me sign it yesterday after you left."

"Is it good?"

Liam shook his head. "I don't even know. I didn't even read it. Didn't even glance at it. Just signed it."

"See?" Sophia said. "Nothing to worry about. You got a fucking contract. They threaten to sue you, you threaten right back. Slap them with a discrimination suit so fast they'll be wishing it was 1955 again when dinosaurs and racist, homophobic, white men ruled the world."

"But even if they can't fire me, what if fans hate me after? Or the other players? Or if the owners hate me?" Joey asked.

"I don't fucking know, Jojo. But I'm sure you can figure out something else to do while living off the fucking millions of dollars you have in the bank. It's not like you're looking at poverty, even if they find some way to break your contract."

"Did you even talk to a lawyer?" Alex asked. "To your manager? Your agent?" Everyone turned to look at him.

"Excellent question," Deano said, giving Alex an air high-five from across the room.

"No. At least I didn't," Joey said. "Did you?" he asked Liam.

"I did, remember?" Liam answered. "My lawyer and agent both said they couldn't find any ruling against it."

Joey shook his head slowly. "No. I guess I forgot. I've been so worried," he touched his left ear unconsciously. Liam grabbed his hand and held it. "About everything," Joey said to him.

Sophia sighed. "Look, I know. You were scared. But the truth is, both of you are big emo babies who are way too worried about what other people think of you."

"Don't sugarcoat it, Soph," Joey said. "Tell us what you really think."

"I think you're both emotionally-stunted drama queens who keep everything bottled up inside and think nobody notices. Like you're some kind of androids who can only have 'nice' feelings and a perfect life. Well, I got news for you. We notice. So how about you both man up, tell the world you're in love and if they don't like it they can kiss your ass. And then maybe in the future when stuff gets confusing, you pick up the goddamn phone and say 'hey, Soph, I need to talk.' But not now, because I'm going to bed." She turned to Sergei. "You, big guy, where's the best place to sleep around here?"

"Couch," he said, startled. "In den. Nice and quiet and dark. No babies. No cats."

"The cats can come with. I kinda want to pet one, see what it feels like. Take me there."

Alex's face was pink with suppressed laughter. Sergei said something in Russian that made him laugh out loud.

"What did he say?" Gina asked.

"He said he's half-terrified and half-in-love with your sisters," Alex translated.

"They have that effect on everyone," Liam said. "Their husbands are very brave, and possibly insane, men."

"You should see this one's grandmother," Lorenzo said, pointing at Liam. "She is a firecracker, my Brigit."

"Your Brigit?" Natalie asked.

When the attention turned to Lorenzo, Liam grabbed Joey's hand and squeezed. "Come on, let's go somewhere private. We need to talk."

They made their way carefully around the edges of the room, trying not to draw attention to themselves.

"Making a run for it?" Alex whispered when they got close to him.

"Yes."

"I don't blame you. Go hide upstairs. Pick any room but the nursery. I'll cover for you."

"You're a lifesaver," Liam said with a quick kiss to his cheek.

30

LIAM

THE WINDOW SEAT IN THE MASTER BEDROOM LOOKED LIKE THE perfect place to hide from everyone and have a serious discussion. Joey sat down on the padded bench with a sigh and leaned his head against the wall. "I'm exhausted. I woke up at three and couldn't get back to sleep so I went for a drive."

"I didn't sleep much last night either. Had a long talk with Michelle." Liam had too much nervous energy to sit. He paced the length of the big room.

"Yeah? How did that go?"

"About the same as this. She gave me the same speech as Sophia did, minus the watermelon thing. Though I'm sure after the baby comes, she'll add that to her repertoire. But that's not what we have to talk about."

"I know."

Liam stood in front of Joey. "You have to deal with whatever is going on in your head. You know that right? It could be serious."

"I know, don't you think I know? I just wanted to wait until after the season. If this is the end of my career, I wanted to go out with a win."

"Joey, it could be the end of…" He couldn't say it. His throat physically closed against the words.

Joey stared out the window, his finger tracing patterns on the glass. "I know," he whispered. "I'm scared."

"I'm fucking terrified. I can't," he swallowed, turned away from Joey and paced again until he could speak. "I'm terrified I'm going to lose you. You're too important."

"You guys can win without me," Joey said, "You've got a great team."

Liam threw his hands up in the air in frustration. He'd had no idea of the depth of Joey's insecurity issues. None. He didn't think anyone did, except maybe Lollo. When things were settled, he was getting the kid into therapy. "Jesus Christ, What is wrong with you?" he shouted. "Not to the fucking team. *Fuck* the team. To your mother, your family, *my* mother for crissake. To me."

"Yeah?" Joey asked, looking up at Liam.

Liam sat down next to him. "Yeah to me, moron. I love you, and it fucking terrifies me. How many times do I have to say it until you believe me? Do I have to beat it into your ass?"

Joey lips quirked in a small smile. "Probably. But not right now. I'm still a little sore from the other night."

"Sorry." Liam tried not to smile.

"No, you're not."

"Not really. Come here." He tugged Joey towards him, turning him until they sat with Joey's back against Liam's chest, their legs inter-twined on the bench. Whenever things between them got too real, Joey always seemed poised for flight. Liam felt like he had to trap Joey to make him stay, make him listen. He could do that; he'd tie him to the bed if he had to.

"This is what's going to happen." He wrapped his arms around Joey's chest and spoke softly into his ear. "You're going to call the coach, tell him what's going on, and then get a whole series of doctor's appointments set up."

"I already did. This morning," Joey said tentatively as if he expected Liam to be mad at him.

"You did? That's great! Was he pissed?"

"He wasn't happy I'd hid it so long, that's for sure. I thought it was, you know, because he wouldn't have traded for me if he'd known."

"Did you say that?"

Joey shrugged, embarrassed.

"Let me guess. You tried to make a joke about it, and he read you the riot act."

"Pretty much. Said I was a person first, then a hockey player. And that he'd known me since I was a kid, and if I thought, etc., etc. You can imagine the rest. Long story short, I'm going to meet the doc at the hospital later today to start some tests. It might be nothing, just part of the panic attacks."

"If it is, great. Amazing. We'll get you some anti-anxiety meds and therapy."

"They told me I should take them, back in high school," Joey confessed.

"They who?" This was the first Liam was hearing about any they.

"School counselors, the usual." Joey laid his head back against Liam's chest.

"Really? I didn't know. Why didn't you say anything?"

"Say what? Sometimes I'm a moron who gets worried about stupid shit and I can't deal with life?

Liam kissed Joey's temple. "Therapy, Jojo. Lots of therapy."

Joey ran his fingers over the back of Liam's hand, intertwining them, tracing lightly over his scarred knuckles. "I'm worried about the drugs and drug testing. And what coaches will think. Who's going to want to hire me if they think I'm halfway to having a breakdown every night?"

"You think you'd be the only professional athlete on mood stabilizers? Don't answer that, I'm sure you do. You're not, trust me. There's lists of approved meds, and if what works best for you isn't on the list, then we apply for a therapeutic use exemption."

"And if that doesn't work?"

Liam took a few deep, calming breaths. He was definitely going to have to do some research on anxiety disorders. He could tell Joey truly wasn't trying to be difficult and wasn't just throwing up roadblocks for no reason. He was seriously concerned.

"The answer is then we try something else. Quit hockey, like Sophia said. I don't care. I'll walk away from all this. I'll walk away from hockey forever to be with you. You get traded one day, I'll move to where you go."

"Why?" Joey asked. "Why would you give all this all up for me? Everything you wanted?"

"I think you know why."

"Because I'm worth it?"

"Because *we're* worth it. The life I envision with you, what I think we can have together, is the most important thing I've ever felt in my entire life. If you don't think so, I can't make you." God he would be gutted if Joey chose hockey over their relationship. "But if you think it's worth a shot, you have to decide what you're willing to risk."

"I've been in love with you forever," Joey confessed.

Liam's arms tightened around Joey. He'd never felt this sappy before. It was almost sickening.

"Don't let it go to your head," Joey said, elbowing him lightly in the gut. "It's probably the brain damage making me feel this way. I get cured, and you're out on the streets."

"You don't need the whole world to love you," Liam said.

"Yeah, I know, I just need you." He said it like he was repeating a poem he'd had to memorize for class.

"No, you idiot. You need to love you. No amount of love from outside – from me, from the fans – is ever going to be enough. Besides, how are you gonna love somebody else if you don't love yourself?"

Joey twisted around in Liam's arms to stare at him. "You did not watch Ru Paul all by yourself."

Liam laughed. "I couldn't sleep last night. I needed something to watch. Ru Paul just sucked me in."

"I'll suck you in," Joey said, kneeling between Liam's legs on the window bench.

Liam looked affronted. "Your Nonno is downstairs!"

"Yeah, and I think he was next door making whoopie with your grandma on Christmas Eve when we were fooling around."

Liam shoved him off the bench. "That's it. You've killed the mood. Now all I can think about is Nonno Lollo and Nana having sex. I may never be in the mood again. I'm going to need therapy."

Joey laughed loudly from the floor. "Oh, really?" He stood up. "So, if I did this." He pulled his shirt off, throwing it behind him. "You wouldn't care?"

"Nope. You've killed my libido."

"Oh, okay." Joey unbuttoned his jeans and slid the zipper down slowly.

Liam grinned, then swung his legs off the window seat.

"I'm just going to," Joey pushed his jeans down over his ass and down his legs, "see what kind of a shower Pergov has in his bathroom." He stepped out of his jeans. "Tell everyone I'll be down in a little bit." He turned his back to Liam and walked away.

Liam pounced, tackling him to the floor.

"Careful with the merchandise!" Joey said through breathless laughter. "I'm very valuable."

"You're a brat," Liam said, latching on to the skin of Joey's neck with his teeth.

Joey moaned and tilted his chin so Liam could have better access.

"Love me?" Liam asked, his mouth a hair's breadth from Joey's ear.

"Oh, yeah. A lot," Joey answered, body tense below Liam's.

"We doing this then, right? No more waffling?"

"Not even pancaking. Want me to take out an ad on the Jumbotron next game?"

"Kind of. Yeah."

Joey pushed off from the floor, catching Liam by surprise and rolling them until Joey sat on top of him. Liam's hands reached for all that bare skin. Damn it, he was never going to be able to resist touching his boy when there was bare skin for the touching.

Joey smirked and wiggled his bubble butt against Liam's cock, which was beginning to show its approval of this turn of events. "Want to check out that shower with me?"

"Oh, yeah," Liam said. "A lot."

Joey hopped up and reached down a hand to Liam. "Come on then, Old Man. What are you waiting for?"

Liam took the offered hand up, and then used it to drag Joey tightly against him. "When we're alone again, I'll show you how old I am."

Joey laughed and then wrapped his arms around Liam and kissed him until he was dizzy. "Let's go shower before someone comes looking for us. You know they're dying to know what we're saying up here."

"We're going to owe Sergei and Alex so big after this," Liam said as he followed Joey into the bathroom. The shower was just as massive as he'd hoped, with multiple shower heads and a bench running along the side. "Sex bathroom!" he said happily.

"It will be now," Joey said and he shut the door behind them.

WHEN THEY FINALLY MADE IT back downstairs, there were claps and cheers from the small crowd still occupying the living room.

"Did you boys kiss and make up?" Angie asked.

"They have wet hair and I'm pretty sure that's not the t-shirt Judy had on when they went upstairs," Deano helpfully pointed out. "So I'm thinking they did."

"Yeah, yeah. I borrowed one of Alex's. Mine got wet. Is there any more coffee?" Liam asked. "I'm tired."

"Oh, did your boy wear you out?" Patrick asked.

Liam glared at his brother. "I will kill you. After the playoffs." The rest of the house was suspiciously quiet. His family must have driven Sergei and Alex out. Gina and Torvill had apparently come to some kind of détente as the cat was curled up asleep on her lap. Gina sat absolutely still, as if afraid to disturb her. "Where is everyone else?" he asked.

"Soph's still sleeping. Alex put Nonno in the guest room; he was exhausted. And then he and Sergei took the babies somewhere. Sergei said we were welcome to stay as long as we wanted. I like him," Angie said.

"Everyone likes Sergei," Liam said. "It's physically impossible not to."

"How long are you guys staying?" Joey asked. "Not that I'm trying to get rid of you or anything."

"I gotta leave soon," Deano said. "I have to be back by the morning."

"I figured," Joey said. "I'm surprised you could get away."

"Family emergency. They can live without their backup goalie for one game."

"But Nonno's going to stay," Gina said.

"Really?" Joey looked so happy that Liam had to hug him. "That's awesome."

They grabbed some of the remaining bagels and went out on the deck. It was a gorgeous spring day, with blue skies and the sun glinting off the water like diamonds.

"This is nice," Gina said, settling into one of the outdoor couches. "I miss you guys. I can't wait until the off-season when we can all be together again. We going to try for a week or two at the house?"

"That's the plan. Except Nico. But that's what you get for playing a sport over the summer. Bad life plan," Deano said, stretching out on one of the loungers.

"Baby should be here by then," Angie said, then stopped, looking at Liam with a guilty expression on her face.

"It's fine. We had a good talk last night. Still pissed at Nico, but it won't be forever. I thought you hated Michelle, anyway, Ange," Liam said.

"Nah, it was stupid shit left over from high school. I let it go. She really needs a friend. And a family since her bitch mom isn't talking to her."

"Don't worry," Gina said "I'm sure Nico's money will go a long way to softening her mother up. If not, we can always stage an intervention. We have a good track record." She smiled.

"You know," Joey said, "There are ways to handle relationships issues like this. Locking people into a bar bathroom isn't one of them."

"Technically we locked the door," Liam pointed out.

Joey grinned. "*You* locked the door. *I* was trying to get out."

Liam stepped closer. "I don't recall you trying too hard."

"See?" Patrick shouted. "See what I have to live with? It's gross. I changed my mind. For the sake of my brain, we should be trying to keep them apart. I've heard things I can't unhear, seen things I can't unsee."

"Yeah, Paddy, the whole world knows what you saw." Liam gave him the older brother death stare combined with the disappointed coach stare.

Patrick withered. "I said I was sorry a million times," he grumbled quietly.

"I think it's going to take a few more," Angie said.

"I don't wanna go," Gina said. "I want to stay here and live in this house and pet the cats and hold the babies."

"You have your own kids," Natalie pointed out.

"Yeah, but they're all used up. These are still new. Plus you all left me. You all hit fourteen and bam, gone to boarding school. Except for me and Ange, and she even went to college out of state."

The other kids exchanged silent looks, and then tackled Gina, taking her down in a group hug. Torvill screeched and tore out of the room.

After a few minutes of teary-eyed hugs and *we loves yous*, Gina dug her way out from under the pile of family. "Okay, Okay. Get off me, you lunatics. I'm a fucking delicate desert flower."

"Good Lord, Joey," Liam said, realization dawning again. "I'd already been playing in the league three years when you were fourteen. Now I feel like a cradle robber."

"Jojo's your boy toy," Patrick snickered.

"According to Hubs, he's my Sugar Daddy," Liam said.

Joey's jaw dropped. "Did he really say that?"

"Not to my face. I overheard him talking to D yesterday. They were trying to figure out if I was some kind of male cougar and could you be a sugar daddy if you were younger than me. They sounded really concerned." He could laugh about it now, mainly because he knew that Hubs and DiDiomete weren't cruel kids, they were just nineteen-year-old jocks with a love of locker room humor.

"Oh my god," Joey said. "I'm so gonna go own that. Maybe I'll get a t-shirt that says Sugar Daddy, and get you one that says Boy Toy."

"You do that, and I will call a reporter for Deadspin and tell them that you wet the bed until you were thirteen and had to sleep in adult diapers," Liam threatened.

"Lies!" Joey gasped. "You wouldn't!"

"I might," Liam answered.

"You won't," Patrick said. "Joey was always your favorite, since the day he was born. Which, if you remember, was about six months before I was," Patrick said. "You were not as impressed with me."

"I'm still not," Liam said. "But Joey wasn't my favorite or anything. I hated you all. And, again, I still do."

Everybody laughed.

"Please," Natalie said. "You let him get away with stuff none of us could. He followed you around like a puppy and before he could walk, you carried him."

"Remember Jojo saying he was going to marry Liam?" Angie asked. "He must have been like three or four."

"Oh, yeah," Gina said. "I'd forgotten about that."

"I did not!" Joey said.

"You did too. You even borrowed my Ken dolls to have a pretend wedding," Gina said. "We'd gone to some cousin's wedding, I forget who, and you were *so* impressed. You spent the next two months telling everyone that you were going to marry Liam because he was nice, and pretty, and let you play with his toys."

"Well, he is pretty," Joey said. "Nice…eh."

"I'll let you play with my toys," Liam said with a smirk. "If you let me play with yours."

"It's noon now," Gina said. "Can we break out the cocktails? Not to stereotype, but that Russian giant must have some vodka in the freezer."

"If we drink every time someone in this family has issues, we're going to become alcoholics," Liam said.

"Hasn't happened yet," Angie pointed out.

Joey slid down on the couch and laid his head in Liam's lap. "I'm so ready for a nap," he said.

Liam smiled and ran his fingers through Joey's hair, massaging his scalp. "You tired, babe?"

"Mmm hmm," Joey answered. "But don't stop, it feels so good."

Patrick rolled his eyes. "Oh my God. They're about two seconds away from sucking each other's faces off. We should go before they start. It's loud guys. So loud." He faked sobbing.

"Feel free to get your own place if you have complaints," Liam suggested. "Or, I don't know, stay at the hotel the team will pay for?"

"We can be quiet," Joey protested.

Natalie laughed. "Nobody in his family can even *spell* the word quiet."

"We were quiet when--" Liam slapped a hand over his mouth before he could finish.

"When?" Gina prompted.

Natalie gasped. "Oh, don't tell me…"

"Told you so," Deano said. He holds out his hand, palm up. "Pay up."

"Don't tell you what?" Gina asked getting frustrated.

"Deano bet me a hundred dollars that they were having sex in the bathroom in that bar in Tampa," Natalie explained. "I said no way Judy would have sex in a nasty bathroom."

Liam shrugged. "He makes me do crazy things."

"I told you that it was *too* quiet in there," Deano said. "They weren't yelling, and I didn't imagine they were shooting the breeze in a bathroom."

Natalie shrugged. "Put in on my tab, Deano. I don't have any cash."

"I'll pay him for you, Nat," Liam offered. "It's the least I can do."

"Get your sugar daddy to pay," she suggested.

"I lost two hundred," Gina said. "Cover me?"

Liam nodded.

EVENTUALLY THE FAMILY left with promises to come back soon. Liam, Joey and Enzo agreed there was no point talking about the medical issues until they had some concrete information.

Joey suffered through a series of tests and MRIs and the diagnosis came back - an acoustic neuroma, a small benign tumor on the nerves of his inner ear. Not life threatening, but potentially career-ending. Even after removal, the doctor's couldn't promise Joey wouldn't suffer balance and hearing problems for the rest of his life.

With the playoffs underway, Liam couldn't be with Joey for his operation. Nonno stayed, and Joey's mother flew out to nurse him through his recovery.

They watched the games on the TV, often joined by Alex and the WAGS during away games. Joey grew closer to Alex, and his mother acquired a couple more surrogate daughters.

Joey found the best surgeons money could buy, and he recovered in record time. The Thunder had advanced into the last round of the Conference Finals, facing off against the San Jose sharks, when Joey got the okay to get on the ice again. It was one of the best days of his life.

31

LIAM

From NHL.COM –

LUCIANO BACK IN THE GAME

Number 46 JOEY LUCIANO returns to the ice tonight in his first game with the Seattle Thunder since undergoing surgery for an acoustic neuroma. Under the supervision of a physician, Luciano has been practicing with the team for the last week.

"We're completely behind Joey's return," Coach Williams said. "He's been cleared to play and the team is looking forward to playing him again."

Luciano joined the Thunder from the Rangers in a two-way trade that saw the Thunder giving up two defencemen and a third round draft pick in exchange for the power center.

"Of course, I'm excited to be back," Luciano said. "But the guys have been kicking ass just fine without me."

The Thunder face the San Jose Sharks tonight for game six of the Western Conference finals. The Thunder lead the series three games to two.

"CHANGE!" LIAM YELLED FROM BEHIND THE BENCH, TAKING advantage of Anderson sending the puck down the length of the ice to the Sharks' defensive zone to call for a line change.

They were fifty-one seconds into the penalty kill. Triple-D had drawn a two-minute penalty for cross-checking a Shark in retaliation for a hard hit on Joey earlier in the period. While Liam appreciated the gesture, his timing sucked. D had gone to the box with two-minutes fourteen seconds left on the clock. It was the third period of game six. The score was tied two-two. Each team had scored once the previous periods.

Joey had scored both goals. The crowd had gone wild, screaming *Looch, Looch!* for a solid ten seconds.

If the Thunder won this, they won the Western Conference and were headed for the Cup. A Shark win would force a game seven.

Liam had been praying for one more goal. He did not want the game going into overtime. Joey seemed to be holding up great, but the last thing he needed was to play another twenty-minute period.

Paul, Robbie, Joey, and Wheels were over the boards before Liam finished yelling.

Joey shot across the ice, the Sharks' d-men converging on him. Rhodes headed for the puck carrier as he sped across the blue line towards the Thunder's net. The fastest skater on the team, Robbie played a particularly offensive defense that made him perfect for the PK team.

Dyson and Wheels covered the other two Sharks forwards.

Passing the Sharks' forward, Robbie flipped a one-eighty, yelled for Wheels, and ripped the puck away with a textbook perfect poke check. His stick flashed out lightning-quick as he took possession of the puck and sent it flying across the ice to Wheels at the very edge of the neutral zone.

As soon as the puck hit his tape, Wheels skated over the blue line into the Thunder offensive zone. "Go!" he shouted, faking a pass to Paul who was coming up quick on his left. The fake pulled the Sharks' guy covering him just far enough off center for Wheels to deke the puck through the guy's skates. While Paul covered his own man, forcing him away from the puck, Robbie checked the Sharks' player closing in on Joey.

Wheels spun around and fired a shot at Joey.

Joey raised his stick, and brought it down hard, meeting the puck the instant it crossed in front of him and one-timing it directly to the net. The puck zipped past the Sharks' defense, flew over the netminder's shoulder, and slammed into the metal pipe with a loud clang.

The crowd held its breath for the half-second it took for the puck to go back down and drop perfectly into the net.

Joey got his hat trick.

The lamp lit, the horn blew, and the fucking stadium *erupted* along with the Thunder bench. Players leaped to their feet, yelling and slamming their sticks against the ground.

"That's what I'm fucking *talking* about!" Joey shouted as hats rained down onto the ice, and the clock stopped with twenty-nine seconds left in the game and the Thunder up by one.

"Fucking right, boys!" Liam shouted as Robbie slammed into Joey, nearly taking him to the ground with the strength of his hug. "Fucking right!"

Coach Williams gave a silent fist pump, but he was grinning like a loon. They all knew it wasn't over until it was over. Plenty of goals had been scored in the last thirty seconds of a game and they still had fifteen seconds of five-on-four left. But *damn* it felt good to be leading.

Joey and the guys on the ice skated past the bench for their celebratory fist bumps, then circled back to join the team while the officials cleared the ice.

"Fucking A boys," Andy said. "We got twenty-nine seconds left. First line in. Keep up the pressure, run 'em hard. Watch the fucking turnovers. Pergov's a wall tonight but let's stop them before they can bring the puck to the net."

"Sven, Marsha, you ready for this?" Sven usually played first pairing with Wheels. Tyson Marchment was a strong third pairing d-man. "You keep them busy, you stick to your man tighter than a tick on a dog's butt."

"Yes coach!" they both yelled.

The teams lined up for the centerline face off, and the puck dropped.

Heart-pounding, Liam's gaze jumped from the clock to his boys. Both teams fought viciously for possession, with bodies slamming into the boards and sticks flying as they battled in the corners. But the first conference championship since the team's founding was so close they could taste it, and the Thunder were on fire. The Sharks never came near scoring, and when the clock ran down, the Thunder had won the Western Conference Playoffs.

Horns blared, cowbells rang, and the crowd screamed. Confetti rained down from the rafters, and the rest of the team skated out to the ice shouting and screaming with joy.

AFTER THE HANDSHAKE LINE, and the awards ceremony and the initial media circus, the celebration moved into the locker room.

Liam smiled so much, his cheeks ached. He was so damn proud of his team. They had played their hearts out the entire season, and now they were taking him to the Cup finals. Unfuckingbelievable.

He couldn't risk making eye contact with Joey, knowing it would be almost impossible to see him and not throw him into the nearest wall and kiss the life out of him, media or no media.

From the looks on their faces, Robbie and Paul were just as bad off. Liam was one second away from telling them his office was empty, when he saw them slipping off together. Thank god. He wasn't quite ready for footage of two of his players making out with each other to hit the internet.

Players in various stages of undress were getting interviewed and drinking champagne, Joey had stripped down to his compression shorts and shirt before getting cornered by a handful of reporters at his cubby. He was smiling ear-to-ear; his hair still short after being shaved for the brain surgery Liam tried not to think about, and downplayed to the press, plastered to his head with sweat.

"Coach!" he yelled, pointing across the room at Coach Williams. "You owe me a blanket!" The cameras turned to Andy.

"I'll get you a whole fucking alpaca, Looch," Andy yelled back, his smile just as wide.

"He said he'd have his daughter make me a blanket if we won the cup," Joey explained. "She's got alpacas!" Joey's head turned and his eyes locked on Liam's.

His smile knocked the breath out of Liam's lungs.

"I really want to pet an alpaca," he said just for Liam.

Holy shit was Liam in love with him.

The reporters yelled his name, one on top of the other, until the woman from one of the Seattle news shows won the battle. "Joey," she said, shoving her record under his nose.

"Yeah?"

"There's rumors you're involved in a relationship with Liam O'Reilly, the defensive coach. Do you have anything to say about those rumors?" She had to yell the last part over the very loud objections from the coach and half the players.

Liam's heart stopped as Joey's gaze locked on his again. Later, he would swear the room had gone silent. Joey smiled at him again. He grinned back, shaking his head in amused surrender. Whatever. He could give a fuck what anybody else thought about them or his relationship with Joey.

Joey leaned back, crossed his arms over his chest and gave him their most charming smile. "Fucking right, I am."

Coach Williams dropped his head into his hands, his shoulders shaking. Liam wasn't sure if he was crying or laughing, or possibly both at the same time.

Pandemonium reigned again as reporters converged on him

and Joey, questions flying at him faster than he could process. He saw fingers flying over phone keypads and he knew the info would be out before he could blink. He let the questions roll over him, not even trying to answer them as he watched Joey play the reporters like a violin, charming and disarming them with his smile and seducing them with his eyes and his body.

"Liam, is a player/coach relationship against the rules?"

"Liam, Do the owners/GM/League/your mother know?"

"Liam, Do the other players know? What do they think?"

"Liam, Do you think there will be trouble down the road? Is this setting a bad precedent?"

Liam ignored them all. "Joey!" he barked over the roar of the crowd. Silence did fall then, as everyone in the room turned wide-eyed to look at him.

"What?" Joey asked, looking across the room, no trace of worry on his face.

"Do you want to get married?"

There were gasps and whispered exclamations of *holy shit* from his boys.

"What?" Joey asked again, standing up. His eyes flashed dangerously.

"Will you marry me?" Liam asked again, smile growing.

The crowd parted like the Red Sea as Joey crossed the room. "Are you fucking kidding me" he asked.

There was a pained inhale, and Patrick choked on laughter. Bent over, arms crossed over his stomach, Patrick was in hysterics. "Oh my god, Judy. Fucking god," he gasped out. "Aunt Jeanie is gonna *kill* you."

Probably, but he didn't care. "Well?" he asked Joey.

Joey shoved his shoulder. "That's not how you do it, moron. That's not how you ask someone to marry you."

"Jesus, it's a simple yes or no question," Liam yelled, throwing his arms up.

Patrick's laughter had dissolved into desperate gasps for air.

"A hundred he says no," McVicker called out.

"Two hundred he says yes," someone challenged.

Sergei ran over to the whiteboard on the wall and starting scribbling down the bets.

"You're simple," Joey said, shaking his head. "Fucking idiot. How could you do this to me? How could you put me in this spot? What if I say no?"

Liam reached for Joey, pulling him against him. "Then I look like an idiot on national television. If I'm an idiot, I'm an idiot. I'm willing to make a fool of myself for you."

Joey shook his head, disengaging from Liam, but grabbing for his hand as he pulled away. "Man, I just… That is so uncool. That's just…it's embarrassing is what it is. Getting all sappy on me. In front of ESPN, too."

"Fuck you. I'll be sappy whenever I want. I don't give a shit. I love you."

More bets rang out and Sergei wrote them down.

"But now you're being such a brat, I take it back."

"Fuck you," Joey said with a laugh. "No take backs."

"Yeah, no take backs," McVicker said. "We all heard you."

Liam rolled his eyes. "Fine. The offer still stands. I'll marry you if we win the Cup. How's that for incentive?"

Joey frowned in confusion. "Wait? How does that work? Why am *I* the one that needs incentive to win the cup? That doesn't even make sense? We'll win whether or not you force me to marry you."

"So, is that a yes or a no?" Liam asked. The whole team quieted, waiting for Joey's answer. Personally, Liam didn't care. Joey would say yes, eventually. They'd get married eventually.

"We'll talk," Joey said.

"No fair!" Wheels called. "We need a yes or no." He pointed to the bet board.

Joey gave him the finger without looking at him, directing it at the team in general. "We'll talk alone. In private." A flash of heat in Joey's eyes was the only warning he got before Joey leaned in and kissed him in front of god, ESPN, and the world. "I love you, too, you uptight idiot."

EPILOGUE

NHL.com – June

The Washington Capitals win the Stanley Cup!

After defeating the Seattle Thunder in game six, the Capitals brought home the Cup for the first time in the team's forty-four year history….

NONNO LOLLO posted in **ONE BIG HAPPY**:

I'm going to do it, kids. Wish me luck!

JOEY: Good luck, Nonno!

GINA: Go get it, Tiger! Rwarrr!

ANGIE: I don't think all this excitement is good for your heart!

NONNO LOLLO: It's the best thing in the world for my heart.

SOPHIA: awwww

NATALIE: That's so romantic, Nonno!

PATRICK: Don't do it! It's a trap!

LIAM: Don't listen to him, no one should.

PATRICK: You should talk, Judy. How many times for you?

PATRICK: Any luck yet?

JOEY: Nope

LIAM: Just a matter of time. I hope you have better luck, Nonno!

NONNO: I got to go! Good bye!

LUNGS WORKING TO GET OXYGEN, JOEY THUDDED HIS HEAD BACK against the pillows. "Wait, stop," he said as his phone chimed with a barrage of notifications. He groaned loudly as Liam slid slowly down Joey's cock, ass clenching the whole way. "Jesus Christ," he cursed. He was so close. Had been so close for so long it hurt. And there was nothing he could do about it.

Liam had propped Joey up on the bed 'so he could watch' and tied his hands to the headboard. He blew him until he was rock hard, and then straddled him, riding him like a cowboy on a bucking bronco.

Joey's heart pounded in his chest, the pulse points in his wrists and neck and solar plexus throbbing. His balls had pulled up so far and so tight, they might never come back down again.

Liam swiveled his hips in a tight circle and Joey's back arched off the bed. "The phone," he shouted. "Gotta, gotta, fuck me, check the phone." Sweat ran down his temples and burned his eyes. His legs trembled.

"Really?" Liam asked, stroking his own hard cock and making a show of it, the bastard.

"What if it's Lollo?" Joey gasped out. The phone was binging and vibrating like crazy.

"Fine," Liam said. "Hold on, I'll get it." He leaned forward, stopping to kiss Joey passionately as he reached for the phone. "Can't. Quite. Reach," he said, sliding further up Joey's cock with each word. "Don't come," he warned as Joey throbbed hard inside him.

Joey clenched his jaw and sucked in air through his teeth.

Liam picked up the phone, looked at it, and smiled.

"Well?" Joey said.

Liam turned the phone so Joey could read the texts.

NONNO LOLLO posted in **ONE BIG HAPPY**:

SHE SAID YES!!!

A string of congratulations followed.

"Yes!" Joey said. Nonno had been so nervous about asking Brigit to marry him. Joey didn't blame him. Liam's grandmother was scary. "I'm so happy for him."

Liam rocked his hips back and forth as he typed in a message. "God, you feel so fucking good," he said closing his eyes.

Liam put the phone back, and leaned forward to untie Joey's wrists.

"Thank god," Joey said. Ignoring the ache in his wrists, he grabbed Liam and pushed him sideways, manhandling him until he was on his back. "You drive me fucking crazy," he said as he hooked his arm under Liam's knees and pushed his legs back.

Liam stared at him, his blue eyes dark with arousal.

Hands trembling, Joey guided his cock to Liam's entrance, sliding all the way in with one slow thrust. They both groaned.

Liam reached up and pulled Joey down to him. His arms and legs wrapped around Joey as much as they could, as he trapped Joey against his body. Joey felt his cock sliding against his abdomen with every thrust.

Their movements slowed, Liam's fingers clenched around his hair, his mouth pressed against Joey's neck as he marked him as his.

They breathed heavily, harshly, the only other sounds the creak of the bed frame and the ceaseless crashing of the ocean against the Nantucket beach.

"Joey," Liam gasped, hips rising to meet Joey's thrusts. "Love you. God, I love you."

"I love you, too," Joey said, voice strained. Every fucking thing about Liam was unbelievable. The feel of his skin and muscles, the taste of his mouth, the sound of his helpless moans, and the silken vice of his body as Joey sank into it over and over. Perfect. He was perfect and Joey wanted this moment to last forever.

"Ask me," He panted against the soft skin of Liam's neck. They were barely moving now, locked together and rocking gently on the bed. Cool salt air wafted over them from the open windows, drying the sweat off their skin. "Ask me again," he pleaded.

"Joey," Liam said, his hands coming up to cup Joey's face. He pressed his open mouth against Joey's, both of them too far gone to kiss. "Joey Luciano, will you marry me?"

"Yes," Joey said, tears springing to his eyes and sliding down his cheeks. "Of course I will."

"I knew you would," he said panting. Liam's broken laugh turned into a gasp, sliding into a long, pained moan as Joey pulled almost all the way out.

"Jerk," Joey said, slamming home. He pulled out of Liam's grasp, and pushing Liam's legs almost to his shoulders, fucked him fast and hard until Liam cried out, hands flying to the headboard.

"Oh, yes. Fuck me, come on, fuck me. Make me come."

Joey kept thrusting, lower back aching, sweat dripping off his body. Liam grabbed his cock, stripping it fast, muscles getting tighter and tighter, high pitched gasps falling from his lips.

Joey's balls throbbed painfully. Liam's leg slipped out of Joey's grasp, falling to the bed, and they both yelled as the change of angle forced Joey deep into Liam.

Liam sucked in a pained breath, and then came with a shout. Joey's hips slammed against him over and over, fucking him through it as his own orgasm ripped through him. He collapsed down on top of Liam, shuddering and trembling as his orgasm continued, the pleasure bordering on pain as his body kept thrusting and his cock kept pulsing.

Liam's fingernails dug into Joey's upper arms as he gave a shout and shot the last of his release between them.

"Holy fuck," Joey said, resting his forehead against Liam's. "Oh my god. I think I broke something."

Liam kissed him, and then gently shoved him onto his back next to him.

"Oh my god," Joey repeated.

"Fucking amazing." Liam's chest heaved as the waited for their breathing to even out and their heartbeats to slow back to normal. Liam ran his hand across his stomach and grimaced. "We're gross."

Joey nodded. "Worth it." It was. They were. Worth everything.

They lay in silence, listening to the waves crashing on the beach until Liam elbowed him gently in the side. "Hey," he said.

Joey turned his head. "What?"

"No take backs." Liam said seriously. Joey could tell he was a little unsure, probably due to Joey saying no the past three times. He didn't really have a good answer as to why except that it had never felt right before. Tonight, it had felt perfect.

"No take backs," he said solemnly. He rolled on to his side and kissed Liam gently. "I promise."

"Good."

Joey rolled back to the bed, eyes closed. Liam reached for his hand and Joey grabbed, holding on tight. "We should shower," he said.

"Umm," Liam murmured in agreement. "Hungry?"

Joey shrugged. "I could eat." He could always eat. "But not right now. I want it to be us for just a little longer. He knew the family would be gathering in the main house, to celebrate Enzo and Brig-it's engagement. He wanted to be there, sharing in their joy and their love. They would eat too much and break open the champagne. They'd toast to Enzo and Brigit. Liam would tell them Joey finally said yes and there would be congratulations and tears and laughter and taunting and money changing hands.

Everything as it should be. Joey wouldn't change a thing.

But for right now, he was content to stay here, in this room, in this moment, with this man, where, for once, everything was perfect.

A PREVIEW OF PROS & CONS OF VENGEANCE

FIVE JOBS. FIVE CHANCES FOR REDEMPTION. One thing's for sure: these men are no angels.

There's nothing like being blackmailed by a dead man to really bring a group of cons together. And what a group we are: a hacker, a thief, a con artist, a thug, and a Federal agent with an axe to grind. The deal is simple, we do the jobs and Charlie's lawyer wipes the slate clean for each of us, one at a time.

BUY ON AMAZON OR READ IN KU

~An Interested Party~

"All in all, Charlie picked a decent place to die."

Palm trees swayed beneath a cloudless sky, and as I sucked in a salt-tinged breath of air, I felt the telltale tingle of an imminent sunburn on the few millimeters of my skin not covered by prosthetics, fake hair, or long, polyester robes.

You had to love Florida. It was gorgeous when it wasn't trying to kill you. Even the rows of headstones in the cemetery seemed somehow cheery.

The woman beside me turned from her steady contemplation of the mourners ringing the newest gravesite and darted a quick look around, making sure no one had overheard.

Pfft. Like I would have let that happen.

"Are you being serious right now?" she hissed. "Keep your voice down, *Father*, before you blow your cover."

I stroked my long, gray beard, partly to make sure it was still securely attached to my face, and forgave her for questioning me. It was the priestly thing to do, and I was all about method acting.

"I'm just *say-ing*," I sing-songed back. "Sun shining, birds singing a high, mournful song for that extra touch of drama. A-plus funeral atmosphere. Ten out of ten. Charlie would have approved."

A man in the gathering narrowed his eyes at me suspiciously, and I returned his look with a benevolent smile, raising my hand in a blessing. The man promptly looked away.

"You're an *idiot*, and I swear to God if anyone recognizes you and pulls a gun, I'm leaving you to fend for yourself. Understand?"

Ah, Miranda. She never tolerated my bullshit for long, which was one of the reasons I loved her. "Perfectly."

She nodded once, then resumed studying the black-clad men and women who stood chatting in small groups. "And it's hot as balls out here. Far from my idea of perfect."

"It's Sarasota in August, Ms. Bosley. *Hot as balls* is the only flavor weather comes in this time of year, unless you know someone who works miracles." I snorted. "Doubt they're big on miracles where poor Charlie ended up." I tilted my head down and widened my eyes meaningfully.

"Hey! That's my *friend* you're talking about, asshole. You don't give a shit that Charlie's gone, but I'm... gonna miss him," she admitted. Her eyes looked suspiciously shiny.

I sighed, rocking slightly on the balls of my feet. "It's not that I won't *miss* him, Randa." For one thing, I'd miss his gorgeous house with the enormous swimming pool that overlooked the beach. Sunsets from that pool were *perfection*. And for another, Charlie was a world-renowned thief and information broker whose name was always spoken with respect. The world would be a heck of a lot colder and lonelier for me without Charlie and his reputation opening doors. But I wasn't exactly the sentimental type, and I doubted I'd spend a lot of time grieving the loss. I'd see this one final job done for old time's sake, and then I'd ghost.

I figured Miranda wouldn't appreciate me mentioning any of that, though. Not while she was being all *melancholy*.

"It's just that... I think the best things about Charlie Bingham are things that will live on, you know?" I offered lamely.

She darted me a look, checking for sincerity, and I blinked guilelessly back at her. She sniffed.

"Also? It's worth noting that you're a giant, squishy marshmallow full of *feelings*."

She gasped. "Take that back!"

I folded my hands piously. "I'm pretty sure it's a sin to lie while impersonating a priest."

"You are insufferable," she said, shaking her head, but I talked over her.

"And the truth is, Miranda Bosley, beneath that sharky, lawyer-ish facade..."

"I think the word you're looking for is *professional.*"

"You *care* about your clients."

"Charlie was an exception," Miranda said in a low voice. She narrowed her eyes at me. "The one and *only* exception."

"Oh, come on," I protested, nodding at a cute redhead who'd taken a seat in the third row back from Charlie's casket. I tried to give her the serious look of a man concerned with the state of her soul, but I'm not gonna lie, all I could see was her purse sitting unattended beneath her seat. It's like people *begged* to be robbed sometimes. "You were Charlie's attorney for, what? Five years? Six? You've known me for a whole decade! And you *love* me!"

"So you say." She looked me up and down, taking in every detail of my outfit before exhaling a subtle huff of disgust. "But you insisted on proceeding with this ridiculous scheme..."

"Ridiculous?" I scoffed under my breath. "Listen, Randa, Charlie's time was up and everyone knew it. Lots of people wanna get right with their conscience before they check out. Balance the scales and right the wrong they've done in their lives. I don't think that's ridiculous, I think it's admirable! I'm glad to be a part of it." Laying it on a bit thick there, perhaps. I stroked my beard once more, briefly contemplating growing one for real. It was an oddly soothing gesture. "I can't help it if I'm enjoying myself along the way, babe. You know me."

"Yeah. Yeah, I know you, alright. And I knew Charlie." She turned toward me, putting her back to the crowd, and her hazel eyes drilled into mine. "Charlie should have planned to fade into *obscurity*, like all the really good thieves do. Instead, we're here having this *spectacle* of a funeral and blackmailing people into doing his work for him."

"Dude. Harsh," I chided. "Have some respect for the deceased."

"Not harsh, *accurate*," she corrected, spinning back around and blanking her face. "I can't believe either of us are involved in this. You do get that it's insanely dangerous, right?"

"Miranda," I said in my most placating voice. "Honestly, it's gonna be fine…"

"Jesus, just look at the men in this crowd, the men we practically *forced* to come here! That's Ridge Pfeiffer." She nodded at the cherubic blond in the front row who sat with the preternatural stillness I'd only ever witnessed in truly exceptional thieves. "He'd steal your soul and be two states away before you knew it was missing, friend. And then there are Castille Alvarez and Wesley Bond over there."

I followed her glance to a lone tree a few paces away, where a disgustingly handsome, black-haired, broad-shouldered, Paul Bunyan of a man stood protectively over a short, twitchy dude with dark red hair. I always thought Alvarez should have been a model, it would have been the perfect cover. Model slash assassin for hire. I guess there were worse faces to see with your last breath.

"You know Steele could kill you ten different ways you could scream for help, and Bond could make a laser beam that would fry your corpse out of chewing gum and a magnifying glass."

I snorted.

"And don't forget Carson Grieves."

I frowned as I eyed the crowd more closely. "I don't see him yet."

"Brown and brown, third row, pretending to salivate over the blonde in the low-cut blouse."

"Ohhh. Damn," I muttered, reluctantly impressed. "He's good."

"You sound surprised," she chided. "You shouldn't be. Best grifter in the business. Fucker could shoot you in broad daylight and convince everyone here they'd never seen him before in their lives."

I snorted. "Miranda, darling, why am I dying in each of these scenarios?"

"Because it's fucking *dangerous!*" she hissed, even as she smiled and nodded at some signal from the funeral director on the other side of the gathering. "These men are not here to pay their respects to Charlie Bingham. They're not here out of some prurient curiosity. They're here because *Charlie* had dirt on them, because *you* invited them, and because *I* threatened to expose them if they didn't show up and play nice."

She turned to face me again. "And here *you* are, standing at Charlie's grave dressed up like... like... fucking *Rasputin-meets-Santa Claus*." She touched her hand to the heavy silver cross that hung from my neck. "Sometimes I wonder if you're *trying* to get caught. To follow Charlie into that grave."

I blinked, stung. The woman was too fucking insightful, catching on to shit I'd barely ever acknowledged to myself.

I grabbed her hand and held it lightly, a priest giving comfort to a grieving friend.

"First of all, I'm not getting caught," I told her absolutely. "That is *not* on the agenda, okay? I have *never* been caught, and I don't plan to start now. I'm a ghost, an afterthought. Charlie's invisible little elf. I'm not on anybody's radar." I looked around at the guys she'd mentioned, the men we'd invited here. They were men like me. Men like Charlie. Dangerous, but decent. Criminals, but ones who stuck firmly to their own moral codes. That's why Charlie had chosen them. "It's safer for everyone if they never find out who I am or how I'm connected to Charlie, and I won't jeopardize that. I'm not getting involved with Charlie's missions except from afar."

She looked at me for a long moment, then nodded.

"And second, I *might* be channeling Rasputin," I allowed, touching a finger to the hair above my temple. "But only in a Tyra Banks, *Rasputin-but-make-it-fashion* kind of way."

A helpless laugh escaped her, quickly turning to a sob. She rubbed her forehead. "Do you ever take anything seriously?" she demanded.

I sighed. "You *know* I do, Randa-Panda," I told her. "I take every part of this seriously. I took *Charlie* seriously. I take Alvarez, Pfeiffer, Grieves, Bond, and Agent Shook seriously. But I take the jobs they need to do, Charlie's unfinished business, even more seriously. And I'm thinking of this as Charlie's last hurrah, babe. One last con. We're gonna send him out in style. Yeah?"

She sucked in a deep breath and tugged at the hem of her black suit jacket like she was steadying herself.

"Once more," she said, without a trace of her earlier emotion. "Let me note that it's hot as balls out here."

I pressed my lips together to hide a smile as Miranda slipped back into lawyer mode. God, why was it that I always viewed serious, worrying, rule-following people as such a *challenge?*

"Quit your whining," I told her, stroking my beard again. "I'm sweating my ass off under this cassock."

"You could take it off. Even priests have to make accommodations for the heat."

"No can do," I said sorrowfully. "I've got nothing on underneath."

It took her a second, but when she finally processed my statement, her eyes widened and her jaw hung open for half a moment.

"You... you're not." She shook her head minutely. "You're *not* naked under there."

I wasn't, not entirely, but the look on her face made the lie worthwhile. "Wanna check?"

She looked so horrified I nearly burst into laughter. Her eyes narrowed. "Your continued existence makes me question that whole *survival of the fittest* thing."

"Nine lives like a cat," I told her with a small smile.

"Only eight left if you manage to pull this off, *Father*."

The undertaker signaled again, gesturing me toward the unassuming podium set up at the front of the gathering. *Showtime.*

I turned to Miranda. "You do your part, and I'll do mine. For Charlie."

"For Charlie," she echoed, but as she turned to walk away, a man approached us.

Tall, with dark hair tinged silver at the temples, he had one of those lean, rugged, model-perfect faces where the jut of his jaw and cheekbones could cut diamonds. My heart recognized him first, pounding in my chest before my mind had fully identified him.

Miranda's eyes widened at the same moment mine did, but likely for different reasons.

"Ms. Bosley," the man said politely. His eyes barely flicked to mine. "Father."

His voice was a deep, rumbling bass I'd heard in my dreams a million times. Though of course, the things he said when he invaded my sleep were far dirtier, and he sure as hell never called me Father... though I may have called *him* Daddy. Every morning after one of those dreams, when I woke up sweaty and aroused and *alone*, I'd tell myself that his voice couldn't possibly be as deep as I'd remembered, that my mind had been playing tricks on me.

But I was wrong. If anything, it was even more gravelly-sexy than I'd recalled.

"Father?" Miranda said sharply, widening her eyes.

Damn. While I'd been remembering my wet dreams, the man - Special Agent Leonard Shook - had been waiting for my reply.

"Pardon," I said, making my voice a little higher than it naturally was, and adding the slight Russian accent that was a perfect mimic of my grandmother's. "The heat. It... makes me light-headed."

Leo's brow furrowed, and he reached out one large hand to grasp my elbow, as though I might faint. "Are you alright? Would you like to take a seat?"

"No, no," I said, shaking my head, while the little demon in the back of my brain insisted, *Yes, please. Preferably on your lap.* "I'll be fine."

"Perhaps remove the robe?" Leo offered, and Miranda made a strangled noise.

"No, but thank you. It wouldn't be appropriate."

"Heat stroke trumps formality," Leo replied matter-of-factly. He reached for the hem of my cassock.

"No! No, my child," I backed up a pace. Did Russian Orthodox priests say *my child*? I couldn't recall. Suddenly I felt unprepared, caught out, exposed.

Maybe Miranda was right. Maybe I hadn't taken today seriously enough. I'd told myself it was important to come here, to see without being seen, so I could assess the situation and help Miranda behind the scenes later. I'd figured these robes would make me practically invisible – no one in this crowd of fences and crooks was likely to look too closely at a man of the cloth.

But then, I hadn't counted on Leo. Jesus *fuck*. Why did this man get to me more than any other ever had?

I wasn't sure exactly where or when my crush on Leo Shook had begun, but I know it was before I'd ever seen him in person. He'd been Charlie's nemesis, always half a pace behind, and I swear, the cat-and-mouse antics were so amusing that even though I was nominally Team Charlie, I wasn't sure who I rooted for harder sometimes.

I took a deep breath. "There," I said in my high-pitched accent. "Much better."

"If you're sure," he said, unconvinced.

"Perhaps skip your remarks, Father," Miranda suggested. "I'm happy to say a few words about the departed on your behalf, and you can keep the funeral rites private?"

I nodded, taking the out she offered. "Perhaps, yes."

"I admit… I wasn't aware that Charles Bingham was a particularly religious man." Leo eyed Miranda skeptically.

Thank God he'd turned to *her* for answers. I wasn't sure I would have been able to stand up under that look. But Miranda, in her contrary way, absorbed his suspicion and used it to strengthen her backbone.

"There were many things about my client that you didn't know, Agent Shook."

"Apparently. Didn't know Charlie was a blackmailer, for one thing."

"Blackmail is an ugly term," she said. "And an inaccurate one in this case. It's simply a business deal."

"Business," he repeated. "With who? Charlie's dead. Dental records confirmed it."

And wasn't it curious how sad he sounded about that? We made a heck of a love triangle: me, Leo Shook, and Charlie Bingham.

"I've been authorized to negotiate the terms of the agreement on behalf of the Bingham estate, along with another interested party."

"An *interested party*," Leo snorted. "Christ. And who the fuck might that be?" He tossed me an apologetic glance. "Pardon my language, Father."

That would be *me*, Mr. Interested Party himself, the man behind the curtain. The man who'd been left the task of redeeming Charlie Bingham and playing invisible puppet master to five professional cons.

I waved away Leo's apology and glanced down, focusing all my attention on the way the shiny black toe of my shoe peeped out from below my robe.

"Discretion is the most valuable service I provide my clients, Agent Shook," Miranda said.

"I don't give a good goddamn about your attorney-client privilege,"

Leo snapped. "I want to know how many people Charlie told what he knows about me. Or *thinks* he knows."

"Right this moment, only I know." Miranda studied her fingernails. "As I was saying, on behalf of the estate, I'm prepared to offer you and a select few others a job in exchange for certain... sensitive information you might find important." Miranda shrugged lightly, as though she weren't coercing a federal agent in a cemetery in front of five dozen witnesses. The woman had more guts than anyone I knew; way more than Charlie had ever had; hell, more than the entire group of mourners put together. She also had a healthy respect for the law, which was why she was so damn careful about breaking it. "You have right of first refusal, and if you choose not to take it, then other individuals will be given the opportunity to bid for those goods."

"Those goods, meaning pictures of..."

Miranda cut him off with a sharp noise. "Not here, Agent Shook. We're having a select gathering back at the Bingham house after the service. You can ask your questions then."

"A select gathering."

Leo was like a parrot today - very unlike the calm, collected Agent Shook I'd come to know through Charlie. I would have been more amused if my heart weren't still beating a mile a minute from the threat of being caught, and beads of sweat weren't literally rolling down my legs and puddling in my oh-so-proper shoes.

"*Very* select," she agreed. "You won't want to miss it. The house is up on Gulf Shore Road under the name of..."

"Bigolb-Autumn Enterprises. I know," he sighed so matter-of-factly I couldn't help but dart a glance at his face.

He knew where Charlie had lived? He knew the stupid name of Charlie's shell corporation? *How?*

Miranda was startled and showed it. "Do tell."

"I've known for a long while," he said, sounding tired. He shook his head ruefully. "Only Charlie Bingham would create a corporation called *Big Old Bottom Enterprises* and think he could keep it a secret from everyone."

But it *had* been a secret. Not even the two or three people Charlie trusted with the truth had ever figured it out until he told them. Leo Shook was more perceptive than I'd given him credit for. And Charlie had been closer to getting caught than he'd ever dreamed.

Miranda and I exchanged a glance. Mine said *holy shit*, and hers said *I told you this was dangerous, you idiot.*

This was worrisome. And yeah, fine, it was also a total fucking turn-on.

Leo ran a hand through his black hair. "I'll look forward to our discussion at the house, then," he said, in a tone that suggested it would not be a pleasant or peaceful discussion.

He turned to me. "Will you be at the house, Father?"

"Oh, me? No. No! Heavens, no," I tittered, painting an accent on every syllable. Even though I desperately wanted to be there, to see everyone's reactions in person, I knew it would be smarter for me to watch the proceedings from a distance. At least for now.

Leo nodded. "Well, then. Bless, Father?" he requested solemnly.

Jesus Christ. Of course the man was conversant in Russian Orthodox etiquette. *Of course he was.*

It was only thanks to the dozens and dozens of masses I'd attended with my Babushka Sonia that my mouth formed the words of the blessing, more muscle memory than conscious thought. I raised my hand, then offered it to him, as was customary, and he took it in both of his, lifting it to his lips for a kiss.

"Take care," Leo said, returning my hand to me. He nodded curtly at Miranda and turned away, taking a seat next to Ridge Pfeiffer.

I clenched my hand into a fist so tight I could feel the rapid beat of my pulse in each of my fingers. One simple touch and he'd turned my stomach inside out.

Miranda was right; Charlie's last con was a dangerous game, dangerous for all of us. But it was too late to turn back now.

ALSO BY A.E. WASP

ABOUT THE AUTHOR

A dreamer and an idealist, Amy writes about people finding connection in a world that can seem lonely and magic in a world than can seem all too mundane. She invites readers into her characters' lives and worlds when they are their most vulnerable, their most human, living with the same hopes and fears we all have. She invites her readers to reach out and share how her characters have touched their lives or how the found families they have gathered around them have shaped their worlds.

Born on Long Island, NY, Amy has lived in Los Angeles, London, and Bangkok. She currently lives in a town that looks suspiciously like Red Deer, Colorado.

SEE INTO MY BRAIN AT PINTEREST
SIGN UP FOR MY NEWSLETTER
AND GET A FREE SUBSCRIBERS' ONLY STORY

Follow me!
aewasp.com
amy@aewasp.com

38242449R00269

Printed in Great Britain
by Amazon